To Luca
Happy 'Big' Birthday!
With love
Helen

THE INTERNET PARTY

A Novel by

HELEN FULLER

Copyright © Helen Fuller 2014

First Published in 2014 by Helen Fuller Publisher - helenfullerpublisher@gmail.com

Paperback ISBN 978-0-9929162-1-3
.epub ISBN 978-0-9929162-0-6
.mobi ISBN 978-0-9929162-2-0

For my parents
Joy and Irving Rogers
Who made me the person I am

Josh Walker is a man passionate about bringing power back to ordinary people disillusioned with politics.

As his political ambitions go from strength to strength, he realises his family life is under threat ...

PROLOGUE

Josh Walker's Diary – March 21ˢᵗ

The sun is shining and the birds are singing. It's the first day of spring. In a few months I'll be forty. It's time to reflect. What have I done with my life? Well, so far not a lot really, depending how you look at it. I haven't saved the world yet, which is what I intended to do from around the age of thirteen. But I do have a respectable career, which is what people would expect of a man of my age. Some might say I was successful. At least I have a job and that's something you can't take for granted these days.

Another question. Have I lived up to my parents' expectations? My mother's, yes. She would be pleased that I'm alive, in good health (as far as I know) and have a roof over my head. I don't think she'd mind that it's my partner Kim's roof rather than mine. Mum would have liked Kim and her children, Dan and Izzy. I think she would want me to have my own children. Maybe I will one day.

What about my father? Have I lived up to his expectations? I suppose he may have expected me to save the world by now. Perhaps not the whole world, but at least a small part of it.

Sometimes I wonder what is the point of existence. Is that all it is – existence? I know that I want to achieve something apart from going to work each day. Will I seize the moment or let it pass? I have a feeling that something monumental is about to happen. This is my time to make a difference to the lives of others. When? How? I don't yet know. But it will happen.

CHAPTER
ONE

Josh sat in his study in his favourite brown leather armchair and looked out of the sunlit window at the back garden. He surveyed the overgrown mass of green vegetation and felt a twinge of guilt, but he managed to ignore it. Gardening was not something he usually did. He liked to read a daily newspaper and keep himself informed. He would cook, clean and wash his own clothes but he was a bit of a dreamer, a restless spirit.

Josh listened as the front door opened. He could tell it was Kim. He heard her drop her bags onto the wooden floor. There was a crackle of plastic. She must have called in at the supermarket on her way back from work.

'Anyone at home?' called Kim.

'I'm in here,' replied Josh.

Kim kicked off her shoes, threw her coat over the banister at the bottom of the stairs and shuffled along the hallway. Then she collapsed onto the large green sofa in the TV room as Josh came out of his study to greet her.

'Hi,' said Josh. 'Did you vote?'

Kim smoothed her wayward dark brown curls back from her face.

'What sort of welcome is that?' She was tired and in no mood for an interrogation.

'Sorry,' said Josh as he bent down and kissed Kim gently on her left cheek. 'How was your day? Would you like a cup of tea?' Josh rested his left hand briefly on her shoulder. 'Well did you vote?'

Kim shrugged him off. 'I forgot. I'll go later. Has Izzy phoned?' she said quickly, trying to change the subject.

'No.'

Josh felt slightly uneasy at the mention of Izzy and

his mouth closed firmly. Kim's daughter had been eight years old when she first came into his life and for a long time she'd been delightful. But more recently she'd turned into a stroppy teenager. As far as Izzy was concerned, reaching the age of thirteen entitled her to stay out as late as possible and go wherever she wanted with whoever she liked. Izzy's teenage years had so far consisted of regular bouts of moodiness and, at times, irrational behaviour, which she and even Kim excused as being caused by hormones. She'd got in with the 'It' crowd of girls in her year at school who all wore thick black eye make-up and hoisted their skirts up as high as possible.

Izzy had already found herself involved in a shoplifting incident where a friend she was with called Jessica was apprehended as they left a department store. A pair of cheap earrings were found in Jessica's bag which she had 'forgotten' to pay for. Fortunately, the store manager had taken a benevolent approach and let Jessica off with a warning. Izzy had been horrified and had vowed never to let such a thing happen again.

While Kim had been upset and angry with Izzy for several days, Josh had been more sympathetic. He hadn't been an angel himself as a teenager. He could remember smoking behind the school bike sheds and missing the odd games lesson without an excuse. Josh's flirtation with smoking hadn't lasted very long because it made him feel ill. He'd had a few brushes with alcohol as he progressed through his teens but none that had got him into too much trouble. Sometimes Josh would stand up for Izzy when he thought Kim was being too hard on her. The trouble was that it led to arguments with Kim and he would suddenly become the target while Izzy quietly slipped out of the room.

'I'm worried about her,' said Kim. 'She should be back by now. I told her that if she wasn't going to athletics training after school she should come straight home.'

Josh felt himself mellow. Things were easier for him. He had a ready-made family and he lived in a comfortable Edwardian semi-detached house overlooking a park. Well, they weren't his exactly. They belonged to Kim but he got the benefits and so what if he also experienced the rough edges – living with Izzy.

'I'm worried about her too,' said Josh. He leaned forward and his lips parted into a smile. 'Please go and vote. You know how important it is. Do it for me. I'll go and find Izzy.'

Josh tilted his head slightly to one side and his mop of dark brown hair fell across his face. He pushed it back as he bent down and put his arm around Kim. She reached out for his hand and held it for a few seconds. Their eyes met in a moment of understanding.

'Ok,' said Kim. Being the mother of two teenage children and working full time as a social worker was taking its toll. She needed Josh's help but she didn't want to be made to feel as if she had to earn it.

'Come on,' said Josh. 'I'll drop you off at the polling station and then I'll look for Izzy. Where is she likely to be?'

'I've called her mobile but it's either switched off or run out of battery. She's probably in the park or maybe in the shopping centre. I've tried calling a few of her friends but can't get through to them either.'

'I'm sure Izzy's ok,' said Josh reassuringly. 'You know what she's like. No news is good news. She's probably in the shopping centre and has lost track of time. The shops are open late tonight. Why don't you have a look around on your way back from the polling station?'

Kim's face relaxed as she smiled at Josh. 'I expect you're right. When I was Izzy's age my parents had no way of contacting me. I used to walk back from school in the pitch black in winter across a deserted common and I don't think they ever worried about me. But I feel that I should be able to speak to Izzy on her mobile whenever I want to and if I can't, I assume that something dreadful has happened to her. Crazy really.'

Kim pulled herself up from the deep and comforting warmth of the sofa. She made her way back along the hallway, slipped on her shoes, grabbed her coat and waited for Josh by the front door.

CHAPTER
TWO

Josh caught sight of Kim in his rear-view mirror as his car pulled away from the church hall that was being used as a polling station. The back of her coat was crumpled and her hair was dishevelled. She seemed to stoop as she walked slowly towards the double doors of the church hall. Josh felt a pang of guilt mixed with sadness. Kim needed a rest and he'd insisted that she go and vote. But he knew she would be annoyed with herself the next day if she didn't get round to voting. She cared about the type of society her children were growing up in and wanted to influence which political party got elected.

Josh first met Kim five and a half years ago on the first day of the autumn term at the university where he worked as a lecturer. He'd been about to start delivering his first lecture of the academic year in social policy. He was casting his eyes around the bustling crowd of new students who were hurrying to find a seat when Kim walked into the lecture hall. Josh noticed her immediately. She wasn't dressed like most of the other students in a uniform of ragged jeans, worn sneakers and oversized hooded jackets or sweaters.

As Kim looked around the lecture hall for somewhere to sit, Josh was drawn to her petite figure with its tamed mass of dark brown curls and English rose complexion. She was wearing a smart black skirt with an emerald green sweater and black knee high leather boots. Unlike the assorted rucksacks and large cheap handbags worn by most of the students, Kim was carrying a shiny black leather briefcase.

Josh tried not to make it obvious as he watched Kim walk down the steps at the side of the lecture hall and place herself a couple of rows back from the front. He surreptitiously examined her face as she cast her eyes down and removed a pad of paper from her briefcase. When Kim looked up Josh could see that her eyes were a beautiful green colour. He guessed that she was in her early thirties, although there was a freshness and youthfulness about her that disguised her age. As Josh turned on his computer ready to start his lecture, he hoped that the woman with the emerald sweater and green eyes would be in his tutorial group.

A few days later Kim Clark walked into Josh Walker's office and into his life. Over the following weeks Kim challenged Josh intellectually, charmed and humoured him, which made him even more attracted to her. There was a meeting of minds between the two of them when tutor group discussions took place that left some of the other students miles behind.

At the time when they met, Kim had been married to Richard, a corporate lawyer working as a partner in a big firm of solicitors in the City of London. Richard had been in his late thirties and probably earning several hundred thousand pounds a year. An image of Richard popped up into Josh's mind. He was a tall man with a shock of blond hair tinted with grey. His body was toned and his face had the healthy glow of a successful sportsman. Richard had been a double Blue at Cambridge University. He'd been captain of the first fifteen rugby team, played water polo and took great delight in telling everyone that he'd rowed against Oxford University in the boat race and been a member of the winning team. Apart from sport, Richard's life revolved around drinking and socialising with his clients.

As Josh drove around the streets of Wimbledon looking out for Izzy's slight frame, he wondered how Kim could have been attracted to him after being married to Richard. They were both tall and slim but there the similarity ended. Where Richard was fair skinned and gregarious in personality, Josh's complexion was dark and he was by nature contemplative and reserved. Furthermore, Josh had little interest in sport but preferred to go to the theatre or an art exhibition. Richard received in pay and benefits around ten times what Josh earned in a year, even including the extra money he got from writing the odd article for newspapers or magazines. Kim had once told him that she'd been attracted to him because of his integrity and vulnerability. She'd also described Josh as kind and supportive.

On the day when Kim had joined Josh's tutor group she'd been financially secure and full of life. She had arranged for her two young children, Dan and Izzy, to be cared for by a nanny and a part-time housekeeper had helped with cooking, cleaning, washing and shopping. Then in one day Kim's life changed forever.

Kim had met Sarah, the wife of Richard's partner, Mike, at a few social functions held at the law firm where the two men both worked in the corporate finance department. The wives had soon found that they shared much in common including children of similar ages and a keen interest in helping their local communities. But beyond that they had an immediate affinity in the way that women sometimes do. Kim and Sarah would often call each other after a difficult evening getting their children to bed or when a child was ill. Meanwhile, their husbands would be working through the night on some international corporate deal.

One morning Kim woke up early to find that Richard hadn't returned from an important meeting the night before. She checked her phone and found a text message from Sarah. **'Call me asap! Sx'**

Kim ran through her contacts and found Sarah's mobile number. She answered after a couple of rings.

'Kim. I need to tell you something about Richard but you have to promise you won't say I told you or Mike will kill me.'

'Kill you?'

'Well, divorce me at the very least.'

'Ok, I promise but why are you whispering?'

'Because he's here, asleep.'

'Who? Richard?'

'No, Mike.'

Kim was wondering where her husband came into this and why Sarah was telling her that Mike was at home asleep, as he should be, when she was struck by a thunderbolt that hit her in the chest and threatened to squeeze all life out of her.

'Richard's been having an affair.'

Those words were to ring out loudly in Kim's mind time and time again for years after her friend had whispered them.

'I can't say any more now but Richard didn't come home last night because he was at his secretary's flat.'

'Elaine' muttered Kim. She was always so helpful over the phone.

'Quite honestly, between you and me, a lot of them are at it,' said Sarah. 'I reckon that around fifteen per cent of the partners are having affairs at any time, with their secretaries, trainee solicitors, paralegals, even clients. And it's not just the male partners. The women are just as bad.'

Kim sat rigid and could hardly speak.

'When did the affair start?' Kim tried to ask but only got as far as 'When?'

'I don't know exactly but I think it's been going on for over a year.'

Kim gasped.

'I'm so sorry. I felt I had to tell you. But please don't say it was me. Let's meet soon. Talk to Richard.'

Sarah's words resonated around Kim's brain. 'Talk to Richard'. Why? What would be the point? She could never ever trust him again.

Kim's life changed overnight when she threw Richard out of the house. She piled up all of his belongings in their front garden, including his sports trophies and the huge wooden oars that he had hung proudly from the ceiling in the hallway from his time at Cambridge. Then Kim phoned him at work and told him to come and fetch his things. Richard had been in an important meeting at the time so he'd called a removal company and they did the job for him. After the meeting he had tried to get back into the house but by then Kim had changed the locks on the front door.

That was the end of Kim and Richard. It was also the end of her comfortable life. From then on she was on her own. Richard would no longer pay for a nanny and a housekeeper and Kim had to go to court to get enough money to live on. He paid for Dan and Izzy to be fed and clothed and he settled their school fees. Any other expenditure, whether for school trips, holidays or family entertainment had to be justified to Richard.

Josh saw Kim gradually turn a little sour, although he still found her attractive. As a mature student Kim did not relate to most of the other undergraduates in her year group as friends, because of their differences in age and life experience. She often stayed behind after tutorials with Josh and began to confide in him. They would sit in his office and over a cup of coffee Kim would complain about Richard and his mean attitude to money and how she felt belittled by the divorce process.

Kim would seek advice from Josh on how to deal with Izzy, who had reacted badly to her father being ejected from the family home. As a single man with not even a property to his name, let alone a child, he felt ill equipped to advise Kim on anything. So he sat and listened and she talked, often for hours each week. Kim came to rely more and more on Josh for support and he grew to love her. After she and Richard had been separated for a year Josh dared to ask her out on a date rather than just as friends. A year later they were living together in the house Kim had shared with Richard.

To the outside world Josh was known as 'Kim's lodger', a description he disliked but could do nothing about for fear of his own meagre finances being taken into account in the very messy divorce proceedings that seemed destined to last for a long time. As part of the pretence that he and Kim were not involved in a relationship he had his own bedroom. Not even Dan or Izzy were allowed to witness his nightly forays into Kim's bed in case one of them accidentally gave the game away.

This subterfuge generally enhanced his and Kim's love life, giving Josh the rush of excitement he had felt about sex as a young man. As they giggled and fumbled under the duvet, Josh would feel free and uninhibited. But sometimes he experienced a slight tinge of embarrassment as he crept along the hallway in the dark on his way to 'Kim's bedroom'.

As Josh drove around the outside of the park peering through the tall black metal railings for any sign of a group of teenagers that might include Izzy, he wished he could earn more money than the salary he received from the university and the few thousand pounds he earned each year from writing and editing articles on social policy.

Kim was often exhausted, by her work, her kids and the strain of her ongoing divorce. Josh wanted to rescue her and turn her back into the woman he'd first met when she'd enrolled as a student on his course. He felt he had no hope of doing anything with his life that would earn him a lot of money. He was approaching forty and the whole of his career had so far been spent in lecturing and academic study, neither of which were well paid. In this respect he'd followed in the footsteps of his father, who had originally qualified as a teacher, then trained teachers himself and finally lectured at a university.

Josh had grown up in a family where public service had been more important than the pursuit of wealth. In fact in some ways the concept of wealth had been alien, even frowned upon. Josh sometimes wondered if his view of the world as a child had been unreal. It had involved an idealistic, Christian Socialist image of humanity as being basically fair and good while caring for the welfare of others. As Josh had grown older he had realised this was not the case at all. He now often felt that the majority of human beings were self-interested and greedy. They had to be made to do what was right and fair by laws and sanctions. Or maybe it was governments and powerful businesses and individuals that caused people to behave as they did.

Josh found himself so deep in thought that he had forgotten to look for Izzy. He stopped his ancient silver Saab convertible by the park gates and shouted her name. The evening light was fading and Josh could see a few shadowy figures dotted around. The dark silhouettes seemed almost to float just above the ground. There was no response to Josh's call so he got back into his car and drove off in the direction of Wimbledon Common, another area regularly frequented by teenagers.

It was dark now and the back streets were eerily quiet and bathed in the gentle orange glow that came from tall street lamps. The rush hour traffic had subsided and people were in their homes eating meals and watching television, having returned from work or school. Josh could hardly believe that this was the day of an election. He thought back to his childhood, something he'd found himself doing a lot recently. Where were the election posters in people's front windows? Where were the election vans, loudspeakers blaring through the streets urging people out of their homes to vote? Josh had only seen a couple of posters throughout the whole time he'd been driving around searching for Izzy.

Josh remembered the streets where he'd grown up in Bristol. Nearly every house had proudly displayed a red, yellow or blue poster in its front window declaring its occupants to be Labour, Liberal or Conservative. Election vans, adorned with the bright colours of each party, loudspeakers blaring out the campaign messages of their candidates, trawled through the streets urging people to vote. As a child Josh had loved the carnival atmosphere of an election, the procession of noisy vans and the rosettes made of shiny ribbon worn with pride by the candidates and their supporters. An army of volunteers would 'knock up' potential voters, offering them lifts to the nearest polling station if they had not yet voted.

Josh recalled the excitement he'd felt as he delivered leaflets with his father and the local Member of Parliament, who was campaigning to be elected for another term. There were times when he would sit at the back of a cold church hall where a public meeting was taking place, drawing pictures in a notebook or examining particles of dust with a small magnifying glass. He never complained as his father had told him that important political matters were being discussed and he must be quiet.

Josh's thoughts turned to the present and how politics had changed over the years. Many people today seemed firmly intent on abstaining, as if not voting was somehow virtuous and a valid choice to make. He could understand how disillusioned voters felt with politicians of all parties. The expenses scandal, when numerous Members of Parliament had been exposed as at best negligent and at worst fraudulent in respect of their claims for expenses had destroyed what little faith the electorate had left. MPs' claims for the cost of building islands in their back gardens for their ducks and for repaying non-existent mortgages on homes they'd never lived in had made politicians more unpopular than estate agents, lawyers and even bankers. They were regarded as less trustworthy than the reality TV stars who strutted their stuff across the screens of the great British public night after night.

Most people only ever saw politicians on television where their speeches were carefully prepared and edited. Even that was a rare event, as political commentators took up most of the available airtime with their deliberations about what may or may not be the case or about to happen in the world of politics. Josh had known the names of most government ministers throughout his youth but now he could only name a few. Television had turned politics into a presidential style where the Prime Minister was king, dictator and president all rolled into one. It was therefore hardly surprising that the electorate felt detached from politicians.

Wimbledon Common was deserted apart from the odd lone dog-walker skirting its edges and the street lamps in the surrounding roads gave it an eerie glow. Josh strained his eyes to look into the darkness but all he could see was a light mist that clouded his vision. There was no possibility of Izzy being out and about in such a hostile place for a young woman. She must be at home by now he thought to himself as he turned his car around and drove in the direction of the town centre.

Josh hoped Izzy was safe but Kim hadn't called him to say that she was. A nagging doubt appeared in his mind that he found hard to extinguish. Izzy had been pushing the boundaries recently and taking risks by mixing with a different crowd of people and going to new places without telling Kim. Josh had recently seen Izzy and a couple of her friends with a group of older boys that he hadn't recognised. Kim had once asked Josh to try and check whether Izzy had met someone on the internet but he hadn't been able to access the laptop Richard had given her.

There were so many stories in the media of teenage girls being groomed for sex by older men who'd pretended to be younger than they were and built up relationships over weeks or months without their parents having any idea. With the thought that Izzy may have been abducted refusing to go away, Josh jammed his foot onto the accelerator and sped in the direction of home.

CHAPTER
THREE

Josh's nostrils quivered as he inhaled the deep aromas of garlic and tomatoes coming from the kitchen. He closed the front door and headed in the direction of the food, realising that he hadn't eaten for hours. Kim had her sleeves rolled up and was busy chopping onion on a large wooden board. A saucepan full to the brim with bright red sauce sizzled on the hob and a huge pan of pasta sat hissing away beside it. The kitchen was filled with steam and lines of moisture ran down its old-fashioned picture window.

Kim looked flushed and relaxed as she turned to face Josh and greeted him warmly with a smile and a wave of the wooden spoon she was holding.

'Izzy's ok,' she said quickly. 'And before you ask, yes, I did vote.'

'Thank goodness,' said Josh. Kim raised her eyebrows. 'I mean about Izzy,' he grinned.

Kim took a sip from a large glass of red wine and waved Josh in the direction of an empty glass that stood next to a half full bottle of cabernet sauvignon on the long pine kitchen table. He picked up the glass and filled it with wine.

'Cheers,' said Josh. He inhaled its warm tones, swirled the liquid around the glass and then took a large gulp. He could feel the alcohol oozing through his body. Josh didn't think of himself as a big drinker but he did like a good red wine.

'So, where is Her Majesty?' Josh almost breathed the words as he shifted a pile of papers to his right and parked himself on the edge of the kitchen table. It was always covered in documents interspersed with post it notes of different colours, shapes and sizes. There were letters from Dan and Izzy's school, junk mail that someone in the house had decided would be useful but then forgot about and old magazines and newspapers that were still unread. Unfortunately important papers such as bills and documents relating to Kim's divorce would often get caught up in the morass of paperwork and disappear forever.

Josh's pet name for Izzy was 'Her Majesty' but he never said it to her face. In fact he had several different names for her, which were designed to show how he felt about her at the time. Kim usually responded positively to Josh when he called Izzy by one of his pet names, sharing the joke.

'Izzy's round at Georgia's,' said Kim in a matter of fact way.

'Nice of her to let us know when I was searching the whole of Wimbledon for her,' replied Josh.

'You left your mobile here,' said Kim. 'I did try to call you.'

Josh could feel her bristle. He didn't want to start a fight and certainly not a fight about Izzy. He had found himself getting into arguments with Kim more often now that Izzy was a teenager. He thought back to when he'd come into Kim's life. Izzy had just turned eight and her older brother, Dan, was twelve years old. Josh had treated both of them with kid gloves. He hadn't had much contact with children before he met Kim. A couple of years later he found himself living with her and taking responsibility for her offspring.

Kim's ex-husband, Richard, hadn't had much to do with Dan and Izzy when they were growing up because of his 'oh-so-important' job as a City solicitor. Nevertheless both children had been devastated by his departure from the family home. Josh had never tried to replace Richard but he'd made an effort to be as good a substitute father, older brother or friend as he knew how. He was always willing to talk to Dan and Izzy and he gave them regular lifts to all their various activities.

Josh watched Kim as she added chopped onion to the sizzling mass of red sauce. He thought that perhaps the onion should have been cooked before the tomatoes but he decided to say nothing. Kim had a 'shove it all in together' style of cooking that was born of necessity. Josh was able to cook but hardly ever did so because he often got distracted listening to radio or watching TV and meals therefore took too long to get ready.

Kim turned off the pasta and reduced the temperature of the sauce. Still wearing her long black and white striped cooking apron, she pulled up a chair and sat at the far end of the kitchen table from where Josh was sitting.

'I hope you don't mind but I've invited a couple of people around for a drink later,' said Kim as she stared into her glass of wine. 'They'll be here about nine o'clock.'

Josh paused for a moment. 'Oh no. Did you have to? I know it's your house but I do live here.'

After he spoke Josh realised he had sounded more put out than he'd intended.

'Well, I'm telling you now,' said Kim calmly. 'Anyway, you don't have to speak to them.'

'I want to watch the local election results on TV,' said Josh.

'They don't even start until after midnight,' said Kim. She smiled reassuringly and looked him straight in the eye.

'Who are these people anyway?' he mumbled.

'Maggie and Bruno. You know, the new couple who moved in on Saturday, two doors down.'

Josh had been busy over the weekend putting the finishing touches to a research paper. He'd been working to a tight deadline that was fast approaching so had spent most of Saturday and Sunday in his study. He smoothed his hair back and furrowed his brow as if he was in deep thought.

'Oh yes,' he said. He vaguely remembered Kim

having mentioned something about people moving into the dilapidated house a few doors down the road. It had been empty since its elderly occupant had died several months ago. Josh had seen inside the house only once, when her nephew had come to collect a piece of furniture, but had been unable to move it on his own. He thought back to the faded wallpaper and bare floorboards, the ceiling damaged by rainwater from a leaking roof. He certainly didn't envy his new neighbours as he contemplated the huge renovation task that awaited them.

'Maggie and Bruno are really nice people,' said Kim as she refilled her glass and stood up to check on the pasta sauce.

'I'm sure they are,' said Josh, smiling. He did not share Kim's enthusiasm for neighbours. She was forever in and out of other people's houses. She wasn't nosey but loved being part of 'the local community'.

'Maggie has her own public relations company and I think Bruno's a surveyor, something to do with property anyway.'

'Great, probably an estate agent,' said Josh. He slipped off the side of the kitchen table where he'd been perched in an uncomfortable position, stretched his legs and helped himself to a second glass of wine. He pulled out a chair and sat down.

'Now if you'd told me that a writer, artist, historian or a fellow academic had moved into the road and would be gracing us with their presence, I might have sounded more enthusiastic about tonight's get-together,' said Josh.

'What's wrong with a surveyor and someone in PR?'

'Boring.'

'Well, at least they're not solicitors or accountants like most of our neighbours.'

'That's true.'

'Anyway, you're just an inverted snob and you know you'll enjoy yourself if you can be bothered to make an effort,' said Kim.

Suddenly Izzy burst into the kitchen. She threw her arms around Kim and flashed Josh one of her huge smiles. Her face was flushed and she was out of breath.

'I said I'd be back before eight and here I am,' said Izzy triumphantly. Kim kissed her daughter on the forehead and smoothed her delicate light brown, wavy hair away from her face so that it lay loosely on her shoulders. In some ways Izzy resembled her mother. She had a fair complexion and a round face, hazel eyes and a slim body. But she had elements of her father's features too such as a wide forehead and mouth with lips turned up at the corners.

'So you are,' said Kim gently.

Josh started to clear the table ready for dinner to be served. He shunted the piles of papers up to one end and went to get knives, forks and spoons from a drawer to lay four place settings.

'We had a mock election at school today,' said Izzy. She grinned with excitement as she sloshed water into a glass, spilling several drops on the table.

'That sounds interesting. Who won?' said Josh.

'UKIP,' said Izzy.

Josh stopped what he was doing and stared at her. 'UKIP?' he spluttered.

Izzy wrinkled her nose, raised her eyebrows and shrugged her shoulders. 'Yeah, the guy was really hot. He's in the Upper Sixth, plays first fifteen rugby and he looked dead fit in his pink shirt.'

Josh noticed that Kim had a smile on her face. He wondered if her daughter was joking.

Izzy paused for a moment and then said, 'What does UKIP stand for?'

'The United Kingdom Independence Party,' said Josh. He gave Izzy a quizzical look.

'It's just as well you don't get to vote until you're eighteen,' said Kim.

'Are you serious?' said Josh. He'd stopped laying the table and stood facing Izzy.

'What d'you mean?' she said, looking worried but with a tone of voice that indicated she was ready to stand up for herself. 'I didn't say I voted for him.'

'Come on guys,' said Kim. 'Let's have a civilised family dinner for a change.'

Izzy noisily pulled up a chair and plonked herself down at the table.

'I suppose I'm going to get a politics lesson, am I?' She looked Josh squarely in the eye. He knew she was challenging him to an argument.

He also knew that Kim would not want to spend the next half an hour listening to him arguing with Izzy. Josh caught sight of Kim's expression that clearly sent out the message to him, 'Don't you dare!' So he got on with laying the table.

'I expect you're tired aren't you,' said Kim to Izzy. 'How was school today?' She quickly shoved a plate of steaming pasta in front of her daughter. 'Eat,' she said. Izzy ate and for a minute or two nobody spoke.

'Where's Dan?' asked Izzy in between mouthfuls of pasta.

'Playing cricket', said Josh quickly before Kim could answer. 'He'll be back soon.' Josh felt his voice soften as he spoke. He never set out to cause friction between himself and Izzy but they often argued, much to Kim's dismay. Josh felt she was becoming tired of their regular evening clashes.

'How come Dan never gets made to come home early for dinner?' said Izzy. It's sport, sport, sport. He's obsessed.'

'He's seventeen years old,' said Kim. 'He'll soon be an adult and able to do exactly what he wants.'

Josh watched her spooning out pasta. She was stooping slightly and her shoulders were hunched in such a way that she looked older than her years.

'I'm going out later to meet Sophie,' said Izzy. She didn't look up but concentrated on her dinner.

'I'm sorry Madam, but you're not going anywhere,' said Kim. 'It's a school night. Haven't you any homework to do? You've got exams coming up in a couple of weeks.'

Josh felt a strong urge to support Kim in her admonishment of her daughter. If he'd been Izzy's father he would have 'put his foot down' as his own father used to say. But Izzy had made Josh more than aware that he was not her father in any shape or form. Sometimes she allowed him to be a sounding board or even her mentor when she was involved in a difficult issue at school. On occasions she even treated him as a friend, but never a father figure. Richard had a very special place in his little girl's heart, even though he seemed to have no idea how much she cared for him.

In Josh's opinion (which he kept to himself) Richard was an inadequate father. He showered Izzy with presents every time they met but always forgot her birthday unless Kim reminded him. He saw Izzy at times and in places that suited him, such as in top London restaurants. But he never went to see her play netball, which she loved, or watch her take part in a school play. Josh, on the other hand, helped Izzy with her homework, acted as a taxi service for herself and her friends and always offered a shoulder to cry on when she'd been let down by Richard. Josh regarded his own father as a measure by which to judge all others and he was pretty sure his came out on top. What Josh tried to do in his substitute father role for Dan and Izzy was to be the rock that his father was for him.

Izzy had stopped talking and was pushing pieces of tube-shaped pasta around her plate as if she were playing a game of chess. Josh knew she would be planning her next move.

'Izzy', he said gently. 'I understand that you would rather be out with your friends but your mother has your best interests at heart.'

She did not look up but continued to poke her food around on the plate when suddenly Kim grabbed it.

'Stop playing with it,' she shouted. 'If you're not going to eat any more...' Kim's words tailed off as she virtually threw the plate in the sink. Then she sat back down heavily on her chair and continued eating. Izzy looked up as if nothing had happened. Josh was surprised, as he'd expected her to make a scene.

'I really can't see the point of passing exams. I'm going to be a celebrity.'

'That's enough,' Kim interrupted. Josh could see from her expression that she was seething with anger just below the surface. 'Your father's paying a lot of money for your education.'

'Dick can afford it,' said Izzy, throwing a wicked look at Josh.

'Don't call him Dick,' shouted Kim.

'Why not? Everyone else calls their parents by their first names.'

Izzy knows exactly which buttons to press to wind up her mother, thought Josh. Kim sighed and turned her back on them both as she cleared up pans, plates and cutlery ready to be washed up.

CHAPTER
FOUR

Josh watched as Izzy tipped a small pile of salt onto her placemat and made patterns with her finger. He glanced at Kim who was busy at the kitchen sink thrusting sticky pans into the deep soapy water.

'So who do you think should win the next general election?' said Josh casually.

Izzy sighed loudly and then looked up from what she was doing and put on a false smile. 'I don't really care,' she said. 'They're all the same, politicians, a bunch of liars and so ugly.'

Izzy leaned back in her chair so that its front legs came off the ground. She rocked backwards and forwards holding onto the kitchen table with both hands. Josh shot a glance at Kim, who was concentrating on loading the dishwasher, blissfully ignorant of her daughter's precarious position. Josh frowned at Izzy and she responded by pulling herself forward so that the chair landed back on four legs with a bump.

'I'd rather vote in a TV talent show than in a proper election. Actually, I bet more people will vote in TV talent shows this year than they will in the next election. I'll lay money on it.'

'So what do you care about apart from who wins television talent contests, or should I say 'no talent' contests?' said Josh, smiling. He was enjoying teasing Izzy. She pretended to ignore him.

'Climate change, pollution, animals being exterminated...I mean extinct.'

'All of those involve politicians having to make difficult decisions,' said Josh. 'Each of the political parties has different views on these sorts of issues.'

'Do they?' said Izzy. Josh couldn't tell whether she was being facetious or not.

'Do you learn much about politics at school?' he said.

'Not really. We did a bit in PSHE.'

Josh looked quizzical.

'P S H E,' said Izzy, emphasising each letter.

'Remind me what that is.'

'Personal... Social... and... Health...Education.' Izzy rolled her eyes.

'Thanks. I suppose it's difficult for your generation to keep up with what each party stands for. Half the time they don't know themselves,' said Josh.

Izzy laughed. At last he had her attention.

'Take the Conservative Party,' said Josh, turning over the palm of his left hand as if he were offering something to Izzy. She leaned towards him, slightly furrowing her brow and concentrating hard.

'Is that the one with the hot leader? Rides a bike and then has a car following him with all his stuff.'

'Well I wouldn't exactly describe him as hot,' said Josh. At one point he didn't even know what his policies were.'

'Why not?'

'Because his party was carrying out something called a 'review'. When he became leader of the Conservative Party he decided to find out what people wanted him to do in the future.' Izzy opened her eyes wide, raised her eyebrows and nodded. Josh continued. 'So he set up what are called working groups to find out.'

'You mean he actually cares what people want?' said Izzy.

'Well, he has his own ideas about what they should want.'

'What about the other parties?'

'As you probably know, the Labour Party was in

government for a long time. When the new leader was elected some people thought he might introduce new policies. But most people would say that Labour Party policy hasn't changed much,' said Josh.

Izzy frowned slightly and concentrated on what Josh was saying with a serious expression on her face.

'What exactly is a policy?'

Josh paused for a moment and cast his eyes around the room as if he were searching for something. 'It's a view about something, a standpoint, a set of beliefs about the way people should lead their lives.'

'So, does everyone in each party think the same thing and do all the parties have different policies?' asked Izzy.

'No,' said Josh. 'Some of the parties agree with each other on some things. For example, in 2003 the Labour Party and the Conservatives both wanted to invade Iraq, but there were members of each party who disagreed.'

'What did they do?' asked Izzy.

'Some of them just went along with what they were told to do by their party leader.'

'Even though they disagreed?' said Izzy looking confused.

'Even though they disagreed,' repeated Josh. 'Except that a couple of Members of Parliament who were in the Cabinet resigned so they could speak out against their own party.'

'It sounds complicated,' said Izzy. 'I thought a cabinet was wooden like a cupboard.'

'You're right.' Josh laughed. 'Some MPs probably need to be shut away in cupboards to keep them out of trouble. The Cabinet I was talking about is the name given to the group of MPs who govern the country. It's called democracy. You get to vote in a general election every five years and once a government is elected, you're stuck with them until they decide to call another election.'

'You can write to your MP though,' said Izzy. 'We did that at school about climate change and, what was the other thing? Oh, I know, fair trade chocolate.' She looked pleased with herself.

'But your MP doesn't have to do what you want even if everyone in his or her constituency wanted the same thing as you,' said Josh.

'Oh,' said Izzy, looking confused.

'That's because an MP is a representative as opposed to a delegate,' said Josh, emphasising the words. 'A representative is someone who is supposed to listen to what their constituents want but they then make up their own mind how to vote.'

'So what's a…' Izzy's voice tailed off.

'Delegate,' said Josh. 'A delegate has to vote how they are told to vote by the majority of people they represent.'

'Can you give me an example?'

Josh watched as Kim, having finished washing up, slid quietly along the side of the kitchen and out into the hallway. Had he seen her wink at him as she disappeared through the doorway or was he imagining things? He looked back at Izzy. Her hands cupped her face as she leaned forward and rested her elbows on the kitchen table. At that precious moment Josh had Izzy's undivided attention.

'Well,' he said, leaning forward to meet her gaze. 'Take the death penalty, for example.' Izzy's eyes widened.

'We don't have that in this country, do we?' she said.

'No. We used to but it was abolished. Some other countries still use the death penalty.'

'Like the USA,' said Izzy. 'I've seen it in films.'

'That's right,' said Josh. 'It's still used in some states.' He paused for a moment. 'Well, what if most of the electorate in Wimbledon wanted the death penalty brought back for murders committed by terrorists? If an MP was a delegate then they would have to vote in Parliament for that to happen, even if they disagreed.'

'But if the MP was a representative they could decide for themselves,' said Izzy excitedly.

'Exactly,' said Josh.

'But that's not really democracy, is it?' she said.

'It's the type of democracy we have in this country and it's been going for a long time.'

'That doesn't make it the right kind of democracy,' said Izzy with a wide grin on her face. She tilted her chair so that it rested on its two back legs and held onto the kitchen table as she rocked backwards and forwards. Josh knew that if Kim had been in the room she would have been shouting at Izzy to stop immediately in case she broke her back, or the chair, or both. Josh was half tempted to say something feeble like 'Izzy, you'd better stop doing that. You know your mother wouldn't be happy if you were to injure yourself.' But he did not want to lose this moment.

It was rare for anyone to engage in anything resembling a political discussion in Kim's house, as everyone was so busy rushing about to his or her various activities. On the few occasions when they all sat down together at the table to eat, conversation usually revolved around what each of them had been doing or intended to do. Josh felt he had a duty to inform Dan and Izzy about politics whenever he could as his own father had done with him.

'There are lots of anomalies in politics,' said Josh, trying not to sound patronising.

'Anomalies?' said Izzy, jerking her chair forward so that it again rested on four legs. Josh breathed a sigh of relief.

'You've probably studied them in your English lessons,' he said.

'I think we did. But I can't remember what they are.' She poured herself a glass of water and took a few delicate sips.

'An anomaly is where something isn't quite the way it should be. The definition is abnormal or irregular,' said Josh.

'Can you give me an example?' said Izzy, still looking confused.

Josh had momentarily forgotten that he was not talking to one of his students but to a thirteen year old.

'Ok.'

Izzy turned her chair towards Josh and listened carefully.

'In 2010 the government decided to sell off the forests in this country that are owned by the public, even though most people disagreed.'

Izzy's eyes opened wide. 'How could the government do that when most people didn't want them to?' she squealed, waving her hands in the air.

'That's politicians for you,' said Josh calmly. 'But an organisation called 38 Degrees set up an online petition and half a million people signed it so the government had to back down. They would have got away with it otherwise.' He looked at Izzy and thought how small and vulnerable she was. Her eyes were watering slightly at the sides and her sad expression had taken some of the colour from her usual rosy complexion.

'That's really bad,' said Izzy slowly.

'What's really bad?' echoed a deep male voice.

Josh turned to see Dan as he lumbered into the kitchen and dumped his school rucksack and huge cricket bag onto the floor. He pulled out a chair next to Izzy and collapsed into it while allowing one of his large hands to tousle her hair.

'You made us jump,' she protested, fanning herself with both hands, as if she were taking part in an American teen sitcom. Izzy's face glowed with love for her older brother. Josh's father described Dan as a 'strapping lad'. It was a phrase that was hardly used these days but suited him well. He was tall and blond with a muscular and athletic build. Izzy's friends swooned over Dan whenever they saw him and she derived a certain status among her peers for having such a 'hot' brother.

Dan had a handsome face that Josh often thought had features resembling those of a Greek god. He was a kind and calm human being. After Richard's swift and enforced departure from the family home Dan had quickly assumed the role of head of the household. He became Kim's protector and often acted as a father figure for Izzy. Most of the time Dan and Izzy got on well, but when he told her to do something she didn't want to do sparks would fly and Izzy would accuse Kim of favouring her son, which on occasions was true.

'Your dinner's in the oven,' said Josh.

Dan grabbed himself a plate and piled so much pasta onto it that several pieces fell onto the floor. Josh raised his eyebrows but decided not to say anything.

'So, did I interrupt some important discussion?' said Dan cheekily as he sat down at the table and began to stuff pasta into his mouth.

'We were talking about politics,' said Josh.

Dan pretended to choke on his food and poured himself a large glass of water. 'Politics,' he spluttered. 'You're discussing politics…with Izzy! Excuse me if I'm wrong but I thought all she knew about voting involved TV talent shows.'

'Very funny,' said Izzy, folding her arms firmly across her chest. She knew Dan was teasing her but she still felt quite cross that he might think she wasn't very bright. Josh knew Dan was taking advantage of the fact that he was four years older than Izzy. He liked to show his sister who was boss every so often in true male fashion. Josh tried to dissipate the tension between them.

'Actually, we were having a very informed discussion,' he said.

'Before you came in and interrupted us,' added Izzy.

Dan smiled at her. He loved the attention he got from teasing his sister. As he heaped salad onto his plate Kim came into the kitchen. She tousled his hair and he pretended to shrug off her display of affection.

'I didn't hear you come in,' said Kim. 'Did you win the match?'

'Of course,' said Dan with a smile on his face.

Josh felt as if he were standing on the sidelines at some sporting event. He could sense the chemistry that existed between Kim and Dan, a feeling of closeness and mutual understanding that excluded all others. He shot a glance at Izzy. She seemed to have lost some more of the colour from her cheeks and was now looking a little awkward as she examined her nails.

'Izzy. Do you want some fruit?' said Kim.

'No thanks. I'm not hungry.' Izzy stood up from her chair. 'I've got to get my coursework done.'

'No messing around on your computer or mobile until you've done your homework,' said Kim. She stood facing Izzy with her hands on her hips and a slight frown on her face. Josh felt warmth and compassion for her. Kim was a good mother.

'We'll finish our discussion another time,' said Josh. He winked at Izzy. She smiled and quietly slid out of the kitchen and into the hallway unnoticed by either her mother or brother, who were now deep in conversation. Kim and Izzy were too alike to be close and Izzy blamed her mother for her father's absence, even though it was him who had the affair. That was it in a nutshell, thought Josh. He turned to Dan.

'So which party do you think will get the most votes in the local elections today?' said Josh, leaning back in his chair with his hands behind his head. Dan helped himself to the largest apple in the fruit bowl, examined it and took a huge bite. Drops of juice glistened at the sides of his wide mouth. There was silence for a few seconds while he finished chewing.

'I'm not sure,' said Dan. 'I reckon a lot of people will stay at home and not vote at all.'

'You mean, like a protest?' said Kim.

'Yeah,' said Dan as he took another large bite of apple. Only one more bite and it would be gone, thought Josh.

'Some people will abstain because they're unhappy with what the government is doing about the economy, cuts to public services and creeping privatisation, that sort of thing,' said Kim.

'There's also the issue of immigration,' said Josh. 'That's going to be a big deal for voters in some parts of the country.'

'Do you think UKIP or the BNP will get many votes?' said Dan.

'I hope not,' said Kim. 'I'm really worried about UKIP. Some of them come over as quite plausible but their views are very right wing.'

'They'll win some seats, especially in places where people can't get jobs or housing,' said Josh. 'It always suits politicians to blame immigrants for social problems.'

'I think everyone is disillusioned with politicians of all parties,' said Kim. 'None of them seem to have any answers to the country's economic problems. Most of them come over in the media as out of touch with the public. They talk in sound bites and never answer the questions that are put to them.'

'I don't really understand why people aren't more interested in politics,' said Josh. 'Everyone's much more aware of environmental issues, genocide, racism and what's going on in the world than ever before. And yet people seem to feel disempowered, as if they don't have the ability to influence the world around them.'

'Well, they don't, do they?' said Kim. 'You can

vote once every three or four years in a local election. But central government seems to run local government these days so that's pretty much a waste of a vote. Then in general elections you can vote only once every five years. Oh yes, you can of course write to your MP to ask him or her to vote in a particular way or to take up some issue on your behalf. But you can't actually influence the course of British politics.'

'That's why people join pressure groups or sign petitions,' said Dan. 'Look how many people are writing blogs on the Internet or setting up on line petitions to campaign on particular issues. It's the only way to get your view across and actually achieve something. Hacked Off have been really successful in putting pressure on the government to do something about phone hacking because so many people signed up to their online petition.'

'Not to mention Twitter and all those people who are changing the course of history in the Middle East because they've been able to communicate quickly and easily,' said Kim.

'I don't know,' said Josh. 'There's a sort of emotional detachment from party politics these days. I see it in my students and I saw it when I was talking to Izzy earlier. The reason why people vote in TV talent shows is that they feel they can influence the outcome. It's different with politics. People can't be bothered to vote because they don't think their votes will make a difference to their daily existence.'

'Bread and circuses,' said Dan loudly. 'We've been studying Karl Marx's theories at school. He was a famous German philosopher who wrote about politics. He said that as long as people are given bread and circuses they don't care how they're governed. That was in the 19th century of course. Today it would be alcohol and TV.'

'That's right,' said Kim. 'What people care about today is which celebrity is neglecting their children or whether their favourite footballer is having an affair.'

'I think teenagers should be allowed to vote,' said Dan.

'They'd just copy their parents or do what their friends told them to do,' said Kim.

'I disagree,' said Josh. 'I knew a lot about politics when I was a teenager. I grew up in a political family. My father stood for Parliament but didn't get elected. So he decided to go into local politics instead and became a Bristol city councillor.'

'Why was that?' said Dan.

'Because my mother said she didn't want to be the wife of an MP. She hated all the events she was expected to attend, having to be nice to people she had no interest in and the prospect of either moving to live in London or spending long periods of time away from my father. My paternal grandfather was also involved in politics. He was only eighteen when he helped to found the South-East Bristol branch of the Labour Party and he was a member until he died at the age of ninety-seven. He was employed as a parliamentary agent and looked after the affairs of two local MPs in succession. He was also a Bristol city councillor for many years and was the secretary of his local party until he was ninety-three.'

'Wow, that's old,' said Dan. Josh nodded.

'I used to go to political meetings when I was a young child,' said Josh. Dan raised his eyebrows. 'I delivered leaflets with my father and canvassed votes for the local MP. I had a fantastic childhood. I felt as if I really mattered.' Images flooded into Josh's mind of him riding in the election van, loudspeakers blaring through the streets, people waving and meetings where politicians held forth in loud and impassioned voices with cake and orange squash to follow. It had been a near perfect childhood.

'Oh well,' said Dan, pushing himself up from the table. 'The only battles I want to fight are those on the rugby field or cricket pitch.' Dan grabbed his two heavy bags and moved slowly towards the kitchen door.

'Wait a minute,' said Kim. 'I need to talk to you about a couple of things.' She beckoned to Dan to sit back down at the table. Josh felt it was time to leave so that Kim could talk to her son alone. She relied on Dan for emotional support, even though the burden was too great for him at times.

Josh slipped quietly out of the kitchen, along the hallway and into his study. He turned on the small TV that was perched precariously on a wooden table in the far corner of the room. The news had just started and various political commentators were giving their opinions and making predictions about the local election results that were still several hours away. Josh stretched out his legs and made himself comfortable in his favourite brown leather armchair. The news would be on for at least an hour and he had no desire to be elsewhere.

CHAPTER
FIVE

Josh was still sitting comfortably in his study watching the news when he thought he heard the front doorbell ring so he turned the sound down on the TV. It was probably one of Dan's friends coming to pick him up, or perhaps Kim had popped out to see a neighbour and forgotten her keys. Something in his subconscious was bothering him but he could not work out what it was. Just as Josh was beginning to think that perhaps he was supposed to be somewhere else, a picture appeared on the TV screen that caught his eye and the thought passed. He turned up the sound and looked at his mobile phone. It was nine fifteen.

Suddenly the door to Josh's study burst open and Kim thrust her head into the room. She looked tense and meaningful. Josh jumped up from his chair. 'What is it?'

'They're here. I thought you'd be ready,' said Kim through her teeth. She looked him up and down like a disapproving schoolteacher.

'Who?'

'Maggie and Bruno, they're in the living room,' whispered Kim.

Josh's brain whirred around and then he remembered her plan for the evening. 'Sorry, I forgot they were coming.'

Kim's head disappeared around the door and, as she walked through the kitchen, he could hear her sighing. Josh felt uncomfortable as his feet slid along the hallway in the direction of the living room. He was about to join a party he didn't want to be at with people he had no interest in. He felt tempted to return to his study and lock himself inside for the whole evening. But that would have been extremely childish and Josh was trying to patch up his relationship with Kim, which had not been going well for a couple of months. They hardly ever socialised with one another and they spent little time on their own together in the house. She would be very upset if he refused to meet her new friends.

Josh could hear the sound of voices as he stood for a moment outside the stripped pine door at the entrance to the living room. He had a strong desire to creep quietly up the stairs and pretend to be ill. Kim must have been listening for his footsteps as he heard her say, 'Josh. Come and meet our new neighbours.' He knew there was no escape. He eased himself into the room and stood to face the assembled company. All three of them stared at him and he quickly looked down to see if his flies were undone. Thankfully no, but there was a large red stain on the front of his rather crumpled grey and white work shirt. It was Kim's pasta sauce.

'Sorry,' said Josh, smiling sheepishly. 'I forgot to change. I've been watching the news and, you know, the election pundits, I lost track of time.'

Josh felt stupid standing there in front of three people making excuses. Suddenly he was rescued by a strikingly pretty blonde woman, who leaped up from the brown leather sofa.

'Hi, I'm Maggie.' The vision of loveliness offered her hand to Josh and he was tempted to kiss it but he resisted and shook it firmly but gently. Their eyes met for a moment and then she looked away.

'Hi,' said Josh, turning to face the large man who had also got up from the sofa and was now standing beside Maggie.

'Bruno,' he said, shaking Josh's hand firmly. A little too firmly, thought Josh as he lowered himself into a dilapidated armchair that had belonged to his grandfather. He sank down into it and made himself comfortable while Kim poured him a large glass of red wine. She got up to pass it to him and he noticed that she had changed her clothes. Kim's newly washed hair that was still slightly damp lay in shiny brown ringlets on her shoulders and, unusually for Kim, she was wearing make-up. Josh smiled warmly at her as she passed him the glass of wine. The living room was looking tidy for a change and she had laid out nuts, crisps and dips in small glass bowls. Josh felt a pang of guilt that while Kim had been busying herself preparing for the arrival of her guests, he had been watching TV.

'Kim was telling us about her Friends of the Park group. It sounds amazing,' said Maggie enthusiastically. She was sitting next to Bruno with the right side of her body firmly pressed against his left side. The sofa was old and after years of Dan and Izzy jumping on it, despite being told not to, it dipped in the middle so that people sitting on it found themselves pressed together. Josh wished for a moment that he could change places with Bruno and then he felt guilty.

'Yeah, the Friends of the Park have been great for the local community, really brought people together, young and old, families and single people, different religions and cultures,' said Josh.

'The Friends' annual picnic is in a few weeks time. I hope you'll both come,' said Kim. Josh watched as she chatted away to Maggie about the joys of the summer picnic. There would be a barbecue for everyone who lived in the roads around the park, children's races and face painting followed by home-made cakes and cups of tea.

While Bruno listened attentively to Maggie and Kim's conversation Josh examined him surreptitiously. He had strong features and thick eyebrows, what could only be described as a Roman nose and a swarthy complexion.

Josh wondered if he had Spanish or Italian blood somewhere in his ancestry. Bruno's eyes were such a deep shade of brown they could almost be described as black. His teeth were gleaming white and his large lips curled up slightly at the corners. His dark brown wavy hair almost touched the collar of his light blue open necked shirt, which

Josh noticed had not two but three buttons undone to reveal the upper half of a muscular chest. Bruno's dark grey pinstriped trousers hid what Josh assumed were strong and powerful legs. Josh thought he must have played rugby at some point in his life. He was handsome when he smiled, not so much because of his features but due to the manner in which he held himself. Bruno was calm and self-assured in a way that Josh was not and that made him feel slightly awkward. He seemed older than Maggie, perhaps nearer to forty than thirty.

Josh would have liked to question Bruno about his background, his career and most important of all his political beliefs. But Kim had told him firmly before the evening began that there were to be no arguments over politics and that he should not be 'too deep'. Deep, thought Josh. He enjoyed being deep. He hated superficial chit-chat about doing up houses or what schools his friends should try to get their darling sons or daughters into. In fact, all the usual middle class dinner party subjects were abhorrent to him, which is why he and Kim never held their own dinner parties and were rarely invited to other people's.

'So, how long have you lived in Horatio Road?' said Maggie.

'Three years,' said Josh. 'Ten years,' said Kim simultaneously. Maggie looked surprised. 'Oh,' she said.

'It's my house,' explained Kim. 'I bought it with my husband, soon to be ex-husband. We're going through a messy divorce.' Kim had killed the conversation. Suddenly Bruno came to her rescue.

'We're about to gut our house. The builders start work next week. It was supposed to happen before we moved in but the company we've contracted to do the renovations got delayed on another job, so we'll be living in a building site for a while.'

Josh had absolutely no interest in what Bruno and Maggie were going to have done to their house. He looked at Kim, whose mind appeared to be elsewhere and who had a forlorn expression on her face. She's probably thinking about divorcing Richard, thought Josh. He mustered up as much enthusiasm as he could for a discussion about home improvements.

'What are you having done?'

'Everything,' said Maggie excitedly as she leaned forward to face Josh, who now had a clear view down the front of her crisp white shirt. He hoped that no one had noticed him looking.

'We're having everything ripped out, new windows, wiring, plumbing, a huge, all glass, rear extension and a loft extension.' Maggie stopped to catch her breath and then went on to describe in more detail the grand plan for her new home. Josh poured her another glass of wine. That must be her third, at least, he thought. The wine was making Maggie animated and her face had a warm glow. Josh thought she looked beautiful.

'Would you like something to eat?' Kim asked Maggie and Bruno, bringing Josh back to reality. They looked like two excited children who had just been offered an ice cream each.

'Yes please,' they said in unison. 'We came straight from work, as you can see,' said Maggie.

She was dressed in a pair of well-cut black trousers and a tight fitting white shirt that showed off her slim and toned figure. Her black leather shoes had high heels and Josh guessed that she was perhaps not as tall as he'd first thought when she had stood up to greet him. Maggie's hair was naturally blonde and wavy and it settled on her shoulders as if every strand had been individually placed in its correct position. Not in a false way as if she had fixed it with spray but because she'd been born with perfect hair. Maggie's bright blue eyes were piercing and whenever she looked at Josh he felt that she could see his thoughts as they passed across his mind. Two smart suit jackets hung on either end of the sofa having been discarded as the temperature in the room increased in direct proportion to the quantity of wine being consumed. Josh looked down at his creased chinos, worn loafers and stained shirt and felt decidedly scruffy.

'I was going to freeze it but it's better fresh,' said Kim as she handed Maggie and Bruno a plate each of steaming pasta. 'Parmesan?' They both nodded.

'Umm, homemade food,' said Bruno.

'We don't cook much. We both work really long hours so we eat out a lot,' explained Maggie.

Josh could see that Bruno was quietly observing his surroundings while he ate. He looked as if he was weighing up Josh and Kim, deciding whether he would make time for them in the future.

'Have you done much to your house?' Maggie asked Kim in between mouthfuls of pasta.

'Not really. The bathroom literally fell to pieces just after we moved in so we had to replace it. That's about all we've done. We need to update the kitchen and the whole place needs decorating. But it's all about money, isn't it?'

Maggie picked up on the tone of defeatism in Kim's voice. 'I love the original features in this room, don't you?' she said cheerfully. She nudged Bruno so hard in the ribs that he almost dropped his plate of pasta in his lap. 'Mmm,' he agreed, nodding his head but unable to speak because his mouth was full of food.

Josh looked surreptitiously at the grandfather clock in the corner of the room, so as not to make it obvious that he was checking the time. As usual it had stopped because no one had bothered to wind it up. He was now on his fourth glass of wine and although he was enjoying the evening more than he thought he would, he was anxious to watch the local election results on TV.

'You would not believe what people have done to their houses around here,' said Kim, who was keen to keep the conversation going. She'd forgotten how much she enjoyed having people round and did not want Maggie and Bruno to leave. Much to Josh's dismay Kim then went on to describe all the different types of extension that had been built by her neighbours. He was even more disappointed to see that Bruno in particular seemed mesmerised by what Kim was saying.

'You bought your house at a good time,' said Bruno. 'Prices have gone up a lot over the last ten years.'

'You're a surveyor, aren't you?' said Kim.

'That's right. I started my own business a few years ago. It's going ok, despite the recession.'

'It needs to go ok. We've got a huge mortgage,' Maggie interrupted. Bruno shot her a disapproving look that she ignored. Josh felt it was time he joined in the conversation so as not to look rude. He hoped they would run out of subjects to discuss soon.

'So, are you involved in the property business?' Josh asked Maggie.

'No,' she replied, stretching out the 'o' sound. 'I'm in Public Relations. I run a business communications consultancy.' Josh had no idea what a business communications consultancy was and he'd no desire to find out, but he loved having Maggie's attention. She's getting drunk, he thought, and smiled to himself. He had already identified Maggie as a woman who could let her hair down and have a good time and he liked her for it. Kim was so uptight these days, always worried about her kids, divorce, finances or job. The list was endless. She found it hard to enjoy life.

'What do you do?' said Maggie, slightly slurring her speech and looking straight at Josh.

'I'm a lecturer in social policy.'

'Oh, a lecherer in what?'

Josh realised that Maggie had no idea what he what he was talking about so he reeled off his standard explanation … lectures, research, tutorials. At the same time he was thinking, not much pay and very little status both inside and outside the walls of the university. Josh thought back to his youth and how highly regarded his father had been in the local community, first as a teacher and then as a lecturer. Society was very different today, thought Josh. Money and status had become so intertwined that in order to have status, people had to have a substantial amount of money.

Josh's thoughts strayed for a few moments and when he re-joined the conversation it had moved on.

'You're a social worker. Wow, that must be hard. I could never do your job,' said Maggie, looking at Kim.

'Overworked and underpaid,' said Kim.

That's public service in the twenty-first century, thought Josh. He was desperate to talk politics and had drunk sufficient alcohol to feel brave enough to do so, despite Kim's earlier warning.

'So, who do you think will win in the local election today?' Josh asked no one in particular.

'Do you mean in Wimbledon?' said Bruno. He leaned forward clasping his two hands together. Big hands, thought Josh. Bruno had a serious expression on his face and his brow furrowed so that he almost looked like he was frowning. Josh began to feel nervous and the thought crossed his mind that perhaps it wasn't such a good idea to start a discussion about politics. He looked at Maggie who had her legs curled up on the sofa in a seductive pose. She seemed relaxed and happy as she gently swished her wine around in its glass.

'We're in Trinity Ward, right?' said Bruno.

'Yeah,' said Josh.

'I'm not really sure how the voting works in local elections,' said Bruno looking a little embarrassed. He was a surveyor and he should know how the voting system worked. Josh managed to hide his surprise that a man could have reached Bruno's age but not know much about politics. But he was secretly pleased as this gave him the perfect opportunity to demonstrate his own knowledge.

'There are twenty wards in the London Borough of Merton. Each ward elects three councillors. In the last local election three councillors from the Conservative Party were elected in this ward. Who knows what will happen tonight?' said Josh.

'I reckon that the Labour Party will lose seats because traditional voters won't come out and vote. Some of them might even vote for UKIP. I think more people are willing to risk voting for minority parties than ever before. I voted for the Green Party,' said Kim.

Josh stared at her in surprise. So much for not talking about politics, he thought to himself as she continued to speak.

'I usually vote Labour but I'm cross with them for being so spineless. Why aren't they coming up with solutions to the country's economic problems? All they do is criticise the policies of the other parties. No-one seems to realise that we need a different type of society. We've got to stop being obsessed with 'growth' and start thinking about what makes people live happy and fulfilling lives.'

It must be the drink, thought Josh. 'Vino Veritas' – If you've drunk wine, you'll speak the truth or something like that. It was years since Josh had studied Latin.

'I was brought up as a Conservative,' Maggie suddenly announced slurring her speech slightly. 'But I'm fed up with them. Sometimes I think I'll vote for the Liberal Democrats. Then one of them says something crass and I think, how could these people run the country?'

As Maggie continued with her monologue Josh noticed how she liked to be in charge of the conversation. Meanwhile Bruno seemed prepared to take a back seat and let her get on with it.

'My parents were friends of the Thatchers,' said Maggie in a posher voice than the one she had been using so far. 'Hence my name.'

'I don't like the leader of the Conservative Party,' said Bruno pointedly. 'He's too smooth and I don't think he's got much substance. He's a PR man, not a prime minister.'

'That's not fair,' said Maggie, turning to face Bruno. 'Anyway, there's nothing wrong with PR.'

Josh was enjoying the scene unfolding before his eyes but he decided to intervene in the argument that was developing between Maggie and Bruno before things became unpleasant and Kim's neighbourly evening got ruined.

'I don't suppose you know much about the political situation in Merton as you've only just moved here. It's quite interesting because we have one ward of independents,' said Josh.

'Independents?' said Maggie, who had now turned her attention from Bruno to Josh.

'Yes, a group of residents in Merton Park.'

'What do you mean by independent?' said Bruno.

'Well, several years ago when the Conservative Party had control of the Council they wanted to put a ring road through Merton Park. It's an area of family housing that's quite attractive and relatively peaceful and the residents were very angry. So a group of local people stood as councillors and got elected. I'm not sure exactly how but they managed to stop the ring road from being built.'

Josh noticed that Bruno seemed more interested in the conversation than he had previously.

'They didn't actually form a political party to start with but just stood as individuals. Then the law changed and they were required to form a party,' said Kim.

'That's really interesting,' said Bruno.

'What's even more interesting is that Merton Park has elected independent councillors ever since and at the last local election they held the balance of power between the Labour and Conservative parties,' said Josh, who was enjoying having an audience.

'You mean there's a hung council. How does that work exactly?' said Maggie.

'Well, at the last election the Labour Party had one more councillor than the Conservative Party so they formed the administration. However, they can't make any decisions without the independents agreeing. So, a group of three people, who represent one geographical area are effectively in charge of the council.'

'And most of the time they vote with the Labour Party so the Conservative Party can't do what they want to do,' said Kim.

'So that's a hung council,' said Bruno.

'What about the Liberal Democrats? Didn't they get any seats?' asked Maggie.

'Only one, I think. They're not very popular around here like they are in some parts of the country.' Josh was enjoying the attention he was getting. 'You might be interested to know that parliamentary democracy began in Merton in 1236.'

'Really,' said Maggie.

'Yes,' said Josh. 'The first ever statute was passed by Parliament at a place called Merton Priory in the area now known as Colliers Wood during the reign of Henry the Third. The Priory was destroyed by Henry the Eighth in 1538 when he ordered the destruction of all the monasteries, by which time Parliament had moved elsewhere. Now there's a giant supermarket on the site.'

'Anyone for coffee?' said Kim. She had just realised that she'd drunk too much wine and needed to sober up ready for work the next day. They all nodded and Kim disappeared into the hallway.

'I'll give you a hand,' said Bruno, easing himself off the sofa and following her out of the room.

CHAPTER
SIX

Josh and Maggie stared at each other in silence for a few seconds as if they were connected by an electric current. Josh wondered what time it was. He never wore a watch. In fact he didn't even own a watch. He'd given up wearing one as a teenager. He had lost several watches at school and eventually decided that he didn't need one. He could always find someone to ask the time but he never needed to as, after years of practice, he had perfected the art of estimating the time and mostly he got it right.

'Do you know what time it is?' Josh asked Maggie in order to break the silence that had crept between them. She leaned forward and once again Josh caught himself examining her breasts. The large amount of wine he had allowed himself to consume over the course of the evening had loosened his inhibitions. He watched as Maggie grabbed a mobile phone from her handbag and checked the time.

One o'clock, thought Josh.

'Ten past one,' said Maggie. He smiled.

'The election results should be coming through by now,' said Josh. Despite the sexually charged atmosphere he felt in Maggie's presence he was desperate to watch the usual pontification of election punditry on TV.

'Great,' said Maggie easing herself off the sofa. She got up, wobbled a bit and then steadied herself by grabbing the arm of Josh's chair. 'Let's go and watch TV,' she said, slightly slurring her words. This was music to Josh's ears. He stood up and somewhat brazenly slid his hand into hers. Then he led Maggie along the hallway towards the door to the kitchen. As they passed by Josh caught sight of Kim and Bruno, who appeared to be deep in conversation, while Kim poured coffee into brightly coloured mugs. To his relief they seemed to be absorbed by each other's company and the guilt he had been preparing to feel never materialised. When they reached the TV room Maggie settled herself down at one end of the rather dilapidated giant sofa, which was covered with a thick green velvety throw.

'Sorry about the mess,' said Josh as he picked up Izzy's magazines from where they'd been scattered in a pile on the floor. He flicked his eyes across the room and they landed on an empty yoghurt pot and a glass half full of what looked like orange juice perched on a shelf just below a large black flat screen TV.

'Teenagers!' said Josh, rolling his eyes and with a tone of disapproval in his voice. Maggie laughed. 'You were one once.'

Josh raised his eyebrows, moved the yoghurt pot and glass to a table at the far end of the room, picked up the remote control and switched on the TV. He sat down on the sofa as close to Maggie as he felt he could without appearing to invade her body space. He could smell the warmth of her perfume and it made him feel happy.

An hour or two passed and every so often Kim and Bruno would appear at the door of the TV room to ask about the election results or offer more coffee. Then they would disappear again. Meanwhile a flurry of information flowed across the TV screen showing the voting patterns around the UK. Computer models predicting the ultimate outcome of the local elections based on voting results so far glowed in a myriad of colours before their eyes. A large map with flashing lights popped up on the screen from time to time to indicate which political party had won council seats in different parts of the UK. Josh and Maggie watched and chatted, listened and debated, laughed and argued and completely lost track of time.

'The Conservative Party's lost loads of seats to UKIP,' said Maggie.

'But the Labour Party and Liberal Democrats haven't done that well either. There's been a really low turn out of voters,' said Josh.

'Why do you think that is?' said Maggie twirling a lock of her hair and adjusting her position on the sofa so that she sat closer to Josh.

'The continuing recession, bankers' bonuses, cuts to the NHS and public services generally, the lack of jobs for young people, no social housing to speak of, the list is endless.'

Maggie nodded sleepily as her eyes kept closing and reopening.

'I think people are just fed up with politicians generally,' said Maggie. She was sitting upright rubbing her eyes. Her hair was untidy and her mascara had smudged so that she looked as if she had two black eyes. She still looked beautiful, thought Josh.

'You're right. I think we've reached a point in time where people really have had enough of politicians.'

'The government treats people like idiots,' said Maggie. 'The Internet and social media have been really good for democracy. It's impossible for politicians to pull the wool over people's eyes any more. Everything's wide open.'

'That's true,' agreed Josh.

'So who would you want to win if there was a general election?' asked Maggie.

'The Labour Party, I suppose. Maybe the Greens if they could get enough votes, which under a first past the post voting system like we have in national elections, they wouldn't. I don't know,' pondered Josh. As he spoke his brow furrowed and he pushed his hair back from his face anxiously.

It was true, he thought, he had voted for the Labour Party for the best part of his life. He'd been brought up in a staunchly Labour household. As a teenager and young adult he had been proud to call himself a socialist. But over the years he'd changed and he was now less sure of his political beliefs than at any other time in his life. Josh felt that in some ways the Labour Party had become more conservative in their policies than the Conservative Party. All three of the major parties were struggling to occupy what was known as the 'middle ground'. Public perception of all politicians, whatever party they belonged to was that they were out for themselves. What was democracy for most people anyway? The chance to vote once every five years.

In reality it was only worth voting for one of the two main parties as no other party could possibly win an outright majority. Without proportional representation none of the smaller parties would ever have much influence in Parliament. That was why people had stopped belonging to political parties and were joining single issue pressure groups instead like Hacked Off. The Internet and social media had become instruments of democracy. They'd given people a voice that could reach out to others. Internet petitions drove politicians to change their policies when they realised the strength of public opinion on certain issues.

'How about you? Who would you want to win if there was a general election tomorrow?' Josh asked Maggie.

'Well,' she replied in an elongated tone. Shades of Bridget Jones, thought Josh. 'I grew up in Tunbridge Wells, that heartland of Middle England Conservatism. I went to a girls' grammar school, my parents are farmers and staunch members of the Conservative Party.' Maggie spoke with slightly slurred speech and an intense smile on her face and then paused.

'So you'd want the Tories to win?' said Josh in a matter of fact manner.

'No,' replied Maggie emphatically. 'I would not.' Josh waited for her to continue. 'I have always voted Conservative in the past but I don't want to in the future.'

'Why not?'

'Because, like you, I am fed up with the lot of them. Most politicians are self-centred, out of touch, second rate individuals whose only ambition is to succeed in gaining more power.'

'Strong words. You sound like you really mean what you say.'

'Both my parents were involved in local politics when I was a child,' said Maggie. 'You know, garden parties, the odd meeting with the local MP. All very tame country bumpkin stuff. I had a childhood ambition to go into politics myself. I liked the idea of being someone important, being listened to, getting things done.'

'I felt I had an obligation to change the world for the better when I was growing up. I honestly thought I would be able to solve all the world's problems. Life seemed so simple then,' said Josh with a tinge of sadness in his voice.

'What did your parents do?' asked Maggie.

'My father was a teacher and then he went on to train teachers when I was growing up. My mother was a secretary, although she could have been a professional opera singer if she'd been prepared to move to London as a young woman. But she'd got to know my father and I think she wanted a family. She worked at the BBC as a production assistant for a while but she gave it up to have me.'

'Ah,' said Maggie looking kindly at Josh. She gently touched his arm and he felt a tingle of pleasure. They said nothing for a few minutes as a flurry of election results flew across the TV screen. The pundits got somewhat overexcited and confused as to which party had won which seat. The political commentator chairing the programme listened avidly to the voice talking to him through his earpiece and corrected the pundits when necessary.

'The trouble is that I don't agree with most of the traditional Conservative Party policies,' said Maggie. 'You know, low taxation at the expense of good public services, the sort of unregulated financial transactions that got us into the economic mess we're in now, policies that are anti-European. But I could never support the Labour Party.'

'What I would really like to do is to vote on all the major issues that need to be decided by politicians on a regular basis,' said Josh.

'How could you do that?' said Maggie moving towards him so that her left thigh touched his right knee sending a shiver of excitement through his body.

'Oh, I don't know,' said Josh. 'Be a member of a giant virtual parliament like in the film Star Wars.'

'You can't be serious,' laughed Maggie. Josh smiled as he imagined himself in a long black cloak floating in space holding forth about something of huge galactic importance.

'I just feel that I've got no real influence over the decisions that are made by politicians and that I could make better decisions than they do most of the time.'

'I'm sure a lot of people feel the same way as you do,' said Maggie. 'They can write to their MP or local councillor, go on a protest march, sign a petition and that's about it. Even if an MP or councillor gets loads of letters and e-mails saying he should do X, he can still do Y because he is a representative and not a delegate.'

Josh had never seen Maggie look so serious, even to the point of looking worried. Then she threw her head back and laughed.

'I know. We could have a parliament like a television talent show where anyone can vote anything they like. I bet loads more people would vote in elections if they could do it online or over the phone. There are loads of voting Apps around.'

'That's not a bad idea,' said Josh. He was sitting in a contemplative pose with his hands cradled together. 'The irony is that I honestly think people feel they have some control over the contestants in reality TV programmes in a way that they don't feel in control of their own lives.'

'What do you mean?' said Maggie.

'By voting in a TV programme like Big Brother people actually feel that they can decide if someone gets evicted or not. What chance do you think people feel they have to vote out an MP or to change a party's policies?' said Josh.

'Oh, I see,' said Maggie, rubbing her eyes.

'You look tired,' said Josh, gently touching her cheek. He had half-expected her to flinch but she raised her hand and held it over his for a few seconds. He felt a rush of warmth and affection, as if a deep and mutual understanding had been reached between them.

'I'm not tired,' Maggie protested, stifling a yawn. 'Well, I am, but I want to stay up all night.'

'Not sure if I'm up to that,' said Josh. Then he regretted saying something that made him sound so old.

'I suppose I'd better go,' said Maggie easing herself up from the sofa. 'Let's continue our discussion tomorrow.'

'OK,' said Josh. He thought 'tomorrow' sounded promising. He had forgotten about Kim and Bruno. 'Josh and Maggie, Josh and Maggie.' The words had a certain ring about them. He showed her to the front door with feelings of anticipation and excitement reminiscent of a first date. He was dreaming of a first kiss when suddenly he was jolted back to reality by the sight of Kim and Bruno leaning against each other on the large brown leather sofa in the living room. Their heads were touching and they were fast asleep.

Josh went to wake them but Maggie whispered 'No.' Then before he knew what was happening she kissed him gently on the cheek and disappeared out of the front door. Josh watched as she hurried down the road. Maggie waved when she reached her house and he waved back. Then she vanished inside leaving Josh to his dreams.

CHAPTER
SEVEN

Josh's hangover was bad. In fact it was worse than bad. It was horrendous and, despite several painkillers taken throughout the morning, it showed no sign of abating. Josh looked at the clock on his overly bright computer screen. It was mid-day, which meant he had been sitting in his office at Central London University for just under two hours staring at a blank whiteboard.

Every so often Josh shifted his position and, as he did so his limbs ached and a slight moan escaped from between his lips. A large pile of exam papers sat on his desk demanding his attention, which he was determined to ignore, for today at least. The sunlight streaming through the dirty window reflected on the whiteboard and hurt his eyes and the floating particles of dust in front of his gaze made him feel sick and dizzy. Josh buried his head in his hands to try to make himself feel better, but it didn't help. He had tried every remedy he could think of – large doses of caffeine, chocolate biscuits, lying down. Nothing had worked and he still felt as bad as he had done when his alarm clock had woken him at 7 o'clock that morning.

After staying up virtually all night to watch the election results with Maggie, Josh had slept for precisely two hours and forty-nine minutes. Then he'd got up to go to work to deliver a lecture at nine o'clock. Fortunately for him it was a lecture for first year students on a subject he could have talked about in his sleep. Judging by some of the looks he'd received from the students sitting in the first couple of rows of the lecture hall, they probably thought Josh was asleep. Now he had to wait until two o'clock in the afternoon when he was due to conduct a tutorial with some third year students. He'd thought about making the long and inconvenient journey to the university canteen to get some lunch. But he found the prospect of having to navigate his way through a myriad of corridors and up and down several flights of stairs off-putting to say the least. Furthermore, the possibility of encountering anyone who knew him, let alone having to speak to them filled him with horror.

So Josh stayed sitting at his desk, as still as he could manage, with his eyes firmly shut and that's where he was when the phone on his desk rang so loudly that he thought the fire alarm must have gone off. He lurched towards the phone in an effort to silence it and grabbed the handset with such ferocity that it flew off the end of his desk and fell into pieces on the floor.

Seconds later as Josh had just managed to put the handset together it rang again. He quickly turned down the volume and let it ring until it switched to voicemail.

'Hi Josh. It's Maggie,' went the sing-song voice. 'I hope you don't mind me calling you at work. I just wanted to have a chat with you about something we talked about last night.' Josh scratched his head. He had very little recollection of what he and Maggie had discussed, despite having spent several hours in her company. How embarrassing was this? Josh was nearly forty years old with a respectable job and three dependants. Yet last night he had drunk more than a first year student at a freshers' ball. Maggie had sounded bright and breezy over the phone despite the fact that Josh was sure she had consumed at least a bottle of red wine the night before. The voicemail message continued.

'I've just finished a meeting nearby and I've got a couple of hours free before my next one so I wondered if you'd like to get together for lunch.'

Like to meet up? Of course I'd like to meet up, thought Josh. But today of all days and at this precise moment? His heart sank as he realised he was not up to seeing Maggie for lunch.

'I'll be on my mobile. There's a sandwich place I spotted by the river. Call me and I'll get you what you want. By...ee.'

Maggie's bright and cheerful voice rang inside Josh's empty vessel of a head. How could she sound so lively? It must be her age, thought Josh, or lack of it. How old was she anyway? Late twenties, early thirties? Young enough to have survived a night of revelry and little sleep without suffering any ill effects. He thought back to the time several years ago when he'd been able to stay up all night and still operate effectively as a human being the next day. He longed to meet Maggie again, but not looking like he did now.

Josh hadn't dared to look in the mirror since he'd caught sight of himself that morning while shaving. His face had been an unpleasant grey colour with dark holes where his eyes should have been. His breath smelled of stale red wine and he hadn't had the energy to have a shower. Josh had managed to find some clean clothes but they were hardly smart. A slightly creased pink and purple striped cotton shirt, faded brown cords and a navy blue jumper were the first items of clothing he had laid his hands on. Each item would have looked fine with something else but when Josh looked at what he was wearing, he realised that they did not go together. As he slowly sank into a dismal mood the phone on his desk rang and he grabbed it without thinking.

'Yes,' he said in a gruff voice.

'Josh?'

'Oh. Maggie. Hi.' He tried to sound enthusiastic.

'I forgot to leave you my mobile number.'

'What do you mean?' Josh decided to play stupid.

'I left you a message, on your voicemail. Didn't you get it?'

'No. I've just got back to my desk,' Josh lied.

'Oh. I was wondering if you'd like to meet for lunch. I've got a bit of time to kill.'

'Time to kill, eh,' said Josh teasingly.

'I didn't mean it like that. Look. I'd really like to see you again.'

Josh's spirits rose instantly and he wanted to sound enthusiastic about meeting up with Maggie, but he decided to play it cool.

'OK. I've got about an hour. We can get a sandwich and sit by the river. I could do with some fresh air.'

'Great. I'm right by Hugo's sandwich bar. I'll get the food. Meet you down by the jetty in ten minutes.'

'OK,' said Josh. He liked it when other people organised his life. He eased himself up from the desk. His limbs still ached but his head was feeling better since his mood had been lifted by the prospect of meeting up with Maggie. It would only take him five minutes to walk the short distance between the university and the River Thames.

Josh decided to freshen up. He opened the door of a large cupboard and from the top shelf he removed a small mirror and a comb. He tidied his hair as best he could and then took out a body spray and wafted it all over himself. Josh grabbed his brown leather jacket, locked the door to his office and, checking there was no-one around who might want to speak to him, hurried along the corridor to splash water on his face at the nearest wash basin. Then he quietly slid out of the large glass double doors at the side of the building and into the adjoining street. He could hear Big Ben chiming in the distance and the roar of London traffic all around him. The grey crowded streets enveloped him and he made his way unnoticed in the direction of the Thames.

Josh spotted Maggie a few minutes before she saw him. She was leaning against the long wall that runs the length of the river staring at something in the distance. She was wearing a dark grey trouser suit with a very thin pink stripe in the material. Her blonde hair was in perfect shape in contrast to Josh's brown tousled mop. It fell gently over her shoulders and Josh wanted to bury his hands in it, pull Maggie into his arms and thrust his lips onto her soft sweet mouth. But he didn't dare.

Maggie must have felt Josh's presence as she turned suddenly to face him. He could see her smiling face shining in the sunshine as she waved two small white paper carrier bags, which Josh presumed contained their sandwiches. Once Josh was face to face with Maggie he could see that she was wearing a pink shirt of the same colour as the tiny stripes in her suit. She looked like an immaculate, power-dressing, successful woman of the twenty-first century. Josh felt distinctly out of place in his creased cotton shirt and faded cords, as if he had just turned up at a business meeting in his pyjamas.

'You look great,' Josh spurted out as Maggie moved forward to kiss him gently on his right cheek. He stopped himself from breathing until he could step back a few paces in case she smelt his breath.

'Thanks. Cheese or tuna?'

'You choose. I'm fine with either.'

They sat down on the nearest bench facing the Thames and Maggie handed Josh one of the paper bags.

'Thanks. So what have you been up to this morning?'

'Just a big boring meeting,' said Maggie as she carefully unfolded her tuna sandwich from its wrapper. 'How about you?'

'Just a big boring lecture,' said Josh. They both laughed and each of them took a bite of their sandwiches.

'Thanks for getting me lunch. I'll reciprocate sometime,' said Josh.

Maggie shifted slightly in her seat so that she could turn towards him. He caught a hint of her perfume, which smelt fresh and warm. He turned to face her and caught sight of her breasts, rising up from her open necked shirt.

He quickly turned his eyes away.

'So what do you think of the local election results?' asked Maggie enthusiastically. Before Josh had time to answer she continued. 'It's just like you said it would be. There's been a low turn out of voters and a shift away from the Conservative Party to UKIP, but not many gains for the other main parties.' Josh felt pleased with himself. He had been analysing the election results all morning and his predictions had been right.

'People are obviously fed up with politics. They can't see the point of voting and they don't trust politicians. Fewer people have voted in these local elections than ever before. If you translate the results into what would happen if this were a general election, the current government would be voted out,' said Josh.

'But neither of the other main parties would have got an outright majority either,' said Maggie as she scooped up small pieces of tuna from the front of her shirt. Josh concentrated on her face, which seemed radiant despite her lack of sleep from the night before.

'So, we would have a hung parliament again,' said Josh concentrating on holding his cheese sandwich tightly together as he lifted it to his lips.

'Were there any hung parliaments before 2010?' said Maggie. Josh felt a sudden urge to kiss her, to wrench her tuna sandwich from her lips and embrace her in one of those passionate embraces that take place in feature films. But he drove the thought from his mind and prepared to give her a lesson in social history as if she were one of his students.

'There were hung parliaments in 1929 and 1974 where no party had an overall majority of seats in the House of Commons. That meant the party with the most seats formed a government but they couldn't get much done so another election was called soon after. We had a coalition government in 1915, which was during the First World War, where two parties got together and governed the country. Perhaps it's easier for political parties to do that when there's a serious crisis to deal with such as war.'

'So the two political parties made joint decisions in the best interests of the country rather than in the best interests of themselves,' said Maggie after Josh had finished his lecture. 'Perhaps they should do the same now and we might solve the financial crisis we're in.'

A few moments passed while Josh and Maggie took sips from the small plastic juice bottles she had bought. Pleasure boats came and went, full of tourists wearing brightly coloured anoraks, waving to each other as they passed.

'Let's go on a boat,' said Maggie grasping Josh's arm. He stared at her, not quite sure whether he'd heard her correctly. 'Shall we? Only for half an hour.' Maggie jumped up from her seat. 'Come on. There's a boat that goes on the hour from just over there.' She pointed to a blue and white wooden boat moored next to a jetty a short distance away. Josh didn't move.

'I'm sorry. I'm being bossy. You probably don't feel up to it after last night,' said Maggie. That was the incentive Josh needed to get him up from his seat and onto his feet.

'No, I'm fine.' He nearly fell backwards but steadied himself on the arm of the bench he'd been sitting on. He had got up too quickly and stars were now flying around before his eyes. Today he felt his age but he was determined not to show it in front of Maggie.

'That's a great idea as long as I can get back for a tutorial at two o'clock,' said Josh. He felt Maggie slip her arm into his and guide him towards the jetty where the brightly coloured boat awaited their arrival. Big Ben chimed one o'clock and Josh felt the vibrations as the boat revved up its engine and chugged away from the jetty. The smell of diesel oil engulfed them as the boat moved swiftly upstream into the swirling waters of the Thames.

'I haven't been on one of these for years,' said Josh excitedly, as if he were a child who'd just been presented with a new toy. He tried to remember if he'd ever taken Dan and Izzy on a boat. But the part of his brain that dealt with memory recall was not co-operating after a night of too much alcohol and too little sleep. He felt a pang of guilt. There must have been boat trips, visits to the London Aquarium, the London Dungeon and the London Eye. But he couldn't recall any.

Josh forced himself to think of something else. He and Maggie hadn't spoken for several minutes and yet there seemed no need to speak. The tour guide's voice boomed out as places of interest floated by - Tate Modern art gallery on the right, St Paul's Cathedral in the distance on the left, the Gherkin, or was it a cucumber? Josh closed his eyes between the sights, inhaled the smells of the river and warmed his face in the sunlight. Maggie interspersed the information coming from the tour guide's cockney accent with snippets of her own. She seemed unconcerned that Josh said nothing as they sped along.

At the Tower of London the boat turned around and the tour guide fell silent for a while as they passed the sights they'd already seen on the outward journey.

'Isn't that the jetty where we started?' said Josh, looking anxious. He'd lost all track of time and suddenly remembered the tutorial he had to be back for at two o'clock.

'Don't worry. It's only one fifteen.' Maggie touched his arm reassuringly. 'We're going downstream now, to the Houses of Parliament.' Josh nodded and settled back into his seat as the voice started up again.

'On your left is the South Bank.' Josh looked up to see the National Theatre and the Royal Festival Hall. When had he last been to see a play or a concert? He hadn't been out with Kim on her own for months. He'd been to the odd school play or social gathering at Dan and Izzy's school. But he hadn't taken Kim or her kids to the theatre, ballet or to a classical concert for ages. He resolved to do so in the near future. Just at that moment Maggie tugged his arm.

'Look Josh. The Houses of Parliament.' He looked up at the home of democracy in the United Kingdom as it towered above the boat that had now slowed to a virtual stop. As the tour guide told the story of Guy Fawkes' failed attempt to blow the place up and tourists frantically took photographs before the boat set off again, Josh's thoughts were elsewhere. This wasn't democracy in the true sense. It was party politics, vested interests, conventions and, at its best, hypocrisy. At its worst it was totalitarianism with decisions being made against the wishes of the vast majority of the people most of the time. That was why so few people had voted in the local elections. Because they didn't feel they counted any more.

'A penny for them.' Maggie's voice came from nowhere and disturbed Josh's thoughts. He smiled at her.

'Sorry. I was miles away.'

Maggie looked at him in earnest. 'You know we were talking last night, about how people have been alienated from politicians and the main political parties.' Josh nodded as he tried to remember exactly what he had said to Maggie the night before. She looked straight into his eyes. Whatever she was about to say she must be deadly serious, thought Josh.

'Remember what you told me about the Independent councillors in Merton Park? That they hold the balance of power between the other parties.'

'Yes,' said Josh, who had at last begun to recall something of what had happened the previous night.

'Well, you know you were saying that if the results of yesterday's local elections were translated into what would happen at the next General Election none of the main parties would get an overall majority and there would be a hung parliament again?' said Maggie.

'Yes.' Josh was beginning to see where Maggie's thoughts were leading.

'If at the next General Election lots of people stood as Independent Members of Parliament and enough of them were elected, they might end up holding the balance of power between the main political parties,' said Maggie enthusiastically.

'It's an interesting idea,' said Josh as he watched Big Ben and the Houses of Parliament shrink in size as the boat headed back up the Thames.

'You don't remember, do you?' said Maggie. She looked at Josh as a mother would look at her child when he'd just achieved something amazing, like taking his first steps without realising the enormity of what he'd done.

'It was your idea in the first place, Josh. You suggested it last night.'

'What did I suggest?'

'That we all stand as Independent Members of Parliament.'

'Who?'

'You, me, Bruno, Kim, friends of ours, people in pressure groups who represent the views of millions of people but who have no power over how MPs vote.'

'I must have been drunk,' laughed Josh.

'You were, but you came up with some good ideas.'

'What else did I suggest?'

Maggie looked at him with a cross expression on her face. She was wondering if his memory really was failing him or whether he was teasing her.

'Seriously, I know it makes me sound like an idiot but I can't remember much. I was having such a great time in your company, I lost track of how much I was drinking.'

Josh felt decidedly stupid making such an apology at his age but Maggie smiled reassuringly.

'Well, you said there were people who should be in Parliament, but who would never get in by conventional means like joining one of the main political parties,' said Maggie.

'That's right,' said Josh. 'Like the relatives of young soldiers fighting abroad who want to do something about equipment shortages and inadequate rehabilitation when they return to the UK injured and who feel that politicians take no notice of them.'

Josh was beginning to remember his monologue from the night before. He had argued that the system of selecting prospective parliamentary candidates had become too complicated and subject to vested interests. The only people who seemed to get elected as MPs were career politicians. Most of these had taken years to be selected by the main political parties and they had only been allowed to stand for Parliament because they towed the party line of whichever party they stood for.

'Martin Bell was elected as an independent MP for Tatton in Cheshire in 1997. He was a respected journalist who had worked for years as a war correspondent for the BBC. He stood for Parliament because he disagreed with corruption in politics. The people who elected Martin Bell trusted him and they agreed with his principles. He wasn't being told what to do or say by anyone. He was his own man and he had a conscience,' said Josh.

'That's what we should do,' said Maggie. 'I'm serious.'

'I'll give it some thought,' said Josh. He had been disarmed by Maggie and put on the spot. All of his life he had pontificated about what should or shouldn't happen in the world, but he'd done very little to change anything. Now he was being told to put up or shut up by an attractive, challenging and idealistic young woman around ten years his junior. If he said no he would lose her respect. If he said yes, who knows what might happen.

When the boat reached its jetty Josh and Maggie said their goodbyes and hurried off in opposite directions, Maggie to her meeting and Josh to his tutorial.

CHAPTER EIGHT

Josh found Kim sitting at the kitchen table with a pile of papers strewn across it. He felt considerably better than he had done that morning. The river trip had 'blown the cobwebs away' as his late mother used to say. His afternoon tutorial had been relatively successful with none of his mature students asking difficult questions. In fact only a few students had turned up at all and most of the tutorial had been taken up with a lively discussion of the election results, which he'd enjoyed.

Josh had lived with Kim for long enough to know that the tense, hunched up position of her body indicated anything other than a good mood. She did not look up.

'How are you feeling?' said Josh with as much warmth in his voice as he could muster.

'Not great.' Kim still did not look up. She bent her head forward and rested it on her hands that were propped up on her elbows.

'Is the newspaper around?' said Josh, casting his eyes over the mass of files, letters, forms, payslips and other papers that covered the kitchen table.

'On the stool.' The newspaper sat unopened on a wooden stool at the end of the kitchen. Josh filled the kettle with water, switched it on, grabbed the newspaper and sat diagonally opposite Kim at the kitchen table.

'I'll make us some coffee,' said Josh. He felt the need to appease Kim, although there was no reason why he should. She had the ability to make him feel guilty sometimes, even when he'd done nothing wrong. She also had a tendency to try and put other people into the same state of mind as herself. He couldn't quite understand the workings of Kim's brain, but she seemed to start feeling better as soon as she'd made other people miserable. Josh was determined to remain as buoyant as he had when he entered the room. He'd survived a really bad hangover, managed not to disgrace himself in front of his students and had an enjoyable lunchtime excursion with Maggie. The thought sent a tingle through his body.

'What did you think of our new neighbours?' said Kim. Josh pretended to be engrossed in the newspaper and did not look up.

'Great,' he said, trying not to sound too enthusiastic. 'It was a good evening, apart from the hangover.'

'You seemed to get on well with Maggie.'

Josh didn't detect any tone in Kim's voice to suggest that she thought he'd done anything wrong, but a slight pang of guilt rose up from somewhere in his body.

'What do you mean?' he said, trying not to sound defensive.

'Well, you spent most of the night together.'

'Did we? I didn't really notice. I spent most of the night watching the election results.' Josh had decided to play down his enthusiasm for Maggie. Kim didn't reply so he continued. 'You seemed to get on well with Bruno. Is he going to join your Friends group? It would be useful for you to have a surveyor on board, wouldn't it?'

Josh smiled at Kim in a warm and reassuring way as he made them both cups of coffee. Kim remained silent and Josh wondered for a moment what she was thinking. Did she suspect him of having feelings for Maggie? Did she even care? He and Kim hadn't had a very good relationship for a while, although neither of them had addressed the problem, preferring instead to maintain a veneer of politeness in their relations with each other.

'What are you doing with all those papers?' Josh peered at the letters, bills and other documents laid out in no particular order on the kitchen table. Kim sighed, picked up a letter consisting of several pages and waved it at Josh.

'It's from Richard's divorce lawyer. I've got to answer all these stupid questions,' said Kim angrily as she slammed the letter back down on the table in front of her.

'Well, maybe you shouldn't try and do it now. I mean, after last night. Wait until you feel up to it.'

Kim stabbed the letter several times with her finger.

'There are bloody time limits and I've got to get all this information together in some semblance of order or I'll be penalised.' Kim spat the words out onto the table with such venom that tiny drops of coffee coloured saliva landed on the letter. Kim wiped them off roughly and made the stains worse.

Josh said nothing for a while as he casually flicked through the newspaper. He knew from past experience that this was going to be one of those conversations where whatever he said would be wrong. Kim needed to take her anger out on someone and he just happened to be in the wrong place at the right time. Josh could stay and fight – verbally not physically – to give her the chance to get the anger out of her system. Alternatively, he could excuse himself and leave the next unfortunate person to enter the house – either Dan or Izzy – to bear the brunt of Kim's frustrations. He decided to take the cowardly route.

'I've got some work to do. I'll leave you to get on with it.' Josh moved as quickly as he could in the direction of his study without making it look as if he were escaping, which of course he was.'

'That's great. Thanks for your help, Josh.'

He could hear Kim's shouts as he hurried along the hallway but now that he was safely inside his study with the door firmly closed he felt no need to reply. Kim had so much baggage. That was the problem with their relationship. There were too many people involved in it, namely Richard, Dan and Izzy. Dan didn't cause Josh too many problems as he got on with his own life most of the time. They had similar temperaments in that they were generally calm with a tendency to become withdrawn if there was any tension in the house. Unlike his sister Izzy, Dan was never deliberately confrontational. He could be quite manipulative at times in order to get what he wanted but he was never physically or emotionally demanding. Izzy was Dan's opposite in that her behaviour was often challenging and volatile. She was insecure and lacked confidence, which Josh put down to her unfortunate life circumstances and in particular, her parents' divorce.

Josh felt that Richard's absence from the family home had affected Izzy more than Dan. When he'd first met her she had seemed to be lively, creative and friendly. But as Josh's relationship with Kim progressed and he saw more of Izzy, he realised that she felt deeply insecure and rejected by her father.

Most of the time she played the part of a confident, sociable and popular girl but when she let her guard down Josh could see deep wounds that hurt her on a daily basis. It didn't help that Kim and Izzy were hard on each other, as if they blamed one another for Richard's departure. Josh had decided soon after he'd met Kim that mother and daughter were too alike to be able to live in peaceful harmony. He had therefore developed various strategies by which to manage their relationship.

Whenever Kim and Izzy were involved in a full-blown argument that showed no sign of abating, Josh would intervene so as to deflect their anger onto him. Eventually they would both run out of steam and more often than not, neither of them would remember what they had been arguing about. Once the situation was calm Josh would remove himself from their presence and after a few minutes, each of them would come and make peace with him, although they rarely apologised or accepted responsibility for the argument.

An alternative strategy that Josh had found helpful over the years in dealing with family strife was to distract

Izzy by asking her to attend to an important task, such as a trip to the shops to collect an item that Josh needed urgently. An errand fee would quickly be negotiated and Izzy would disappear out of the house leaving Kim to huff and puff about her daughter's shortcomings until she ran out of steam.

But Josh could never be as capable as Dan at the peace process in the house. Kim had told Josh that Dan hadn't cried when Richard left. He'd put his arms around her and said, 'Don't worry Mum. I'll look after you.' Kim had felt guilty over the years that Dan had assumed such a huge burden of responsibility for her well-being at a young age. But Dan seemed to have survived the absence of his father in a way that Izzy had not. Dan's grades at school were consistently good whereas Izzy's were often bad. Dan never gave his mother any trouble and while some of his friends were experimenting with drink and drugs, Dan was either playing sport or watching it on TV. He was a popular boy with many friends and he excelled at sports of all kinds. He was captain of the first eleven cricket team at school and had won numerous cups and medals in different sports over the years.

Josh sat at his desk pressing his fingers into the keys of his laptop as his thoughts drifted between Kim, Izzy and Dan. He found himself tapping in keywords such as 'political parties', 'independent Members of Parliament', 'how to set up a political party' and 'Martin Bell'.

There were several entries for the war correspondent who had been elected to Parliament as an independent MP on an anti-corruption ticket. Josh looked at the photograph of the man in his trademark light-coloured suit who had caught the public's imagination. He was in the middle of reading that Martin Bell had published a book dealing with the subject of MPs fiddling their expenses called 'A Very British Revolution' when he heard a knock on his study door.

'Come in,' said Josh. He expected to see Kim's sad face but when the door opened it was Dan. Josh felt relieved as he watched the boy in man's clothing quietly pull the door to.

'Take a seat.' Josh pointed him in the direction of his brown leather armchair. Dan eased his large frame into it, gently resting his hands on the arms of the chair and stretching his legs out so that they almost touched Josh's feet. It occurred to him that Dan must have grown taller recently. He was not just a strapping seventeen-year-old. He had a presence that seemed to fill the room. His large oval face had a healthy-looking glow and his wavy fair hair glistened. Dan was tall and mature for his age with a muscular frame developed from years of playing sports. Josh immediately thought of Richard when he looked at his son. The boy gave off the same air of confidence as his father whenever he entered a room. He had a gentle smile on his face and a quizzical look in his greyish blue eyes as he stared at the computer screen.

'How's your mother?' said Josh.

'She's ok. I made her go up to bed.'

'We didn't get much sleep,' said Josh as he swung his chair around to face Dan, blocking his view of the computer screen.

'I know you were both up for most of the night. I could hear you. Mum was still asleep on the sofa when I got up for school. No wonder she's knackered.'

Josh thought he could detect a note of disapproval in Dan's tone of voice. He felt as if he was being reprimanded by a parent but decided not to make an issue of it. After Richard's departure from the family home Dan had assumed the role of Kim's protector despite the fact that she was his mother and many years older than him. Josh respected him for the way he looked after Kim, even though it caused him inconvenience and even embarrassment at times.

'Did you have a cricket match?' said Josh trying to

distract Dan from the subject of last night's revelries.

'Yeah, we played against Dulwich and we won.'

'Did your father come and watch?'

'Does he ever?' Dan shrugged his shoulders and rolled his eyes.

'Did you tell him the match was on?'

'No.'

Josh knew that despite working eighteen-hour days and sometimes all night, Richard would always jump at the opportunity to watch his son take part in any type of sporting activity. Dan knew that too but he rarely told his father when he was playing in a match.

Josh had observed on many occasions that the boy deliberately denied his father the bonding experiences that Richard craved. This was Dan's way of punishing his father. On other occasions he chose to be out of the house when Richard called to see him and he would often make a point of refusing money when his father offered it to him.

Dan preferred to earn his own money by taking on part-time jobs. From the age of sixteen he had worked delivering leaflets and local papers and had looked after friends' pets when they went away on holiday. Recently Dan had been taken on as a cricket coach for a local club. Kim was proud of her son's ability to earn money, which contrasted with Izzy's obsession with spending it. However, she got angry when Dan refused money from Richard in spite of the fact that she understood his desire for revenge.

'What have you been up to today? Were you able to go to work? I mean after last night,' said Dan. Josh again felt as if he were being called to account by his mother or father.

'Actually…' Josh was just about to describe his river trip with Maggie when he decided that it would create the wrong impression. After all, he had only met the woman the night before and here he was the following day meeting her for lunch and going on a boat ride with her like it was their first date. He changed tack.

'I survived a lecture and a tutorial despite having too little sleep and too much to drink,' Josh joked, but the joke fell flat when he saw Dan's face and the disapproving expression that was written all over it. The boy let out a sigh and Josh half expected to be given a good telling off. But either Dan didn't have the energy after his cricket match or he thought it would be unwise to get into an argument. Dan turned and pointed at the computer screen.

'What are you looking at?' he asked.

Josh wavered for a moment as he decided whether to tell Dan the truth or not. He swivelled his chair around so that he was facing the computer screen and blocking the boy's view. At the same time Dan stood up and peered over Josh's shoulder. It was too late for him to click the mouse and switch screens or pretend to be checking his email. As Dan moved closer Josh could feel the warmth of his body freshly doused in Lynx East Africa spray after an afternoon in the blazing sun of the cricket pitch.

'Who's Martin Bell?' Dan was now standing next to Josh, bending his large frame forward and staring quizzically at the image on the screen before him – a man in a smart white suit, his dark brown curly hair neither long nor short, thick dark eyebrows with a friendly and confident expression on his face.

'Martin Bell stood as an independent MP in the 1997 General Election,' said Josh.

'What's an independent MP?'

'An MP who is not a member of any political party.'

'So they vote how they like?' said Dan.

'Yes. They're not bound to vote according to any particular policy like those set out in party manifestos.'

'Why do people want to be elected as independents?' Dan was now standing tall next to Josh, who felt the need to stand up as well. He was a good six inches shorter than the boy and of lighter build. Bending over the computer, Josh clicked the mouse to show him more information about Martin Bell.

'That's really interesting,' said Dan as he bent forward and read the close-knit paragraphs of black lettering on the screen. 'So Martin Bell was the first independent Member of Parliament to be elected since 1951. It says here that the public were fed up with the Conservative government's sleazy image and that both the main opposition parties agreed not to field any candidates in the constituency where Martin Bell got elected.'

'It helped that he was already a media personality. He had been working for years as a war correspondent for the BBC so people were used to seeing him on TV.'

'Not in a white suit though,' said Dan laughing. He moved back to the armchair and sank into it with his legs crossed and his hands together as if he were praying. Josh remained standing and let his eyes stray towards the window. The sun had faded and a warm brown light had settled over the garden. It would soon be dark outside. Josh allowed his thoughts to wander for a moment as he wondered whether Maggie had returned from work.

'Why were you looking him up?' Josh's mind was jolted back to the conversation with Dan. 'Martin Bell.'

Josh considered saying that he was doing some research on independent politicians for a course he was running at the university. But he didn't want to lie to Dan. There were times when he felt he had to lie to Kim or Izzy and he justified this to himself on the grounds that it was in their best interests. But he could not lie to Dan. There was something about the boy that made it impossible to tell him even the smallest of untruths.

'I'm thinking of setting up a new political party. Well not a party exactly, more a collection of honourable and like-minded people who would stand as independent MPs and who would vote in the best interests of the electorate.'

'What would be the point?' said Dan.

'There are in fact several points. The main point if you like is to restore true democracy to the people of this country.'

'How?' Dan came back with a single shot as if he and Josh were playing tennis.

'Well, the way it would work is that people would stand as independent MPs in different parts of the country on a variety of issues.'

'Who would stand as independent MPs?' Dan fired his next question.

'Anyone really. Well, maybe not anyone. I think there would have to be some sort of vetting process but basically good, honest individuals who believe strongly in certain issues.'

'Isn't that what politicians are supposed to be?' said Dan.

'Some of them are good and honest people who vote in Parliament in accordance with their own moral values and the wishes of their constituents. But there are others who have their own interests at heart. They make decisions in order to further their own careers and often for personal financial gain. Many MPs vote in line with what they are told to vote by the Whips, even though they disagree with them.'

'The Whips?' Dan looked confused.

'They are the MPs in each party who are responsible for making sure the other MPs vote according to the policies that have been agreed in the manifesto or in cabinet meetings. They cajole, pressurise, bribe and sometimes even threaten their fellow MPs to vote in a particular way, usually in the way the party leader wants them to vote.'

'What's the point of that?' said Dan.

'The idea is that each whip makes sure a party's line is followed so that decisions are made according to party policy. A problem arises when an MP feels that he or she can't bring themselves to vote in line with their own party's policy.'

'Why might that happen?'

'Perhaps the MP thinks that his or her constituents wouldn't agree with something or maybe their own conscience is telling them to vote in a particular way.'

'Can you think of an example?' Dan's face was glowing with enthusiasm and Josh was enjoying himself too. This was the sort of discussion Josh had been brought up on. Every weekend at lunchtimes he would sit at the dining room table with his mother, father and sister listening to 'The World This Weekend' or 'Any Questions' on BBC Radio Four. It was during these radio programmes that the hot political topics of the day would be discussed by various panellists, including MPs and journalists. At the end of each programme the whole family would settle down to a lively discussion as to which of the speakers had been right or wrong. Josh remembered taking an active part in these discussions from when he was a young child until he left home to go to university.

Even now when he visited his elderly father in Bristol he would find himself talking for hours about the political issues of the day. Josh's childhood and teenage years had been soaked in a sense that he not only had the opportunity to change the world through engaging in politics but he had a positive duty to do so. Politics was in Josh's blood and yet he had never got involved in party political activities or stood for election as a local councillor or MP.

In common with most people today he felt more inclined to support pressure groups campaigning on a single issue like the protection of the environment or saving animals from extinction. Josh felt he had more chance of influencing government policy by joining a campaigning organisation like Hacked Off or 38 Degrees than by belonging to a political party or voting in a local or general election.

'I can think of one,' shouted Dan with excitement as he slapped his hands on his knees and leaned forward.

'What? Sorry. My mind was elsewhere.' Josh looked at the boy's handsome face, desperately trying to remember what they'd been talking about before his thoughts had retreated to his childhood.

'This is a really good example of politicians not voting the way their constituents would have wanted them to vote.'

'What is?' Josh rubbed his eyes. He was hungry and tired and was still feeling the adverse effects of the night before.

'The war in Iraq,' shouted Dan so loudly that Josh flinched as if he had received a blow to his body. 'Most of the British people were against it but both of the main political parties voted to invade the country. How's that for democracy?'

Josh nodded sagely in the teacher-student way he was used to in his working life.

'That's a good example, Dan,' he said, trying not to sound patronising. 'Of course, there were some MPs who voted against the war in Iraq. For example, Robin Cook and Clare Short were both government ministers and they resigned from the Cabinet because they chose to follow their consciences.'

'Robin Cook. Wasn't he the MP who died on top of a mountain?' said Dan.

'Yes, he died in 2005. I'm not sure if he actually died on the mountain or after he was brought down,' said Josh. 'A lot of people respected him for resigning from the Cabinet. Maybe his private life wasn't perfect.' Josh stopped himself from saying any more but it was too late.

'What do you mean?' said Dan.

'Well, he was having an affair with his secretary and then his wife found out.'

There was silence for a few seconds, although to Josh it felt much longer. He wondered what Dan was thinking.

Richard had been having an affair with his secretary for about a year before Kim found out.

'How long had they been married?'

'A long time, twenty-nine years, I believe. They had grown-up children.'

'Did that make him a bad politician?'

'Not really. Lots of MPs have dodgy personal lives but that doesn't make them bad at their jobs. Well, it might make them vulnerable to being blackmailed so that they vote in Parliament in a particular way or give away privileged information.'

'So what skeletons have you got hidden?' Dan laughed loudly. 'I mean if you were to stand as an independent MP.'

Josh didn't have time to defend his reputation as at that moment Kim stuck her head around the door.

'Skeletons. Independent MPs. What are you two plotting?' Kim cuffed Dan over the top of his head.

'Ow.' He pretended to be hurt. Kim perched herself on the edge of Josh's desk and cast her eyes over the computer screen. She turned her nose up and creased her face into a quizzical expression while Josh desperately searched around in his numbed brain for a suitably non-committal response to her question. But before he could think of anything to say Dan piped up.

'Josh is going to stand as an independent MP at the next general election. I was just asking him if he had any skeletons that might come back to haunt him. You know, mistresses, dodgy financial deals, any past history of drug abuse or violent crime.' Dan laughed loudly as he spoke, throwing his head back and waving his arms around in a fit of hilarity.

Josh frowned as he felt Dan's behaviour was demeaning him in front of Kim. This was the one aspect of Dan's character that Josh didn't like, his ability to make Josh feel small. It was as if Dan was saying to him, 'I'm top dog around here and don't you forget it'. Dan's words could certainly have a dampening effect on Josh's ego.

Having closely examined the computer screen, Kim calmly scrutinised the faces of Josh and Dan. She seemed more relaxed than when Josh had seen her earlier at the kitchen table. Her hair had been brushed and there was colour in her cheeks where previously there had been none.

'Let's deal with one thing at a time,' said Kim gently. 'Putting the skeletons to one side, what's all this about you standing as an independent MP, Josh?'

'It's a long story,' he said, hoping that the subject would go away. He was tempted to lie and say that the whole thing had been a joke, but his conscience wouldn't let him.

'I've got plenty of time,' said Kim. 'I'm all ears.'

Josh detected more than a hint of sarcasm in her voice as she folded her arms across her chest and tilted her head to one side, waiting for him to speak. Once he had repeated what he'd described to Dan earlier, starting with Martin Bell and ending with the war in Iraq, Kim was silent for a moment. When she spoke there was an unpleasant tone to her voice that Josh hadn't heard before.

'This is, I assume, some sort of joke, fantasy even, on your part.' She looked him straight in the eye. His emotions went from feeling belittled by Dan to angry and determined in the face of Kim's disdain for his grand plan.

'It's certainly not a fantasy,' said Josh as he stood up straight and puffed his chest out as far as it would go. 'You said yourself that the Merton Park Independents' hold on the balance of power between the Labour Party and the Conservative Party was the best thing that had ever happened to local democracy.'

'I did?'

Josh looked at Kim quizzically as he tried to work out whether she was agreeing with him or was just being facetious.

'Well, what if a group of independent MPs held the balance of power between the main political parties in a general election? That would go some way to restoring democracy, wouldn't it?'

'It's pie in the sky. It's not going to happen, is it Josh? It's just another of your little fantasies.'

Kim slid off the desk and stood face to face with her partner. Dan, who had started this whole business as a smiling assassin now stared anxiously at his mother.

'Mum,' protested Dan. Kim gave him a look that said 'keep out of this mess that you started' and turned back to face Josh.

'Isn't it about time that you grew up and decided what you want out of life? I know what I want and I thought you wanted the same thing.'

Josh looked anxiously at Dan, who was sitting in a rigid position with his hands firmly grasping both arms of his chair, his previously healthy complexion now a pale grey colour. This was neither the time nor the place for a steaming row. Not in front of Dan.

'Look. We're both tired. Let's talk about this another time,' said Josh. He moved forward to put his arm around Kim but she slipped out of his reach before he could make contact. She turned on her heel and disappeared out of the room. Josh thought he could hear her crying as she stomped along the hallway. He heard the front door slam with a huge bang and then there was silence. He looked at Dan for reassurance. The boy shrugged his shoulders.

'I think it's a good idea,' he said. 'You should call yourselves the Internet Party and do everything over the Web. That will cut down on time and money and you'll also save the world's resources. I could make you a website.' Dan stood up, managed a half smile and left the room in a hurry.

Josh closed down his computer and switched on the TV. He watched one of the news channels where four well-known political commentators were discussing the local election results and pontificating about which party might win if there was a general election and people voted in the same way. Josh stared at the screen but couldn't take anything in. He was thinking about Kim and what she'd said. Was he a fantasist, or was he an originator of a new way of thinking? What did she mean when she said that he should decide what he wanted from life? Was Kim unhappy? She said she knew what she wanted, but did he want the same thing?

All these questions would have to be answered, and soon. Josh knew he hadn't been communicating well with Kim for some time. He'd guessed that there were things she wanted to say to him but had been holding back. Kim's divorce proceedings had put a block between them but there was something else that was causing problems in their relationship. Josh resolved to find out what it was. He put all his ideas of becoming an independent MP out of his mind and realised that for the last hour he hadn't once thought about Maggie.

Josh spent the rest of the day holed up in his study with the door firmly closed. He had a drawer in his desk that he used for emergency supplies and had consumed two cartons of apple juice, a flapjack and two bars of chocolate throughout the evening. Since Dan had left Josh's study several hours earlier he hadn't seen a living soul. The familiar shouts and slamming of doors had gradually subsided, which meant that Kim, Dan and Izzy were probably in each of their bedrooms, even if they were not yet asleep.

Josh hadn't heard Kim's voice for at least an hour when she had shouted out that she was going to bed. At last he felt able to leave the safe haven of his study and make his way upstairs. As he walked along the hallway the floorboards seemed to creak more loudly than usual. At the top of the stairs a light shone from under the door to Dan's bedroom and Josh could hear the sound of Coldplay's Paradise playing gently in the background. Dan was probably reading one of his school books or a sports magazine. He was not that keen on novels, preferring to stay grounded in reality, unlike Josh, who liked to escape into fiction at every opportunity.

There was no sound from Izzy's room, which was in darkness with the door slightly open. This was unusual as Izzy invariably fell asleep with a light on and music blaring away. Josh gently pushed the door open. Izzy's bedroom looked as if it had been burgled, with clothes strewn all over her bed and across the floor. The drawers of her dresser had garments bulging out of them in all directions and it looked as if it might topple over at any moment. Having checked that Izzy wasn't buried under the clothes mountain on her bed, Josh switched on her bedside light. He guessed that she must be sleeping over at a friend's house, which she usually did on a Friday or Saturday night. He pushed the items of clothing back into the drawers that were sticking out and closed them as best he could. Then he picked up the clothes from the floor and added them to those that were already on the bed. Finally he closed the blind and propped Izzy's teddy bear, aptly named 'Honey' because of its colour, up against her pillows. Josh sat down at her desk, which was littered with magazines and schoolwork and thought back to when he had first met Izzy. Her transition from child to teenager had been tempestuous and unsettled because of her parents' animosity towards each other.

Josh's relationship with Kim had begun a year after she had kicked Richard out of the family home, so he bore no guilt for Izzy's suffering. Yet sometimes Josh felt the sting of her hatred because he was not her 'real father' as Izzy liked to describe Richard. Josh cast his eyes around the room. Its walls were covered in photographs of Izzy and her friends in a variety of pouting poses. There were mood boards with pictures of various models, perfume bottles, clothes and handbags together with combinations of different words cut out of magazines such as 'Love', 'Glamour' and 'Fashion'.

At times Josh felt a strong sense of responsibility for Izzy's well-being and he would often help her if she got into difficulties with her homework. On some occasions she would even consult him over friendship issues or arguments with her mother. But he did not feel the same kind of responsibility he thought he might if Izzy were his own flesh and blood. Josh had always shied away from having his own children. Whenever a relationship had become serious enough for the subject of children to be raised, he had either ended the relationship himself or made it so clear that children were not on his agenda that the woman in his life at the time would end it herself.

During a brief encounter with a bereavement counsellor after his mother's death Josh had been told that he didn't want children because he still viewed himself as a child. He did not want to grow up and take on responsibility for the life of another human being. Perhaps that was why he'd been attracted to Kim. She had two kids, a decent job and an ex-husband with a lot of money. Kim had been a strong and self-sufficient woman, which Josh had found very attractive. Recently however, the demands of bringing up two teenage children and the pressures of her divorce proceedings had made her less capable, weaker and, Josh hated himself for thinking it, less attractive. The more Kim needed him, the less he desired her.

Every so often Kim would 'throw a fit', as Dan and Izzy described it, shouting and screaming about how she wanted to give up her job and be a stay at home mum. Josh knew that as a university lecturer he would never earn enough for that to happen. Kim seemed resentful that she no longer had the high-powered City solicitor husband earning hundreds of thousands of pounds a year. But at the same time she constantly criticised Richard's lifestyle and blamed the long hours he worked in an egotistical environment for the collapse of their marriage.

Josh took a last look around Izzy's bedroom at the cuddly toys, pictures of music artists he didn't recognise, the piles of cheap jewellery in small dishes and an assortment of chewing gum wrappers strewn over the floor. Where were Izzy's secrets? Did she have a diary hidden away somewhere that contained her hopes and dreams? Josh remembered being given a five-year diary when he was a teenager. He had written in it each night before going to bed and had carefully locked it afterwards with its tiny silver key. He could not recall where the diary was now. Most probably stuffed away in a cardboard box that Josh kept hidden at the back of a cupboard and which contained his school reports and exercise books, old holiday photos and various badges from his activities as a boy scout.

Josh eased himself out of Izzy's chair, switched off her light and trod carefully in the direction of the spare room. He thought about what Dan had said earlier.

The Internet Party would be the perfect name for a political movement that he hoped would appeal to people of all ages and backgrounds. The Internet had empowered humanity in so many ways. Josh resolved that he would make it happen and he'd start tomorrow.

CHAPTER
NINE

'Did you know that minority political parties don't usually do very well in national elections?' said Dan.

'Is that right?' said Josh absent-mindedly as he moved his computer mouse around on its mat.

'Do you want to know why?' said Dan. He knew Josh hadn't been listening.

'What?' Josh looked up from where he'd been staring intently at his computer screen.

'It says here on the Electoral Commission's website that smaller parties only do well when there is proportional representation, like in the European elections.'

'So we can't expect the Internet Party to win many votes in a general election,' said Josh.

'No,' said Dan.

Josh leaned back on his computer chair and put his hands behind his head.

'Well, I don't think that should put us off. Do you?'

Dan shifted himself slightly in Josh's brown leather armchair and clutched the brand new laptop computer that his father had bought him to help with his A' level examinations that were fast approaching. He looked straight at Josh and rolled his eyes.

'No. That's not what I meant. I just thought you'd be interested to know.'

'Have you had a look at the forms?' said Josh as his eyes returned to his computer screen on the desk in front of him.

'Not yet.'

'Well, there seem to be a lot of decisions to be made and forms to be completed before the Internet Party can be registered with the Electoral Commission as a political party.'

'Like what?' said Dan as he tapped various keys on his computer in order to get himself onto the Commission's website.

'We'll need to check that they're happy with the name.'

'What does the website say about names?' said Dan.

'The name of a political party has to be six words or less and can't be obscene.'

Dan laughed out loud and then blushed slightly as a few words came into his mind.

'The name can't be too nationalistic, so the British Party or the English Party are no good.'

'That's a shame,' said Dan, jokingly. 'How about the UK Internet Party?'

'That would be ok, except it sounds a bit like the UK Independence Party and there's already one with that name. You're not supposed to have parties with similar names in case the electorate get confused and vote for the wrong one by mistake.'

'Sounds like a good idea to me.' Dan rubbed his forehead. 'I know. Let's try and think of a name that everyone would vote for, like the Free Chocolate Party or the No Tax Party.' Dan smiled broadly and Josh imagined all the wild and wonderful names flying about in the boy's mind.

'There's already a Monster Raving Loony Party,' said Josh.

'Seriously?' Dan's eyes opened wide.

'Yes and people really do vote for its candidates.'

Dan guffawed loudly and almost slipped off his chair with the hilarity of it all. Meanwhile Josh kept thinking of the huge task ahead. All the forms to be completed, systems to be set up for monitoring donations, rules and regulations to be followed to avoid falling foul of the Electoral Commission.

'How about the Apathy Party or the Do Not Vote Party or None of the Others Party?'

'No Dan. None of those names would be allowed. We'll have to find out if the Internet Party is an acceptable name and if not, we'll have to think again. Now let's get on with what else has to be done.'

'Ok boss,' said Dan. He settled back into his chair and waited patiently to be told what would happen next.

Josh was enjoying Dan's company. The boy had thrown himself into the Internet Party with enormous enthusiasm and had been very supportive of Josh as he struggled with all the formalities of setting up a political party from scratch.

Maggie had more than enough to do with running her PR business and managing the fast and furious building project that was unfolding two doors down the road. Somehow she'd organised a large team of builders over a period of three months to virtually transform her house from a derelict building site into a modern show home. To Josh's amazement the builders had finished a loft extension within six weeks, including a new slate roof with gleaming solar panels. There had been a flurry of excitement over the installation of solar panels as no one else had them in the road. Maggie had proudly reported to Josh that the shell of the massive kitchen extension that went right across the back of the house, complete with huge glass bifolding doors had been finished in eight weeks. He hadn't taken much of an interest at the time as he'd been too busy dealing with the creation of the Internet Party.

Although Josh had initially been somewhat reluctant to turn his fantasy into reality, he now felt fully committed to the idea of a new political party. The juggernaut of idealism that he'd kept hidden for years was now hurtling forwards at a tremendous pace. He'd agreed with Maggie that she would put her time and energy into getting her house renovations completed so that the Internet Party could use her home as its headquarters before the General Election that was fast approaching. Bruno hadn't been keen on the idea of his newly refurbished home being occupied by a band of volunteers for several weeks but Maggie had given him no choice. That seemed to Josh to be the dynamic of their relationship.

'What else has to be done apart from getting the Electoral Commission to agree the name?' said Dan.

'We have to draw up a constitution and register the names of the party leader and treasurer.'

'Who's going to be leader? You or Maggie?'

Josh sighed and shifted in his seat. A few seconds passed before he spoke.

'I'll probably put my name down as I'll be dealing with all the official stuff while Maggie runs the day-to-day operations.'

Dan nodded but was silent for a few moments. He looked down at his hands.

'Do you think Maggie will be happy with that?'

'What?'

'You know, you being party leader.'

No, thought Josh. Maggie would want her name on the record.

'Well, I'll try and get both our names recorded, as joint party leaders and then we'll see. How about helping me to design some logos? Perhaps you could get your friends to help. How's the website coming along?'

'Really good,' said Dan. 'Mum went ballistic about the amount of time I'd been spending on the Internet Party, so now there's a group of us from school working on the website in our lunch hour. We're nearly finished with the basics.'

Dan's face glowed with pride and enthusiasm but Josh looked worried.

'Oh, I am sorry. I keep forgetting about your exams. I'll get some of the volunteers to work on the logos. I don't want either of us getting into trouble with Kim. Well, no more than we are already.' He winked conspiratorially at Dan, who grinned in response. Then Josh stood up and stretched his arms above his head in a gesture that indicated their meeting was coming to an end. He turned to look down at Dan with a serious expression on his face. When he spoke he realised that his words were directed at himself as well as the boy.

'I can't let my idealism ruin your exams or damage your relationship with your mother.'

'It's ok. I'm really enjoying being...' Dan searched around for the words. 'Being part of something, you know, something big.' He hesitated. 'I just have to make sure I leave enough time for revision.'

'The great thing, Dan, is that you'll actually be able to vote for the Internet Party in the General Election, as you'll be eighteen by then.'

'Certainly will,' said Dan as he stood up to face Josh. 'I suppose I'd better go and do my coursework now.'

'Yes, you must,' said Josh, assuming a fatherly tone. 'Your school work has to be your first priority.'

Dan rolled his eyes and, holding his new laptop computer close to his left side, put up his right hand to receive a high five. Then he lumbered out of the study and was gone. Josh felt a surge of warmth towards Dan and a twinge of guilt that he might have asked too much of the boy who was nearly a man. He vowed to get some of the young and enthusiastic volunteers involved in the design of the website and logos as well as setting up pages on Facebook and Twitter.

Josh and Maggie had made the decision not to draw up the type of formal manifesto held by most political parties. Instead they wanted people to vote for policies on a day-to-day basis and not be hidebound by any particular dictat. But there were plenty of other formalities to be complied with. Josh read through the financial regulations and reporting requirements on the Electoral Commission website. There were strict rules about donations and loans. Josh recalled that some of these had been breached by several of the main political parties in the past. There were rules determining how much money could be spent on election campaigns and requirements about accounts being filed.

Josh could see from the Electoral Commission website that there was going to be a huge amount of work involved in setting up and running a political party. He started to type up the bare bones of a draft constitution to discuss with Maggie later. He set out the various headings - aims and objectives, structure, decision-making, officers and responsibilities, membership requirements and finances. Then he decided to go and see her so they could flesh out the constitution together. There was no point in Josh sitting for hours deciding what he wanted to say, only to have Maggie come along and want to change things.

Josh had decided that turquoise should be the official colour of the Internet Party and he hoped Maggie would agree. Turquoise had been his mother's favourite colour and it conjured up positive images and emotions. He recalled a particular photograph of himself and his mother on holiday in Devon when he was a young boy. They were standing together in a blue sea and his mother was wearing a turquoise coloured dress. She was holding his hand and they were both smiling and trying not to fall over as the waves lapped around their knees. Josh tapped 'turquoise' into Google. He cast his eyes over its various hues ranging from blue to green, opaque to transparent. In some cultures turquoise was thought to have protective qualities and represented victory. That was good enough for Josh and he hoped for Maggie too.

CHAPTER TEN

How's it going?' called Josh from the doorstep of Maggie's house. He could see her through the open front door in a haze of dust at the top of the stairs. He walked into the newly plastered hallway without bothering to knock or ring the doorbell. Josh eased himself past several sheets of plasterboard and some planks of wood, which he recognised as the new skirting board destined for the upstairs bedrooms. He could hear the sound of banging from somewhere inside the house as the bare floorboards he was standing on vibrated and dust rose up into his nostrils.

'Hi,' called Maggie enthusiastically as she caught sight of Josh and hurried downstairs to meet him. She planted a kiss on his cheek and he caught a hint of her perfume mixed with plaster dust, as her tousled hair brushed across his face.

'I've never liked DIY,' said Josh. He'd intended to be humorous but the words made him sound like a grumpy old man. He hoped that Maggie hadn't heard him as she quickly disappeared into the large through lounge, gesturing to him to follow.

'Downstairs is nearly finished. We'll set up our office over here to start with.'

Maggie took Josh by the arm and led him across the rickety floorboards to one end of the large living room with its perfectly plastered walls and brand new ceiling.

'The floors will be finished by the end of next week. We'll have under floor heating in every room downstairs and light oak flooring throughout except for the kitchen area. Did I show you the kitchen tiles?' Josh shook his head. 'Here they are.'

Maggie pointed to a pile of large stone tiles in a corner of the L-shaped kitchen area and Josh smiled.

'You'd make a great estate agent.'

'Thanks. I'll take that as a compliment.'

Maggie gave him one of her winning smiles and he felt a shiver of excitement as their eyes met. Kindred spirits, thought Josh. He felt empowered by Maggie. She was a dynamo driving him forward on their joint quest. He thought how attractive she looked in her faded light blue jeans and loose fitting shirt. Her face was flushed and her hair shone in the sunlight like a golden crown. Josh imagined himself as a knight in shining armour and was about to whisk Maggie away to his castle when his thoughts were interrupted by a knock on the front door.

'Oh good,' said Maggie. 'That'll be the man from BT. The phone isn't working.'

She disappeared into the hallway. Josh looked out of the front window and saw a van parked outside with the familiar BT logo.

'Sorry about the mess. Would you like a cup of tea?' said Maggie as the man followed her into the room. Josh thought she was fussing around him a bit more than was necessary.

'Thanks love, milk and two sugars please.' Maggie hurried off towards the kitchen. 'Hello mate.' The large man nodded at Josh and he nodded back. 'How many lines you got?' Josh looked blank.

'Two live ones and there's one that was disconnected before we moved in,' Maggie shouted from the kitchen. Suddenly there was a loud drilling noise from upstairs and the BT man jumped. Maggie appeared with his tea and Josh decided to be more sociable.

'Hi. I'm Josh.'

'Greg,' said the BT man. He was tall and muscular with short black hair and aged about thirty. Josh pulled himself upright without even realising he was doing so.

'I'll need to check the lines inside the house first. Where are the junction boxes?'

While Maggie showed Greg around Josh examined

the newly plastered walls. They were much smoother than the ones in Kim's house. He thought back to when he'd helped Kim with some decorating just after he'd moved in with her. He had not found the experience at all enjoyable. Life was too short for painting, wallpapering and spending hours in DIY superstores. He would rather read a book, watch a film or meet up with friends.

Josh drifted into the newly refurbished kitchen area. He slid his finger over the dark grey granite work surface leaving a line in the dust. The walls were fresh with gleaming white paint and there were green glass panels between the work surfaces and the light oak cupboards. Josh had just opened one of the cupboard doors when Maggie appeared.

'Nice kitchen,' he said, quickly closing the door and feeling embarrassed.

'Thanks,' said Maggie. 'Coffee?'

Josh smiled and nodded as he perched on one of the silver stools that were tucked under the work surface.

'What's wrong with the phone?'

'Dead,' said Maggie. 'It was ok last night but when I got up this morning, nothing, kaput!'

'So no internet connection either.'

'Sadly no,' said Maggie as she handed Josh a steaming mug of freshly brewed coffee. 'Oh well, at least BT came out quickly. Nancy at number two had to wait for five days when her phone packed up.'

Josh watched Maggie as she sat in a slightly hunched up position on her stool, clutching her coffee mug between her hands as if it might slip out of her grasp at any moment. As the steam wafted up over Maggie's face Josh found himself wondering if she knew how he felt about her. Did the pupils of his eyes dilate when she looked at him? Suddenly Maggie put down her mug and jumped off her stool.

'There's Kim,' she said as she hurried in the direction of the front door. Josh's heart missed a beat and he felt guilty while at the same time annoyed with himself. After all, it wasn't as if he and Maggie had been in flagrante on the bare floorboards of the living room. Not with the BT man fixing telephone wires downstairs and the builders banging around upstairs anyway. Josh felt slightly amused at the thought of him and Maggie having wild and passionate sex in the middle of what was effectively a building site until he saw Kim's face. He stared at her as she stormed into the kitchen wearing her 'I'm not amused' expression bordering on 'I'm very angry.' Maggie hurried along after her.

'Well, here you are,' said Kim with a sneer.

To Josh those four simple words spoke volumes. In his mind what she had actually said was, 'Why the hell did you go out without telling me where you were going and why haven't you got your bloody mobile switched on?' He felt for his phone in his jacket pockets and of course, it wasn't there.

'I tried to call the house but the line was dead,' said Kim sternly.

'Sorry,' said Maggie. She gave Kim a look which said, 'Poor you having to chase around after Josh.'

'I'm sure my mobile was in my jacket from last night. I hope one of the kids hasn't borrowed it,' said Josh as he patted his pockets knowing that it wasn't there but determined to defend himself in front of Maggie. Kim chose to ignore his comment about the possibility of her children borrowing his phone. She would normally have objected but she had more important things on her mind this morning than where Josh's mobile might be.

'There's a journalist at my house,' said Kim. 'He wants to interview you, Josh.'

'Great,' said Maggie clapping her hands together. Kim gave her a look of disapproval.

'Shall I send him round here then?' said Kim, who had already decided to do so.

'Which paper is he from?' said Josh.

'He didn't say,' said Kim crossly.

'I'll come and get him,' said Maggie, feeling the tension between them.

'By the way, Josh,' said Kim as she started to walk out of the kitchen. 'Izzy says you agreed to give her a lift back from Sally's tonight. I'll be at my book club.'

'What time?'

'Six thirty.'

Josh saw Kim and Maggie walk past the front window and he considered what it would be like to have two wives. Suddenly his thoughts were interrupted.

'Excuse me mate,' said Greg, as he appeared in the kitchen doorway. 'Aren't you that fella who's set up a new political party? I saw your picture on the Internet.'

'That's me. It's called the Internet Party.'

'Why did you call it that?'

'The idea is that everyone can use the Internet and it's a good way of getting in touch with people.'

'Like blogs?'

'Basically yes but it's a bit more structured than that. We want people to have a say in what should happen in politics on a regular basis. Not just let the politicians control everything.'

'Yeah, that's what I read on the website. I'm sick of politicians. They promise all these things and when they get elected they do exactly what they want.'

'I'm back.' Josh heard Maggie's cheery voice and then the front door slam with a loud bang. 'Gosh it's windy out there,' she said as she strode into the kitchen smoothing her hair back from her face. 'Josh, Greg, let me introduce you both to Matthew Archer.'

Greg looked awkward as the short, bespectacled, slightly chubby man wearing a stone coloured raincoat shook his hand furiously.

He quickly excused himself by saying he had finished in the house and now had to go up the road to check on some wiring in a junction box.

'Hi Matthew,' said Josh holding out his hand.

'Call me Matt,' said the journalist, eagerly grabbing his hand and shaking it warmly.

'Matt's freelance,' said Maggie. 'He wants to interview both of us. I'm just going to get changed.' She rushed off as she spoke and left the men to circle around weighing each other up, examining the other's appearance. Josh noticed that Matt was wearing an enormous and ostentatious watch. He tried to work out what make it was and guessed that it must be worth over a thousand pounds. Josh directed Matt to the large glass topped dining table in the kitchen area and they both sat down. He watched through the glass as the journalist removed a small recording device and a notebook from his bag.

'Well, Josh, I've looked at your website so I've got some idea of what you want to achieve. But I'd like to know more about the man behind the Internet Party. What drives you? What's your ultimate goal? What kind of life do you live day to day?'

Josh looked at the journalist. This was exactly what he'd expected. Matthew Archer wasn't interested in hearing about Josh's vision of a new kind of democracy. He wanted to know if Josh had ever been in trouble with the law and whether he'd used drugs. But Josh wasn't playing his nasty little game of tabloid journalism so he launched into a speech.

'The whole point of the Internet Party is to restore democracy. Apart from casting a vote in local or national elections every few years, people don't feel they have any role to play in politics. The current voting system has no credibility. Fewer people vote in elections than they do in reality TV shows. Why is this? Because people feel they have more control over who wins or loses a reality TV show than they do over their own lives. All people can do in a general election is to vote for one of two main parties. At least that's how most people feel. They can't vote for a minority party because without proportional representation, it's a wasted vote. Once MPs are elected they can do what they want as there's no system of accountability to the people who elected them.'

'Within reason,' said Matt as he scribbled furiously in his notebook.

'Ok,' continued Josh. 'If a Member of Parliament belongs to a political party, as the vast majority do, he or she will basically follow what's in the party manifesto. But you can't always expect a manifesto to deal with future events, can you?'

The journalist went to speak but Josh continued.

'Once politicians are elected they want to hold onto power at any cost. They blow with the wind if they think it will take them in the direction they want to go. They lie and cheat and hope they won't get caught out. And worst of all, they often don't listen to the people who elected them.' Josh finally ran out of breath.

'So what's different about the Internet Party?' said Matt. 'Aren't you just like The UK Independence Party, the British National Party or the Greens, a one issue party?'

'I wouldn't describe those as one issue parties but no, we aren't like them. We aren't like any other political party. First and foremost we are not career politicians. We are ordinary people going about our day-to-day existence who care more about democracy than self-interest. We want people to have control over their lives. We want them to have a voice, to be able to influence decisions day by day, week by week, not just once every five years.'

'Would you abolish Parliament?' said Matt.

'Yes, in its current form. We would set up a virtual parliament with flexible hours and voting systems and greater access to the views of experts. Parliament would no longer consist of a bunch of career politicians, mostly white middle-aged males, desperate to keep their power, salaries and expenses, absent from debates, ignorant of expert views, manipulated by spin doctors, lobbyists or the Whips and primarily interested in themselves.'

'So what policies do you have?' said Matt. He stopped scribbling in his notepad and leaned back in his chair looking exhausted.

'Trust will replace policy. We currently have a political system where we have hundreds of policies but very little trust. What we need to do is to restore trust.'

Matt raised his eyebrows and started writing again.

'We will have ground rules, a set of values and a framework for making decisions, but policies will be made by the people, not by politicians.'

Josh stopped talking as he saw Maggie coming down the hallway. She was freshly made up with a light pink sheen on her lips that matched the stripes on her white shirt. Her hair had been brushed in golden waves that lay on her shoulders and sparkled as they caught the rays of sunshine streaming in through the mass of glass that stretched along the back of the house. She was wearing new blue jeans that hugged every contour of her toned body and she looked radiant.

As Maggie pulled out a chair and sat down at the dining table Matt stopped writing and gazed at her with his pen poised in the air, as if his hand was suddenly frozen.

'Sorry,' said Maggie sounding slightly out of breath. 'I got caught up with the builders. I had to make some difficult decisions, like where on the bathroom wall to site the loo roll holder.' She laughed and rolled her eyes. 'I'll make some fresh coffee.'

Maggie stood up quickly and the two men watched her turn on the large silver mixer tap and pour water into the shiny black kettle. She turned towards them as she waited for the water to boil.

'Where did you get to?'

Josh couldn't remember what he'd been talking

about before Maggie came into the room and Matt had completely lost interest in the subject under discussion. Both men said nothing but sat basking in the sunshine of Maggie's beautiful personality and appearance. Politics was forgotten as the conversation turned to the cost of kitchens, the importance of retaining original features in Edwardian houses and stories about cowboy builders. Sensing that she had become the centre of attention, Maggie steered the conversation back to politics.

'I'm sick of home improvements. Let's talk about the Internet Party.'

As Maggie outlined her vision of democracy for the twenty-first century and Matt enthusiastically jotted down notes, Josh indulged in a bit of daydreaming. He imagined that he and Maggie were on an atoll in the Maldives, alone on a golden beach, with the warm sun caressing their bodies and the gentle waves of a perfect blue sea lapping at their feet. Josh loved to escape into his thoughts, dreams and fantasies. It was his way of dealing with the harsh realities of life.

Josh often felt responsible for society's ills and inadequate for being unable to make the world a better place. He was conscious of Gandhi's mantra that it was possible to do small things to change the world. But Josh wanted to make big changes. He could see the validity of Kim's efforts to improve the local environment by helping to restore the park opposite her house. But Josh wanted to pass a law to make all local councils restore their parks across the whole country. When his overwhelming sense of social responsibility became too much for him, Josh would abandon all plans for making the world a better place and escape into his fantasies. He looked at Matt and Maggie as if he were watching a film. He could see Matt gazing up into Maggie's eyes as he assiduously recorded her words.

'That's right, isn't it?'

Josh's wandering thoughts were brought back

sharply into focus as he found Maggie staring straight at him with her hands firmly on her hips. Her face and neck were flushed with excitement. He nodded and smiled warmly in a gesture of reassurance. Maggie visibly relaxed and Josh hoped she hadn't realised that he wasn't listening to a word she said. Suddenly Matt checked the time on his watch and jumped up from his chair.

'I'd better get going. My parking meter ran out twenty minutes ago. What are the traffic wardens like round here?'

Josh and Maggie exchanged glances and grimaced at each other.

'Pretty evil,' said Maggie.

Matt shoved his notebook and recording device into his bag.

'I've got enough to be going on with,' he said, and slung his raincoat over his left arm while holding out his right hand. Josh shook it and felt a connection. This is what the Internet Party has to offer, thought Josh - hope, excitement and a fresh approach. When Maggie placed a kiss on Matt's left cheek Josh thought he saw the man blush and jealousy seeped through his veins.

'I'll be in touch.'

Matt waved as he hurried off down the road. As soon as he was out of sight, Maggie jumped up and down, clapping her hands with excitement and hugged Josh with such enthusiasm that they both toppled over onto the bare floorboards of the living room. They held each other tightly and Josh felt Maggie's warmth flowing into his body as he breathed in the scent of her hair and gently kissed her head. Suddenly there was a loud knock on the front door and the sound of heavy footsteps coming down the hallway. Josh and Maggie managed to sit up before the man from BT strode into the room, but neither of them could stop laughing.

Greg stood shifting awkwardly from one foot to the

other while Josh and Maggie struggled to their feet. 'I'm done. Everything should be working now.'

'Thanks,' said Maggie, smoothing down her hair and her shirt.

'Cheers,' said Greg as he moved towards the door of the living room. Then he disappeared down the hallway closely followed by Maggie.

Josh brushed the dust from his clothes and looked around for something that might tell him what time it was. He thought it was probably about six o'clock. The green digital numbers on the black oven in the kitchen flashed 17:55 hours. That meant he had thirty-five minutes left before he had to collect Izzy.

Maggie had managed to compose herself before she came back into the room and Josh realised that the moment for intimacy between the two of them had sadly passed. He allowed himself to imagine what might have happened if Greg hadn't appeared when he did. Would he and Maggie have kissed each other on the lips? That would have taken their relationship to a different level.

'I wonder if Matt will get any of the newspapers interested in his story,' said Maggie who now looked quite serious.

'I hope so,' said Josh.

'Well at least he's on our side.'

'You can never tell with journalists.'

They stood in silence for a few seconds, each alone with their thoughts. Then Josh said goodbye and Maggie kissed him lightly on the cheek, but the magic of the afternoon had gone and Josh felt sad as he drove along in his Saab convertible to fulfil his promise to Kim and pick up Izzy.

CHAPTER
ELEVEN

Later that evening Josh was sitting alone in Kim's kitchen.
He always thought of the kitchen as her territory, even
though he did his fair share of the household chores and
they'd lived together for several years. In fact, apart from
Josh's study, most of the house felt as if it belonged to
Kim, which of course it did. In the past Josh hadn't been
bothered by the fact that he had no place of his own. He
had willingly taken on the emotional burden of Kim and her
children from the time he'd moved into her home. Despite
not being well paid, because Josh had a generous nature,
he'd borne some of the financial burden of Kim's family
over the years. This hadn't concerned him until recently.
But now something was nagging away in the back of his
mind. 'You are nearly forty years old and yet you have no
financial security,' said the voice.

Perhaps it was seeing Bruno and Maggie's house
being gutted and renovated to the standard of a show home
that was getting to him. Josh had rejected the possibility
that he might be materialistic enough to be remotely
interested in the period features, designer kitchens and posh
paint colours that adorned the houses of the Wimbledon
bourgeoisie.

It had comforted Josh when he'd estimated the huge
amount of borrowing that Maggie and Bruno must have
taken on to buy and renovate their house. Each of them
had sold their flats in Notting Hill and after paying off their
loans they must have been left with a total sum of around
eight hundred thousand pounds. Josh had worked out that
in order to buy and renovate the house, they must have
taken out a mortgage of around seven hundred thousand
pounds. He couldn't even contemplate what it would be like

to be responsible for repaying such an enormous amount of money, but the thought made him feel better. Josh had never borrowed money for anything and he intended to avoid being saddled with a mortgage for as long as possible.

Before he met Kim he'd lived in a one bedroom rented basement flat in Camberwell. Sometimes he wished he'd stayed there. Life with Kim and her family was becoming increasingly tiresome. She was constantly stressed out about her divorce. Izzy was a volatile teenager, often angry and resentful towards Josh, as if it was somehow his fault that her father had deserted her. At other times she was loving and affectionate towards him, almost to the point of flirtatiousness. All too frequently the fact that Izzy was another man's daughter made things more complicated than if Josh had been her father and that would have been difficult enough.

Kim hadn't said much since he had returned from picking up Izzy. There had been the usual arguments over whether the four of them would be sitting down to dinner together, as Kim always wanted them to do. Unless Izzy had an important piece of information she was determined to share with everyone or dinner consisted of something she was fond of eating, she would often stomp off to her bedroom with a bowl of cereal or park herself in front of the TV and refuse to move. She would never hear a bad word spoken against her father and, apart from the times when Kim actually wanted to start an argument with Izzy, she didn't mention Richard's name in her daughter's presence.

After dinner Dan had left the house for the evening and Izzy was firmly ensconced in her bedroom with One Direction blaring away. Josh could picture her on Facebook relaying the events of the day to her friends, who would also be sitting in front of their computers, while she sent the odd text message to those who were out and about.

Josh was doing his usual trick of hiding his head inside his newspaper when Kim walked into the kitchen to make herself a cup of tea. They hadn't discussed the meeting with Matt over dinner as neither Kim nor Josh had thought it appropriate to bring up the subject in front of Dan and Izzy. But now that Kim had Josh to herself she was anxious to hear what had happened. Usually Josh felt grateful for the small number of opportunities Kim gave him to have quality time with her. The times when they would sit at the large pine kitchen table talking about the day's events over a bottle of red wine. These were the moments in their relationship that Josh relished and which seemed less and less as time went on. But tonight Josh felt uncomfortable in Kim's presence and the last thing he wanted was to answer her questions about his meeting with Matthew Archer.

He felt like escaping to his study, which was the one place where he was entitled not to be bothered by other people. When Josh was in his study with the door closed he was off limits and couldn't be disturbed. He desperately needed to think of a way of getting there now.

Kim sat down at the table and cradled her cup of tea in her hands.

'So how did things go with that journalist?'

'Fine, Matt's ok. He didn't ask too many awkward questions. How was your day?' said Josh trying to change the subject.

Usually Kim was quite happy to tell Josh all about the trials and tribulations of her work or family life but she wasn't going to be distracted from what she wanted to talk about today.

'So what sort of questions did he ask?'

Kim was obviously not going to let the subject of the meeting with the journalist pass. Oh well, thought Josh, I suppose this is the first time I've been interviewed about the Internet Party. He'd been in high spirits after what had felt more like a cosy chat than the grilling he'd expected from Matt. Now his high was in danger of turning into a low. Kim's face looked tense and her stare indicated that she not only wanted answers to her questions, but she wanted them now.

'Well,' said Josh. 'I explained how I came up with the idea of the Internet Party.'

'You and Maggie,' chipped in Kim with emphasis on the word 'and'.

Josh gave Kim a quizzical look. He thought it was strange that Kim wanted Josh to give Maggie credit for anything. The very mention of Maggie usually sent Kim off into a tirade of abuse about some aspect of her lifestyle or appearance so Josh tried to avoid even saying her name. But Josh could sense that tonight Kim's antagonism was firmly directed at him. He decided to ignore her comment.

'The interview wasn't very long and we kept being interrupted by the builders and a man from BT who came to fix the phones.' Josh was trying to play things down without much success.

'You didn't tell Matt anything about me or the kids did you?' Josh thought Kim's words sounded more like an accusation than a question. He felt disarmed by the tone of her voice and the expression on her face. They were assertive almost to the point of being aggressive. 'Did you?'

Josh couldn't remember whether he'd said anything to Matt about his personal life so he decided to play safe.

'No, the subject never came up.'

Kim raised her eyebrows and her sharp green eyes searched his face for any glimpse of a lie.

'So what would you have said if the issue had come up?' Kim wanted the whole truth and nothing but the truth. She was the prosecutor, jury and the judge all rolled into one. Josh was thinking fast. Had he said anything about Kim? There was no reason not to. She was his partner after all.

'I don't know,' he said weakly.

'What do you mean, you don't know? Kim was standing up now and staring down accusingly at Josh.

'Do you mean you don't know what you said or you don't know what you would have said?'

Josh stood up to face Kim.

'I don't know what I would have said.'

Josh spoke forcibly in an attempt to put himself on an equal footing with Kim. He knew from past experience that if she felt she had the upper hand in an argument it would generally turn into a full blown row. Josh hated rows and did everything he could to avoid them.

'We obviously need to sit down and discuss this in a calm and sensible fashion,' said Josh, as if he was talking to one of his students.

'Don't patronise me,' said Kim, sitting back down at the table. She paused for a few moments. 'The thing is, I don't want you to be a celebrity.'

Josh almost laughed at the thought of his picture on the front of Right On magazine or one of the other 'rags' as he liked to call them. But he managed to stop himself when he caught sight of the real anguish on Kim's face. He suddenly felt sorry for her. He had been selfish and self-obsessed and as a result, he'd been blind to the needs of others, especially Kim.

'I'm not a celebrity and I don't intend to become one. The whole point of the Internet Party is that no one becomes godlike. We need to get away from the concept of 'leaders'. No single human being has all the answers. Look at the dangers posed by autocratic leaders all over the world. Decision-making based on dogma and charisma rather than on rational thought and sound democratic principles will always lead to disaster.' Josh stopped speaking. He could see that Kim was weary and in no mood for a political lecture.

'If you speak to anyone in the media in future I don't want you to even mention me, or my children. Is that clear?' said Kim emphatically.

'Yes,' said Josh gently.

'There's my divorce.'

'I know.'

Josh tried to sound reassuring, comforting even. Kim's divorce had been an ongoing saga that he'd tried to keep out of as far as possible. He had read a few books on separation and divorce in an attempt to improve his understanding of Kim's situation. In reality he'd also done so to make life simpler for himself. He had a logical mind and if he could rationalise human behaviour and emotions he found them easier to manage.

Josh knew that divorce involved the type of grief someone might experience following bereavement. After several years of grieving for her lost marriage Kim now felt anger and resentment towards Richard. Suddenly Kim burst into tears and held her head in her hands.

'I don't want you to become famous. I'm afraid I'll lose you. I feel you're already drifting away from me. I hate the Internet Party,' Kim moaned.

Josh was stunned. He thought Kim must be crying because of her divorce, the effect of Richard's departure on Dan and Izzy or concerns about her financial future. But here she was worrying about Josh's new-found celebrity status after only one interview with a journalist. Kim could be utterly irrational at times.

'I'm not a celebrity and I've no intention of becoming one.'

Josh spoke with conviction, loudly and deliberately emphasising each word. Kim looked up at him through a cloud of tears. She stared at the man she thought she loved, the man who until recently had represented something of a secure future for her and her children. Kim's world had been turned upside down, first by Josh's apparent infatuation with Maggie and then by the creation of the Internet Party. She had expected 'Josh's midlife crisis crush on Maggie', as she disparagingly described it to her friends, to pass fairly quickly. She thought Maggie would discourage his attentions after a few days of basking in what Kim supposed she would regard as flattery. But she'd gradually realised that these two self-absorbed individuals had become locked into a mutual quest that drew them together in an intense emotional bond. Kim knew from listening to Josh and Maggie's conversations that they did not hold the same political views. But they shared a set of moral values that seemed to override their differences. It was as if politics could wait until democracy had been restored. Once people's votes counted, politics could be reintroduced to their daily lives.

Kim's mind suddenly became clear, as if her tears had washed away certain blockages to her thinking. She realised that she could no longer trust Josh. When he said that he had no intention of becoming a celebrity he probably meant what he said. But Kim couldn't trust him not to change his mind. Nor could she trust him with Maggie. She would have to wait and see what happened. Josh was on a journey and Kim had no idea where he might end up. But she knew she was going nowhere. She was determined that her own life would continue as it had done before she even met Maggie and Bruno.

Sometimes Josh thought he could read Kim's mind. One of his favourite pastimes was to guess what she was thinking from her facial expressions. But her face was now completely blank, as if the drawbridge to a castle had been pulled up and slammed shut against the wall. Josh had no idea what Kim was thinking and he felt extremely uncomfortable and even a little vulnerable. For the first time since he'd moved in with Kim he wished he had somewhere else to escape to, a place of his own where he could feel secure. He hated confrontation and being made to feel that he was in the wrong, especially when he felt he'd done nothing to justify such a feeling.

Izzy's arrival jolted both Kim and Josh back into the moment. She swaggered into the kitchen with a wide grin on her face and threw her open handbag onto the table spilling some of its contents. Her purse, a small bottle of perfume, pink lip gloss and a packet of gum slid in different directions before coming to a stop.

'Oops,' said Izzy as she grabbed her mobile phone just before it fell off the table and onto the floor. She stuffed her wayward belongings back into her handbag and looked at Kim and Josh. She could sense they were having 'an awkward moment', which was how she described things when they weren't getting along.

'I just saw Maggie on the way back from school,' said Izzy cheerily, thinking that it might help if she were to lighten up the conversation. 'She was telling me about that guy this morning, the journalist. Sounds like you're both gonna be famous.'

Izzy spoke kindly to Josh. He quite liked it when she was in this sort of mood. He hoped that her presence would cheer Kim up. But he was going to have to change the subject.

'Good day at school?' said Josh. Izzy nodded as she pulled out a chair from under the kitchen table and sat down. But she couldn't be diverted from what she wanted to talk about.

'So when are you gonna be in the paper? You need to let me know so I can tell all my friends.' Izzy held onto the table and leaned her chair back so that it stood precariously on its two back legs.

'Don't do that,' said Kim sharply. 'You'll break the chair.'

'Sorree,' replied Izzy, narrowing her eyes and raising her eyebrows at the same time. This was something Josh had tried but never managed to do. She pulled the chair forward onto four legs. 'Did you have your photo taken?'

'Oh for goodness sake,' shouted Kim as she jumped up from her seat and stormed out of the room.

'What's up with her?' said Izzy grimacing at Josh.

He leaned forward and looked into her sweet and innocent hazel eyes.

'Your mother isn't very pleased about the idea of things being written about me in the newspaper. She's a bit stressed out about the fact that the journalist turned up at her door and that there's so much interest in the Internet Party.'

'I think it's great,' said Izzy. She was again rocking back and forth on her chair and was perilously close to tipping backwards and banging her head on the kitchen sink. Josh thought about admonishing her as Kim had done but decided not to.

'I want to be a celebrity,' said Izzy.

Josh smiled. 'What, you mean on the TV, in Right On magazine, that sort of thing?'

'And the rest,' said Izzy. She reeled off a list of magazines that Josh had never even heard of and he realised that she was deadly serious. He felt sad as he was sure Izzy had more to offer the world than the so called celebrities who were splayed across the pages of tabloid newspapers and glossy magazines day after day.

'I'll talk to Mum,' said Izzy. She slammed her chair back down onto the floor, stood up and gave Josh a reassuring pat on the shoulder.

'Thanks,' he said as she picked up her handbag and left the room.

After a few minutes he heard the sound of voices at the top of the house. He decided not to hang around to find out whether he had caused a row between Kim and her daughter. They could argue about something of monumental importance or some trivial matter with equal ferocity and he didn't have the emotional energy for a fight. Josh quietly let himself out of the front door and slowly drifted in the direction of Maggie's house. He immediately felt guilty, but at the same time he was excited by the prospect of seeing her again.

Maggie swung her legs back and forth over the side of the kitchen stool as she stared into space. Her hands were clutching a freshly made cup of steaming hot coffee. Josh held one too and they both sat caressing their mugs as if they were involved in some deeply intense religious ceremony. Fifteen minutes earlier he had turned up unexpectedly at Maggie's front door. He had explained to her that Kim was finding him hard to live with because of his involvement with the Internet Party. They had talked openly and at length about their partners. Josh had been surprised but relieved to hear that Bruno was disturbed by what he described as 'Maggie's obsession' with the Internet Party. He was disappointed that Bruno hadn't gone so far as to accuse her of being obsessed with Josh, or perhaps she was just keeping that to herself for fear of embarrassing him. He had decided not to tell Maggie that Kim was unhappy about the amount of time he was spending at her house.

'I think we need to move up a gear,' said Maggie, at last breaking the silence. She looked at Josh. 'Once Matt's article is published we'll get a rush of interest from the media. The website's already taking loads of hits.'

'What do you mean by moving up a gear?' asked Josh.

He wasn't one for planning ahead. Since his Mother had died he'd tried to live in the moment as much as possible. Sometimes he found himself reliving his past, usually the safe and happy parts of his childhood such as seaside holidays and family gatherings or time spent with friends.

Maggie looked at Josh and wondered what he was thinking. It suited her for him to be passive. She had everything planned out. She needed his ideas, charisma and most of all his maleness. It was a sad fact of life that despite years of feminism and attempts by the law to bring about equality between men and women, men were still taken more seriously as political leaders than the so-called fairer sex. Josh was Maggie's front man but he was malleable enough for her to control. She'd convinced herself that she wasn't using him unfairly and she was comforted by the fact that they were on the same wavelength and were aiming for the same goal. But Maggie also knew that she would have to drive the campaign. After all, she was a strategist by nature.

'Look,' said Maggie, jumping off her stool and standing in front of Josh as if she had a whiteboard behind her that she was about to write on. 'The builders have just about finished. We've got carpets being laid upstairs at the beginning of next week and then this place will be habitable again. Bruno and I don't have much furniture and we can leave most of our stuff in storage until after the general election. I reckon we should start using this place as our headquarters. We can get loads of desks and computers in here.'

Maggie waved her arms around to show Josh where everything would go in her grand plan. 'I'm taking unpaid leave for four weeks and you've got your students' study leave coming up. How long are they off for?'

'Three weeks,' said Josh.

Maggie obviously didn't realise that Josh would still have work to do even if his students were studying for their exams but he decided not to say anything. He could almost see the cogs and wheels of Maggie's thought process whirring around in her brain as she planned their lives in the run-up to the election.

'I think you should move in here,' said Maggie. 'We've got six bedrooms and three bathrooms and it would be fairer to Kim and the kids. You'll be virtually living round here anyway over the next few weeks so you may as well sleep here. You can leave most of your stuff at Kim's and you'll still get to see her. It'll take the heat off you both. I'm not surprised Kim's stressed out. She's got two teenage kids. Have they got exams this summer?'

Josh nodded. 'Dan's got A levels and Izzy's got some sort of tests.' His mind was reeling at Maggie's suggestion that he actually move into her house but he was also starting to feel guilty.

'Kim works full time, doesn't she?' said Maggie.

'Yes,' said Josh sheepishly.

'And she's going through some messy divorce stuff. Well, I wouldn't want all that on my plate, let alone you causing loads of trouble with the Internet Party.'

Maggie really could be very blunt at times, thought Josh. He felt extremely uncomfortable and he found himself shifting in his seat as he tried to think of something appropriate to say. Maggie might just as well have said, 'Josh, you're a selfish bastard. You've taken on a divorced woman and her two kids only to dump them when it suits your own political ambitions.'

'You'll be doing them all a favour if you move out for a few weeks. Keep them out of the spotlight.'

Maggie smiled as she spoke and Josh realised that she wasn't calling him selfish. She understood his needs and desires. The quest he was on was her quest too. Josh wondered what Bruno would think about him moving into the house he shared with Maggie.

As Josh walked slowly back along the road to Kim's house he could smell the scents of early summer on the still evening air. The strongest perfume was of broom with its spiky green branches and clusters of bright yellow flowers. Josh thought back to the evening strolls that he and Kim used to take around the park after work when they first lived together. Sometimes they would go for a meal in a restaurant along Wimbledon Broadway or to a show at the New Wimbledon Theatre. Afterwards they would walk around the outside of the park in the dark inhaling the scent of broom or freshly cut grass.

Josh couldn't remember the last time he and Kim had strolled around the park together. Their lives had become mundane and littered with the demands of others. Josh felt a sense of loss and yet at the same time a feeling of excitement flickered inside his chest. He could tell that change was in the air, the raising of expectations and a demand for more accountability. A revolution was about to take place in the nation's thinking. Once an alternative was presented to the voting population they would grab it and run with it as if nothing else mattered. Power would be restored to the people and with it would come a more democratic society and balanced decision-making no longer based on dogma and self-interest.

Josh suddenly felt in a buoyant mood. The general election was only a few weeks away and a lot could happen in that time. He decided to take a detour through the park. The light was fading and he could only just make out the shady silhouettes of a group of teenagers lolling around on a bench near to some large trees. A couple of dog walkers wandered along the serpentine paths that had been laid out in beaux arts style in 1901. Josh breathed in deeply as he listened to the noise of the birds' early evening chatter. The clear sound of a woodpecker rang out over the park and in the distance Josh could hear the familiar whine of a police siren.

Kim was sitting quietly at the kitchen table reading a book when Josh walked into the room. He could tell she was calm, although her eyes were red and swollen. He decided to come straight out with what he had to say.

'Maggie's suggested that I move in with her and Bruno until after the election. We're going to use their house as our headquarters. The next few weeks are going to be full on if the Internet Party is going to have any impact on the results. It will be very disruptive for you and the kids, as there's bound to be a lot of press interest. I think it will be fairer to all of you if I'm not here much.'

Kim said nothing for a while as she examined her nails. Then she looked up at Josh through her red and puffy eyes.

'What does Bruno think about all this?' she said.

'Maggie's going to talk to him tonight. She says he won't have a problem with it. Apparently he's away a lot at the moment working on some project in Birmingham.'

Kim started to speak but then thought better of it.

'Bruno seems pretty laid back. He works long hours and he's often away from home so I don't think it will bother him that much,' said Josh.

'Bruno can stay here if he wants to,' said Kim, much to his surprise. He felt a bit put out that she was being so reasonable about him moving out for a while. He was also slightly unsettled about the prospect of Bruno being invited to move in with Kim, although he couldn't understand why he felt that way. After all here he was being given the chance to spend every sleeping and waking moment in Maggie's presence until after the general election. Anything could happen.

CHAPTER
TWELVE

Izzy let out a scream as she grabbed the Sunday Post from where it had fallen through the letter-box onto the front doormat.

'Josh, Mum, Dan, come and see this,' she shouted at the top of her voice in no particular direction but so that they could all hear her.

Josh appeared from the kitchen. Kim and Dan collided on the upstairs landing and then they both hurried downstairs. Izzy was grinning and clasping the newspaper to her chest. The glossy magazine that she'd been searching for when she picked up the paper lay discarded on the floor, still wrapped in its plastic covering. Once Izzy was sure that she had everyone's attention and the pleas of 'What's all the fuss about?' had died down, she held up the newspaper with its front page facing the assembled company. Josh, Kim and Dan stared in disbelief.

The photograph of Josh took up almost half of the front page. He was pictured sitting on a bench in the park with his legs crossed and stretched out in front of him in a casual pose. He appeared to be either staring into space or at some object in the distance. He was wearing his brown leather jacket, loafers and what appeared to be jeans.

'Man or Mouse? What sort of headline is that?' said Kim, spitting out her words.

'Can I?' said Josh, gently indicating to Izzy that she should pass the paper to him, which she reluctantly did. 'I'll spread it out on the table so we can all see it,' said Josh as he walked along the hallway and into the kitchen followed by the others. He laid the paper out and read the caption to the photograph. 'Man or Mouse?' What the hell was that supposed to mean? Josh noticed that there was some small writing next to his picture that referred the reader to pages two and three for the full story. He turned over to the next page and could hardly believe his eyes. The headline at the top of a double page spread read: 'Is this the man who will bring down the Government and restore Democracy to the British Public?'

'Oh my god,' gasped Izzy. It was her favourite expression of the moment taken from the countless American soaps that she watched on TV. 'Look Mum,' she shouted grabbing Kim's arm. 'There's a picture of you getting shopping out of your car wearing that awful tracksuit. How embarrassing!'

'What a cheek,' said Kim as she peered at the unflattering black and white image of her hoisting two large, reusable cloth carrier bags out of the boot of her dark blue people carrier. She felt shocked that someone had been spying on her with a long lens. The photographer must have been hiding behind a bush in the park, judging from the angle from which the photo had been taken. She felt sick and angry.

'Oh great,' said Josh as he spotted an old school photograph of himself in the bottom right hand corner of the second page. 'Where the hell did they get that from?'

'One of your arch enemies, judging by what you look like?' said Dan, speaking for the first time since the drama unfolded. Dan and Izzy held their hands over their mouths as they tried not to laugh at the sight of Josh as a spotty teenager. His cheerful face, partially hidden by a mop of dark and untidy hair, beamed out from the page as he stood in an awkward pose wearing slightly undersized school uniform.

'How old were you when that picture was taken?' asked Dan.

'About thirteen or fourteen,' replied Josh. He was still in a state of disbelief at the huge amount of newspaper coverage he'd been given.

'I just can't believe this,' said Kim as she stood in a defiant pose with her hands firmly on her hips, skim-reading the lengthy typewritten columns for any reference to herself or her kids. 'Did you know about it?' Kim looked accusingly at Josh.

'Of course not. Do you honestly think I wouldn't tell you?' Kim gave him a look of disbelief.

'There's nothing about us, Dan.' Izzy made a sad face.

'Good,' said Dan. 'I don't want to be in the newspaper.'

'I do,' protested Izzy. 'I want to be famous. I want to be in Right On magazine and on those programmes on TV where you show people round your house.' Izzy twirled around and waved her arms in true celebrity style.

'There's so much in here that's wrong. It's outrageous,' said Josh as he traced the forefinger of his left hand carefully down the edge of each column.

'Like what?' said Dan.

'Well, according to this article, I might be a dangerous anarchist.'

'What's an anarchist?' said Izzy.

'It's someone who doesn't believe in government,' said Dan.

'But I'm also described as a modern day Oliver Cromwell and he wasn't an anarchist. He just wanted to change the rules of government,' said Josh.

'I'll bet you wish someone from the paper had come round to speak to you before they printed all this,' said Izzy. She rested her hand gently on Josh's forearm in a gesture of solidarity.

'They don't usually do that,' Dan announced with an air of authority that made him seem much older than his seventeen years. 'If journalists spoke to people before they printed things about them, they'd have to print the truth.' Izzy stared at Dan with her eyes wide open. She had always assumed that everything she read in newspapers and magazines was true.

'So why do papers print lies?' she asked.

'To make money of course,' said Kim. She continued her search to see if the paper had written anything about her.

'You don't exactly look your best in that photo, Mum,' said Dan.

'Well, what do you expect? I am not accustomed to putting on my best clothes and full makeup for grocery shopping.' Kim's angry tone caused Dan and Izzy to exchange glances.

'I suppose it could have been worse,' said Josh as he filled the kettle with water from the tap.

'Oh yes,' agreed Kim in a facetious tone of voice. 'The paper could have published a picture of me in my swimsuit. I remember one newspaper printing a photo of Cherie Blair, the wife of the Prime Minister at the time getting into or out of a boat on holiday. The accompanying article made a huge fuss of the fact that she was wearing the same swimsuit she'd worn when she'd been photographed in the previous year getting in or out of the same boat.'

'I remember that picture,' said Josh. 'The press had it in for her and they chose to print the most unflattering poses they could get.'

'They basically tried to ridicule her. Most photos made her look overweight and shots would be deliberately taken with her tossing her head back and her mouth wide open,' said Kim.

'It's like those photos in Right On magazine. You know, the ones of models, pop artists and film stars,' said Izzy.

'I know what you mean. The pictures of supermodels with greasy hair, no makeup and scruffy clothes,' said Dan.

'Not to mention large spots on their faces and their bums hanging out of too small bikini bottoms,' laughed Izzy.

'I suppose there is a funny side to all this. But on a serious note we're going to have to come up with a strategy for dealing with the media in the future,' said Josh.

'Can't you ask Maggie? She runs a PR company. I'm surprised she didn't see this coming.' Josh noted the caustic tone in Kim's voice and decided to ignore her.

'I'm going to have to talk to a lawyer. I'll speak to the guys in the Law Faculty at work and see if they can recommend someone. I'm not putting up with being called an anarchist,' said Josh.

'I think we should get a CCTV camera fixed to the front of the house so we can see if anyone's watching,' said Dan.

'It might come to that,' said Josh.

'Well I'm not happy about all this,' said Kim waving her right arm over the newspaper in a dismissive manner. 'I think I'll go out of the house with a black bin bag over my head in future.' Izzy giggled at an image that appeared in her mind of her mother fumbling her way to her car half covered in a large black bag.

'That would play right into the hands of the media. You'd be described as a bag lady. That would do wonders for my image,' said Josh.

'The bag lady and the mouse,' said Dan laughing.

'Why did the newspaper call you a mouse?' said Izzy.

'I suppose it's a play on words, as in computer mouse, or perhaps the Post is questioning whether I'm a brave or timid person. There's an old saying. Are you a man or a mouse? In other words, are you brave enough to stand up for yourself? Newspapers sometimes try to be clever with their headlines.'

Josh turned the words over in his mind for a few seconds. He hadn't really thought about his image before now. He had always assumed that people saw him in the same way and as he wanted to be seen. He realised that he'd been naive and that he was now playing a different game from the one he'd played for most of his life.

He would have to be more careful about what he said and did and would even have to think about what clothes he wore. This was something Josh had never done before. His wardrobe contained only a few items of clothing, which he wore over and over again until they became threadbare. His work as a lecturer allowed him to wear clothes that were casual and timeless such as faded polo shirts and chinos in the summer and shapeless sweaters in the winter. Most of Josh's students looked scruffier than he did so he never felt the need to dress up unless he had to attend a university function, in which case he would drag out his brown cord suit from the back of his wardrobe and find an old white shirt to wear.

After seeing himself on the front of the Sunday Post Josh realised that he was going to need help with his image and a new set of clothing. 'I'll call Maggie and see if she can come over. I wonder if she's seen the Post,' said Josh.

'I've got cricket training in half an hour,' said Dan.

'Well get your kit ready and I'll run you up to the club as soon as we've spoken to Maggie,' said Josh. He always took Dan to cricket training on a Sunday morning. It was his way of showing the boy that he cared for him and he enjoyed Dan's company. It also earned him points with Kim, who was generally exhausted by the weekend from dealing with the emotional demands of her clients all week.

'Maggie's probably not even awake yet,' murmured Kim under her breath.

'Hi Maggie, it's Josh. Sorry to disturb you but could I ask you a favour? Have you seen the Sunday Post?' Josh cupped his hand over the phone and whispered, 'I think I woke her up. She's going downstairs to get the paper.'

'I expect they were having sex, Maggie and Bruno,' said Izzy loudly. The others stared at her in horror and Josh jammed his hand over the mouthpiece. 'It's something people do on a Sunday morning if they don't have kids.'

'Izzy,' protested Dan, whose face had turned from a healthy pink to bright red in colour at the mention of the word 'sex'. But there was no stopping her.

'It's true. I read it in a magazine at the doctor's surgery.' Izzy suddenly realised from the looks on the faces of Josh and Kim that she was treading on dangerous ground. Her mouth slammed shut and she said no more. There was silence for a while as Josh tried to remember the last time he and Kim had made love on a Sunday morning. He looked at Kim, who was staring into space and wondered what she was thinking. He felt a pang of guilt. He'd been self-absorbed to the point of selfishness over recent weeks and had spent little time addressing her needs. The Internet Party had become all-consuming and Josh was only just managing to fulfil his obligations at work, let alone those he had at home. He suddenly realised that his relationship with Kim was on hold pending the outcome of the election.

'Maggie's coming round now,' said Josh.

'How very kind of her,' said Kim in a sarcastic tone.

Josh knew she was spoiling for a fight but he was determined not to get involved in one just before Maggie arrived, which she did in a matter of seconds. He couldn't stop himself from smiling broadly at her as she burst into the kitchen, closely followed by Dan and Izzy, who had both rushed to open the front door.

Kim didn't turn around to greet Maggie but looked casually over her shoulder as she fumbled about at the sink trying to give the impression of being busy. Josh registered a flicker of a smile emanate from Kim's tight lips. It was a greeting that indicated to Maggie that she was not welcome but her presence would be tolerated because it was required.

Maggie looked flushed from having run along the street. She sat down at the kitchen table and scrutinised the newspaper, clutching the edges of the printed pages.

Josh's eyes settled on Maggie's chest. She had

obviously thrown on her close fitting mauve tracksuit in a hurry and Josh could see that she wasn't wearing a bra underneath. He quickly averted his eyes and looked at Kim, who, to his relief, was making a pot of coffee and still had her back turned. Then he caught sight of Dan, who was standing in a rigid position with his eyes transfixed on Maggie. Josh felt uncomfortable at the thought that his seventeen-year-old 'stepson' might have designs on the woman of his dreams. He quickly worked out the age difference between her and Dan. Then he calculated the difference in age between himself and Maggie and wished he hadn't.

'Thanks very much,' she said, deliberately emphasising each word and smiling warmly as she accepted the steaming cup of coffee Kim presented to her.

'What do you think about the article?' said Josh.

'Well, there are a few things that need correcting, as you probably realise. But it isn't too damaging and the publicity will be good for the Internet Party.'

'As in there's no such thing as bad publicity,' said Dan, trying to get Maggie's attention.

'I quite like the photo,' she said, holding up the large picture of Josh on the front page of the paper.

'It's not exactly flattering,' he said.

'It's a lot better than mine,' said Kim. Maggie looked awkward for a moment and then spoke reassuringly.

'Newspaper photos are rarely flattering and are usually extremely unflattering, so you haven't done too badly.'

'Next time I'll wear dark glasses and a blonde wig. In fact there won't even be a next time because I'll become a recluse. I won't even go out of the house.' Kim looked agitated and clenched her fists, tightly pressing them into her lap.

'Poor Mum,' said Izzy, kindly placing an arm around her mother's shoulder.

'I'm not even in the Internet Party. I just happen to live with someone who is,' said Kim.

'That's the trouble with the media,' said Maggie gently. 'They're not very discerning as to who they take pictures of and they certainly don't care who they upset.'

'Will I be in the newspapers, Maggie?' piped up Izzy, waving her arms around enthusiastically.

'You shouldn't be.'

'Oh,' said Izzy, looking disappointed. Why not?'

'Because you're too young. Newspapers and magazines aren't allowed to go around taking photographs of people who are under sixteen. Not without the permission of their parents.'

'That's not fair. I want to have my picture in the paper.' Izzy clenched her fists at her sides and stamped her feet.

'It's a rule that exists for your own protection,' explained Maggie.

'I don't see why my privacy isn't worth protecting,' Kim interrupted, staring at Maggie in a hostile manner.

'Under British law there is no right to privacy.'

'So can papers print anything they like about people?' asked Dan, smiling and trying to attract Maggie's attention.

'Newspapers, magazines, TV and radio stations. They are all bound by codes of conduct which regulate what they can or can't say about people,' said Maggie, smiling back so warmly that she made Dan blush with embarrassment.

'Are they supposed to print the truth?' said Izzy.

Maggie smiled and looked straight at Josh. He smiled back and for a moment he felt a connection, a meeting of minds.

'The truth,' laughed Kim. 'Would that be the absolute truth or relative truth?' She stood with her arms held out at her sides, palms facing upwards, with a quizzical look on her face. Izzy looked confused.

'This is getting interesting. I love philosophy,' said Dan, pulling a chair out from under the table and sitting as close as he could get to Maggie without making it obvious.

Maggie decided to ignore Kim and Dan. She didn't want to get involved in a deep and meaningful discussion about honesty and lies and how perceptions of the truth might differ. It was early on a Sunday morning and she wanted to return to her nice warm bed, drink a cup of coffee and have a leisurely look at the Sunday papers, even if they didn't always tell the truth. So without looking at anyone in particular Maggie explained how newspapers were subject to regulation. If someone felt that a newspaper had acted improperly they could send a complaint to the regulator and have it investigated.

'We need to make two decisions,' said Maggie. 'The first is what we should do about this article. There are a few inaccuracies but I don't think they warrant a complaint being made.'

'We can put a statement on the Internet Party's website correcting what the paper got wrong,' said Josh.

'And email a copy to the Sunday Post,' added Dan enthusiastically, hoping to impress Maggie.

'We should also email copies to all of the other papers. The weekly newspapers often pick up stories from the Sunday papers and put their own slant on them.'

'That's all we need,' said Kim, rolling her eyes in exasperation.

'What was the other decision?' asked Izzy, raising her hand in the air to get Maggie's attention. 'You said we had to make two decisions.'

'Thanks for reminding me.' She sent the girl one of her beaming smiles showing her perfect white teeth and Izzy beamed right back. 'The other thing we have to decide is a plan of action for the future.'

'What do you mean exactly?' said Kim in a

challenging tone of voice. She was not going to be told what to do by Maggie.

'Well, this is just the beginning. We are a few weeks away from the election and there are bound to be other stories published by the media. Not just newspapers but magazines, radio stations and maybe even TV channels.'

'Yippee,' cheered Izzy. 'Fame at last.' She danced around the kitchen. Josh stared down at his feet and tried to imagine just how much media interest might unfold over the coming weeks. Then he looked up at Kim and saw that she was standing with her arms firmly crossed, leaning against the kitchen sink and she was frowning.

'You mean there's going to be a lot more of this,' Kim hissed through her teeth as she glanced back and forth at Josh and Maggie, but they both ignored her.

'You're right Maggie. We need a plan of action,' said Josh. 'What do you suggest?'

'Don't talk to journalists, but if you have to then only with one of our people present and a recording device. Generally, I think it's best to avoid the media. We can send out statements by email and put them on our website if we've got something to say.'

'What about the paparazzi? Shall we all go around in disguise or do we have to make sure that we're wearing our best designer clothes and full make-up before we go out of the front door?' Kim sneered.

'As any of us, and I'm including myself and Bruno in all of this, could be photographed at any time, we need to make sure we're giving the right impression when we're out and about,' said Maggie.

'Well I for one don't have the money to buy a new wardrobe of clothing. In fact, even if I did, I wouldn't change my style of clothes. I'm not being dictated to as to what I can and can't wear. And I'm not having cosmetic surgery, or dying my hair. Not for anyone.'

Kim looked pointedly at Josh and then stormed out

of the kitchen. As she left, quickly followed by Izzy, Josh could see tears welling up in her eyes. Guilt and more guilt, he thought.

'What was all that about?' said Dan, who was genuinely unsure as to what had made his mother so upset. He looked back and forth between Josh and Maggie, neither of whom met his stares. Eventually Josh spoke.

'The thing is, Dan.' He paused for a few seconds. 'Kim, your mother, is quite understandably unhappy about being dragged into the public eye just because she and I live under the same roof.' Dan nodded.

'Bruno will feel the same if his photo gets published or if anything is written about him. He's a very private person,' said Maggie reassuringly. At the mention of Bruno's name both Josh and Dan fell silent, each alone with his thoughts.

'Hey. I've got to get to cricket.' Dan suddenly leaped up from his seat. 'I'll get a lift from my mate down the road.' He gave Maggie one of his cool mature smiles, nodded at Josh and dashed from the room.

'Thanks,' said Josh after him. He felt a sense of relief that he wouldn't have to run the gauntlet of answering questions about the article at the cricket club.

'I know a few 'friendly' journalists,' said Maggie.

'How friendly?' said Josh with a tone of disbelief.

Maggie leaned forward over the kitchen table with her arms folded and her chest pushed hard against them so that the shape of her breasts lay openly displayed beneath her thin tracksuit top, the zip threatening to burst open at any moment. Josh willed himself to look away and managed to find something on a kitchen surface that warranted his attention.

'Well, every journalist on every newspaper under the sun is going to have an agenda of some sort or an angle they what to put on things. What we have to do is to find a journalist who is on our side and who is prepared to tell the story we want the public to hear,' said Maggie.

'OK, I'll leave that one to you. You're the PR expert.'

'I'll speak to you later,' said Maggie, as she eased herself up from the kitchen table. 'Bruno's been out to buy croissants and I said I'd only be ten minutes.'

Josh felt a rush of jealousy at the mention of Bruno's name. He wanted Maggie to stay and eat croissants with him. The two of them could plan their PR strategy over a leisurely breakfast and later they could go to bed and make love.

Suddenly Maggie's arms were around Josh's neck and her face was as close to his as it had ever been. He stared at the fresh and youthful beauty before him hardly believing his luck. Had she read his mind?

'Cheer up Josh. The article wasn't that bad and the picture of you in the park made you look cool and mysterious.'

'What about the school photo?' said Josh raising his eyebrows. He was experiencing an almost uncontrollable desire to grab Maggie around her waist and pull her tightly towards him so that their bodies moulded into one. But something was stopping him.

'It's cute,' said Maggie.

'Cute!' Josh objected.

'We were all teenagers once,' said Maggie reassuringly. She kissed him on the cheek and he smelt her aroma. Not the perfume she usually wore but a mixture of freshly laundered towels and hair shampoo with the scent of a meadow full of flowers.

'I'll call you later,' said Maggie and then she was gone. Josh heard her words from what seemed miles away. He felt a sense of loneliness and isolation that reached deep into his soul. He also felt exposed and scared as if he had just stumbled into the entrance to a huge dark cavern. He wanted Maggie with him. She made him feel safe.

Josh folded up the Sunday Post and took it with him

into his study. He opened up the Internet Party website. The web address had been displayed at the end of the newspaper article so he'd expected to see some feedback on the site. But he was completely taken aback by the number of emails people had sent. He scrolled down and saw that many had been sent in the early hours of Sunday morning when the article had been posted on line. Some were from people living abroad and a few were abusive but most were complimentary and encouraging about the Internet Party.

Josh kept scrolling down the emails waiting for a subject title to catch his eye. There was no way that he could read all of them, let alone send a reply. He would have to do a blanket response for the time being thanking everyone for their interest and sending out more information about the Internet Party. Then the emails would need to be copied to the party's growing band of helpers so that a more personal response could be given. Josh suddenly felt overwhelmed by the huge amount of attention he had received. A feeling of sickness came over him so he stopped looking at the computer screen and stared out of the window. His vision blurred for a few seconds and he found himself blinking in a frantic effort to correct it. Josh's breathing was fast and shallow so he gulped in air in an effort to catch his breath. A wave of panic engulfed him so that he experienced palpitations and his limbs became weak.

Josh moved carefully from his computer chair in the study to the sofa in the TV room, holding onto pieces of furniture to stop himself from falling over. He collapsed into the soft green velvet, folded his arms across his face and concentrated on the darkness before him. The blinds were still drawn and the sofa embraced and cocooned his body. Josh's breathing slowed and he felt calmer. He decided to stay where he was for a while and fought to block out the images that kept appearing in his mind – the glowing computer screen with its myriad of unopened emails and the pictures of him in the Sunday Post.

CHAPTER THIRTEEN

Josh heard footsteps coming down the stairs and along the hallway in the direction of the TV room. He had been lying on the sofa with the palms of his hands placed firmly over his eyes for what seemed hours. The footsteps stopped in the middle of the room and Josh felt he was being watched. He removed his left palm from his face and opened his left eye. Izzy was standing with her arms folded staring down at him with an impatient look.

'What's wrong with you?' She spoke in the tone of voice a parent might use when accosting a slovenly teenager.

'Nothing,' protested Josh. He quickly removed his other palm from his right eye, opened it and blinked at the light that seeped into the room from either side of the blinds covering its two windows.

'Well, why are you lying down?'

'I was resting and thinking.'

'What were you thinking about?' Izzy asked in a more gentle tone.

'The article in the Sunday Post.' Josh heard her breathe in sharply. There was a pause and then she spoke.

'Mum's very upset about it.' Izzy put a strong emphasis on the word 'very' to ensure that Josh understood the importance of the matter.

'So am I,' he said, rather more loudly than he'd intended. He swung his legs off the sofa, rubbed his eyes and ran his fingers through his untidy mass of dark hair.

'But it's your fault.' Izzy stared at Josh accusingly.

'What's my fault?'

'Mum's photo in the paper.' Josh almost laughed out loud at the stupid suggestion she had made but he just managed to stop himself.

'Look Izzy. It's not my fault that some photographer decided to take a picture of your mother getting her shopping out of her car. What about that awful photo of me as a spotty teenager?'

Izzy dropped her guard for a second and Josh thought he saw a flicker of a smile pass over her lips before she quickly regained her composure in her determination to win this battle.

'But it's your choice, Josh. You decided to set up the Internet Party with Maggie. So it's not surprising that someone is going to want to take pictures of you. But mum's not anything to do with it and it's not fair that she should have all this hassle.'

Josh was beginning to wonder whether he wanted the aggravation of being called to account all the time. Before the Internet Party came into being he'd led a pretty humdrum existence. Hardly anyone had known who he was and only a few people had cared about what he did with his time. Now he not only had to account to his immediate family for how he chose to live his life, it seemed as if he had to answer to the whole world.

'Izzy, Kim is my partner. We live together. It's therefore inevitable that she's going to get caught up in what I do with my life.'

Josh could have continued his lecture by explaining to Izzy that he had to put up with things he didn't like about living with Kim, in her house and with her children. For example, he often had to deal with Dan and Izzy's father, Richard. That was a major downside to being in a relationship with Kim. He had to listen to her moaning about the trials and tribulations of her ongoing divorce, her constant lack of money and the punishing demands of her job as a social worker. He had to act as a taxi driver for Kim's kids and put up with her frequent arguments with her daughter. Josh wanted to be able to explain to Izzy that if you were in a relationship with someone you had to take the rough with the smooth. But he knew he couldn't discuss such matters without upsetting her and that would make a bad situation worse.

'Well, I don't think mum's going to forgive you this time.' Izzy looked genuinely worried and Josh wanted to put his arms around her and give her a hug. But he generally shied away from open displays of affection. On the odd occasion Izzy would throw her arms around him when she was particularly excited about something but he never initiated contact with her in case it was misconstrued.

'Maggie is coming round later with a plan so we can make sure your mum doesn't get upset again.'

Josh got up from the sofa and walked purposefully into his study to indicate to Izzy that the subject they had been discussing was now closed. She followed and stood behind him as he flicked the computer mouse to clear the screensaver.

'Wow. Look at all those emails.' Izzy leaned over the desk and watched as Josh scrolled up and down deciding which to open, what to delete or report as spam.

'I like Maggie,' said Izzy as she walked over to the window and pressed her nose against the glass. She breathed hot air onto it, rounding her mouth as she did so and then moved back to watch the rings of steam disappear. Josh decided not to respond to Izzy's words.

'I don't think mum likes Maggie.'

'Why on earth not?' said Josh sounding genuinely surprised. He could not imagine anyone disliking Maggie. He turned to watch Izzy making rings of steam on the window.

'I think she's jealous.'

'Who?'

'Mum.'

'Why?'

'You spend a lot of time with Maggie and you get

on really well.'

'But I love your mother.' Josh spurted out the words as much to his own surprise as to Izzy's. He had become so obsessed with the Internet Party over recent weeks that he'd rarely examined his feelings for Kim. He felt reassured that he did still love her. But he knew that he was also falling in love with Maggie.

'Mum doesn't think you'll win the election,' said Izzy turning her head around to look at Josh.

'You mean she doesn't want me to.' She gave him a disapproving look. 'Where is Kim anyhow?'

'Gone to see Vicky, you know, in Princess Road.'

'Did she have a black bin liner over her head? At least if we see any pictures of someone wearing a bin-bag in the paper we'll know it's Kim,' said Josh.

'Ha Ha,' said Izzy. Then she moved towards him and her round face looked a little sad. 'Seriously Josh, I don't want you and mum to break up over this Internet Party business.' She looked him straight in the eye.

'Izzy. The general election will be over in a few weeks and then everything will go back to normal. The journalists will have other things to write about. The Internet Party may win some seats in Parliament or it may not. I may become an MP or I may not. Whatever happens, your mother and I will still be together.'

As Josh spoke he questioned whether he really meant what he was saying. But Izzy had heard what she wanted to hear. Not for Kim but for herself. She did not want to lose Josh from her life. Suddenly she bent down and kissed him on his left cheek.

'I've gotta go to dance practice. Laters!' Izzy bounded out of the room like a young puppy in search of a new toy.

'Laters,' Josh muttered to himself. This was Izzy's latest expression no doubt gleaned from some dreadful American TV programme of the 'Oh My God' genre. He suddenly felt a huge weight of responsibility upon him, not for his own life but for Izzy's.

For the first time ever he realised that Izzy had begun to look upon him as a father figure.

Josh tried to put this thought out of his mind by concentrating on the vast number of unopened emails before his eyes. Part of him wanted to delegate the task of examining the emails to Maggie's band of volunteers who worked at her house. The whole of the ground floor and four of the six bedrooms had been turned into a headquarters for the Internet Party. But Josh's childlike curiosity got the better of him and he decided to go through the messages on the screen slowly and methodically.

He wanted to know what people thought of the Internet Party. So far most of the emails he'd received had been positive. In fact, over the last few weeks he'd been buoyed up by the enthusiasm and goodwill of those who had sent him emails and posted comments on the website. The Internet Party had touched a nerve in the British population. It had reawakened people's interest in politics. Suddenly people believed that they could make a difference to their own lives and the lives of others.

Josh recalled the excitement he had felt at times as a child living in a political family. Lively discussions over Sunday lunch had often made Josh feel empowered to change aspects of the world that he found unacceptable such as poverty, inequality and injustice. Sitting around the dining room table in his parents' 1930's semi-detached red-brick house in Bristol, Josh, his younger sister, Rebecca and their parents would discuss the political issues of the day.

Turning away for a moment from his computer screen with its overpowering magnetism, Josh pictured the house where he had spent most of his childhood. It sat at the end of a terrace of similar properties except that his had a large garden that stretched all around the side of the house. The garden had been full of apple and pear trees when he'd moved there at the age of six. Josh and his sister had whiled away their childhood making tree houses and dens in which to play imaginary games. The bottom of the garden had been dark and overgrown with two ramshackle wooden sheds side by side. The smaller shed was used for garden implements while the larger one was the perfect den for Josh and all the other children from the neighbourhood. It was here that they played games such as 'Swallows and Amazons' or 'The Secret Seven' taken from books by the same names. Josh remembered how he had been the leader of the Swallows. Next to the den was a tall thin tree trunk known as the 'totem pole', a name taken from the Cowboy films that were frequently watched by children brought up in the nineteen fifties and sixties.

Josh recalled that only one of his friends was brave enough to climb to the top of the pole, a boy of the same age called Chris. He lived in the cul-de-sac at the side of Josh's house and was his best friend and almost like a brother. As Josh wallowed in the memories of his idyllic childhood he felt a rush of warmth and a feeling of belonging to a place that had been filled with love and hope. It was inevitable that after such a happy childhood, the challenges of adult life would at times be uncomfortable and disappointing. Yet only a few weeks ago Josh had once again started to feel that same hope and excitement he'd experienced as a child when his father had talked to him as if he had the power to change the world for the better.

Josh allowed his eyes to be drawn back to his computer screen. He opened an email. It was a message of support from a Mr Khan in Bradford, a former Conservative Party supporter who had become disillusioned with MPs of all parties. He was worried about the increasing popularity of UKIP and the danger of their anti-immigration policies creating disharmony between different racial groups.

Josh flicked open another email. A Mrs Hopkins from Swansea in Wales wanted to be considered as a candidate for the Internet Party. She had attached a short autobiography in which she described herself as a thirty-two year-old single parent from a mining family. She had recently completed an Open University degree course that had restored her self-confidence after a poor education and unhappy marriage. Traditionally a Labour Party supporter, she felt that they weren't standing up for working people in the way that they should be. Mrs Hopkins said she worked full time as a hospital administrator and therefore had no time to climb the career politicians' ladder. But she had valuable life experience and sound judgment, two things she felt most politicians lacked. Josh smiled and sent short and encouraging messages of thanks, saying he would forward their emails to a member of the Internet Party who would be in touch with them soon.

Most of the emails were positive and contained messages of support. Many of them made useful comments and suggestions. They came from all over the United Kingdom and from many different parts of the world. Josh was interested to see that there had been a rush of emails from the USA, Canada and Australia following the article in the Sunday Post. There were a few abusive messages, most of them short and to the point. Josh was upset by the first few that he'd read and had therefore taken time to reply to them and explain why the sender should reconsider his or her view. But he'd soon learned his lesson.

'Do not engage with lunatics.' Maggie's advice to Josh had been crystal clear and he'd ignored it. The more he communicated with the abusers the more abuse he received. Most of it consisted of the standard four-letter words telling Josh where he could shove his Internet Party. But the next email he opened gave him a nasty shock. It had been sent at six minutes past midnight, just after the article in the Sunday Post would have gone online. Josh looked closely at the email address, a unique combination of letters and numbers that gave no clue as to the identity of the sender. The words were written in English and the message was clear. It was a death threat.

'Sleep with one eye open or your life may be shorter than you plan it to be.'

Josh felt a chill that went deep into his soul. He sat staring at the words on the screen for a few seconds and then pressed the 'delete' button. 'Are you sure you want to delete this message?'

'Yes, I am sure.' Josh spoke the words out loud and pressed 'enter'. The offending email disappeared. But he knew it was still there lurking in the depths of his computer. He got up and looked out of the window hoping to erase his memory with a more pleasant image. Josh's favourite blackbird was nowhere to be seen. He tried to pull himself together and came up with the idea that whoever sent the death threat was a random sender who had probably tapped in loads of email addresses without knowing who they belonged to. After all, there was nothing in the message itself to indicate that it had been intended for him, Josh, the so-called 'leader' of the Internet Party.

He scrolled down the list of emails to see if he recognised any of the senders' addresses. What he needed now was familiarity in the form of a reassuring message of support from a friend. Suddenly one subject heading caught his eye.

Remember Me? – Hi from Christine

Josh hesitated for a moment as he turned the name 'Christine' over in his mind. His thoughts switched from the unwelcome task of trying to imagine what someone capable of sending an anonymous death threat might look like to the more familiar occupation of recalling memories of the females he'd met that he held deep in his subconscious.

Josh closed his eyes and repeated the name 'Christine'. An image of a woman he'd become friends with in his first year at university called Christina floated into his mind. She had been slim with dark shoulder length hair and an English rose sort of complexion with fine features and a charming smile. Her friends had called her Chrissie. Josh had kept in touch with her over the years by sending the odd Christmas card. But she was never known as Christine.

Then he remembered Kris, a mature student he'd taught in his current job a few years ago. Her first name was Christine but she'd insisted that people call her Kris with a K. She was one of the most annoying people Josh had ever met. His experience of mature students generally fell into two categories. One type was reckless and irresponsible, using their university experience to relive their teenage years by cutting corners on their academic work and indulging in rampant sex and wild parties. The other type were overly conscientious, had unrealistically high expectations of their lecturers, refused to engage in any part of the university experience and spent most of their time complaining. Kris had fallen into the second category.

Josh felt uncomfortable as he recalled the end of term summer party at which Kris had asked him out. She'd first of all explained that she understood how unprofessional it would have been for him to embark upon a physical and emotional relationship with her while she was still his student. Now that the course had ended she could see no reason why they shouldn't 'get it together'. Josh had been surprised and somewhat flattered but had quickly explained that he'd recently met someone else, which was untrue but the kindest way of rejecting Kris. Unfortunately, undeterred by his words and rather the worse for drink, she'd grabbed his arm and pulled him towards her. As she'd lunged forward to kiss him he'd involuntarily sidestepped to avoid her and she had toppled over into some bushes. Josh had helped her up and apologised profusely but the damage was done.

Kris had written him a letter afterwards in which she described how disappointed she had been by his 'unprofessional, disrespectful and childish behaviour.' Josh felt a sense of trepidation as he opened the email. There had been one significant Christine in Josh's past life. But he'd compartmentalised his memories of her to a part of his mind that he rarely visited. He hardly dared to hope that it was from her.

'Hi Josh. I don't suppose you'll remember me but I remember you. I saw the article about you in the Sunday Post. Nice picture! It brought back happy memories. Well done you for 'catching the imagination of the British public.' What else have you been doing over the last 20 years? I'm a partner in a firm of solicitors in Sussex. I get up to London quite often. It would be great to meet up.
Best
Christine'

Josh felt a mixture of excitement, panic and guilt. Why guilt? He hadn't seen Christine since he'd been in the last term of his first year at Exeter University. He'd met her at a freshers' party. She was two years older than Josh and had been in the last year of her law degree. She had no reason to be interested in him but he'd noticed her immediately. Unlike most of the other students at the party Christine had been smartly dressed in black trousers with a crisp white blouse that showed off her toned figure. She had perfectly cut short brown hair, dark eyebrows and beautiful brown eyes that made her look warm, kind and sexy.

Josh had been sitting with a group of freshers he didn't know well or have much in common with and had been idly looking around the room when his eyes fixed on Christine. She was standing at the bar talking to a group of friends in an animated fashion. Without thinking Josh stood up and headed towards the bar. He positioned himself next to Christine, leaned casually on the side of the bar and smiled at her. To his delight she smiled back. 'You're not a fresher are you,' said Josh. Christine had replied that she was on the Events Committee for the Students Union and that she'd helped to organise the party.

Josh recalled the tingle of pleasure he'd felt when Christine had turned away from her group of friends and talked to him. How he had relived that moment over the years. He recalled the first rush of true love, his sexual awakening and the confidence in his own being that Christine had given him in the months they had spent together. Time had helped to heal the overwhelming pain and relieve the intense feelings of failure and rejection that Josh had experienced at the end of his relationship with Christine. But while the pain had subsided, the crushing of Josh's confidence and the damage to his self-worth had never been repaired. He had been in love for the first and the last time when he'd been in love with Christine. He had found himself able to love other women but he'd never again experienced being 'in love'.

The circumstances of Josh's break-up with Christine were almost too painful to relive. As he stared at the email his emotions went wild. He felt pleased that Christine had got back in touch with him but the anger and resentment she had caused all those years ago suddenly resurfaced and taunted him. He felt curious. What did she look like? Had she aged well? Would he still feel attracted to her? Why should he contact her at all? Wasn't his life complicated enough? Had she got in touch with him merely because she'd seen him in the newspaper? Or had she wanted to see him for years but never found a way of tracking him down before now?

Questions, questions, questions rushed in and out of his mind. Had Christine loved him as much as he'd loved her? Josh knew that he had not been her first sexual partner but she had been his first true love and his awakening as a sexual being.

As Josh hesitated with his finger poised over the computer mouse, deciding whether to allow Christine back into his life, he heard the back door slam and the sound of footsteps coming along the hallway. He froze as Kim walked into his study. Her face was flushed and she looked pleased with herself. As she bent down to look at the computer screen Josh automatically closed the window to remove Christine's e-mail from view. Then he felt cross with himself for having done so. After all, what did he have to hide?

'What are you up to?' said Kim.

'What do you mean?' said Josh anxiously. He sounded defensive but Kim was in far too good a mood to notice. She put her arms around Josh's neck and hugged him.

'I've had such a good time at Vicky's house. She had a few girlfriends round and they were hilarious. They made me see the funny side of this Sunday Post business.'

'Good,' said Josh. He wanted to say something else but words failed him.

'Where's Izzy?' said Kim.

'Dance practice.'

'Oh yes, I'd forgotten about that.'

Fortunately for Josh, Kim didn't pursue her line of inquiry as to how he'd been occupying his time. She disappeared into the kitchen to make them both a cup of tea, happily humming to herself as she went. Josh reopened Christine's email and placed it in a folder. He also printed out a copy and put it under some papers in his desk drawer. Josh had no idea why. He never printed off emails, seeing it as a waste of the world's resources. Josh scrolled down the list, quickly reading each one and placing them in folders. There were no more death threats and by the end of the afternoon he felt buoyed up again by the huge level of support he'd received from members of the public.

The article in the Sunday Post had generated seven hundred and sixty-nine positive messages of support, thirteen expressions of interest in standing as candidates for the Internet Party and fifty offers of help. In contrast the five negative emails and single death threat that Josh had decided was a hoax anyway had dwindled into insignificance. Later that evening various volunteers at Maggie's house would open the folders and collate the information they contained. Names and email addresses would be listed so that supporters could be contacted in the future. Josh had not opened a folder for death threats and he had no intention of doing so. He'd convinced himself it was a 'one off' and had decided not to mention it to anyone.

CHAPTER
FOURTEEN

By the time Maggie arrived at Kim's house later that evening it had a relaxed and happy atmosphere. Vicky and her friends had managed to convince Kim that the photo of her in the Post was not at all unflattering. In fact over dinner and after several glasses of wine Josh and Kim had laughed about the photos and certain aspects of the article. Maggie turned up as agreed at eight o'clock looking flushed and radiant, freshly made up and wearing smart black trousers and a perfectly pressed light blue shirt. Her hair was shining and she'd blown it dry in soft waves that lay gently on her shoulders. Josh heard himself take in a sharp breath as Maggie strode into the kitchen and pulled up a chair at the table. She'd arrived without a bag and obviously had somewhere else to go. In her right hand was a perfectly white piece of A4 paper with what appeared to be a freshly printed list in black writing. She held it slightly away from her as if the ink was not quite dry.

'Hi everyone.' Maggie nodded at Josh, Kim, Dan and Izzy in turn, her warm smile displaying her glistening white teeth. 'I'm in a bit of a rush so I'll run through this quickly if that's ok.' She waved the piece of paper in the air.

No-one said anything but they all looked at Maggie intently, waiting patiently for her to speak again.

'Right, I've talked to a few people I know in PR and I've come up with a media strategy. So that we can avoid the type of situation we had today with the Sunday Post.'

Maggie stopped speaking for a few seconds and looked around the table at the expectant faces. None of them spoke.

'So, this is what we will all need to do over the next

few weeks until the election is over.'

Maggie held up the white piece of paper in front of her face and slowly read out the list of commandments.

'Number one. Do not speak to journalists or anyone else in the media either intentionally or accidentally. I have arranged for someone to identify journalists who are supportive of what we are trying to do and I will organise briefings for them.

Number two. Dress smartly and be aware of your appearance and behaviour at all times in case you are photographed or filmed.'

'Filmed,' squealed Izzy. 'You mean TV cameras. That sort of thing.'

'Yes,' said Maggie. 'It's unlikely but it's possible that as the Internet Party becomes more of a serious threat to the established parties, TV stations might get interested.'

'Yippee,' said Izzy loudly, clapping her hands. Kim gave her a disapproving look.

Dan stared lovingly at Maggie. He'd been listening to her speak but he hadn't taken much notice of what she'd said. Josh looked down at the table as the reality of what his increasing public profile might actually entail finally sank in. He was in danger of becoming public property with both his actions and inactions being scrutinised in minute detail. Josh was not familiar with the concept of accountability, either at home or at work, let alone in a public forum.

Maggie continued with her list.

'Number three. Waste Management. Otherwise known as rubbish.'

No-one laughed and Kim looked increasingly annoyed. Izzy screwed up her face in a quizzical expression to indicate that she had no idea what Maggie was talking about. Dan was at last listening, sitting upright in his chair and tapping the fingers of his left hand quietly on the kitchen table to aid his concentration. Josh cupped his chin in his hands and rested his elbows on the table. He waited with trepidation to hear what Maggie had to say on the subject of waste management.

'From now on you must not put anything personal in the recycling boxes. Shred everything and I mean everything. Not just the obvious things like bank statements, letters or work documents but the not so obvious. For example, letters from your schools.' Maggie nodded in the direction of Dan and Izzy.

'Why letters from their schools?' said Kim suddenly breaking her silence.

'Because it's best that the media don't find out which schools Dan and Izzy go to.'

'But why?' said Kim looking anxious.

'Because there's always a risk of unscrupulous journalists trying to make a story out of which schools the kids of politicians are sent to. There's also the possibility of reporters talking to parents or other pupils at the school gates to try and get information out of them.'

'So what. Anyway Dan and Izzy aren't Josh's kids,' said Kim beginning to sound belligerent. Maggie looked worried.

'Please Kim. This is advice I've been given by people in the know.' Maggie put the white piece of paper onto the table and shrugged her shoulders with her palms upturned. 'Shall I go on?' She looked straight at Josh.

'Yes,' he replied.

'Apart from the stuff that goes in the recycling boxes you'll need to be careful about what you put in the black bags. Basically anything personal needs to go straight to the dump. As the election gets nearer there will be a real risk of your rubbish being examined either by journalists or by private investigators.'

'What on earth for?' Josh blurted out loudly. He could hardly believe what he'd heard.

'So they can collect dirt, excuse the pun. The tabloids love to discredit people. Most of their pages are devoted to digging the dirt on politicians and celebrities.'

Josh shot a glance at Kim. She had her arms tightly crossed over her chest and she was glaring at Maggie. Like a volcano about to erupt, thought Josh.

'So what exactly should we avoid putting in the rubbish?' Kim hissed through her teeth.

'Basically anything that gives away information,' said Maggie. She didn't look at Kim but glanced around the kitchen as if she wasn't speaking to anyone in particular.

'I know,' Izzy piped up, much to Josh's relief. 'Medicine bottles.'

'What are you on about?' said Dan. Izzy gave him one of her withering looks.

'If one of us was getting medicine from the doctor and we threw the bottle in the bin it would have our name on it.' Izzy took a deep breath as everyone else in the room looked straight at her. 'So, if anyone got hold of the empty bottle, a journalist or private investigator, he would know what medicine one of us was taking.'

'Good example,' said Maggie enthusiastically. She smiled at Izzy who beamed back looking pleased with the attention.

'I can't believe that anyone is going to be interested in what medicine any of us takes,' said Dan.

'You'd be surprised,' said Maggie. She looked at her watch and shifted in her seat. 'Now moving on swiftly to the last item on my list, the issue of phone calls and text messages.'

'You're not going to tell us that our phones are being tapped are you?' Kim laughed out loud.

Maggie looked a little hurt, checked the time on her watch and smoothed her hands over her hips.

'Well, actually they might be,' she said quietly.

'Oh my god,' shouted Izzy waving her hands in front of her face as if she was fanning herself like a character in an American sitcom.

'Reporters might be hacking into my voicemail like they did with that teenage girl Milly Dowler who got abducted and murdered.'

'That was terrible,' said Kim angrily. 'Her poor parents thought she was still alive because of what that newspaper did.'

'Yes. I saw them on TV giving evidence at the Leveson Inquiry. It was heart-rending,' said Josh.

'Well, at least the newspapers have been exposed for what they are. Guardians of free speech, truth and democracy? That's a joke!' said Kim.

'You, I mean we, just have to be careful. The same principle applies to emails, photos and other stuff on the computer. Someone could hack in and get access to material that's damaging to the Internet Party.'

Dan's face went bright red in colour as he remembered some embarrassing photos a friend had emailed to him that morning.

'Is there anything you'd like to share with us, Dan?' said Kim. His face got even redder.

'I've got to rush. I'll catch up with you all soon.' Maggie smiled and waved as she jumped up from her chair. She headed for the door and then she was gone. The piece of white paper with its list of commandments in black ink stared up from the table.

'Thanks, Maggie. I'll see you out,' Josh shouted after her. He grabbed the list and stood up. He was desperate to escape. He could feel a row brewing with Kim. But he heard the front door slam before he'd left the kitchen. Fortunately for Josh, Kim was in the process of grilling Dan about exactly what it was on his computer that had made him so embarrassed while Izzy, unusually quiet for a change, sat with a smug expression on her face taking great delight in the fact that her brother was being told off. Josh saw the opportunity to disappear and slid off down the hallway, carefully holding the piece of paper.

Once Josh was safe in his study with the door firmly closed, he decided to revisit the email from Christine. He'd been bothered by its existence and hadn't yet replied, so she had no idea whether he'd even received it. He could press the 'delete' button and consign Christine back into the depths of his memory. Alternatively, he could send her a reply.

Josh sat staring at the wording of the email hoping to find an excuse for not responding to it. But the cheerful greeting and the enthusiasm Christine had expressed for the Internet Party made it impossible to ignore. Josh clicked on 'write' and began to type.

'Hi Christine
Good to hear from you. Can't believe it's been so long since we met. Things are pretty hectic with the Internet Party. Thanks for your encouragement. Just to bring you up to date with my life, I live with my partner Kim and her 2 teenage kids. A few relationships before that but nothing lasted very long (serial monogamy!?). No kids of my own (probably just as well). I lecture in social policy (yawn) at Central London University. Not exactly well paid but the students are mostly ok. Mum died 10 years ago after suffering from dementia for many years. It took me a long time to come to terms with her not being there any more. Dad is in good health and is enjoying life at the ripe old age of 86. Well, that's me in a nutshell.'

Josh debated over how to end and finally decided to keep it simple, so he typed the words:

'Hope all is well with you.
Best
Josh'

He hesitated for a moment, considered whether to click on 'cancel' and then pushed the 'send' button. His computer made a ping type of noise and the words, 'Your email has been sent' flashed onto the screen. Josh felt a mixture of emotions that included excitement, trepidation and guilt. But why should he feel guilty? He hadn't sent a marriage proposal or even an invitation to meet up. He'd made it clear to Christine that he was in a relationship. So why should he feel uncomfortable?

Somewhere in his mind was the thought that Kim wouldn't approve of him making contact with Christine but he ignored it and stared out of the window into the garden. He cast his eyes over the rickety fence that foxes had made holes in, its overgrown shrubbery and its complete lack of colour apart from green. It's all to do with money, thought Josh. Maggie's brand new landscaped garden must have cost thousands of pounds to put together. She and Bruno had good jobs and the ability to borrow large sums of money. Kim had children to feed and clothe.

Josh was suddenly startled by the words, 'You have email', which leaped out at him from his computer. He quickly turned down the volume and gingerly clicked 'open'. Christine's reply was short and sweet.

'Hi Josh
Great to hear back from you – at last! Thought perhaps you might be too important to speak to me (joke). I'm coming up to London next Wednesday morning as I have to do some legal work for my partner. I'll be finished by about twelve. Can you meet for lunch? It would be great to chat about old times.
Best
Christine'

Josh felt a shiver of excitement as he took in the cheery, light hearted tone of Christine's words. No danger there, he thought. She's got a partner and it sounds like she has a good job. She seems pretty normal. Josh tried to recall if he was booked up for Wednesday lunchtime. It was Sunday and he hadn't looked at his work diary for a couple of days.

He knew he wouldn't have any lectures or tutorials but sometimes he agreed to meet students at lunchtimes to discuss their assignments. In fact, having made such arrangements, he often forgot about them so he couldn't rely on his memory and would have to check the diary on his desk when he got into work. Kim frequently criticised Josh for not putting appointments on his phone but he never seemed to get round to doing so. I'll have to check that Maggie hasn't arranged any interviews with journalists on Wednesday, thought Josh. He decided not to allow himself time to agonise over his next move and clicked on 'reply'.

'Christine
Lunch sounds great. Keep Wednesday free and I'll check to see if I've got any appointments at work or with the Internet Party that no-one's told me about. I'll be back in touch soon.
Josh'

Christine's response was instant.

'Ok. Let me know. Look forward to seeing you. Haven't changed a bit in 20 years – ha ha! Christine'

A tingle went up Josh's spine. Memories from the past came flooding back. His first meeting with Christine, how cool and confident she'd been as she stood at the student bar, how smartly dressed she'd looked, quite unlike the other students. How she'd been instantly interested in Josh when he boldly introduced himself, how they'd spent the whole evening together, chatting and dancing, relaxed in each other's company as if they'd known each other for years. At the end of the evening they'd shared a kiss on the steps of Christine's block of student flats and that was when Josh had fallen in love for the first time, fresh-faced and with his whole life ahead of him. He closed his eyes and tried to conjure up the emotions he'd felt at that moment, the lighting of a fire within him and the deep and all consuming love for the confident and attractive woman whose lips were pressed to his. It was a feeling Josh had dared to think might never end and one that he wanted to experience again.

CHAPTER
FIFTEEN

Josh had agonised over whether to have lunch with Christine. He'd left it to the last possible moment before emailing her to confirm that he'd meet her at a sandwich bar they both knew in Covent Garden. Josh had half hoped that some important matter might arise at work or that Maggie would demand his presence elsewhere but nothing materialised to stand in his way. Part of him wanted to keep his memories of his first true love intact to avoid the risk of them being spoilt forever. But Josh's curiosity had got the better of him. So he had emailed Christine with a brief description of what he'd be wearing - a dark blue linen suit, an open necked light blue shirt and brown loafers.

Josh knew Christine had seen photographs of him in newspapers and on the Internet Party website, so he didn't need to worry about whether she'd be disappointed by how he'd changed over the years. But he had no idea what Christine would look like apart from the fact that she'd emailed him to say she would be wearing a red jacket, a white shirt and black trousers.

Josh had been tempted to ask Christine to send him a photo of herself before their meeting. But he felt this might give the wrong impression, as if he still had designs on her. After all it was Christine who had ended their relationship. She had slept with someone else after a drunken party to celebrate the end of her final exams. Josh had made the fatal mistake of not being there to make sure she spent the night with him. Instead he'd been at his parents' home in Bristol feeling depressed after a disastrous first year of studying law, which he'd found tortuously dull. Josh had been sure that he'd done badly in his first year exams so he'd retreated to the security of his parents' home to lick his wounds and wait for his results.

It was only when Josh returned to university the day after the fateful party of the night before and Christine told him she'd slept with someone else that he realised how much he loved her. She had said that she couldn't continue the relationship because of what she'd done. Perhaps this had been her way of letting him down gently and an attempt to make him feel better about himself. If it was, it singularly failed. Josh had felt as if he'd been hit by a car. The pain had been unbearable. Christine's rejection had been the worst thing that had ever happened to him. He hadn't dared to let her see how hurt he was. So for the last three weeks of term, while all the students were enjoying themselves after their exam results Josh played it cool. He never once showed Christine how much he cared for her and how he missed her in every moment of every day. He'd often wondered over the years whether he should have behaved differently. Perhaps he should have pleaded with her to take him back and forgiven her for what she'd done.

Christine had seemed impressed by how Josh had coped with her rejection of him. She'd even invited him to her twenty-first birthday party in her home town of East Grinstead in Sussex. Josh had thought about it over the years and wondered why he'd even bothered to go. Perhaps he'd had the faintest of hopes that Christine would change her mind and ask to go back out with him.

The pain had etched the events permanently into his memory. He chose not to revisit them most of the time, but now that he was contemplating his reunion with Christine, they'd resurfaced and seemed as clear as yesterday. Josh had spent a painful car journey travelling from Exeter to East Grinstead. Not painful in the physical sense but on an emotional level. He could clearly recall sitting in the back of the car looking out over fields bathed in early summer sunlight. It was late May or early June and the rhododendrons were in full bloom with blotches of pink, white, purple and red littering the landscape.

When Josh had arrived at Christine's parents' house before the party she'd behaved as if nothing had ever happened between them. She'd treated him as a dear old friend and kissed him on the cheek, shown him where to put his things in the spare room and then rushed off to greet another guest, leaving Josh feeling empty and numb. This sensation had lasted all through the party and into the following day.

Josh still had a vivid memory of his last dance with Christine. She had asked him to dance 'because he looked so miserable'. Not because she wanted him back in her life. Josh had never forgotten the track that had been playing as their bodies swayed together for the last time and he inhaled as much of her scent as his lungs would allow. It was 'When will I see you again?' by the Three Degrees. He could still remember the words and when he heard the song on the radio it would conjure up a picture of the dance he'd wanted to last forever.

Josh hadn't been able to sleep after the party. He'd tossed and turned and considered creeping into Christine's bedroom. But he hadn't dared to risk being caught by her parents or worse, to suffer rejection for a second time. Josh had got up with the dawn chorus and had gone to sit in a field at the back of Christine's house until he felt he could face the day. He half hoped that she'd come to find him so he could at least be alone with her before they parted forever. But she never came.

At the end of her final year at university Christine went off to law school in Guildford to train to become a solicitor and Josh changed his course to Politics and Philosophy. This was much better suited to both his personality and his way of thinking. He had found the study of academic law to be turgid, pedantic and often scientific in its approach.

Josh's decision to study law had been based on a strong sense of social justice and a desire to learn about the legal system in its wider context of society as a whole. He wanted to know why certain laws had been passed and what legislation should be introduced in the future to deal with the ills of society. His ambition to become a lawyer had arisen from the desire to help people and to make society a better place. Josh soon came to realise that many of the students on his course had only one ambition, which was to make as much money as possible. Their careers were already laid out for them in 'Daddy's law firm in the City' or 'Uncle's barristers' chambers.'

Josh had regarded many of the law students as alien beings, especially those who had attended private boarding schools. Some of them drove around in brand new sports cars bought for them by 'Daddy and Mummy'. They wore cloth caps and green 'wellies', otherwise known as Wellington boots. They spoke with plummy accents and frequently said 'Ya' very loudly instead of 'Yes'. The 'Ya-Yas', as they were often described, lived in cottages in the countryside outside Exeter and held dinner parties for their friends. This was Josh's first experience of people with privileged backgrounds and a great deal of money and he often felt intimidated by them.

The confidence and self-esteem Josh had gained throughout his school years as he succeeded with his academic work and eventually became head boy did not equip him for the challenges he'd face at university. He often felt as if he had to play a game to fit in with the people around him, or put on an act and become a different type of person from the one that he truly was. Josh gradually became a chameleon, adapting his personality to fit in with those around him, just as he would have to do in the outside world. But having been himself from as young as he could remember, he found it hard to become someone else. Perhaps that's why he'd chosen an academic career as it had enabled him to be as true as he could possibly be to himself.

It had taken Josh years to recover from the hurt he'd felt at the end of his relationship with Christine. He'd thrown himself into a succession of relationships with other women to try and recover his confidence and self-esteem. But he'd found that he could not repeat the intense and all consuming feelings of sexual abandonment and the negation of self that he'd experienced with Christine. Over the years Josh had considered trying to make contact with her in the hope of rekindling the flame of desire. But the fear of rejection had stopped him.

While Josh walked along the Strand he half hoped that Christine would disappoint him, that she'd look old and grey, overweight and unkempt. As he approached Sandwich Corner, where they'd agreed to meet, a strange and unfamiliar sensation crept over his body. He hesitated for a minute as he tried to determine what he was feeling. It was a mixture of elation and trepidation. Josh was playing a part in a film where boy meets girl. It was a feeling of sexual excitement and fear. He took a couple of deep breaths to steady his mind. Then he strode forward on autopilot to avoid the risk of running in the opposite direction.

Josh pushed open the door of the sandwich bar. It was busy inside and the queue at the counter stretched almost to the door. Christine had offered to get there first to find them both a seat as he had a lecture that didn't finish until one o'clock. It was now twenty past one. Josh caught sight of Christine before she saw him. She was sitting in a far corner and was looking down at her mobile phone. He was surprised when he felt a sense of relief to see that her hair was brown rather than grey and that she looked neither overweight nor badly dressed.

As he carefully eased his way past the queue of people, Christine stood up and waved. Her face looked much the same as he remembered, apart from a few laughter lines and a tinge of grey around her temples. Her skin was slightly tanned and she had the same soft brown eyes that

Josh had pictured many times over the years. Her lips were thinner than he'd recalled, although she'd made the best of them with clear pink lipstick. But when Christine smiled a change came over Josh. He'd forgotten her smile. A warm sensation engulfed him, finding its way into every part of his body. He stood transfixed for a few seconds and then forced himself to move forwards. He was now only a short distance from where she was standing.

Christine stood with her arms outstretched and her head tilted to one side. She looked welcoming with her gleaming hair, tanned skin and smart clothes. A few seconds later Josh found himself with his arms wrapped around Christine's toned body and his lips pressed firmly against her right cheek. He inhaled the warm aroma of her perfume, a heady mixture of summer flowers and dark nights spent in exotic places.

He felt the sensation of soft cashmere as his chin touched her red jacket. As Christine held Josh tightly in her arms he could feel her fingertips gently caressing the back of his neck. Was this some sort of sign? Was she trying to tell him something? When he felt her arms slacken he released her from his embrace and stepped slightly back. Josh felt as if he'd come home.

'You haven't changed a bit,' said Christine cheekily.

'That's just what I was going to say.' Josh laughed.

They smiled at each other and then looked down at their menus.

'So what have you been up to for...' Christine paused. 'How many years is it since we last met?'

'Too many,' said Josh.

'Actually, I know quite a bit about you. I've even read your Wikipedia entry.'

'Oh yes, Maggie wrote that. She's in PR.'

'It is rather like an advert for the leader of a political party.'

Josh smiled and raised his eyebrows. Then just as

he was about to speak, a waiter arrived to take their orders. A chicken wrap and sparkling water for Christine and a cheese sandwich and apple juice for Josh.

'I like the Internet Party's website,' said Christine.

'Thanks. We're getting thousands of hits every day.'

'I'm not surprised. I agree with what you're trying to do. If we don't re-engage the public in meaningful political thought and activity we're going to be in big trouble. Politics will be hijacked by ignorant buffoons.'

'Some people might say that's already happening,' said Josh.

'I can think of a few,' said Christine. She smiled and seemed to radiate warmth into the atmosphere.

'Do you remember when I stood for that position on the student council in my first year?'

Christine laughed. 'You didn't win, did you?'

'No. I remember a very traditional ex-public school boy won who used to wear jeans tucked into his cowboy boots.'

'Oh yes, there were a lot of those.'

'I was elected as chairman of the staff student committee in my third year but that was after you'd left,' said Josh.

Christine smiled and as always, he found himself smiling back. He remembered how affectionate they'd been with each other. She had brought out the best in him. He pictured himself in her student bedsit, writing out his manifesto as Christine massaged his shoulders and spoke encouraging words. She touched his hand and looked deep into his eyes, bringing him gently back to the present.

'Don't think about it,' she said.

'What?'

'The past'

'How did you know I was?'

'I'm sorry I treated you badly. I wasn't ready for commitment. I was leaving Exeter, going to law school.

I didn't realise what we had until years later when my marriage broke down.'

Josh was trying to think what to say when Christine jumped up from the table. 'Sorry, I've got to go. I'm supposed to be at a meeting in five minutes.'

'Don't worry. I'll settle up. You can jump in a taxi.'

Christine bent down and gently kissed Josh on the cheek.

'I've really enjoyed meeting up. You must succeed in your quest and keep in touch.'

Josh stood and waved as Christine and her red jacket disappeared out of the sandwich bar in a flash. He sat down and while he finished his drink he thought about what she'd said. Christine was on his side. She agreed with what he was doing and she wanted him to succeed.

CHAPTER
SIXTEEN

'Someone's been in my house,' shouted Kim from the top of the stairs.

Josh, Dan and Izzy, who were all seated at the kitchen table, exchanged glances. Dan rolled his eyes and Izzy opened hers wide while Josh's eyes narrowed. They all waited for what they knew would be a longer and louder shout.

'Did you hear me?   Someone's been in this hooouuussse.'

Dan stood up, walked towards the kitchen door and disappeared into the hallway. Josh knew that he should have gone to find out what all the fuss was about, but he couldn't bring himself to get up from the table.

'Mum. Come down. We heard you,' called Dan from the bottom of the stairs.

Josh caught Izzy's eye and they both shrugged their shoulders as they shared a look of bewilderment.

'But how do you know?' protested Dan from halfway up the stairs.

'Because I can sense it,' Kim shouted in reply. Josh could tell from the tone of her voice that she was extremely agitated.

'Is anything missing?' Dan's voice was quieter now and Josh strained to hear what was being said. It sounded as if Kim and Dan had gone into one of the bedrooms.

'What is she going on about?' said Izzy with her eyes still wide open.

'I have absolutely no idea.'

They listened for a few minutes as cupboard doors were opened and slammed shut again as Kim and Dan moved from room to room. Josh assumed some sort of a search was going on. Perhaps Izzy had misappropriated a piece of Kim's favourite clothing or jewellery. This was something that Izzy had taken to doing recently and it made Kim very annoyed. Suddenly Izzy stood up and moved quickly towards the kitchen door.

'I suppose I'd better go and see what's happening.'

'I should stay here if I were you,' said Josh. 'You'll only add to the chaos.'

'What do you mean, add to the chaos?' Izzy looked put out and hurt as she stood staring at him with her hands firmly on her hips.

'I'm sorry,' said Josh, who'd forgotten just how sensitive Izzy could be when she was told not to do something. 'What I meant was that when your mother is in one of her moods she's likely to have a go at you for no particular reason. I thought you might want to avoid that.'

Josh hesitated for a moment and then smiled conspiratorially. 'I'm keeping my head down.' He put his arms up over his head as if he was protecting himself from an imminent attack. Izzy laughed and looked a little more relaxed.

'But I want to know what they're doing.' She jiggled around on the spot and pouted her lips.

'Let's just wait patiently until they come downstairs,' said Josh.

'Oh, all right.'

Izzy plonked herself back down at the table opposite Josh and they both listened as Kim and Dan moved from room to room for what must have been only a few minutes, yet seemed much longer. Words drifted down from upstairs, but without the sentences to which they should have been attached.

'Look'

'There'

'Like that'

'This morning'

'Moved'

By the time Kim and Dan came downstairs Kim had stopped shouting but she still looked agitated and worried. Dan guided her to a seat at the kitchen table.

'Someone's been in this house, Josh.'

Kim's eyes pleaded with him and her face looked pale and anxious.

Josh glanced at Izzy in an attempt to warn Kim to be careful what she said in front of her young and impressionable daughter. Her judgment had been lacking recently. He spoke quietly and calmly.

'What exactly do you mean by someone's been in the house? People are coming and going all the time, especially the kids' friends.'

'You don't mean a burglar, do you?' Izzy interrupted. She appeared shocked and frightened. 'Have you checked my room?' She jumped up from her seat. 'My laptop, my jewellery, I need to go and see if it's still there.'

Josh frowned at Kim for upsetting Izzy, but he knew that at times like this she didn't care who she upset.

'We've checked your room, Izzy,' said Dan reassuringly. 'Nothing's missing as far as we can tell, but it's in a bit of a mess.'

Josh thought how much he valued Dan's ability to bring calm to most situations.

'You didn't mean a burglar, did you Mum?' Dan spoke in a serious and pointed manner as he looked straight at Kim. A few seconds passed. 'Did you,' he repeated in a tone that indicated she did not.

'No. I didn't mean a burglar,' said Kim reluctantly. 'However, I do know that someone's been poking around in this house and I intend to find out who it is.'

'But nothing's been taken,' said Dan in exasperation.

Josh decided it was time to step up to the crease. He spoke gently to Kim. 'What makes you think anyone has been in the house?'

'I can just feel it. Things have been moved. You know. Disturbed.'

Josh was beginning to wonder whether it was Kim who was disturbed. Perhaps the strain she was under was making her delusional.

Izzy had been sitting in silence wringing her hands when she suddenly jumped up and rushed towards the door. 'I don't care what anyone says. I'm going to check my room,' she announced as she disappeared into the hallway. Dan let out a sigh and followed her.

'Josh. I'm not being paranoid,' pleaded Kim. 'I wouldn't upset the kids like this if I wasn't deadly serious. I don't know how anyone could get into the house when we're not here, but I honestly believe someone has.'

Josh noticed that there were tiny beads of perspiration in a kind of arc across Kim's forehead. She looked tired and her face seemed to have acquired more wrinkles since he'd seen her last. There was a line of grey where her hair parted as she hadn't found the time to colour it for several weeks.

Kim stared at Josh with a quizzical look on her face. He wondered if she saw him as he saw himself. What was she thinking? Sometimes he wanted to ask her. A penny for your thoughts, his grandmother would say to him as a child. It was a phrase you never heard today. Lost with a generation that had died. Josh had always felt embarrassed when his grandmother had asked him what he was thinking, even if it was entirely innocent.

'What is it Josh? Why have you gone all quiet?' Kim eyed him suspiciously.

'I was just thinking,' said Josh. 'I suppose we need to carry out a thorough search of the house to see if anything is missing.'

Kim looked relieved. Small patches of colour returned to her cheeks and the wrinkles on her forehead diminished in size.

'I'll check my study,' said Josh getting up from the

table. The thought crossed his mind that perhaps he should give Kim a sign of reassurance, a gentle touch on the arm or kiss on the cheek. But he felt uncomfortable as to how she might react.

Josh stood in the doorway to his study and looked for signs that someone had been poking around. He was not wholly convinced that Kim was right. How could she possibly tell what had been moved in a house that was so disorganised? As usual there were piles of papers on virtually every surface and the house was cluttered with the detritus of teenagers' lives. Sports kit and school bags lay discarded in the middle of the hallway or dumped on sofas and chairs. Clothes were left hanging on whatever piece of furniture happened to be nearby when they were taken off or were thrown onto the floor. In a corner of the living room sat a pile of plastic carrier bags full of unfiled paperwork, old school uniform that no longer fitted and clothes to be mended or recycled.

Kim's bedroom was the most disorganised room in the house, as anything that didn't have a place elsewhere ended up there. The wardrobe was full to bursting with garments that she never made the time to sort out. She'd therefore taken to piling up the clothes she wore regularly on two large wooden armchairs. All the other surfaces were littered with heaps of books and magazines. If the bed hadn't been needed for sleep, it too would have become a dumping ground. But each night any items that had found their way onto the bed were moved elsewhere.

Josh's study was the opposite of Kim's bedroom. It was clean and tidy with papers organised neatly into piles, carefully placed in metal trays stacked on top of each other and clearly labelled 'Action', 'Information' and 'Filing'. The last of the three trays was usually empty as he had a policy of filing most of his paperwork as soon as he'd dealt with it. During rows Kim would often accuse Josh of being anal retentive and he would describe her as slovenly. Kim

167

was usually defensive and would argue that she could always find what she needed from one of her stacks of papers or plastic bags. There was one proviso to this generalisation, which was that nobody had interfered with any of her belongings by moving or reorganising them. Dan and Izzy took great delight in proving Kim wrong whenever they got the opportunity.

As Josh surveyed each piece of office furniture he knew that someone had been inside his study. This was not unusual. Izzy was a fairly regular visitor whenever she was in need of a pen, pencil, stapler, hole punch or other item of stationery. She had her own but they were generally buried underneath piles of paper on her desk or hidden under mountains of clothes on her bedroom floor. Josh would know at once if Izzy had raided his office. His computer chair would be pushed aside so that she could get to what she wanted as quickly as possible. His desk would look untidy and at least one piece of essential office equipment would be missing.

But today Josh's chair was in its usual place tucked under his desk. All items of stationery were neatly lined up in the order of their height from left to right. Nothing was obviously missing and yet Josh felt uncomfortable, almost as if someone was watching him. He sat down at his desk and looked through the few pieces of paper in the metal trays. They seemed to be in order. If anyone had been through his papers, he or she had been careful to replace them exactly as they'd been found.

Josh pulled out his desk drawers one by one and examined their contents. The bottom drawer was large and he usually kept it locked. He opened a tin box that he kept on a shelf and took out a small key. He turned it over a few times in his hand and then inserted it into the lock. The key wouldn't turn. The drawer was already unlocked. Josh hesitated for a few seconds. His stomach was churning and he felt hot as he gently eased the drawer open.

At first glance everything seemed to be in its usual place. But as he looked through the contents of the drawer, Josh started to feel anxious. He'd hidden the hard copies of the emails he'd received from Christine at the bottom of the drawer. They were gone. But worst of all, Josh's diaries were missing, the small leather-bound books into which he carefully placed his thoughts and dreams. Not on a daily basis but whenever he felt the need. Nobody knew about Josh's diaries. A feeling of panic came over him. He tried to think back to what he'd written over the last few weeks, months and even years.

Josh had expressed his innermost thoughts on the creamy white paper encased in stiff brown leather. He'd described his feelings for Maggie, his dreams for the Internet Party, how he felt his relationship with Kim was falling apart and his recent meeting with Christine. Josh had gained a feeling of peace as he wrote down his thoughts, almost as if he were engaged in meditation. Problems had resolved themselves on the cream coloured pages as his spidery handwriting told its story. But now his mind was in turmoil as his thoughts thrashed around like those of a drowning man.

Josh took a few long deep breaths and forced himself to look out of the window. There was no sign of the comforting blackbird in the garden, only green vegetation speckled with sunlight. Who had opened the drawer? Josh asked himself this question over and over again, as if the longer he did so, the more likely it would be that an answer would present itself. Had Kim found the key and taken the diaries? Josh knew she no longer trusted him. On a few occasions recently he'd noticed that she'd been trying to see what password he was tapping into his laptop computer as he sat at the kitchen table. She knew he'd received an email from Christine as Josh had naively told her about it one day when he thought they'd been getting on quite well. But since then Kim had been so suspicious about 'all of these women crawling out of the woodwork', as she liked to describe the former girlfriends who had contacted him through the Internet Party website that Josh hadn't dared to tell her about the other emails he'd received, let alone the fact that he'd met Christine for lunch.

Suddenly a rational voice popped up in his head. If Kim had taken the diaries or copies of the emails, she would have looked at them immediately and be shouting and screaming at him by now. If Izzy had taken them she would have delivered them straight to Kim with the same result. Josh was beginning to think that Kim was right. Perhaps a stranger had been inside the house. A shiver went down his spine.

He knew the house wasn't as secure as it should be. Maggie had told him so three weeks ago. 'You must get an alarm fitted if nothing else,' Maggie had said as she turned on her heel and left after their disagreement. Josh had never been concerned about home security. He had few personal possessions and hardly any that were valuable. Kim's house had original Edwardian windows that were either stuck firmly shut with layers of old paint or could only be opened with extreme force and a lot of noise. The outside of the house hadn't been decorated for several years and some of the paint was peeling off the window frames and stone surrounds. The front garden was overgrown and thick net curtains hung at the windows. Josh had always felt confident that no burglar would be interested in breaking into the house. Both the front and back doors had five lever security locks, as required by Kim's household contents insurance policy, but they were rarely used. The house was therefore only protected by somewhat inadequate locks, which could easily be jemmied or opened with a credit card.

When Josh had locked himself out once and called a locksmith, the burly young man, with tattoos all down his arms, had taken exactly two seconds to open the front door. In contrast to Kim's humble abode, the house Maggie shared with Bruno, her 'headquarters' or 'control centre', as it had become known, had maximum security. It was protected with key-operated locks on all of its windows, London bars and several high specification locks on its doors, a sophisticated alarm system that was linked to a monitoring station and CCTV cameras that covered the front and back of the house.

Josh felt foolish and naive. Maggie had warned him several times that the media might take 'unusual steps' to find out information about him. Apparently this was a phrase used by journalists to describe activity that was either illegal or bordering on illegal such as phone hacking and impersonation. Maggie was a trained journalist and she'd worked for various newspapers and magazines before she'd set up her own PR firm. She knew her enemy well. Josh felt embarrassed that he'd acted like an ostrich with its head firmly buried in the sand. He hadn't wanted to face the unpleasant aspects of becoming a high profile public figure. But now reality was staring him in the face following the theft of his diaries and emails.

He shuddered when he thought of what the Sunday papers might print if one of their reporters got hold of the contents of even one of his leather-bound books. He could imagine the headline: 'Shock, horror and disappointment as charismatic leader of the Internet Party is revealed to be romantically involved with at least three women. The Sunday Ridicule exclusively reports that while Josh Walker, 39 (newspapers are always obsessed with people's ages and usually get them wrong) appears to live a happy family life with Kim Clark, 38 and her teenage children, all is not as it seems. He is reported to have had a secret meeting with Christine Lewis, 43 (a guess and actually wrong – she is 41) a former girlfriend who tracked him down on Friends Reunited (wrong – it was the Internet Party website, but who cares?). At the same time Mr Walker is reported to be secretly lusting after his Deputy Leader, Maggie Bryant,

31' (guaranteed to annoy her as she hates being called his 'deputy').

Josh tried to imagine what would be worse – being confronted by Kim, who would undoubtedly kick him out of the house, probably for ever and maybe even banish him completely from her life and the lives of her children, or suffering the humiliation of facing Maggie.

He knew she'd be upset because of the potential damage to the Internet Party. He allowed himself to think she'd be flattered by his romantic intentions, but she might also be very angry about the salacious nature of his thoughts that he'd espoused in his diaries. Josh wasn't sure about Christine. He reckoned she'd react well to the publicity and would probably be quite pleased with the attention she'd receive. Why else had she got in touch with him after so many years? Although Josh had at first felt pleased by Christine's desire to meet up with him, deep down he suspected that she'd been influenced by his new found fame.

Josh's deliberations were interrupted when Izzy burst into the room. She stood rigid in front of him for a few seconds with her hazel eyes wide open, as if she'd suffered a shock.

'Mum's moving out.'

Josh gave Izzy a quizzical look. 'Moving out?'

'Yes. She's packing her things into suitcases.'

Josh was wondering if he'd stepped into some sort of family TV comedy show like Outnumbered or the Inbetweeners, except that by the look on Izzy's face it must be tragedy bordering on farce. She was still standing in a fixed position with her skinny arms stuck out at a forty-five degree angle from her sides and her palms stretched open. Her shoulders were hunched up half way into a shrug.

'Did Kim, your mum, say she was moving out?' Josh spoke gently and leaned forward slightly.

'No.'

'Well maybe she's having a clear out.'

Izzy moved her head slowly from side to side several times and frowned at Josh. They both knew that Kim rarely cleared things out. On a few occasions Josh had helped Dan and Izzy sort out their bedrooms and take unwanted clothes and possessions to the Oxfam shop around the corner. But this was a rare event as, if Kim found out, she would get annoyed and accuse Josh of interfering. The children did not have the same hoarding instincts as their mother and they found this aspect of her hard to live with.

Josh had rationalised Kim's behaviour by attributing it to a need to be in control of her life after the shock of her betrayal by Richard, who she'd loved and trusted for many years. Izzy would simply state that her mother must have been a squirrel in a previous life and Dan would say nothing but Josh guessed he sometimes found it difficult to understand her.

Josh knew that Izzy desperately wanted him to accompany her upstairs to see what Kim was doing. Despite the fact that he didn't want to, it was inevitable that he would have to do so. Izzy rarely took no for an answer. They crept quietly up the stairs with Josh leading the way and Izzy only a step behind him. He listened to her irregular breathing as they made their way along the landing in the direction of Kim's bedroom. The door was slightly ajar and Josh could hear the sound of muttering and of things being moved around the room. He tiptoed towards the doorway and gestured to Izzy to keep quiet and follow him. They both watched as Kim carefully packed her most precious belongings into a large battered suitcase.

'Did you find anything missing?' said Josh as he walked into the room, closely followed by Izzy. Kim turned suddenly to face them, as she was jolted out of her own little world. She rested on her heels and eyed them suspiciously.

'You made me jump. Were you spying on me?'

'Of course not,' said Josh.

'Did you find anything missing?' asked Kim. She

looked worried. He hesitated for a few seconds.

'What do you mean?' Josh was playing for time. He wasn't sure what to say. He couldn't tell the truth. Kim didn't even know about his diaries, or the missing emails. He wasn't going to tell her about them now. But what if he were to make something up? Perhaps he should say that a valuable item had been taken. But he couldn't think of anything and he was beginning to feel hot. His cheeks were burning. He was worried that he looked embarrassed, as if he were a naughty boy who'd been caught out by his mother.

'Was there anything missing from your study?'

'No,' he lied with conviction. 'How about you?'

'I'm still not sure. But I'm not taking any chances. I'm putting some of my stuff in that Yellow Box storage place.'

Josh turned his head to where Izzy was standing diagonally behind him and gave her a look which said, 'There you are, your mother is not moving out. She's just gone slightly mad and is putting some of her 'stuff' into storage.' Izzy visibly relaxed, rushed past him and forced herself into her mother's arms. Kim looked surprised and reluctantly embraced her daughter. Then Josh watched, as she seemed to be taken over by a wave of love and affection for Izzy. She hugged her tightly and kissed her on top of her head. He felt an almost overwhelming urge to join in but he knew it was not his place to do so.

After a few minutes Izzy extracted herself from her mother's arms. 'Can I give you some of my stuff to go into storage? Please Mum.'

'Of course you can,' said Kim kindly.

Izzy disappeared to her room and Josh took the opportunity to confront Kim.

'Is this really necessary?' he whispered.

'Yes, I'm afraid it is.'

'But you said nothing was missing.'

'I said I hadn't found anything missing yet,' hissed Kim through gritted teeth.

Josh was about to speak when Izzy rushed back into the room clutching her coin collection, a gold charm bracelet given to her by her grandfather and various ornaments. She handed them carefully to Kim.

'I've got some old clothes I can wrap them in. You can help me.'

Josh knew when he wasn't wanted. He would continue his conversation with Kim when Izzy was asleep in bed.

'I'll leave you to it. I'm going to get some fresh air,' he said casually, trying to give the impression for Izzy's benefit that all was well with the world, when clearly it was not.

Minutes later Josh was breathing in the aroma of yellow broom in the park as he tried to clear his mind. He made a mental list of things to do the following day. First of all he'd speak to Maggie about an alarm for Kim's house. The Internet Party would have to pay. The next item on his list was to carry out a more thorough search of the house to see what else was missing. Finally, he needed to call a lawyer about the possibility of the contents of the diaries being publicised by the media.

As Josh sat down on a bench in the shade under a tree a worrying thought came into his mind. He quickly stood up again. What if someone wanted to blackmail him? He had no money to speak of, just a few thousand pounds of savings he'd inherited from his dear mother. Whoever had taken the diaries and copies of the emails must realise that he wasn't well off. So why had they been removed from his desk and who'd taken them? Did someone intend to try and put pressure on him to stop the Internet Party in its tracks? Questions flooded into his mind as he paced around the park and deliberately avoided anyone who might want to stop and chat.

After several laps of the park Josh felt calmer and he sat down on one of the newly installed wooden benches. It felt warm and comforting. He leaned back and closed his eyes as he felt the sun on his face. He concentrated on his breathing and attempted to relax his taut muscles. Josh listened to the sounds of laughter and the joyous shouts of children having fun. He opened his eyes and squinted for a moment as they adjusted to a burst of sunlight. He watched as small boys and girls ran in and out of bushes playing hide and seek or sped past on tiny scooters. Bicycles circled this way and that as they negotiated the twists and turns of the pathways. Groups of teenagers draped themselves over benches in hidden corners of the park, encapsulated in their own separate worlds. Twenty-something females, scantily clad in bikinis, compensated for living in flats without gardens by sunning themselves, as if the whole park belonged to them.

An elderly couple nodded at Josh as they slowly passed him by. He noticed that their feet hardly left the ground as they carefully shuffled along the newly laid, perfectly flat, sandstone-coloured paths. Josh recalled how only a year ago the old tarmac pathways had been cracked and uneven. There had been only four benches in the park and they had been broken and covered in graffiti. Now there were over twenty, made of wood with metal frames painted a gentle sea green colour. Before the park was restored the grass had been littered with rubbish and broken glass. Now it was a beautiful and safe oasis. In the middle stood a drinking fountain made of speckled grey coloured granite in the shape of an urn on a pedestal. Before the restoration the urn had been dethroned with its top knocked off and it had lain lonely and neglected in the gardeners' compound. But now it looked majestic and resplendent in the sunlight, surrounded by a happy group of children who seemed transfixed by the stream of water escaping from the spouts of its shiny brass taps whenever they were pressed.

Kim and the other members of her Friends group had campaigned long and hard to persuade the local council to apply for a grant from the Heritage Lottery Fund to restore the park. The whole project had taken nine years to complete from start to finish and had cost around one and a half million pounds. Kim had been on a quest and everyone agreed that it was her resolute determination that had made a difference and ensured the success of the project. Josh recalled how Kim's group had lobbied the local councillors and secured their support. Then they'd called a public meeting, which had been attended by one hundred and fifty local residents. The police and local government officers had turned up and by the end of the meeting everyone had agreed that the park should be restored. After several years of form filling, the appointment of landscape architects, surveyors, a project manager and building contractor, the restoration took place and the park became transformed. It now stood as a shining example of what a group of ordinary local residents can achieve when they set their minds to something with a strong sense of social purpose.

As the evening approached, various dog walkers appeared with a selection of pooches. These were joined by a stream of joggers, determined to de-stress and rejuvenate their tired souls. Josh felt a glow of pride as he watched the sea of faces ebb and flow. Some were familiar and others were not. He was proud of the efforts that Kim and her Friends group had made over the years to put pressure on the local council to help to restore the park. Here was a tangible success story. The restoration had been an achievable objective and all the time and trouble had been worthwhile. Josh wondered if he'd set his own ambitions too high. Were people laughing about him behind his back and saying, 'Who does he think he is? What makes him suitable to be an MP?' There were two ways of making a difference in the world, thought Josh, the small, realistic ways and those that were large and often unrealistic. Suddenly he wished he could turn the clock back and return to a life of anonymity. But there would be no going back. The pain and embarrassment he would suffer for withdrawing from the race would be far greater than for losing.

As soon as Josh heard the click of the park ranger shutting one of the four sets of gates he immediately stood up. Then he quickly made his way through the dim light that now engulfed him and out of the park. He decided to go straight away to see Maggie, as he needed to talk to her about getting an alarm fitted at Kim's house. He resolved not to mention the business about his diaries and the emails, but to be as vague as possible. Josh wondered whether Kim had found that any of her belongings were missing. Perhaps whoever had stolen his diaries had taken other things to make it look as if the house had been burgled. She must have called the police by now. It occurred to Josh that he should get the key to his desk drawers checked for fingerprints. But he knew that whoever had been in the house was a professional. The thought made him shiver as he hurried towards the bright lights of Maggie's safe fortress.

Once Josh was in his room he checked his emails. He was pleased to see one from Christine.

'Hi Josh. Thanks for lunch. Sorry I had to rush off. Let's do it again sometime. Keep up the fight! Let me know how you're doing. Christine x'

He liked the idea of meeting up again. He could remember why he'd loved her so much and probably still did. How much? He wasn't sure.

CHAPTER
SEVENTEEN

Josh sat in his study. His mind was blank. Well, as blank as it could be with all that was going on. In fact, blank was probably the wrong word. 'Numb' would be a better description, exhausted almost to the point of burn out. He tried to focus on his favourite blackbird but his eyes refused to stir from their blurred existence, tired from hours of staring at a computer screen. Josh could hear the TV blaring away in the next room. He pictured Izzy splayed across the green velvet sofa, an empty yoghurt pot perched precariously on its arm. It was her breakfast time and she'd just emerged from a late night of fast and furious messaging of her friends on her phone and computer, often at the same time. The list of websites was endless that massaged the egos of Izzy and her friends. Pouting prima donnas with their fingers pressed to their lips like the famous picture of Marilyn Monroe.

Suddenly a voice with a broad northern accent boomed out from the next room. 'Ziggy is in the diary room.' A thought formed in Josh's mind. Izzy is watching Big Brother. It was a TV programme he rarely caught sight of and never willingly consumed. But when Izzy was in the house and Big Brother was in season the TV was inevitably switched on and often turned up to full volume. Josh felt a pang of guilt and disappointment in himself. Was this a sign of old age, he thought, the inability to appreciate a TV programme belonging to another generation?

Josh's mind flashed back to a Monty Python TV programme involving a dead parrot that he'd watched with his father. Did a sketch about a dead parrot have any greater artistic merit or moral value than a collection of carefully chosen misfits being watched twenty-four hours a day like goldfish in a bowl? Josh's mind exploded with the delight of past memories. He and his father had been great fans of the Monty Python series on TV, where men in suits and bowler hats did silly walks, lumberjacks sang songs and there was a giant hedgehog called Dinsdale. Josh laughed out loud and for more than a few seconds he couldn't stop.

'Ziggy and Leonara are in the garden,' said Big Brother. Why did the people who lived in the Big Brother house have such weird names, thought Josh? He heaved himself up from his chair and wandered into the TV room. Izzy was draped across the sofa with her pink pyjamas crumpled around her body and her eyes glued to the screen. After a few seconds she gave him a hostile look as if to say, What are you doing here? She stared at him until he began to feel uncomfortable. Perhaps he'd done the wrong thing by invading Izzy's space.

'So, what's new?' said Josh, casually looking at the TV.

'I can't tell you what's been happening,' said Izzy. 'It's too complicated if you haven't been watching every day.' She kept her eyes fixed to the screen, anxious not to miss anything.

'When I was your age I used to watch a programme featuring a dead parrot on top of a television, men in suits and bowler hats doing silly walks, lumberjacks singing songs and a giant hedgehog called Dinsdale,' said Josh.

'What?' said Izzy.

'Nothing,' he replied as he walked slowly out of the room.

'Weird,' mumbled Izzy when she thought he was out of earshot. Josh smiled. His memories had given him a pleasant warm feeling and he wanted it to continue. He needed to escape for a while. Apart from his study there was nowhere he felt he could relax. Maggie's house was a barrage of computer screens running day and night, people coming and going, phones ringing. He spent most of his time there now that he was no longer 'officially' living at Kim's place. Josh's emotions were in constant turmoil. Sometimes he felt like a homeless person. At other times he felt high with the intense massaging of his ego by the numerous journalists and other media people who plagued him on a daily basis.

Josh felt a strong desire to go back to his roots in Bristol, to rediscover his true self. But first he needed to speak to Kim, who'd been remarkably stressed recently because of all the media attention Josh was receiving. She'd taken to looking out of the window every few minutes to check whether a reporter or photographer might be spying on her from the park opposite. Whenever a car parked outside the house Kim would note down its registration number and a description of anyone inside. On one occasion Josh had even found her looking out of an upstairs window through a pair of binoculars. She had been very embarrassed when he'd come into the room and had tried to make light of what she was doing by pretending to be checking that they were working properly.

Josh found Kim in her bedroom. Well, it was her bedroom for the time being, while he was staying at Maggie's house. Just until the election is over, thought Josh. He could hardly imagine life after the election. It was like a great wave, far in the distance, imperceptibly edging nearer. As Josh entered the room Kim looked up.

'What are you doing?' he said casually.

'I'm just sorting out stuff to go to the second hand shop at the school. I thought I'd clear out some of Dan's old clothes while he's away on the cricket tour this week. He grows out of them so quickly.'

Kim glanced at Josh for a second and then went back to stuffing clothes into a variety of brightly coloured plastic bags. He took a few paces over to the bedroom window and looked out over the park. It was glistening in the sunlight and he felt his spirits lift, which gave him the confidence to say what he'd been intending to say but wasn't sure whether he'd actually do so.

'Kim.' She looked up. 'I was wondering whether to go down to Bristol to see Dad for the day. I haven't seen him for months.'

'Good idea.'

Kim sounded enthusiastic, perhaps a little too keen in fact. Josh suspected that she would be relieved to have him out of her way for a while. He thought about the times he'd made love to her, in this bedroom on the large bed that was almost always covered in clothes, books and magazines. He felt no desire to do so now and in any case, Kim would object on the grounds that Izzy was downstairs and might appear at any moment. Oh how the presence of children killed off passion in even the strongest of relationships, thought Josh, let alone one under intense strain like his and Kim's. He picked his way back across the room towards the door, stepping carefully over various objects that were scattered over the floor.

'How will you get away without being followed?' said Kim as she piled the plastic bags filled with clothes into a heap.

'What?' said Josh. Kim beckoned to him and went to stand by the large bay window waiting for him to follow. She had bought thick net curtains and put them up all over the house immediately after her first experience of a journalist trying to take photographs through her living-room window. Josh had found the net curtains suffocating, as if he were a fly trapped in a spider's web, but he hadn't dared to object. It was, after all, Kim's house. She pointed to a silver people carrier with darkened windows that was parked diagonally opposite the house.

'It's been there for a few hours.'

Josh felt like saying, 'So what?' But he didn't want to antagonise her. 'I'll slip out the back, in a black bin liner.'

'Very funny,' said Kim.

Josh thought he saw the glint of a smile, but it faded as quickly as it began.

'I'll call Vicky. If she's at home you can get out through her place.'

The words 'get out' said it all, he thought. Kim felt imprisoned, besieged and oppressed. But the pressure felt by Kim did not help Josh. It made him feel suffocated. But worse than that, it made him feel responsible and accountable. Responsible for how Kim felt and accountable for the actions that had made her so unhappy.

Ten minutes later Josh was dressed in the most unobtrusive casual clothing he could find among the belongings that he'd left at Kim's house. Carrying a small rucksack and grabbing a black baseball cap from the back of Dan's bedroom door as he passed, which he pulled as far down over his eyes as he could without making vision impossible, he quietly opened the back door. At exactly the same time and in accordance with the plan that had been agreed with Josh a few minutes earlier, Kim rushed out of the front door and jumped into her car. She revved up the engine and hurriedly drove off as the driver of the silver people carrier galvanised himself into action and sped after her. Kim smiled as she thought how disappointed he would be when he realised he had followed her to the supermarket nearby.

Josh made his way quietly down the garden path and let himself out of the rickety gate into the narrow lane that ran along the back of Kim's house. The lane had heavy iron gates at each end to prevent anyone gaining access apart from the people who lived in the houses that backed onto the lane, who each had a key. The tall iron gates had sharp spikes on top to deter intruders from climbing over them. Fortunately Vicky was at home so Kim had arranged for Josh to escape through her house. She lived in a property that backed onto Kim's and was a loyal member of the burgeoning Friends of the Park group.

Vicky flung her back door open and disarmed Josh somewhat by throwing her arms around his neck and hugging him tightly. She was a large woman with a mop of blonde hair that she usually wore half pinned up on her head and half falling over her face. She had a warm smile and a generous nature and was a woman who could be trusted.

'Josh. How are you?' said Vicky in her sing song voice.

'Fine, thanks,' he said, though he didn't feel fine at all. But he wasn't going to get involved in a discussion about his health or welfare. He just wanted to get away as fast as possible. Josh gently extricated himself from Vicky's embrace and adjusted Dan's baseball cap. He saw that she was wearing a bright green smock, black leggings and orange rubber clogs. On anyone else such garish clothes would have looked ridiculous, but they suited her.

'So, you're off to Bristol to see your Dad,' said Vicky as she guided Josh through her bright and colourful kitchen, haphazardly decorated with paintings and other assorted artwork of her three children.

Great, thought Josh. Vicky knows I'm going to Bristol. His face must have registered his displeasure at Kim's lack of confidentiality.

'Don't worry. I can keep a secret.'

Josh had never been able to understand why women felt compelled to tell each other everything. Well, that was the impression he'd gained from speaking to Kim. He'd been told about her friends' marital problems, their husbands' work issues and their children's experiences with sex, drugs and alcohol. Josh sometimes worried about what Kim might have told her friends about him. Men were different and he often wished they weren't. Women seemed to have a camaraderie, which buoyed them up in times of adversity that was based on neither the consumption of large amounts of alcohol nor endless discussions about sport.

Josh felt uncomfortable that at a time when the media were constantly digging for dirt, Kim had to be so open.

Vicky wrapped herself in a large patchwork jacket that looked more like a quilt and grabbed a brown leather bag from the bottom of the stairs.

'I'll go out to the car to make sure no-one's around. You can borrow Jake's hoodie if you want to. It'll go with the cap.' She gestured to a massive light grey hooded tracksuit top that had been thrown unceremoniously onto a brown wooden chest in the hallway. Jake was Vicky's larger than life fourteen- year-old son.

'I think I'll give that a miss, thanks,' Josh laughed as he gradually felt more relaxed. You couldn't feel uptight in Vicky's house. It was warm, colourful and full of love. The walls were bright yellow and the furniture was russet red.

'How is Jake?'

'Oh well, you know. He's fourteen.'

Now it was Vicky's turn not to want to give anything away. That was the strange thing about living in a 'community', as Kim liked to call the people who resided in the roads around the park. Josh would often know something about a neighbour or a friend of Kim's that he knew they didn't know he knew. Life could get quite complicated at times. For example, Josh knew that Jake was having a few problems with his schoolwork and that his mother suspected he might be experimenting with drugs. But she wasn't going to tell Josh. He watched Vicky as she wandered out to her car. He saw her glance around and then she beckoned him to join her. Josh slammed the front door and, looking straight ahead, moved towards the car. Nobody jumped out of a bush or from behind a parked vehicle to take his photo and no cars pulled out behind them as he and Vicky set off on the short journey to Wimbledon station.

Josh breathed a misplaced sigh of relief as he sank down into the deep leather seat in the back of Vicky's car.

He felt safely hidden behind the blacked out windows. Had he known that a woman sitting in a parked car they'd just passed was at that very moment speaking about him on her mobile phone to a man waiting outside Wimbledon station, Josh would not have felt so relaxed. A few minutes later as he bought his train ticket and a newspaper, the man watched from behind a magazine. Then he followed Josh as he climbed onto a District Line Tube train bound for Paddington.

As the train rattled past Wimbledon Park, the All England Club and other familiar sights, Josh realised that this was the first time he'd been able to get away since he and Maggie had started the Internet Party. He wondered if he'd have gone ahead with it all if he'd known what would be involved – the wrecking of his private life, the possibly irrevocable damage to his relationship with Kim, the constant feeling of having his actions scrutinised, his words analysed, his appearance judged and his whole being questioned. If this was what politicians had to face on a daily basis, why would anyone wish to be one? Yet he himself had chosen to be a politician, with all that it entailed.

CHAPTER
EIGHTEEN

As the high speed train pulled out of Paddington on its journey to South Wales, Josh felt comforted by the gentle lilt of the Welsh accent reading out a list of the stations on the way.

'This is the eleven forty-five train to Swansea calling at Reading, Swindon, Bristol Parkway, Newport, Cardiff Central, Bridgend, Port Talbot Parkway, Neath and Swansea.'

Josh settled himself into a seat by the window and stared out as concrete gave way to grass and the rolling countryside stretched in all directions. He breathed easily and his mind, as it so often did these days, wandered back into his past. He pictured himself aged around eight being taken up and down the country roads from Bristol to the constituency in Marlborough, Wiltshire where his father was standing as the prospective MP. Josh's mother had driven a battered Hillman Estate car which had rattled along with uncomfortable seats and leaking windows. He remembered the scarf his sister had knitted on these arduous and monotonous journeys. It had been very long and had consisted of sections made out of wool of different colours. The scarf had started narrow at one end, but by the time it was finished it had increased in size to three times its original width at the other end. It had taken his sister many hours to finish the scarf while their father canvassed for votes.

It seemed only a matter of minutes after leaving Paddington before the train pulled into Reading station, then Swindon and finally Bristol Parkway. Josh grabbed his rucksack and made his way along the carriage towards the nearest exit. The man who was following him got out at the other end of the carriage and, keeping a safe distance, mingled with the crowd that slowly trickled down the stairs and out of the station.

Josh stepped lightly into a waiting taxi and felt a sense of belonging as the driver chattered away in a broad Bristol accent. He couldn't work out exactly why people looked different from how they were in London. Perhaps it was the type of clothes they wore, the environment they lived in or maybe it was simply their genetic make-up. The air definitely felt fresher despite a huge increase in the number of cars from the time when Josh had lived in Bristol. The man who had followed him from London had disappeared but now another man was tailing Josh's taxi in a family saloon. This was the type of car that would not stand out at all or cause any suspicion that its occupants might be involved in anything underhand.

Josh felt happier than he had for several months and was oblivious to the fact that, in addition to the dark blue family saloon, another car was following him at a safe distance so as not to be seen. Josh's taxi turned left into Gloucester Road and the saloon continued straight ahead. The other car, a silver hatchback, took up pole position immediately behind the taxi. Josh felt excited by the anticipation of seeing his old school again.

The taxi passed nondescript 1930's terraced housing and rows of small shops huddled together, an uninspiring red-brick church, more shops and then the school appeared as the taxi came out of a bend in the road. It comprised several white coloured stone-clad buildings from the 1950's, which Josh was sure had been made of red brick when they'd first been built. The white colour made them look somewhat futuristic and extra buildings had been added where once the playing fields seemed to stretch forever. As the taxi passed the school's front gates he saw that its name had been changed from Monks Park Comprehensive to the Orchard School. This made him feel slightly uncomfortable, as if someone had changed a part of his past life without telling him.

Josh had been a political animal as a teenager. He wasn't sure whether this was entirely due to his upbringing or if his personality came into the equation. The question of nature versus nurture often occupied his thoughts and he wondered if he would have been a socialist if he'd been brought up in a conservative household like Maggie. Between the ages of about thirteen and eighteen Josh had been a rebel and a revolutionary, challenging authority and seeking change. But he'd also been respected and valued by his teachers and headmaster and had been popular with his fellow pupils. Josh smiled as he pictured himself selling radical student newspapers outside the school gates.

One school governor who was a member of the Conservative Party had complained vociferously to the headmaster that her son had been forced to buy a paper. But Josh didn't even know who the governor's son was and the headmaster had believed Josh when he said he would never have forced anyone to buy a paper. Josh had been so well respected by the staff that he'd been elected as a 'pupil governor' when the local council introduced a scheme for pupils and their parents to sit on school governing bodies. He remembered having made various useful suggestions, one of which was to close the gap in a fence near to a parade of shops. This hadn't gone down too well with a small group of his fellow pupils who used the hole to escape through to go and buy cigarettes.

Josh felt a surge of pride as he recalled being elected as Head Boy by a majority of the teachers and pupils in the sixth form of the school. However, it didn't take him long to decide that the positions of Head Girl and Head Boy were elitist and outdated. So he proposed the formation of a democratically elected Sixth Form Council with himself as the chairman and his proposal was accepted. This really irritated his younger sister who, three years later, was elected as chair of the Sixth Form Council. She argued that she should be able to call herself Head Girl instead when she applied to universities. The headmaster at the time took a sympathetic and pragmatic approach and agreed that to the outside world she could describe herself as Head Girl.

Josh cast his mind back to the teachers he'd respected and valued throughout his school years. He could picture their faces and recall the catchphrases they used to inspire their pupils. Unlike most of his peers, Josh had enjoyed Latin because his teacher had been so challenging and enthusiastic. Mrs Bond was petite, slim and smart with reddish brown hair and bright red lipstick. She wore tailored clothes and had a natural air of authority. Nobody misbehaved in Mrs Bond's class and everyone got good results in Latin.

Josh tried to remember the names of other teachers who'd impressed him. One male history teacher, whose name escaped him, had excited Josh with political discussions and debates about issues that lay well outside the narrow syllabus he was supposed to be teaching. An English teacher called Mr Lake had taken Josh and his classmates on wonderful trips to see Shakespearian plays in Stratford Upon Avon.

As Josh revelled in the memories of his time at school he truly felt they'd been the happiest days of his life. It was a cliché but he knew he'd been fortunate to have a charmed existence as a child and teenager. So many happy memories flooded into Josh's mind at once that he felt dizzy for a while – faces he recognised of teachers and friends, sporting events, drama productions and discos. It almost seemed as if seven years of his life had flashed past in a moment.

Then the school was gone and the long straight road that had first been built by Romans lay ahead slicing its way through the green blanket of Horfield Common. It looked like a huge patch of pastry the colour of felt on a snooker table, criss-crossed by roads and dotted with houses. Josh looked out of the car window across the whole of Bristol to the rolling Mendip hills in the distance. Then the taxi passed the playground where he and his sister had spent hours of their time as children. He pictured the swings, the seesaw and the witch's hat roundabout they'd played on and another roundabout that had gone so fast it had made him dizzy.

They'd all been replaced by new and safer equipment to comply with health and safety rules, no doubt. The dingy shelter where Josh and his friends had whiled away their time had been demolished. He could almost sense its dank smell somewhere deep in his memory and picture the initials carved deeply into its dark wood.

The taxi left the common behind and passed a huge Tesco that had been built on a school playing field. Josh looked at what had been a newsagent's shop where he'd stopped each day on his way back from school to buy sweets. It had gone out of business when the supermarket arrived. He looked at the small hardware shop that had turned into a giant builder's merchants. For a moment he felt negative about so-called progress. As the taxi turned into the road where his father lived it could hardly get through the traffic. Josh thought back to when there were hardly any cars in the road. He and his friends had played in the cul-de-sac that adjoined his house for hours on end without any worry of being run over.

Josh looked at his father's house with pride as the taxi stopped outside. Not because it was at all grand but because it was his family home. He'd never felt able to make a permanent home elsewhere. He had lived in rented flats before he'd met Kim and had never thought of her house as home. The taxi drove off and Josh failed to notice the silver hatchback that had parked further down the road. He surveyed the front of the house and saw that his father had recently installed new windows. The house stood proudly on a corner plot surrounded by a thick, dark green laurel hedge. A caravan that had been made in the same year in which Josh had been born, stood in the far corner of the back garden. He thought of the happy holidays the family had spent travelling around the UK and a few countries in Europe.

Josh rang the doorbell and listened as its chimes resonated throughout the house. He had his own key but preferred not to use it as a mark of respect for his father. Somehow it didn't seem quite right to let himself into a house that he no longer lived in. Josh could see the large frame of his father approaching through the frosted glass in the front door. It opened and he smiled as his father welcomed him over the threshold.

'Hello son.' He held out his hand and drew Josh towards him. The two men firmly embraced each other for a few seconds. Josh had always regarded his father as a mentor and guide through life's labyrinth. They had similar personalities and this gave them a good understanding of each other. In fact, for many years Josh had idolised his father while disobeying him at times. His sister had enjoyed a more volatile relationship with their father. She'd been confrontational as a child and particularly as a teenager. Josh had watched as she battled against their parents, knowing that in the end she would have to succumb to their wishes. He on the other hand would often agree to do what was required of him and then do the opposite when their backs were turned. This was not something Josh was proud of and, as he got older he felt incredulous at some of the things he'd done as a child and teenager and got away with.

At times Josh felt tempted to own up and purge himself of the shame attached to his past misdeeds but he knew his father would be hurt and disappointed. Even at the age of thirty-nine he felt the need for his father's unconditional love and approval as much as when he was a child. Josh wandered around the garden while his father made them both cups of coffee. He had a vivid memory of the first time he saw the house when he was six years old. The walls of the front room had been covered in red wallpaper with a circular white swirly pattern. It had stuck in his mind ever since like the pattern that stays with you when you look at a bright light and then close your eyes. His mother had replaced the red wallpaper with something less startling as soon as the family moved into the house.

Josh sat down on a bench at the end of the garden and listened to the sound of buzzing bees and birds twittering in the trees. He tried to conjure up the feeling of complete freedom he'd experienced as a child when playing with his friends in this garden. He had been a member of a gang. Not the type of gang that dealt in drugs from street corners or used knives to gain 'respect', but a group of local kids who spent endless days playing imaginary games. Josh and his friends would often disappear onto Horfield Common or into each other's back gardens from dawn until dusk with homemade cheese sandwiches and bottles of orange squash. On other occasions they'd set up camp in one of the two wooden sheds at the bottom of Josh's garden that would become secret caverns or pirate ships.

He watched his father walk slowly across the garden carefully carrying two cups of steaming coffee. He stood up, took one of the cups and gestured to his father to sit down. For a few minutes his father questioned him about his work and family life and Josh caught up with who, out of his father's elderly friends had recently been taken ill or died. Then, as always, the conversation turned to politics.

'So you want to bring power back to the masses,' said Josh's father after hearing a lengthy explanation from his son as to what he wanted the Internet Party to achieve. 'But can you trust the masses to make good decisions? One of the arguments against delegative as opposed to representative democracy is that people would want to do stupid things like reintroduce the death penalty.'

'I have faith that people wouldn't make that sort of decision,' said Josh emphatically. 'Look at what happened when the Prime Minister wanted to attack Syria to teach Assad a lesson for using chemical weapons against his own people. The polls showed that over seventy per cent of people questioned disagreed with such action. Thousands sent emails to their MPs and the government had to back down. That's an example of internet democracy being a force for good.'

'Perhaps I'm getting cynical in my old age,' said Josh's father.

'And maybe I'm still an idealist.'

There was a short silence between the two men as each reflected on the words they'd spoken to the other. Josh felt revitalised after a rest in the fresh air. He would have been happy to sit quietly for a while taking in the sights and smells of the garden with its brightly coloured flowers and budding shrubs. But his father wasn't going to let this opportunity pass. He hardly ever had his son to himself. If he went up to London and stayed in Kim's house Josh would be distracted by the needs of others and he couldn't recall the last time his son had come to visit him in Bristol.

'The Internet is giving people the opportunity to gain knowledge, power and influence like never before,' said Josh. 'Doctors are being called to account by their patients, who are researching their symptoms and possible treatments on line and even diagnosing their own illnesses. Communication and decision-making is moving faster than it's ever moved before.'

Josh could see that his father's eyes were almost closed. It was time for his afternoon nap. But Josh was in full flow and determined to continue his speech.

'I want to see a new and different type of Parliament. The 'gentleman's club' has to be replaced with something that people can relate to. The current system is archaic. Some would say it borders on farce. People haranguing each other across the despatch box with the speaker shouting 'Order', 'Order' and no-one taking any notice.'

Josh raised his voice as he shouted 'Order!' and his father's eyes opened wide.

'Sorry. I was nodding off.'

'Parliament needs new premises with computer screens and video conferencing facilities so that if MPs are in their constituencies or abroad they can still take part in debates. There should be civilised working hours to encourage family life and MPs should be able to vote online. They must have access to the best information that technology can provide at the touch of a button. We need to replace dogma with pragmatism based on agreed principles of social justice. The aim of the Internet Party is to create a more open and egalitarian society at the touch of a button.'

Josh's father wiped a tear from his eye.

'I'm proud of you, son, very proud.' He pulled a large white handkerchief from his trouser pocket and blew his nose loudly. 'Your mother was proud of you too.' Josh's father sniffed. 'Sometimes I feel sorry for you, Josh.'

'Why?'

'Because you were born into a family with a strong sense of social responsibility.'

'That's not such a bad thing.'

'But it can be a burden, Josh. As you know, I haven't made a lot of money throughout my life. But I have solved a huge number of problems for many people. I like to think that when I was a local councillor I helped to bring about social change and made a positive difference to people's lives.'

'I'm sure you did,' said Josh.

'So did your grandfather. He was on the Bristol City Council for over thirty years. He neglected his own financial affairs because he was so busy standing up for his constituents' rights to decent housing and education or writing letters of protest to the local paper.'

'I'm proud of you and Grandpa,' said Josh. The words he spoke made him feel slightly embarrassed. This was not the type of conversation they usually had. Nevertheless Josh and his father spent the last hour of his visit reminiscing about his paternal grandparents. He'd enjoyed spending time with them as he was growing up. They were both committed socialists who devoted their lives to others. Josh had felt special when he visited them, as if he was part of a political dynasty. He'd enjoyed the excitement of the chase and the satisfaction of victory when an election had been won. He wondered whether those early experiences were driving him now.

When it was time for Josh to return to London he found it hard to drag himself away from the happy memories that surrounded him. But most of all he would miss the deep friendship and unconditional love of his father. Perhaps that was why he'd avoided having his own children. Because he felt he would never be as good a father as his father was to him. Josh's spirits had been lifted by the comfortable surroundings of his childhood and by his meeting with his father. There was just one element of sadness to his visit, the absence of his mother. He could feel her presence in the house even though she'd died over ten years ago. Everywhere there were reminders of her creative and artistic nature. Her paintings of familiar scenes and places the family had visited over the years hung on every wall. Patchwork cushions she'd made adorned each chair as timeless reminders of her industrious nature and desire to make a comfortable home for her family.

Josh allowed himself a moment of sadness and reflected upon the beautiful and talented woman that he'd been proud to call his mother. On his last visit Josh's father had given him a tiny autograph book that had belonged to her. It contained the signatures and good wishes of many people she had worked with at the BBC as she left to give birth to Josh, her first child. There had been no automatic washing machines to make his mother's life easier with a baby. Only a mangle and buckets of cloth nappies. Josh felt a pang of guilt that he hadn't made the sacrifices that his parents had made to bring him into the world, precious child that he was.

There were no cars following the taxi that took Josh to Bristol Parkway for his journey back to London. He was so preoccupied with his thoughts that he didn't notice that the silver people carrier parked a few doors from his father's house had completely blacked out windows.

Josh was in the spare room at Maggie's house. He'd arrived back from his trip to see his father in a buoyant mood and hadn't wanted to spoil it by going back to Kim's home and getting involved in some domestic crisis. Instead he'd managed to slip quietly into Maggie's house while she was out and had crept up the stairs to the smallest room on the first floor, unnoticed by the industrious band of volunteers who were beavering away downstairs. This was the only room in the house, apart from Maggie and Bruno's bedroom that was not being used as office space or storage for the Internet Party. The room had been allocated to Josh to use whenever he wanted.

He had just opened up his laptop computer when his mobile phone rang. He looked at the number. It was his father.

'You won't believe what's just happened, Josh. I've been door-stepped, by a journalist. The cheek of the young fellow. He turned up at the front door and seemed quite pleasant to start with. He said he was writing an article about you and that he'd like to interview me. Well, I didn't want to do or say the wrong thing like refuse to speak to him or slam the door in his face. So, I very stupidly invited him in and I thought I'd tell him lots of positive things about

197

you. Like how idealistic you were as a child and that you're not interested in fame or money. How determined you are to bring about greater democracy and re-engage ordinary people with politics. I naively thought the man might even be interested in some of the things I've done in my life that may have influenced you to become the socially minded individual you are today. Well, I should have known better.'

Josh's father paused for breath.

'Slow down a bit, Dad. I'm trying to take all of this in. What's the name of the journalist and which paper does he work for?'

'He said his name is James Smith and that he works for the Echo, but I wouldn't believe a word of it.'

'Did he show you any ID?'

'No. I didn't give him the chance.'

'Why not?'

'Because as soon as he started asking me questions about whether you'd been badly behaved at school or taken drugs or got into trouble with the police I showed him the front door quicker than you can say, How's your father?'

Josh smiled as he pictured his tall and distinguished father hustling the journalist out of his house. But then he felt sad at the trouble he'd caused and worried that he must have been followed.

'Did he take a photo of you?'

'I didn't let him.'

'Good,' said Josh.

'The silly man could have got all kinds of interesting information out of me if he'd played his cards right. But oh no, he had to be looking for dirt.'

'I'm really sorry, Dad. I've come across several people like that in the media.' Josh sighed. He was feeling weighed down by the consequences of his actions for people who were close to him, people whose feelings and wellbeing he cared about. He was beginning to wonder how important his political ambitions actually were.

'Look, son. No harm done. It goes with the territory. I remember being hounded by journalists when I stood for Parliament. I should have known better than to open the door to the man.' Josh's father paused for a moment. 'Now there's one thing I do have to say to you. A small piece of advice. Smarten yourself up a bit, son. I know you're trying to keep a low profile but that baseball cap and the scruffy clothes you were wearing today were ridiculous. I can only assume they were some sort of disguise. Ditch them, Josh. Be proud of who you are. Don't let people intimidate you. Wear smart clothes even if they're casual. If you haven't got enough money to buy some decent clothes, I'll give you some.'

'Dad,' Josh protested, but his father was in full flow.

'And get a decent haircut. You've already had your photo in the newspaper. You'll be on TV soon, although not on one of those awful reality shows, I hope.' Josh's father laughed. 'These people don't frighten me, journalists and the like. I've never felt intimidated by anyone and I don't intend to start now.'

'Thanks for the advice, Dad.' Josh tried to sound grateful, which he genuinely was. He just felt odd being given such a talking to by his father. It made him feel like a child again.

'Also, tell your family and friends not to speak to journalists.'

Josh nodded. He would have to be more careful in future. He'd have to start following Maggie's advice about 'playing the game'. He would have to be a man rather than a mouse and shape up to the challenges ahead. He'd start playing the game and would play to win.

CHAPTER
NINETEEN

Josh typed 'Internet Party' into Google and watched as a myriad of results appeared on his computer screen. His eyes searched for the Internet Party's website, which he opened and scrolled down to see what was new. The weather had been grey and chilly and Josh had been holed up inside his study for what seemed hours. In fact it was only two hours since he'd finished eating a hefty Sunday lunch kindly prepared by Kim. Like Josh she had an old fashioned view of Sundays and wanted to make them family days as much as possible.

In reality the only time that Kim, Dan, Izzy and Josh spent together on the 'day of rest' was the hour or two when they sat down to lunch. In the morning Dan usually had a rugby or cricket match depending on the time of year. Izzy often went to a dance or drama group and she could be out of the house all day if there was an impending production that she had to rehearse for. On some Sundays Dan and Izzy would have to go to their father's house, although such visits seemed to be less frequent as they became older and more independent.

Josh had enjoyed the lunch that Kim had prepared which had consisted of organic chicken with broccoli, carrots, parsnips, roast potatoes and sprouts. Josh loved sprouts as they reminded him of Christmas dinners when he was a child. The apple crumble he'd eaten with its thick and creamy custard sat heavily in his stomach making him feel warm and comfortable inside. Josh carefully scrolled down the Google entries to see if the Internet Party had hit the headlines that day. The media seemed to be watching closely as the 'fairy tale unfolded'. This was the phrase they'd used to describe the 'rags to riches' story of a political party that had 'come from nowhere' and 'captured the public's imagination.' According to the media the Internet Party was gradually 'restoring the public's confidence in politics' and was destined to 'return power to the people.'

There had been a few negative comments with headlines such as 'Who are these Internet Party people?' 'Can we trust them?' 'What are their policies?' 'Do they even have any policies?' But most of the time media coverage had been upbeat and positive. In fact the political pundits were engaging in a whole new debate about what form British democracy should take in the twenty first century. As Josh scrolled down his computer screen, page after page highlighted the lively debates going on between journalists and members of the public as to how people should be able to exercise their democratic rights to exert control over their lives.

Josh cast his eyes over some of the blogs that had sprung up around the Internet Party. There were a few that he found worrying. One or two suggested that the party would be a catalyst for the reintroduction of the death penalty, repatriation of all immigrants and other policies of those on the far right of the political spectrum. Ironically others put forward the view that the party would be the vehicle to bring about a socialist state. One blog referred to 'a Trojan horse being planted inside the walls of centrist politics ready to burst open with a wave of societal change not seen since the days of Oliver Cromwell.' Another blog suggested that to elect members of the Internet Party to Parliament would result in anarchy that would threaten every aspect of British society from nursery schools to the Monarchy.

Josh laughed out loud when he read such ridiculous spouting off. He felt that a number of people had misunderstood the Internet Party's simple message, which was that the balance of power in society needed to be restored from the politicians to the electorate. Finally, after quickly checking through the day's headlines, he clicked onto the party's website. Its turquoise hues were attractive and welcoming. With a slight touch of vanity Josh felt that the photo of him on the home page did not really do him justice, but he didn't intend to embarrass himself by asking to get it changed to one that was more flattering. In contrast he thought Maggie's photo made her look like a film star or a supermodel.

Josh looked to see what was new. Someone had listed all the positive articles that had appeared in newspapers and magazines over the last few days. There were photos of the prospective candidates who had been signed up to stand for Parliament at the forthcoming election. As Josh had been involved in their selection he skimmed over their details. Then he checked on how many hits there had been on the website so far that day. A figure of two hundred thousand nine hundred and sixteen was shown on the screen. The total number of hits since the website was set up amounted to around twenty five million, although the figure was growing all the time.

The Internet Party's message seemed to be catching the attention of journalists in Europe and North America. Josh felt a rush of pride at what he and the other members had created. But at the same time he was beginning to experience another emotion, one that he could not yet describe. Was it surprise, anxiety or fear? There was an element of disbelief every time he switched his computer on and looked at the Internet Party's website, but that did not make him feel uncomfortable.

As Josh tried to identify the emotion that eluded him, he heard a phone ring from somewhere deep in the body of the house. That wasn't unusual these days as most calls were for Dan or Izzy and the sound hardly registered in his mind. Because the home telephone number had always been listed in Kim's married name, which she no longer used, nobody from the media had managed to get hold of it. Recently Josh had succeeded in persuading Kim that the number should also be listed as ex-directory due to the fact that more and more journalists were managing to track him down. There had been a few abusive calls recently so a house rule had developed whereby nobody would answer the phone unless they knew the identity of the caller.

Izzy had been persuaded by the argument that most of the calls to the house were from her friends to laboriously tap their numbers into the phone memory together with the contacts of Kim, Dan and Josh. It had taken her several days and she'd expressed her frustration, boredom and a variety of other complaints volubly with moans and groans to the point where Josh had felt obliged to pay her handsomely for the job. He smiled as he remembered the look on Izzy's face after a particularly difficult moment when she'd threatened to delete all of the input numbers. Dan had accused her of blackmail but Josh suspected that he'd been jealous of the payment she'd received.

He heard the phone ring again.

'I'll get it,' shouted Kim. He listened as she hurried down the hallway to the kitchen. Josh counted nine rings before the answerphone clicked in and he heard the dulcet tones of an anonymous female voice.

'Hello. Your call cannot be taken at the moment so please leave a message after the tone'. There was a humming noise and the caller rang off without saying anything.

'Where's the frigging phone?' Josh could hear Kim's irate voice loudly through his study door. He wasn't sure whether Dan or Izzy were at home but frigging was a word Kim used when they were around so as not to set a bad example by saying what she really wanted to say. Josh had been buried inside his study since lunchtime and was unaware of the comings and goings in the rest of the house. He now felt obliged to open the door.

'It's not in here,' Josh called.

'What?' Kim shouted from upstairs.

Then the phone rang again. Josh stood up and went to the stand in the kitchen where the handset should have been. He looked at the small screen to see who was calling but it registered as 'Number Withheld'. That always made him suspicious. Recently there had been a number of times where the caller cut off as soon as the answerphone clicked in. Kim thought it was probably one of Dan's many female admirers who was too shy to be identified. Josh could hear the sound of someone banging on a door upstairs.

'It's not in here,' shouted Izzy above the sound of music in her room.

'I can hear it. Open the door,' Kim yelled back.

Josh pictured the scene unfolding upstairs. Izzy would be searching frantically through piles of discarded clothes, empty diet coke bottles, used make-up wipes, dirty tissues and school folders bursting at the seams. Kim would be standing outside Izzy's locked bedroom door fuming on several counts – her daughter's disorganised state of existence, her refusal to open the door and the fact that the phone lay buried somewhere out of reach. The phone stopped ringing and the music coming from Izzy's room got louder as she opened the door. Then he heard her voice.

'It's for Josh.'

'Next time put it back.'

Izzy's door slammed shut and he heard Kim stomping down the stairs as he hurried into the hallway to meet her. He would normally have refused to take the phone without knowing the identity of the caller. But the look on Kim's face gave him no choice. She was obviously in no mood for a refusal.

'Who is it?' Josh mouthed as she thrust the phone at him. Kim shrugged and quickly walked away. It occurred to him that he could pretend to be cut off but that would just delay things as the unknown person would no doubt call back. He was also curious as to who it was that kept withholding their number.

A brisk male voice with a Scottish accent ascertained that he was speaking to 'Mr Walker'. The man sounded annoyed that it had taken him so long to get through. Then he identified himself. Josh felt weak and had to sit down.

'This is the office of the Prime Minister. My name is Hamish Stoke and I'm calling because the Prime Minister has asked me to arrange for you to attend a meeting with him.'

Josh gasped and found himself unable to speak for several seconds.

'Hello. Are you still there?' Hamish Stoke sounded even more annoyed.

'When, where, how?' said Josh.

'Here, of course. Number Ten Downing Street, tomorrow morning at nine o'clock. Transport can be arranged if you wish.' Hamish Stoke's voice softened slightly. 'Of course, if that's inconvenient we can arrange the meeting for another time. I'll give you my direct dial number. Feel free to call me whenever you wish.'

'I'll check my diary and get right back to you,' Josh spluttered into the phone trying desperately to sound cool and failing miserably.

'You do that please Mr Walker. Goodbye.'

Josh clicked the handset to its 'off' position and checked that the call had disconnected before carefully placing it in its holder. He stared at the phone half expecting it to ring again at any moment. Then he slid quietly into his study and collapsed into the armchair. He needed to speak to Maggie. She would know what to do. Josh could hear the sound of newspapers rustling in the TV room. He knew that Kim would be reading the Sunday papers. He was aware of the sound of music drifting down through the floorboards from Izzy's bedroom upstairs. She had reduced the volume after the missing phone incident. She's keeping her head down, thought Josh.

It had only taken him a few seconds to decide not to

mention the call from the Prime Minister's office to Kim. Life was stressful enough for her at present. She'd made her position clear on several occasions. She did not like Josh being involved in politics and she wanted herself and her kids kept out of it too. He knew that Kim thought the Internet Party would make no impact at the forthcoming election and would then fizzle out as quickly as it began. Josh hadn't argued against this view in order to keep the peace with Kim. But everything pointed to the opposite view. It appeared to him that the Internet Party was destined to have a major impact.

Josh caught sight of Maggie through her living room window as he made his way up the path to her front door. She was lying sprawled across her black leather sofa. She must have seen him coming as the shiny black door mysteriously opened before he'd reached it.

'Hello stranger,' said Maggie popping her head round the door and cheerily raising a half full glass of white wine. She gestured to Josh that he should follow her into the living room and eased herself back into exactly the same position on the sofa that she'd been in when he'd caught sight of her through the window. As Maggie's curved and toned body sank into the soft warm leather Josh wished he was the sofa.

'Can I get you a drink?' She waved her glass at Josh before taking a gentle sip. 'A late lunch,' she added quickly. He shook his head.

'I've been looking at the website,' said Josh. He felt himself relax into the red leather armchair.

'Did you see anything interesting? I haven't looked at it today.' Maggie shifted her body so that her feet were propped up on one arm of the sofa while her head was resting on the other.

'Nothing special,' said Josh. His hands were clasped together and his legs were stretched out in front of him. He examined his shoes and saw that they were scuffed and worn.

He decided to buy a new pair the following day. Josh found that being in Maggie's presence made him feel scruffy. She was one of those people who always looked immaculate no matter what she wore. Today she was wearing a faded pair of jeans and a polo shirt that looked as if it had shrunk in the wash. Her hair was dishevelled and she wore no make up. Josh's love for Maggie welled up inside him so that he wanted to leap across the room, lift her into his arms and whisk her upstairs to the nearest bedroom. But as he'd received no sign of encouragement from her that he should do any such thing, he stayed firmly in his seat.

'So what's new?' said Maggie. Josh wondered if she could see that something was bothering him.

'I had a strange call today,' said Josh.

'Tell me about it. We've been getting them all week.' Mention of the word 'we' suddenly made him feel uncomfortable.

'It was someone from the Prime Minister's office.' Josh spoke the words slowly and deliberately in a half hearted attempt to bolster his own self esteem in face of the realisation that Maggie still shared a large part of her life with Bruno, a part he knew little about.

'The Prime Minister's office,' shouted Maggie, moving quickly into a sitting position as if the man himself might walk into the room at any moment. Then she started to laugh hysterically, swaying backwards and forwards and making a running on the spot type of motion with her feet. Eventually, after managing to calm herself down, she took a sip of wine, nearly choked and punching the air with her right fist, shouted 'Yes!'

Maggie leaned forward and stared eagerly at Josh. 'Come on then. Tell me what they said.'

'It wasn't a 'they'. It was a Hamish Stoke.'

'Oh, a Hamish Stoke. And who is he when he's at home?' said Maggie in her 'posh' accent mimicking her mother's old-fashioned turn of phrase.

'Haven't a clue,' said Josh and they both laughed, enjoying the moment. 'I didn't get that far. I said I'd call the guy back.'

'What! You said you'd call the Prime Minister back, at your convenience, on your own terms,' Maggie continued in her posh accent. 'How hilarious!' She was now up on her bare feet pacing around on her newly varnished wooden floor.

'Well, I suppose we should feel honoured,' said Josh, trying to sound serious. 'Perhaps he sees us as a threat.'

Josh shrugged his shoulders. Nobody really knew what impact the Internet Party might have. Political commentators had come up with all kinds of weird and wonderful theories over the last few weeks. But on the whole they were a conservative bunch with a small 'c' and their general view was that the Internet Party would create a ripple rather than a wave.

The consensus was that the concept was good and that the emergence of a new political party when people were disillusioned with politicians was timely. If it achieved nothing else, the Internet Party would act as a wake up call to the complacent and sometimes dishonest Members of Parliament who abused their authority and let down the people who elected them.

Josh had observed a change for good in the way the Internet was being used as an instrument of democracy. It was often a vehicle for fraud and abuse, but it could also be a tool for discovering the truth. It was becoming harder for the government to hide its mistakes or abuses of power as emails and other so called 'privileged documents' found their way from civil service computers onto the Worldwide Web to be read by millions of people. Oppressive and undemocratic governments in foreign countries could no longer repress dissent as photographs and film of demonstrations were posted on YouTube from the mobile phones of demonstrators or bystanders.

'We need a plan Josh,' said Maggie.

'What kind of plan?'

'We've got to decide how to handle this business with the Prime Minister. What exactly did Hamish Stoke say?'

It had occurred to Josh that the call could easily have been a hoax. He had felt uneasy from the moment he'd first spoken to the man who called himself Hamish Stoke and he had no intention of calling him back.

'How do we know this isn't someone having a laugh?' said Maggie reading Josh's mind.

'Exactly'.

Maggie paused for a moment and took the last sip of her wine. She had a thoughtful expression on her face, as if she was considering various options. Then she put her glass down on the wooden floor and stood up. Her too small polo shirt had ridden up to expose a perfect waist and Josh couldn't help watching as she tried to pull it down to meet the top of her jeans.

'Have you got the number?'

Josh nodded and fished around in the pockets of his dark brown leather jacket for the yellow post-it note he'd written the number on. He handed it to Maggie.

'I'll call and pretend I'm your secretary.' She smiled conspiratorially and reached for the note. Josh smiled back raising his eyebrows in an expression of mock surprise. He loved Maggie's fearless approach to life. Suddenly he saw that she had a phone in her hand.

'Is that Hamish Stoke's office?' Maggie spoke with confidence and an air of authority. 'It's Mr Walker's secretary. Would you mind telling Mr Stoke that Mr Walker would be delighted to meet the Prime Minister. However, Mr Walker is unable to come to Number Ten Downing Street. He would therefore like to invite the Prime Minister to number thirty-three Horatio Road, Wimbledon. Yes, that's right, South West Nineteen. Goodbye.'

Maggie ran her tongue across her lips and grinned like a cat licking itself after eating cream. She sat back down on the sofa and carefully placed the phone beside her.

'I can't believe you just did that,' said Josh. He sounded horrified and his face was fixed in a stunned expression with his eyes wide open.

'It's not that bad. All I did was to invite him here.'

Maggie had suddenly lost her cool. Gone was the confident, capable and fearless stance and for the first time since Josh had met her, she looked vulnerable. He felt a surge of warmth towards Maggie. He wanted to jump up from his chair, fling his arms around her and smother her in kisses. But his body remained motionless and somehow detached from his mind.

'What if he feels we've snubbed him? After all, he is the Prime Minister and one of the most important people in the country,' said Josh.

Maggie nervously ran her fingers through her hair and refused to look at Josh. 'I didn't think you should go to see him. It would send the wrong message to our supporters.'

Maggie paused for a few seconds and then she managed to regain her sense of purpose. She looked Josh in the eye as if she was challenging him to disagree with what she was about to say. 'The Prime Minister wants to see you, right?' As Josh opened his mouth to speak, Maggie interrupted. 'He must have an agenda, a reason for inviting you. But he's not going to tell you what it is, is he?'

'I suppose not,' said Josh. 'I wonder why he wants to meet up.' Maggie shrugged her shoulders and opened her arms wide to indicate that she had no idea and he'd better come up with some suggestions. Josh cleared his throat and paused for a moment to give himself time to think before speaking.

'Well, the Prime Minister will want to make the point that he is in charge of running the country.' Maggie nodded encouragingly so Josh continued. 'And he'll want to send a message to the electorate that he's not about to give up power to anyone else, let alone a bunch of amateurs who have cobbled together last-minute-political-party.com.'

'Exactly,' said Maggie, who'd now regained her cool. 'I can picture you being escorted to the door of Ten Downing Street by the Prime Minister's bodyguards. The door opens and you disappear inside. Half an hour later you re-emerge into the glare of flash photography and you are quickly hurried away. Shortly afterwards the Prime Minister appears and in his usual calm manner he reassures the waiting media that you, the leader of the Internet Party, have accepted that you are no threat to his power. Democracy is intact and it shall remain so when he is re-elected.'

Josh clapped his hands and laughed. 'But why go to the trouble of meeting me? He could just issue a press statement.'

'He's probably curious and he may even feel a teeny-weeny bit scared,' said Maggie.

Now they were both laughing. She wiped a tear from her eye and held up her right hand. Josh met it with his left hand in a triumphant gesture of solidarity.

'Listen,' said Maggie. By inviting the Prime Minister to come here we are agreeing to his request for a meeting. We are also showing him that we are to be taken seriously and, most important, we will be in control.'

'I'll bet you he won't come,' said Josh. He leaned back in his chair, stretched his legs out in front of him and rested his hands behind his head.

'How much?' said Maggie.

'What?'

'How much do you want to bet?'

Josh was not a betting man. He put on a pained expression as if he had something of great importance on his mind. He was beginning to feel a little overwhelmed by

Maggie's strong presence.

'I'd better get going. I said I'd give Izzy a lift to her play rehearsal.'

'Chicken!'

Maggie's parting shot resounded in Josh's head as he walked back to Kim's house. He thought about what she'd said. Just how courageous was he? He felt overwhelmed on occasions by Maggie's strength of purpose and her clear vision. Was he just being carried along by events over which he had no control? He was on the front line, portrayed by the media as the leader of the Internet Party. But he hadn't put himself in that position. The media had created that role for him and he hadn't objected. But it was Maggie who was really in charge. She was the true leader.

Josh stood outside Kim's front door and searched his jacket pockets for his keys. There were none to be found and his phone was also missing. He rang the doorbell and within seconds the front door flew open. Kim's face was a greyish colour and she had red rims around her eyes. She looked like she'd been crying.

'Sorry, I lost track of time,' said Josh.

'We need to talk,' said Kim as she marched along the hallway and into the kitchen with Josh in her wake. She stood by the kitchen sink with her arms folded and stared at him in disbelief.

'It's Sunday,' said Kim. 'It's the one day of the week when I try to bring us all together.' She emphasised the words, 'I try'.

Josh started to feel uncomfortable. He knew Kim intended to make him feel guilty but what he actually felt was resentment.

'You know Izzy wanted you to take her to the play rehearsal this evening.' Kim emphasised the word 'you'. 'I know it may not seem like a big deal to you but she's already been let down by one father.'

Now Josh was feeling angry. How dare she try and

make him responsible for Richard's failings. He'd enough of a problem dealing with his own.

'Look,' said Josh sounding cross. 'I'm sorry I'm late. I got a call from the Prime Minister's office requesting a meeting with me and I had to talk to Maggie.'

Kim was silent for a moment while she thought about what he'd said.

'The Prime Minister's office.' She spoke the words slowly. 'Well, I don't care who wants a meeting with you. Family comes first.'

Josh could sense that Kim wanted to say a lot more. She looked as if she might explode at any moment. Fortunately, Izzy shouted from the top of the stairs that she was ready to leave and gave him the chance to escape. She'd been running late herself as she tried on various outfits and discarded them onto the floor before deciding which one to wear. When Josh met Izzy by the front door he gave away no sign of the row that had been simmering between him and her mother.

As his car pulled away from the kerb with Izzy chattering happily beside him he felt a mixture of emotions. Josh was proud that Izzy enjoyed his company and wanted to spend time with him, even if it meant giving her endless lifts to see her friends and to numerous activities. He felt glad that he was part of Kim's family, but he disliked the resentment she harboured in relation to his involvement with the Internet Party.

After Josh had delivered Izzy to her play rehearsal he decided to confront Kim. He wouldn't do so tonight. There was too much tension and anger in the air. He would choose a time when she was in a better mood.

Josh decided to spend the evening at Maggie's house. He would collect Izzy later from her play rehearsal and deliver her back home. Maybe he'd go and speak to Kim then. Josh was shuttling between the two houses all the time now. He often stayed overnight in Maggie's spare room because his evenings were full of meetings with the band of volunteers, whose idealism and enthusiasm filled him with hope and gave him the energy to continue with his quest.

As usual on a Sunday night the house was quiet. Bruno had left earlier in the evening to fly to Manchester, where he had a meeting first thing on Monday morning about some important building project. The volunteers were spending time with their friends and families or were preparing themselves for work or their studies at school, college or university the next day. Josh settled himself down on the small bed and opened his laptop. He looked at the time on the screen and calculated that he had about an hour before going to collect Izzy. He scrolled down his emails, checking the subject headings for any that looked interesting.

One caught his eye. It read **'Extremely Urgent Warning for Mr Walker.'** Josh's heart sank. He didn't recognise the email address but that was nothing unusual. It was the word 'warning' that worried him. The anonymous death threat he'd received hadn't been repeated. He had, however, been sent a collection of weird and wonderful suggestions by various unknown senders as to what he could do with the Internet Party. Josh had discussed these with the police and they'd reassured him that it was standard practice for aspiring politicians to be subjected to various forms of abuse by members of the public. The existence of email, Twitter and other social media had made it easy for people to send abusive messages to MPs and other public figures whose contact details were now freely available.

Josh took a deep breath and read it.

'Mr Walker,
Who do you think you are? Have you no idea what will happen to you if you continue with this Internet Party nonsense? Nobody will vote for you but you are putting

your family at risk. **Do you honestly think that those
in power are going to let you take it from them? Have
you not heard of MI5 and MI6? They are watching
your every move, listening to your phone conversations,
hacking into your e-mail. Have you met up with a
woman from your past recently? Have you visited a
close relative? The secret services will know everything
about you, past and present. They have access to your
medical records and will be talking to people about you
on social media, pretending to be your friends. You have
been warned. Watch your back!'**

    Josh tried to keep calm. He read the email over
and over again. Was this a warning or a threat? Was the
message a hoax or was there truth in those words? Josh felt
very alone and yet he knew he would have to discuss it with
others.

    He'd been naive and so wrapped up in the idealism
of what he was trying to achieve that he'd become blinkered.
Hadn't he considered the possibility that someone might
want to harm him? If he had then he'd discounted the
thought as quickly as it had arisen. Anger welled up
inside Josh because he hadn't considered the safety of his
immediate family – Kim, Dan and Izzy, his father and sister
and her family. Then there was Maggie and her parents.
What about their safety? Had Maggie taken steps to protect
them? The game was moving to a different level, the rules
were changing and the stakes were higher. Josh could feel
palpitations in his chest. Perhaps it was time to engage
a private security firm. Kim would object to any further
invasion of her privacy. But how would she react to the
suggestion that her children might be at risk, either from
some madman, or worse, from people who were sane.

CHAPTER TWENTY

Izzy's scream was the loudest Josh had ever heard. It sent piercing shots in all directions throughout the house and seemed to last forever. Next he heard shouting, crying, the sound of unidentifiable objects being thrown around and doors being slammed shut. Josh felt in a state of shock and for a few moments he couldn't move out of his chair. Then he heard the sound of footsteps running down the hallway and Izzy burst into his study. She was hysterical. Her face was red and stained with tears and she kept wiping her hands down the front of her clothes, which she only did when she was extremely anxious. Izzy was shaking and staring with her eyes wide open. Josh stood up and held her arms for a moment.

'What's the matter, Izzy? Calm down.'

'Da-Dad,' she stuttered. It must be something serious, thought Josh. She only ever called him Dad during moments of extreme stress, usually after some monumental row with her mother.

'It's Mu-mm-mum.' She kept smoothing her clothes with the palms of her hands and jiggling her feet about.

'Come on Izzy. What's wrong?' Josh tried to sound calm and reassuring, despite the fact that a feeling of panic was slowly welling up inside him.

'She's gone mad.'

'Who?'

'Mum.'

Josh steered Izzy into the TV room and sat her gently on the sofa. She was no longer hysterical but was sobbing uncontrollably as she sat bolt upright staring into Josh's eyes, pleading with him to help her. 'You have to do something.'

Josh felt reluctant to leave Izzy.

'Do you want me to go and see her?'

'Ye-ye-yes,' she stammered.

'You stay here then,' said Josh.

Izzy nodded and the pace of her breathing lessened as a feeling of relief began to creep over her. Josh moved quickly and quietly towards the hallway. He could hear sounds from outside the front door. Then suddenly it burst open and Kim bustled in with two black bin liners full of rubbish. She was red in the face and her eyes were glazed over in a way that Josh had never seen before.

Kim was staring straight at him and yet she seemed to be looking through him to a point in the far distance.

'What are you doing?' said Josh gently.

'What does it look like?' replied Kim crossly. Her eyes suddenly seemed to come back into focus.

'But it's rubbish day. Aren't you supposed to be taking those bags in the opposite direction?'

'I'm not leaving them out there.' Kim spat out the words with what appeared to Josh to be a tinge of madness. Her hair was sticking up in the air and her clothes were arranged in such a way on her body that she looked slightly deranged. She pushed past Josh and took the two black bags full of rubbish out into the back garden. Josh followed and watched as Kim tipped the contents of the bags onto the patio. He caught sight of Izzy standing at the window, her face as white as a sheet, staring in horror at her mother. Kim began to search through the pile of rubbish.

'Are you looking for something?' said Josh. This was the logical explanation for Kim's behaviour. She must have thrown something away by mistake. Kim did not reply but continued to search through the rubbish in a frenzied manner. After a few minutes she started to put the rubbish back into the bags. Josh could see that her hands were covered in a sticky mess of sauce, scraps of food and all the other detritus that finds its way into the rubbish of a family of four each week.

'Careful,' said Josh as he pointed to the top of a tin can that had sharp edges.

Kim stopped what she was doing for a second, carefully wrapped the top in a piece of newspaper and put it back into one of the bags. She neither spoke nor looked up. Josh's eyes scoured the pile of mostly plastic food packaging mixed with cotton wool buds, make-up wipes, pencil sharpenings and a whole myriad of items that were unrecognisable after several days in the dark heat of the dustbins.

Once Kim had refilled the bags she tied them up carefully and, standing upright with a bag in each hand, she announced to Josh, 'I'm taking these to the dump.'

'Why? The dustmen will be here soon.'

He wished he hadn't spoken when Kim's body stiffened and she snarled, 'To stop people from interfering with them. I don't want anyone looking at our rubbish.'

Josh glanced at Izzy, who was still standing by the window with a forlorn expression on her face. He raised his eyebrows and made a face to indicate that he'd no idea what was going on. Izzy shrugged her shoulders and shook her head as if to say that she didn't know either. Kim ignored both of them, disappeared into the house with the bags and let herself out of the front door. Josh stood still and listened as the boot of her car slammed shut and Kim revved up the engine and screeched off in the direction of the municipal dump.

'I hope she doesn't have an accident,' Josh muttered to himself as he walked slowly back inside the house to see Izzy. He wondered how he would live with the guilt of failing to stop Kim from driving off if she were killed and he berated himself for being so pathetic and non-confrontational. Izzy was standing aimlessly in the middle of Josh's study with a worried expression on her face.

'Your mother's gone to take the rubbish to the

dump,' said Josh as coolly as he could manage. 'I'll get you a drink.' He gently held Izzy's left arm and guided her into the kitchen. 'What would you like?'

'Chocolate milk,' she muttered as she sat down quietly at the kitchen table.

'Tell me what happened,' said Josh as he stirred three large spoonfuls of a chocolate-flavoured powder into a tall glass of milk.

'Mum completely flipped. I've never seen her like that before. She gets angry but she was out of her mind. I thought she was going to kill me.'

Josh sat down next to Izzy and gently put his left arm around her shoulders. She gripped the glass with both hands and took small sips of the soothing liquid.

'Did you have a row?'

'Not to start with. Mum was a bit cross about the shredder. She couldn't get it to work properly. Something had got stuck in it and she thought Dan or I had broken it.' Izzy took another sip of the chocolate milk.

'I said it wasn't me who broke it 'cos I never use it. Then I got a lecture about how I should be shredding everything. Not just personal stuff but homework I don't want, notes from my school, anything with my email address on it. Mum just kept going on and on. She was getting really worked up and it pissed me off. So I said I wasn't going to shred anything and she could do it if she wanted to.'

Izzy took a deep breath and then she removed a tissue from a box on the kitchen table and blew her nose noisily. She clutched the tissue and sighed.

'Why d'you think your mother was getting so upset about the shredder?'

'Cos of that lecture Maggie gave us, like all those things we've got to remember, to make sure people don't find out personal things, you know, the media people, journalists.'

'So what made Kim bring the rubbish bags into the house?'

'There was this guy. He was wearing one of those luminous waistcoats. I think he was from the council but he looked a bit rough.'

'What was he doing?' said Josh.

'Well, mum went to put out the rubbish bags and he was looking through the recycling boxes. She said she saw him put something into a rucksack he was carrying on his back. So she went up and asked him what he was doing.'

'What did he say?'

'He said he was looking for magazines people didn't want. Mum told the guy that he shouldn't take things out of people's recycling boxes and that she would report him to the council. I knew she wouldn't really 'cos she's not like that. She probably felt sorry for him. He didn't speak proper English and I don't suppose he had much money. Anyway, when she came back inside the house I said she was really embarrassing and so what if he wanted our old magazines. Mum got really angry and screamed at me about the shredder and people going through our bins. She kept going on about you being a celebrity and Maggie telling us what we can and can't do. She was shaking me. I thought she was going mad.' Izzy paused and then spoke in a whisper. 'I thought mum was going to kill me. I've never in my life seen her like that. I'm really worried.'

Tears welled up in Izzy's eyes and she began to sob again. Her body seemed to shrink in front of Josh's eyes so that it looked small and crumpled. He held her close to him and his own eyes filled with tears. How could he have brought such sadness into the lives of Kim and Izzy? A feeling of guilt and helplessness crept over him. He had set up the Internet Party with Maggie in order to empower people and improve their lives, not to ruin the lives of the people he loved.

CHAPTER
TWENTY-ONE

It had been a long day and Josh felt exhausted. He'd been lecturing students for most of the morning and had conducted tutorials all afternoon. He added up the hours and worked out that he'd been teaching for seven hours, marking essays for three hours and dealing with administrative work for two – a total of twelve hours. Perhaps that didn't constitute a long day for a City solicitor or investment banker but considering they were paid at least ten times the paltry salary Josh received as a lowly lecturer it seemed like a hard day's work to him.

The highlight of his day had been an email he'd received from Christine. Josh hadn't heard from her since they'd met for lunch, apart from the short message she'd sent thanking him and apologising for rushing off. This email was longer but very much to the point.

'Hi Josh
Sorry not to have been in touch sooner. I've been completely wrapped up in work but I've been keeping my eye on you via social media. You didn't know you were being spied on did you? I can hardly believe you've got over a million followers on Twitter. That's far more than any other political leader in the UK.
This may sound a bit odd but I thought I'd jot down a few facts about my life to try and fill in some of the gaps. Maybe you could do the same so that we don't have to do it when me meet up again.'

Josh read with interest as Christine described how she'd met her husband, a fellow lawyer. She went on to explain that they'd devoted themselves to their careers and let the opportunity to have children slip past, which she now regretted. She was candidly honest about the mistakes she'd made in her marriage and sad that divorce had finally seemed the only option available to them both. As Christine didn't mention a current relationship, Josh assumed she was single. The 'partner' she'd mentioned in her first email had turned out to be one of her business partners, not a boyfriend.

He had made several attempts to reply to the email but had deleted each draft as either they gave too much or too little information. He decided to wait until his spirits had lifted so that he could send a response that was positive as opposed to flat. He hated to admit it but he was feeling sorry for himself after the drama of the previous day.

Josh stared out of the window as the train from Waterloo station to Wimbledon sped past the urban sprawl of London. He considered his lot and carried out a comparison with two of his most highly paid friends. Josh had met Sebastian at university. He was now a partner in a 'magic circle' firm of solicitors in the City. Josh had no idea why the top five firms were called by that name. He made a mental note to ask Sebastian next time they met.

Perhaps it was something to do with money. Law firms didn't generally publish annual accounts, but each year the legal press printed estimates of partners' profit shares. Josh always read the figures with interest but with no concept of what it meant to earn eight hundred thousand pounds a year. That was his last estimate of Sebastian's annual earnings based on figures he'd read in the Times.

The only person Josh knew who earned more than Sebastian was his old friend Mark who worked as an investment banker with an American bank. Before the latest financial crisis the economy had been buoyant and bonuses for bankers had reached dizzy heights. Mark had never talked to Josh about his bonus but every spring he would buy brand new top of the range cars for himself and his wife. He had also invested in property and his 'portfolio' as he liked to call it included a holiday home in Salcombe in Devon worth several million pounds, a villa in Portugal that was on the edge of the largest golf course in the country and an apartment in the most exclusive club complex in Antigua in the Caribbean. There were also three 'buy to let' flats in London and two houses Mark had bought in Nottingham and Oxford where his kids went to university.

Mark had made his fortune by the time he was forty and although Josh suspected that it had shrunk during the last recession, he was still extremely rich by most people's standards. Josh recalled a statistic he'd read recently in an article about pay. The average wage in the UK was around twenty-seven thousand pounds a year. That made him feel slightly better as he thought of his own salary.

The train was hot and crowded. Josh had been lucky enough to find an empty seat at Waterloo but by the time the train reached Vauxhall there was standing room only. As the train pulled out of the station he caught sight of a pregnant woman carrying a large black briefcase and wearing a dark blue suit who was making her way awkwardly along the carriage towards him. She looked pale and exhausted and Josh immediately felt sorry for her. It occurred to him that someone should give up their seat for her to sit down. But everyone had their eyes fixed on a book, newspaper, hand held computer, reading device or mobile phone or otherwise kept them firmly closed. Josh suddenly felt compelled to stand up and offer his seat to the woman. However, just as he did so the train lurched to one side and he banged into a large sweaty workman who gave him an aggressive stare.

'Sorry mate,' said Josh as he gestured to the woman to sit down while trying to guard the empty seat from anyone else who might try to muscle in. A few people raised their eyes in his direction. He noticed that their faces were dull and lifeless.

'Thanks,' said the woman as she carefully lowered herself into the seat and tucked her briefcase under her legs.

She smiled at Josh and as he smiled back he felt a warm sensation spread over his body as he revelled in the pleasure of a moment's kindness.

When the train reached Wimbledon station Josh put on his sunglasses and baseball cap in a half-hearted attempt to disguise his identity. He was becoming used to a few people giving him quizzical looks of recognition, but it was not something he wished to encourage. Occasionally strangers would stop him in the street, apologise and say that his face looked familiar in the hope that he would explain who he was. Josh would smile politely, shrug his shoulders and continue on his way leaving the strangers in his wake.

Josh decided to walk along Crown Road and down Holy Road on this particular evening. He took a different route to and from the station each day in an attempt to catch out anyone who might wish to follow him. Since the article in the Sunday Post there had been a few pieces about him in the daily papers, mostly feeding off information on the Internet Party website. But gradually the media seemed to be losing interest.

Josh walked across the park as dusk was falling and the last rays of sunshine shone through the bare trees. He inhaled the scent of freshly cut grass tinged with the smell of broom. Eager to experience more of the sights, sounds and smells of the early evening, Josh stopped at the first bench he came to. He sat and watched for a while as the dog walkers and joggers passed by. In the distance he could hear the timeless sound of an ice cream van's gentle tune. Josh closed his eyes and felt at home.

When he opened them again he caught sight of a blue flashing light near to Kim's house. He couldn't see what type of vehicle it belonged to as the black railings and dense green shrubbery blocked his view. A feeling of paralysis came over Josh as he tried to stand up. It took him a while to regain his composure. He hadn't heard any siren. Josh reached into his left hand pocket for his mobile phone, but it was empty. The sensation of serenity he'd experienced while sitting happily on the bench had evaporated in seconds and he now felt angry with himself for leaving his phone at work. Josh managed to pull himself together and walked as quickly as he could out of the park. As he turned into Horatio Road he saw a police car parked outside Kim's house. His heart sank as he rushed to the front door, fumbled with his keys and let himself in.

The sound of Kim crying resonated throughout the house. Josh walked quickly along the hallway in the direction of conversation he could hear in the kitchen. The voices stopped as he entered the room but Kim's crying got louder when she saw him. She was sitting hunched up at the kitchen table clutching a box of tissues. Her eyes were red and puffy and she was sobbing uncontrollably.

Maggie was sitting to one side of Kim with her arm around her shoulders and Bruno was standing behind them. On the other side sat a female police officer holding a notepad. Josh thought how young she looked. She could easily be the same age as one of his students. The officer was blonde and fairly short with her hair tied back in a ponytail. She was wearing a black bullet proof vest over her white shirt that looked incongruous in Kim's kitchen. She had a pretty face. Too pretty for a police officer, thought Josh and then he rebuked himself for being sexist. The blue-eyed, fair-faced police officer spoke with a strong South London accent.

'You must be Mr Walker.'

'Yes, I am.'

Josh nodded at Bruno and managed a slight smile of nothing more than recognition at Maggie. Kim didn't look up. Was that sympathy he saw in Maggie's eyes or was it pity? Josh immediately thought that something must have happened to his father. Had he fallen and broken a limb? This was Josh's greatest fear, apart from one that was even worse. Josh couldn't even begin to contemplate his father's death.

Suddenly Kim raised her head and turned her red and tear-stained face to look at Josh. He could see that she was angry and distraught.

'Izzy's gone missing and it's your fault.' Kim blurted out the words in Josh's direction like bullets from a gun and he felt their full force in the middle of his chest.

'The police think she may have been kidnapped,' said Maggie quickly in a gentle tone. Josh could tell that she was anxious.

'I need to ask you some questions, Mr Walker. Please sit down,' said the police officer. 'I'm Police Constable Janet Warner from Wimbledon police station. I need to know when you last saw Izzy.'

'Why? Am I a suspect?' Josh blurted out his words without thinking. 'No, sorry, I didn't mean that. I'm just shocked.' What had Kim meant when she said it was Josh's fault that Izzy was missing? He felt he should be the one comforting Kim, not Maggie. But she'd just accused him of being responsible for the disappearance of her daughter. He felt the need to take control of the situation.

'What's the position so far?' Josh addressed this question to everyone at the table as if he were about to start a tutorial discussion with his students.

'As I said, Mr Walker, it would be helpful to know when you last recall seeing Izzy. I'm trying to get a picture of her movements.'

PC Warner held her notepad ready to jot down what Josh said, but he couldn't speak. One day rolled into another in Kim's household and he could hardly remember what he'd had for breakfast, let alone when he'd last seen Kim's kids. In any case he now spent a lot of time at Maggie's house.

'I'll tell you what we've managed to piece together and that might help to jog your memory,' said PC Warner.

Kim had been unable to make contact with Izzy

for several hours. This was not unusual in itself, thought Josh. The advantages of being able to maintain contact with teenagers through their mobile phones were often outweighed by the frustration and worry that arose when they failed to answer voicemail or text messages because their phones were out of credit or battery or they'd forgotten to switch them on.

While Josh listened to the circumstances of Izzy's supposed disappearance he thought back to his own childhood. He'd run away from school once when he was about nine years old. He'd painted the palms of his hands a mucky green colour in an art lesson and the teacher hadn't been impressed. She'd told him to go and wash his hands and not come back. What she'd meant was to go straight out to the playground, as it was nearly break time. Josh had taken her words literally and had gone home, much to his mother's surprise and the headmaster's horror.

He remembered acting impulsively at the time and being annoyed with his teacher for making such a fuss in front of the whole class about a bit of paint. He'd known he was wrong to run away but had decided to do it anyway.

'Then at five o'clock, Ms Clark,' PC Warner continued.

'Please call me Kim.'

'Then at five o'clock Kim received a text message on her mobile from a phone that had a number she didn't recognise. She called straight back but a voice said it was 'unavailable'.'

Josh looked up.

'The text said that Izzy won't be coming back until a set of demands are met,' said PC Warner as she rested her notepad on the table.

'Demands, what demands?' shouted Josh. Everyone turned to look at him.

'We don't know yet,' said PC Warner. 'We were hoping you might be able to shed some light on things.'

'Why me?'

'We thought you might know who has kidnapped Izzy.'

'How on earth would I know?'

'Because Kim says you've been getting strange emails.' PC Warner paused for a few seconds. 'Death threats.'

Something was not quite right but he couldn't tell what it was. He felt as if he was watching himself in a film, an Agatha Christie whodunit or a police drama on TV. The situation felt unreal.

'We think there may be a link between the text message and the emails,' said PC Warner.

'I didn't take them seriously. I assumed they were either a joke or from someone unbalanced but harmless,' said Josh looking sheepish.

Suddenly Kim spoke. Not in the tone that she'd used when she had accused Josh of being responsible for Izzy's disappearance, but with a sense of pity in her voice.

'I feel sorry for you, Josh. You just don't get it, do you? You have no idea of what you've put me and my children through with this Internet Party nonsense.' Kim gave Maggie a meaningful stare and then turned back to face Josh. 'We've been living every day under siege and in a state of paranoia. Each time I leave the house I have to worry whether a photographer from a newspaper is going to take my picture. I can't go to the shops without complete strangers coming up to me and asking what your policies are on this, that or the other. Basically my life is not my own anymore. I'm living in your shadow. I find myself lecturing Dan and Izzy every day, sometimes several times a day, on how they must behave properly at all times so they don't cause you embarrassment by ending up in the newspapers and ruining your chances of being elected as an MP. How do you think that makes them feel? They're teenagers!' Kim looked as if she was about to burst into tears again. 'They should be able to mess around in public without worrying whether they're doing anything that might reduce your chances of winning the election.' Kim paused for breath and looked at Josh in an accusing manner. 'Dan and Izzy aren't even your children.'

Josh felt hurt, as if he'd been punched in the stomach. He looked at the faces staring at him – Kim, Bruno, Maggie and PC Warner. It was as if he was on trial for some heinous crime and they were sitting in judgment.

'I'm sorry. I had no idea you felt that way. You know I love Dan and Izzy as if they were my own children.'

Josh looked from one stony face to another and then settled his gaze on Maggie, imploring her to speak on his behalf, which she did a moment later in her crisp and authoritative middle class accent.

'Look everyone. We've got to deal with where we are now. We need a plan.' She looked at PC Warner, who nodded.

'I'll get copies of the emails,' said Josh as he jumped up and headed towards the door, seeing an opportunity to escape to the security of his study. But Kim's voice stopped him in his tracks.

'I've got them here,' she said, waving a thin, red cardboard folder in the air. Josh returned slowly to his seat with a quizzical expression on his face.

'Where did you find them?' he said, feeling uncomfortable that Kim had invaded the safe territory of his study.

'In your desk,' she replied.

Josh felt himself blush at the thought of what else she might have found while rifling through his desk drawers.

'Can I see the text message?' said Josh. Kim pushed her mobile phone across the kitchen table. He picked it up and the message was clear.

'If u dont stop the IP and do wot we want Izzy isnt comin bac.'

Josh looked at Kim curiously. 'How could anyone get your mobile number?'

'It's in Izzy's contacts,' said Maggie quickly. 'But her phone is switched off.'

'So it can't be traced.'

'No. But the police are contacting the mobile company to find out where Izzy was when she last used her phone.'

'We're also examining CCTV footage. There are cameras all over Wimbledon,' said PC Warner.

'What about the emails? Can you trace the senders?' said Bruno.

'That may be difficult. I'll give them to my colleagues in CID. They'll get on to the internet service providers to see if they're willing to give us the information we need. Otherwise we'll have to go to court to get an order to enable us to trace the computers the emails were sent from. But that will take time.'

There was a stunned silence while the assembled company took in the magnitude of the task ahead. Tracing the mobile phone that the text message had been sent from, which may or may not have been registered with a network provider. Examining CCTV footage for the whole of Wimbledon, which could take several hours and may or may not reveal Izzy's movements before she disappeared. Contacting the mobile phone company to get details of calls she'd made around that time. Calling Izzy's friends to see if they knew where she might be. Tracking down the sender or senders of the threatening emails.

'I'd like to look at Izzy's bedroom, please, to see if there are any signs of why she might be missing. Would you mind showing me where it is, Ms Clark?' said PC Warner.

Kim heaved herself up slowly from her chair as if she was lifting a great weight. Maggie and Bruno moved quickly to help her. Josh got up from his seat.

'I'll help you,' he said as he moved towards the door.

'No,' said Kim emphatically. She glared at Josh, who stood still. 'You go back to Maggie's. You've hardly been here over the last few weeks. You have no idea what Izzy's been doing in her room. Anyway, you must have something really important to do for the Internet Party, so you can go and do that.'

Before Josh could even think of a reply Kim turned to Bruno.

'Would you mind staying?'

'Of course not.'

Josh noticed that whereas Maggie had released Kim from her grasp after helping her to stand, Bruno's large hands were still clasped firmly around Kim's right arm and shoulder in a way that made Josh feel uncomfortable. He opened his mouth to speak and then shut it again without uttering a word.

'Come with me,' said Maggie. 'We'll go and talk to the volunteers about these weird emails you've been getting. Some of the people working for us have computer science degrees. They must be able to help us find out who is sending them.' She gestured to Josh to follow and made her way quickly towards the hallway. He nodded to PC Warner and followed Maggie out of the kitchen.

'I'll be in touch soon, Mr Walker,' PC Warner called after him.

Maggie was almost at her front door when Josh caught up with her.

'Why did you do that?' he said angrily.

Maggie turned to face him.

'I did you a favour, Josh. You needed to get out of Kim's house before she said anything stupid.'

'What could be more stupid than to accuse me of being responsible for Izzy's disappearance? I know I'm not exactly her favourite person at the moment but I love Izzy as if she were my own daughter.'

'I know you do,' said Maggie as she unlocked

her front door. 'But that's not the point. Kim isn't being rational and the police are naturally suspicious.'

'Oh, so I'm guilty of kidnapping and murder am I?'

'Now you're being irrational. Calm down and let's try and find out who sent the emails.'

'I can't. You deal with it. I need to think.'

Josh pushed past Maggie and climbed the stairs two at a time and in a matter of seconds he was inside the spare room with the door firmly shut. He lay on the bed and closed his eyes. The room spun around and tiny specks of light flashed inside his head. He grasped the sides of the bed and tried to breath slowly to calm his mind.

In a large loft room a small girl sat on the floor and examined the marks on her arms. She felt hungry and exhausted. A packet of biscuits lay beside her uneaten. She could hear noises below but, unlike the sounds of her home, they were unfamiliar. Izzy felt empty and alone.

CHAPTER
TWENTY-TWO

Wimbledon police station was only five minutes walk away from Horatio Road. Josh and Kim made their way slowly towards the large red brick building in Crown Road, as if they had no desire ever to reach their destination. They hadn't spoken since Kim had told Josh to leave her house the night before. Neither of them had ever stepped inside the police station, although they'd walked past it virtually every day on their way to work or to the nearby shopping centre. As they gingerly climbed the steps to the entrance, they narrowly missed colliding with two hooded youths who burst through the double doors, swearing and waving pieces of paper in the air.

Josh felt like a goldfish in a bowl as the doors slammed shut behind him. The small square room had large glass panels along three sides, one looking out into the street and the others flanked by empty corridors. He counted that there were ten people in the room including Kim and himself. Some had their heads down and were reading or texting on their mobile phones while others simply stared into space. The room smelled of officialdom.

A male police officer seated behind a glass screen at the end of the room was busy taking down details from a blonde woman wearing a white fake fur coat. Another woman stood nearby whom Josh guessed was a store detective judging by her demeanour. A man of about fifty wearing a dirty grey raincoat was bent over in a far corner of the reception area frantically writing down words in a notepad that were being spoken to him by a woman in broken English. Josh tried to work out what nationality she was. Her accent indicated that she might be Eastern European but he had no idea of which country she originated from.

Josh assumed the man was a duty solicitor. His face looked haggard, no doubt from late night calls to the police station.

Kim looked at her watch. The appointment with Detective Sergeant Mike Spalding had been scheduled for ten o'clock and it was now five minutes to ten. Exactly five minutes later a light brown coloured door opened next to where the police officer was sitting and a slim young man wearing a smart grey pin striped suit stuck his head into the room. His small dark eyes flashed around the reception area and landed upon Kim and Josh.

'Mr and Mrs Walker?'

Josh almost looked around to see who the man was speaking to. He wasn't used to being addressed as Mr Walker. His students and colleagues called him Josh. He saw Kim stand up and move towards the open door and he followed her. She disliked being called Mrs Walker but she didn't correct the young man. Kim had decided to use her maiden name after she separated from Richard. She would still answer to her married name at Dan and Izzy's school, but the rest of the time she was known as Ms Clark.

Josh thought Detective Sergeant Mike Spalding looked about eighteen years old, although he must have been in his twenties. He didn't shake hands or speak but led Kim and Josh along a series of grey corridors to a room with a dark brown wooden plaque on the door. When Josh saw the words 'INTERVIEW ROOM' it suddenly dawned on him that he and Kim might be regarded as suspects in relation to Izzy's disappearance. As they were both ushered into the room his palms started to feel sweaty and he became sure that a guilty expression had crept over his face. He quickly glanced around to find something in which he could catch sight of his own reflection.

One of the walls had a long mirror that stretched all along its top half. Josh stared at the startled face before him. Was that his face? He rarely looked at himself in a mirror. Occasionally he would quickly check his appearance in the small mirror in the hallway before rushing out of the front door or in the bathroom when cleaning his teeth at the start and end of each day. Josh's face looked tired and drawn from having hardly slept the night before. He glanced at Kim, who was standing next to him in front of a large brown wooden table. Her eyes were red and swollen from crying. They looked empty, as if they'd given up every tear they had to give.

Detective Sergeant Mike Spalding gestured to Kim and Josh to sit down at the table. Still no pleasantries from his direction, just minimal formalities to get the job done as quickly as possible. Presumed guilty until proven innocent, thought Josh as he turned the words backwards and forwards in his mind like a meditative chant. Suddenly his musings were interrupted when a young woman came into the room. She was of medium height and looked like a female version of DS Spalding. She had the same spiky brown hair and her dark eyes darted back and forth as she pulled up a chair and sat down at the table next to her fellow officer.

'This is my colleague, Detective Constable Emily Willis.' The young woman nodded, adjusted her black suit jacket and turned her head towards her 'boss'.

'Right,' said DS Spalding. 'Thanks for coming in.' Josh managed a nod while Kim stayed rigid, holding her facial muscles tight as if her face might crumble and fall to the floor in pieces if she were to let go. DS Spalding started up the tape recorder that sat to one side of him on the table. Josh anticipated the words that he'd heard so often when watching police dramas on TV.

'You do not have to say anything. But it may harm your defence if you do not mention when questioned something which you later rely on in Court. Anything you do say may be given in evidence.'

But what Josh in fact heard was DS Spalding

explaining that it was standard operating procedure to record interviews with witnesses as it was much more efficient than writing and would ensure an accurate record. He then went on to state the time, date and location of the interview and the names of those present in the room.

'I just wanted to ask you both for a bit more detail in relation to the events that led up to Izzy's disappearance.'

Events that led up to, events that led up to, Josh repeated to himself in his mind. The police always talked of events leading up to something. It was a roundabout way of asking what had happened. He could hardly remember what he'd eaten for breakfast let alone what else had occurred the day before.

Fortunately for Josh and despite being in a state of extreme shock, Kim was able to recall every tiny detail of the 'events leading up to Izzy's disappearance'. She rose to the occasion and put on her 'best mother in the world performance' by managing to describe exactly what Izzy had been wearing when she'd last seen her daughter and even what they'd said to each other.

According to Kim there had been no row, no cross words had been spoken and she could think of no reason why Izzy might have run away. Josh was impressed with how gently DS Spalding questioned Kim, never once making her upset or suggesting that she'd done anything wrong. Detective Constable Emily Willis had asked Kim a couple of questions, but had spent most of her time bent over sheets of paper with the words 'Witness Statement' written at the top of each page. Her handwriting was a series of squiggles that flew off her pen onto the piece of paper she was writing on. Josh couldn't see Emily's eyes, as they remained facing firmly downwards, but he imagined them darting back and forth as she wrote.

Now it was Josh's turn to answer questions. DS Spalding leaned back in his chair and attempted to make himself appear larger than he was. Josh looked at the young woman and man before him and he felt old. The thought momentarily amused him, but when he saw the expression on DC Willis's face he felt uncomfortable. She was looking straight at him and her dark eyes pierced his soul. He could feel them inside his head searching around for the truth, the whole truth and nothing but the truth. Was that a look of pity he saw on her face or was it a sneer? Perhaps she felt sympathy for Kim or Izzy, maybe even for Josh himself. He couldn't tell what she might be thinking as her face was blank.

DS Spalding adopted a different approach when questioning Josh to the one he'd used to interview Kim. 'Nice Cop' quickly became 'Nasty Cop'. After asking Josh about 'the events leading up to Izzy's disappearance', DS Spalding took a line of questioning that made Josh feel as if he was playing the part of a suspect in a crime thriller.

'Izzy didn't like the Internet Party, did she Mr Walker?'

'We didn't really discuss it.'

'Oh come on, Mr Walker, Izzy was worried that you would leave her mother if you were elected as a Member of Parliament.'

'That's rubbish.' Josh's words spurted out in a more defensive tone than he'd intended.

'Izzy was depressed by the affect your preoccupation with the Internet Party and your absence from the family home was having on her mother.' DS Spalding glanced at Kim and then looked back at Josh. 'Isn't that right Mr Walker?'

Josh turned and looked at Kim for the first time since they'd both entered the interview room. Kim didn't move her head to face him but Josh could see tears welling up in her eyes. He turned away before she might blink and send an avalanche of sadness racing down her cheeks.

'How would you describe your relationship with your step-daughter?'

Josh had never really thought of Izzy as his step-daughter. Izzy was Izzy, a free spirit for whom he felt minimal responsibility most of the time.

'Izzy and I get on well,' said Josh. He spoke with conviction as if he really believed that to be the case. The detective's quizzical look made him wonder if he should say more. He glanced sideways at Kim for reassurance but she stared straight ahead as if in some kind of trance. DS Spalding let out a slow deep breath and shuffled his papers.

'Izzy's disappearance, this is good publicity for you, isn't it Mr Walker? Good publicity for the Internet Party. I expect this will soon be front page news, if it isn't already.'

Josh felt a sudden shock jolting his body as if he'd touched an electric fence. He hadn't looked at the newspaper that morning. Neither had he turned on the TV, radio or computer. He hadn't even checked his phone for messages. Suddenly Kim burst into tears and Josh felt compelled to wrap an arm around her shoulders. She froze but didn't push him away.

'I don't know what you're suggesting but this interview doesn't seem to be getting us any closer to finding Izzy, which was presumably the purpose of us coming here.'

Josh's voice sounded authoritative, as if he was expounding some important political theory to a lecture hall full of students. He felt himself taking control of the situation as he stood up.

'Is that all you need to know because I think I should take Ms Clark home, don't you?'

DS Spalding and DC Willis exchanged glances. This meant nothing to Josh but it must have made sense to each of them as they stood up at exactly the same time and pushed their chairs back to indicate that the interview was over.

'I'm very sorry,' said Emily. She opened a drawer and handed Kim a small packet of tissues. She gave Josh a look of disapproval.

'Thanks for coming in. We'll be in touch,' said DS Spalding as he showed them out of the room and back along the maze of corridors, each indistinguishable from the next. Josh had a host of questions he wanted answers to. Exactly what were the police doing to find Izzy? What should he and Kim do if the kidnapper made contact with them? What should they say if they were approached by the media? But Josh didn't want to prolong the agony any longer.

'A family liaison officer will be in touch with you in the next couple of hours. You can ask them for any information you need. Here's my card,' said DS Spalding. 'Call me at any time.'

Kim and Josh shuffled out of the Police Station hoping they wouldn't be seen by anyone they knew. To their great relief there were no reporters ready to interview them and no photographers to take pictures. Josh felt tempted to drop into the local shopping centre opposite the Police Station and gather up a bundle of newspapers, but he feared that his photograph might be emblazoned across their front pages. He decided that he'd look at them online instead. Josh held Kim's arm as they walked back to her house. He felt unable to say anything until she gave him permission by speaking to him, but she said nothing.

As they turned into Horatio Road Josh's stomach clenched itself into a fist. Richard's brand new red Porsche was parked outside Kim's house next to Josh's murky grey dilapidated Saab convertible. The car had a personalised number plate, RIC H1, which Josh regarded as obscenely ostentatious. Dan called it a 'prick car' and Kim dismissed it as a product of Richard's midlife crisis. Izzy enjoyed riding in the Porsche and defended her father whenever Kim or Dan made fun of him.

'I'll handle this,' said Kim as Josh turned his key in the front door. He stood back to let her into the hallway. He could hear the sound of two male voices with music in the background. Kim walked confidently into the living room while Josh loitered in the hallway.

Suddenly Richard burst out of nowhere and Josh found himself pinned to a wall. Richard was six feet six inches tall with broad shoulders and he weighed sixteen stone. He stank of alcohol and his face was red and covered in sweat. Josh could hardly breathe as Richard lifted his lesser physique off the ground and gripped his throat with both hands. He felt as if he might pass out at any time. He could hear shouting but it seemed far away even though he could see Richard's mouth moving frantically in front of his face.

'You're dead meat. If my daughter isn't found, you're dead meat.'

'Richard, let him go, Richard,' shouted Kim.

'Dad, get off him. Please, you're going to kill him,' pleaded Dan.

As quickly as Richard had grabbed him and thrust him against the wall, Josh found himself falling to the floor. Now Richard was on his knees, holding his head in his hands, sobbing over and over again.

'Izzy, my Izzy.'

With help from Kim and Dan, Josh managed to stand up, although he felt dizzy and his throat hurt. Then the three of them watched as a man so used to presiding over situations he could control, a highly respected corporate lawyer turned into a blubbering wreck.

Josh stood rigid, afraid to move in case Richard attacked him again. Dan glared at his father with an expression of disgust. He had positioned himself so that Richard would have to get past him in order to confront Josh. A few minutes passed and Josh started to feel better.

Once Kim felt that he was no longer in danger, she disappeared into the kitchen, followed by Dan a few seconds later. Richard reminded Josh of the Hunchback of Notre Dame in a cartoon film he'd taken Dan and Izzy to watch at the cinema when they were younger. He waited while the man's large frame gradually stopped shaking and his sobbing subsided. He felt it would be cowardly to leave and he wanted to show Richard that despite almost being strangled to death, he was not a lesser being. After several minutes Richard raised his head and stood to face Josh. His eyes were red and puffy and his blonde hair tinged with grey was plastered across his forehead. Josh thought he looked like a broken man, quite different from the usually upright, smart suited city slicker with coiffed hair. Richard stood up, brushed his hair back from his face, pulled a handkerchief from his trouser pocket and blew his nose loudly.

'I need some air. Come with me Josh,' Richard pleaded. After a minute's silence Josh replied.

'So long as you don't try and kill me again.'

'I'm so sorry,' spluttered Richard. 'I don't know what came over me. I just couldn't help myself.'

'You know I treat Izzy like she's my own daughter. I would never do anything to hurt her or put her life at risk.'

'I know Josh. Please can we …'

Richard pointed to the front door. As he opened it a welcome rush of fresh air filled the hallway. The two men didn't speak as they crossed the road and headed towards the park. Josh was relieved to see that it was full of people, parents playing with their children, men in suits eating their sandwiches and young women sunbathing on the grass. He breathed a sigh of relief. There was no way that Richard would murder him in broad daylight in front of everyone. Josh motioned towards an empty bench and the two men sat down.

'I blame myself for all this. I've been a lousy father,' said Richard. Josh was not about to disagree so he said nothing.

'You can't have it all, Josh. I realise that now. I've lost my wife and my kids.' He wiped a tear from his left eye. 'They'll never forgive me, Josh. I know that. Ok, so I've got a pot of money. Do you know how much I made last year?'

Josh managed to shake his head. He had no desire to hear what was coming next.

'Seven hundred thousand pounds … after tax.'

Josh had no concept of what that figure meant. All he knew was that it would take him well over ten years to earn such an enormous sum of money.'

'Seven hundred thousand pounds, in one year, but I have no relationship with my kids. Dan hates me. Izzy tries to love me but I've hurt her and I keep on hurting her because I can't love Kim any more and Izzy wants us to be a happy family again.' Josh thought about commenting on Richard's monologue but decided that he would probably say something wrong so he kept quiet. Eventually Richard turned to face him.

'Don't do what I did, Josh. I took Kim and the kids for granted. I put all my efforts into being a top city lawyer. I worked sixteen hour days and often all night. I lost my perspective. The law firm became the centre of my universe. I ate all my meals at work, I slept at work, I had affairs in the office and it all seemed normal because everyone else was doing the same thing.'

Josh listened to what Richard was saying. It was a world he had no knowledge of, a world of deals worth millions, of meetings going on all night, of entertaining clients at lap dancing clubs and of drinking vast amounts of champagne costing thousands of pounds.

'You could make the same mistake Josh. You could let the Internet Party take over your life. Perhaps it has already. I know that Kim is unhappy. Izzy told me that politics is changing you. She said that you no longer have any time for her and that you had forgotten to take her to dance practice a couple of times.'

Josh bit his lip as anger started to well up inside him. Who was Richard to criticise Josh for forgetting to take his daughter to her wretched dance practice? Why wasn't

Richard taking his own children to their various activities?

'You are fortunate, Josh. Dan and Izzy respect you because you've shown that you care about them. Don't throw that respect away, just for the sake of five minutes of fame.'

Izzy slept fitfully until she was woken by the dawn. The old mattress on the bare floorboards made her feel as if her limbs were sticks pressing into her body. There was no blind or curtains covering the window and the walls were bare. The mattress was the only piece of furniture in the room. The sleeping bag Izzy had been given was too thin to be warm and she had little flesh on her small frame. Even sleeping in her clothes couldn't stop her from shivering. She felt vulnerable and sad. The day ahead seemed empty and uncertain. Suddenly Izzy froze as she heard the sound of footsteps at the bottom of the stairs leading up to the attic. She tried to slow her breathing to a point where it made no sound at all but started to feel dizzy. She slid down into the sleeping bag and tried to flatten her body into the mattress so that she became invisible. Izzy listened as the footsteps came closer.

CHAPTER
TWENTY-THREE

The monitor for the CCTV cameras sat quietly humming away to itself in one corner of the 'control centre', which was the name that had been given to Maggie's large living area. Josh sat a few feet away staring at one of the computer screens that were lined up along a wall on one side of the room. He sat alone as the rest of Maggie's 'team' had finally crept off to their warm and comfortable beds.

The picture on the monitor switched every few seconds from the front to the back of the house in a wide sweeping motion. It was compulsive viewing, even though there was nothing much to see. Midnight was approaching and Horatio Road was empty apart from a few parked cars. The replica Edwardian streetlight immediately outside the front of the house enabled clear night vision so that anyone walking along the road could be seen, but there was no one out and about tonight. When the picture switched to the back garden it became fuzzy and blurred unless a fox or a cat moved and triggered one of the security lights to switch itself on.

Josh's eyes were suddenly drawn to the monitor as a large car slid slowly across the screen. Seconds later two other vehicles of similar size and shape cruised past the front of the house. Then they were gone. Josh moved his chair closer to the monitor as the fuzz of the back garden seemed to last forever. For some reason he felt uncomfortable, not quite in fight or flight mode, but unsettled, as if he knew someone was watching. The three cars had a sense of eeriness about them. He couldn't be sure because it was dark but he thought they had blacked out windows.

Josh bent forward and pressed a button on the monitor to run the picture back and then he watched as the cars rolled across the screen. He moved the picture forwards and backwards to see if he could spot a face in a window or a distinguishing mark on one of the vehicles.

Josh froze as he reset the monitor. The three dark coloured vehicles were parked in a line immediately outside Maggie's house. He was aware that one part of his mind was telling him to transport his body to the hallway and press the panic button by the front door, but his body refused to move. A more rational part of his mind told him to calm down. If he pressed the panic button the alarm monitoring station would alert the police who'd come rushing round to find three cars parked outside. So what? He could imagine just how facetious and unimpressed they would be after being called out urgently to a scene of three parked cars when they were needed to deal with violent crime elsewhere.

Josh watched as two men wearing dark suits and earpieces got out of the back of the first car. Then he walked quickly into the hallway and stood by the front door. He could pretend that no one was at home and if the men tried to break the door down he could press the panic button. That would create a huge commotion of bells ringing, lights flashing and sirens wailing which would wake up the whole neighbourhood and send people rushing out of their houses into the street.

Josh squinted through the spy hole in the otherwise solid wooden front door. He felt reassured that no one could see him looking out. The two men who were standing on the doorstep were tall and muscular with short hair. They looked shifty in the way that they cast their eyes about, turning their heads backwards and forwards from the door to the street. Yet they also seemed straight laced and official like the secret servicemen Josh had seen on TV guarding US presidents.

One of the men pressed the doorbell and sound rang out through the emptiness of the house. Josh thought how stupid he was to be alone. Maggie had gone to visit her parents overnight in Tunbridge Wells and Bruno was away on business. Josh could easily have persuaded one of the team to stay with him but he had relished being alone until now. The bell rang again and a voice inside his head told him to decide whether to answer the door. If he pretended not to be in the men might break it down and that would put him in a worse position than he was now. Josh swallowed hard and pressed the intercom button.

'Who is it? He spoke with as much authority in his voice as he could muster. The palms of his hands were sweaty and he felt afraid.

'Is that Mr Josh Walker?' The man spoke with an upper class British accent and Josh felt relieved that he was neither American nor Italian. He had expected to hear a voice from an old gangster movie.

'Who are you?' Josh replied.

'Is that Mr Walker?'

'Who wants to speak with him?'

'The Prime Minister.'

There was a short silence in which Josh imagined that he must either be dreaming or that he'd inadvertently sleep walked onto a film set.

'The Prime Minister,' Josh repeated in a tone of surprise and disbelief.

'Yes. The Prime Minister wants a meeting with Mr Walker, now and in private.'

Josh almost laughed out loud. He allowed himself a suppressed chuckle, which made him feel more relaxed.

'If the Prime Minister wants to meet Mr Walker he will have to get out of the car.'

'We were rather hoping that Mr Walker would come to the car,' said the voice with the cut glass accent. Josh assumed that he must be from MI5 or MI6 or perhaps he was just a sharp shooting bodyguard who used to be in the SAS. They must be carrying guns, thought Josh. There was no way that he was going out of the front door and getting into a strange car.

'If the Prime Minister wants to meet me he can come inside the house.'

There was no reply for a while and Josh's view through the spy hole was limited so he ran into the living room and set the CCTV monitor so that it was fixed on the three cars. He could see one of the men bending down and speaking to someone inside the middle car while the other man stood beside him looking up and down the street. Then two other men got out of the front and rear vehicles. They had the same short haircuts and were wearing similar dark suits. One went to the left and the other went to the right and they both disappeared from the frame of the CCTV monitor.

Josh was transfixed and he stayed watching the screen for what seemed hours but must only have been minutes. Then he saw movement and a hunched up figure in a dark suit emerged from the middle car. He could see it was a man but his face was shrouded from view by the two burly secret servicemen, police officers, bodyguards, or whatever they were. Horatio Road had been deserted while the scene unfolded. They chose the right time to come here, thought Josh as he watched the huddle of men slip quietly up the front path. The doorbell rang and Josh moved slowly towards the front door. He looked through the spy hole and saw what he assumed to be the face of the Prime Minister.

He'd only ever seen him before on TV so he took the opportunity of literally being face to face to examine what he saw in more detail. Josh felt as if he was playing a part in a film and this made him feel completely calm when he went to open the front door.

The Prime Minister stood in between his henchmen. 'Mr Walker, I presume.' He shook Josh's hand with a firm grasp, as if to say, 'I'm in charge here.'

'Please call me Josh.'

The Prime Minister nodded and entered the hallway. The two henchmen started to follow but he indicated that they should wait outside. The men stepped back and assumed positions of vigilance. Josh closed the front door and ushered the Prime Minister into the living area with its bank of computer screens, tables and chairs.

'Would you like to sit down?' Josh pointed to the large black leather sofa in the dining area that seamlessly joined the living room.

'You've got a lot of space here. I like high ceilings.' The Prime Minister surveyed the room.

'The house has been extended at the back,' said Josh pointing towards the modern kitchen with its wall to ceiling glass doors.

'It's very cramped at Number Ten.' The Prime Minister smiled, pulled out a chair from the long, glass topped dining table and sat down. He gestured to Josh to do the same.

'I expect you want to know why I'm here.' Josh nodded. 'Well, you wouldn't come to my place so I decided to come to yours.'

Josh ran through what to say in reply. He felt he owed the man an explanation as to why he hadn't been prepared to go to Downing Street. Because he knew that a photo of him entering Number Ten would have been splashed all over the media. How he would be seen to surrender to the status quo by accepting his place as a lesser being, one to be controlled rather than one in control.

'This isn't exactly my place,' said Josh, steering the conversation away from the subject of why he hadn't been prepared to go to Number Ten. 'The house belongs to another member of the Internet Party, a woman called Maggie and her partner Bruno. I expect you've read about her.' The Prime Minister nodded and leaned forward with his arms resting on the glass surface. His expression suddenly became very serious.

'I want to speak to you, Josh, about the forthcoming general election. I can understand why you set up the Internet Party. But the purpose of my visit tonight is to ask you to disband it.'

Josh nearly laughed out loud. The Internet Party currently had over ten million supporters registered online and the number was growing every day. Even if he wanted to close the party down, he was only one individual and there were many who would take his place. The Prime Minister continued his speech.

'I've come here to invite you and your supporters to join my party.' Josh felt a mixture of anger and disbelief at being patronised.

'I'm willing to guarantee you and Maggie safe seats at the next election and I'll offer you a position on the front bench if everything goes according to plan.'

This was the trouble with traditional politicians, thought Josh. They want to manipulate and control people for their own ends. He decided to fight back.

'Do you know how many supporters we have?' said Josh.

'I've seen the Internet Party website.'

'How many people support your party? How many paid-up members do you have? The opinion polls say...'

'I don't take any notice of them,' the Prime Minister sharply interrupted. Politicians only take notice of opinion polls when it suits them, thought Josh.

'Look.' The Prime Minister was beginning to sound cross. 'I'm offering you the chance of real power as a real politician. This isn't some kind of a game. What you're doing could have serious consequences for the stability of this country. We could end up with a hung Parliament, with several small political parties, some very right wing, some very left wing and no cohesion, no proper decision-making and therefore no progress.'

The Prime Minister leaned back and sat staring at

Josh with his arms folded across his chest.

· 'I think what you mean is that for the first time in many years people are going to be able to vote for a new party that might actually win the election, improve people's living standards and restore democracy in this country,' said Josh.

'But my party has improved society,' protested the Prime Minister.

'In my view the majority of politicians in all parties have lost sight of the needs of most of the population. In fact there's a greater divide now between rich and poor than ever before.'

The Prime Minister shifted awkwardly in his seat and the friendly expression he'd worn when he first arrived had left his face.

'So what are these needs that we are supposed to have lost sight of?'

'People need secure jobs in which they are well treated, homes they can afford to buy and maintain, a high standard of education for their children and sufficient good quality food. They need to be in control of their lives and the environments in which they live. People need to be part of a community that cares for and supports its members.'

'Fine words Josh. So you think I and my fellow MPs have lost sight of these things?'

'In my view all politicians have lost sight of the needs of ordinary people, not just those in your party,' said Josh. He was beginning to feel pleased with himself.

'So what does your number two think? Does she agree with your views? I thought she was a Tory.' Josh saw the Prime Minister's lips curl up slightly at the sides in something of a wry smile, or was it a sneer?

'Maggie is not my number two and she's not a Tory. She's my equal, as are all the members and supporters of the Internet Party. She used to vote for the Conservative Party but she feels they have lost their way. Maggie wants to see a return to traditional Conservative principles such as businesses adopting a paternalistic approach to their employees by caring for their welfare and sharing profits with them. She wants companies to provide job security, crèche facilities and decent pensions that cannot be ravaged by asset strippers. Maggie objects to people being treated as commodities by global players who move their businesses overnight to places where there is cheap labour and poor working conditions in pursuit of huge profits, destroying the communities they leave behind. As you know, many of these businesses pay virtually no tax in the countries where they operate while giving their top employees ridiculously high pay and extortionate bonuses.'

The Prime Minister shifted in his seat and yawned. 'So you're an old fashioned socialist and Maggie's a traditional Tory. How can you agree on anything?'

'Actually we agree on most things. We want to bring back our troops from abroad. We intend to set up compulsory national community service for all teenagers during school holidays using school buildings and paying teachers and parents to run the schemes. We believe that people claiming benefits who are fit and able to work should do community work for two days each week to keep up their work ethic. We would halve class sizes, cut all bureaucracy in schools and make sure that children reached a decent standard of education before leaving school. Would you like me to continue or do you want to look at our website? You won't find lots of complicated policies but there are certain core values.'

'Mr Walker. Society is too complicated these days to be run on the basis of core values. There are many threats to the future safety, security and stability of this country. Do you think the people in your party have the necessary skills and experience to confront these?'

'Yes, I do,' said Josh, emphasising each word.

'Well, my offer remains open should you wish to

change your mind,' said the Prime Minister as he pulled himself up from the chair, his gnarled hands resting for a minute on the table. His face looked grey and drawn, his eyes exhausted from lack of sleep.

'I'm very sorry about Izzy. You and your partner must be devastated.' Josh nodded. 'This may not be much comfort to you but I have some idea of what you're going through. I worry about my children constantly, not only their safety but how they're coping with life at Number Ten. People coming and going all the time, a lack of privacy. My wife and I have little time for family life and I know the kids are put under huge strain at times, which I can't often alleviate because I'm always at an important meeting or dealing with some crisis.'

Josh started to speak but the Prime Minister raised his hand to indicate that he hadn't finished his soliloquy.

'They are great levellers, children. They don't care how important you are to the outside world. If they want you to take them anywhere or do something then that's their right. It's hard to keep a balance.'

The Prime Minister walked slowly around the glass table tracing his finger along its edge as he stared at the blank white walls and computer screens.

'The newspapers are the worst, Josh. Be very careful when dealing with the media but particularly journalists. Carry a recording device and use it whenever you speak to a reporter. Don't trust anyone in the media. There will be people who pretend to be your friend but they will stab you in the back. Play their game better than they do and play to win. Every newspaper, TV station, journalist, producer, presenter or whatever guise they appear in has their own agenda. Make sure you know what it is and that you're one step ahead. Insist on being told what questions you're going to be asked before recording or filming begins. Look out for pitfalls. Don't react to traps they set. Manoeuvre yourself around them.'

Josh was beginning to wonder what he'd got himself into.

'You make public life sound like guerrilla warfare.'

The Prime Minister gave a hollow laugh. 'It goes with the territory.'

Josh was starting to feel angry as he thought about the way in which the press had behaved over the phone hacking scandal. All those innocent victims whose lives had been turned upside down, their reputations in tatters after being pilloried for things they hadn't done. He felt sudden fear as to what might happen to him.

'I can't believe the media think that Izzy's disappearance is some sort of publicity stunt,' spluttered Josh.

The Prime Minister looked at him long and hard.

'They don't really think that.'

Josh rubbed his forehead. Suddenly he felt exhausted.

'But that's what's being suggested on the front pages of every newspaper. Some of the online blogs are even saying I've abducted Izzy myself. I'm the wicked stepfather. Next I'll be accused of murder.' Josh closed his eyes and rubbed his face with his hands.

'Get a good lawyer, if you haven't already got one. Sue everyone who defames you. That's the only way to stop them.'

Josh sighed, removed his hands from his face and watched as the Prime Minister walked around the room like a caged animal, half-heartedly looking for a way out. 'I'll give you as much help as I can to find Izzy.'

'Thanks.'

'Think about what I've said. You won't win the election but you'll muddy the waters for the rest of us.'

The two men stood for a few seconds in a shared moment of understanding.

Josh led the Prime Minister to the front door, opened

it, shook his hand and watched as his entourage disappeared back into the night, leaving him to wonder if he'd been dreaming. He stood for a while in front of the CCTV monitor staring at the shady image of the deserted street where the three black cars had waited patiently while he, Josh Walker, had talked with the Prime Minister, the most powerful man in Britain.

He thought how excited Izzy would be if she knew he'd met the Prime Minister. His heart sank as his mind thrashed around trying to find an image of the girl that did not evoke sadness. He tried to conjure up memories of Izzy when she'd played the part of Tinkerbell in a school production of Peter Pan. An image of a small girl wearing a green and gold tunic with pink tights flitted across Josh's mind. Her dance steps had been so light that she appeared to float above the stage.

Where was Izzy now?

Was she still alive?

Josh's mood dropped like a stone from the elevated fantasy of the Prime Minister's visit to the dismal reality of Izzy's disappearance.

CHAPTER TWENTY-FOUR

'Why didn't you call me?' said Maggie crossly.

She spoke so loudly that she almost shouted the words at Josh even though he was only a few feet away from where she was standing. He half opened one eye and watched as her tight white shirt threatened to burst its buttons from the heaviness of her breathing. He had never before seen her look so cross. Maggie stood in her living room with her hands placed firmly on her hips, staring down at Josh as he lay on the black leather sofa. She was wearing light blue jeans and strappy sandals. Her blonde hair lay in waves across her shoulders. Even when it hadn't been brushed it looked as if each lock had been put deliberately into place.

Maggie had returned to London earlier than expected from her parents' house in Tunbridge Wells and had found Josh asleep on her sofa. He still lay there with his limbs refusing to move and with one eye half open.

'I'm hardly going to start phoning you up in the middle of the night, am I?' Josh protested. He sounded exactly as he felt, extremely tired and very annoyed that he'd been woken up so early.

'Yes, you should have called me. I always keep my mobile switched on.' Josh could hear from the tone of Maggie's voice that she was determined to have an argument. He managed to get one eye completely open. He looked around the room and wondered whether the events of the previous night had really happened or if it had all been a dream.

'Why are all these computers on standby? We don't want the Internet Party accused of contributing to climate change, do we?' said Josh.

'Don't try and change the subject. Anyway you were the last person awake in this room last night, so you should have switched them off.'

Maggie sighed pointedly and walked off to make herself coffee in the kitchen. Meanwhile Josh managed to get his other eye fully open and after expending a huge amount of energy, raised the top half of his body into a sitting position. Maggie sat down on a computer chair a few feet away from Josh so that the tantalising smell of freshly brewed coffee drifted past his nostrils. She'd deliberately chosen a chair that was higher than the sofa that Josh was sitting on.

As the Internet Party gained in popularity and received greater attention from the media, Josh had noticed how Maggie was doing more to exert power over the organisation. Now that she was on unpaid leave from her job she seemed to spend every waking moment checking or sending emails or messages on Twitter or Facebook, scouring the media for articles about the Internet Party or directing the activities of the band of volunteers who came and went from her home at all hours of the day and night. Virtually every room was now being used as an office. Josh had lost count of the number of computers in the house. Laptops and files adorned virtually every surface.

The upstairs bedroom where Josh slept was the smallest in the house and overlooked the back garden. The single bed took up half of the room. Then there was a small clothes rail with a few pieces of clothing hanging on it and a suitcase containing every other item of necessity that Josh had brought with him from Kim's house. The room had an atmosphere that felt temporary, which of course it was. Josh didn't really like spending time in Maggie's spare room, but he felt he had no choice in the matter until after the election. He wasn't welcome at Kim's house these days.

'So what else did the Prime Minister say?' demanded Maggie.

Josh tried to remember what he'd already told her. He felt tortured by the aroma of freshly brewed coffee that wafted across the room, but he didn't have the energy to get up and pour himself a cup.

'Bring me a coffee and I'll tell you,' he pleaded in a joking manner. But Maggie sensed that she had the upper hand and she was in no mood for a joke.

'No. You tell me what he said and then I'll make you a coffee.'

Josh knew when he was beaten. He proceeded to give Maggie a full account of the events of the night before. How the three dark coloured ministerial cars had crept up Horatio Road, what the Prime Minister and his entourage of bodyguards had looked like and, as far as he could remember, what had been discussed. Maggie wanted to know every detail down to the colour of the Prime Minister's socks.

'Are you sure they were black? You said before that you thought they were dark blue.'

'Did I? Well, maybe they were.'

'You also said he was wearing a dark blue suit. Are you sure about that?'

Why were some women so obsessed with what people were wearing? He couldn't remember whether the Prime Minister's socks had been black or dark blue and he really didn't care what colour they were. But he didn't want to upset Maggie, especially as he was still waiting for her to bring him a coffee, so he decided to plump for black.

'The suit was definitely dark blue and the socks were black,' said Josh with as much conviction as he could manage.

'And you said his tie was dark red.'

'Definitely.'

If there was one thing Josh was sure of from the night before, it was the colour of the Prime Minister's tie. It always amused him to see politicians wearing ties that bore colours associated with political parties that were not their own. When Josh was a young man, canvassing for votes with his father and grandfather in East Bristol, no self-respecting Labour Party candidate would have worn anything other than a red tie. Blue was a colour that was historically linked with the Conservative Party. However, over the last two decades, as each of the three main parties fought to occupy the so called 'centre ground' in politics, the colours of the ties that members of each party wore had been swapped around, as had many of the parties' policies.

'Did he say anything about Izzy?' said Maggie.

'Who?'

'The PM.'

'Yes, he did, actually.'

'Well, what did he say?'

Maggie spoke impatiently before he'd had a chance to finish his sentence. She obviously hadn't forgiven him and there was no sign that she was going to make him the coffee she'd promised. Josh could have made it for himself, but he still felt in a state of shock and wasn't able to get up from the sofa.

'He was very sympathetic. He said he understood how hard it was for the children of politicians, being in the media spotlight, that sort of thing.'

'What else did he say?'

'He said he knew that Izzy's disappearance wasn't a publicity stunt and that he would give us as much help as he could to find her.'

'What a nice man,' said Maggie with a hint of sarcasm to her voice that Josh felt was unfair. But he wasn't going to argue with her now.

'The Prime Minister also said that the media would print what they wanted, regardless of whether it was true or not.'

'That's just what we need,' said Maggie, rolling her eyes.

'The strange thing was that he didn't look at all like

he does on TV. He seemed much more humble and less in control, almost human,' said Josh with a smile.

Maggie burst out laughing and as Josh joined in he felt a sense of relief that the ice between them had melted. They shared the moment and revelled in the fact that the Internet Party had been shown reverence by the leader of the government.

'I'll get you that coffee I promised,' said Maggie as she slid off the computer chair. She bent down and touched Josh's left shoulder in a reassuring gesture of solidarity, which sent a tingling sensation throughout his body and into his toes. He looked down, half expecting them to be glowing.

Josh hadn't seen Kim since their visit to the police station a few days ago. He decided to use the meeting with the Prime Minister as a reason for dropping in on her and to check about Izzy. He felt buoyed up by the visit and the invitation he'd received. It had given him a feeling of credibility that he hadn't experienced before. Surely Kim would be impressed. Josh wanted her to feel proud of him, even if she didn't agree with what he'd been doing with his life. He walked up to Kim's front door with feelings of trepidation and excitement. Josh suddenly realised that he missed her. He wanted to hug her and bury his face in her soft brown curls. At this precise moment he desired Kim in a way that he hadn't for many weeks, perhaps even months. Maggie and her show home lifestyle somehow seemed shallow and empty when compared with the life he'd shared with Kim.

Josh pressed the front doorbell and after a minute or two he heard the familiar sound of footsteps coming along the hallway. Kim answered the door. She looked well apart from the puffiness beneath her eyes, which gave away the fact that she'd been crying. Not for minutes or hours but every day since Izzy had gone missing. Kim stared at Josh.

'Are you going to let me in?'

He still had his key so he could easily have opened the front door himself. But something had stopped him. Kim paused for a moment before stepping back into the hallway and gesturing to Josh to follow her. He could smell the familiar aroma of garlic, onions and tomatoes emanating from the kitchen. He could hear the sound of two male voices and recognised one as belonging to Dan. The other voice seemed familiar but not immediately recognisable. Josh wanted to ask Kim who the voice belonged to. He longed to be able to walk straight into the kitchen, as he'd done so many times before, sit down at the table with a glass of red wine and discuss the day's events with Kim, Dan and Izzy. But he felt unable to do so because everything had changed.

Kim showed Josh into her front room with its old fashioned green patterned wallpaper and its tired beige carpet. She sat down on one of the armchairs and he sat in the other. Kim hadn't spoken since she'd opened the front door with a straightforward 'Hello.'

'Has there been any news about Izzy?' said Josh.

'Not really. The police came round and asked some more questions but they didn't give anything away. How about you?'

'Nothing. Not even a visit from the police. We've got someone looking at the website twenty four hours a day in case the kidnapper makes contact.'

'Oh,' said Kim.

'Are you ok?'

Kim nodded but she was clearly not ok. Josh could see that she was about to burst into tears. He wanted her to cry so that he could throw his arms around her and draw her close to him. He wanted to run his fingers through her hair and wipe the tears from her face. Josh wanted to reassure her that everything would be alright and that Izzy would be found safe and well. But he knew that he was in no position to make such a promise.

Josh got up from his chair and put his arms out to embrace Kim, but she recoiled with a look of horror on her face. Or was it an expression of disgust? He sat back down in the chair with a jolt as if he'd received an electric shock. The confidence he had felt as he'd set off for Kim's house was quickly ebbing away.

'The Prime Minister came to see me,' said Josh, as much to reassure himself as to try and impress Kim.

'I know. Dan told me.' He could tell by the tone of her voice that she was not impressed.

'Look Josh. I don't know why you've come here. I've hardly seen you over the last couple of weeks. But I've been doing a lot of thinking.' Kim paused and he listened as she took a sharp intake of breath.

'It's over, Josh.   Our relationship, partnership, whatever it was. It's finished. I don't love you any more. I wonder if I ever did. I'm not sure if I even like you. Well, what you've become.'

Josh felt sick to the pit of his stomach. A sensation of numbness crept over his body. Even his brain was numb, incapable of forming logical thoughts. He felt in a state of shock. After a few seconds he managed to speak.

'The Prime Minister's offered to give us whatever help we need to find Izzy.'

'I don't need his help,' said Kim defiantly. Just at that moment a head appeared from around the door. 'Dinner's ready. Oh. Hi Josh. I didn't realise you were here.'

Bruno walked confidently into the room as he spoke and held out his right hand. Josh stood up and took the hand, which felt strong and warm. Bruno looked calm and relaxed in a white, open necked shirt with the sleeves rolled up and the trousers from his dark blue pinstriped suit. Kim ignored the two men as they greeted each other and she quickly left the room.

'I'll see you out. We're about to eat,' said Bruno.

Josh found himself following Bruno out of the room

and along the hallway in the direction of the front door. He glanced back in the hope that the kitchen door might be open, but it was closed. Josh felt in a daze. Most of his belongings were still in this house and yet he clearly wasn't welcome.

'Remember me to Maggie,' said Bruno as he opened the front door.

'I will.'

The two men waved goodbye to each other as Josh set off up the road. What did Bruno mean? Remember me to Maggie. As far as he knew, Bruno and Maggie were still involved in a relationship with each other, although he doubted whether they spent much time together. But that should change after the election, he thought to himself. Josh realised that he hadn't seen much of Bruno recently because he'd either been away on business or staying at Kim's.

After the initial shock Josh had felt when Kim had suggested that Bruno could stay at her house, he'd quickly come round to the idea. It had suited him to get away from the arguments and tensions in Kim's family and to be able to immerse himself in the Internet Party. He had also wanted to be near Maggie. Bruno had accepted Kim's invitation to stay at her house because he'd got fed up with living in what he described as first of all a building site and then an office block. That's what the house he owned with Maggie had become now that it was the headquarters of the Internet Party.

My life is out of control, thought Josh, as he ambled back to his temporary home. Is this what happens to people who get involved in politics? You sign up in the belief that you'll have power, control and the ability to make a difference. But then you find that you are the one who is being controlled, by the media and by people you care about, who you thought cared for you. Josh was relieved to find that Maggie was busy with some of the new volunteers when he got back to her house, so he slipped in quietly and went straight to his room.

He got out a pad of paper and started composing a letter to Kim. He'd been going to send her a text or an email but that seemed too impersonal. He couldn't remember the last time he'd written a letter. After several attempts it read:

Dear Kim

I was shocked and hurt after I saw you today. I love you, Kim. I know that a lot has happened over the last few weeks and that my involvement with the Internet Party has caused you huge upset, damaged our relationship and messed up our family life. I know that you blame me for Izzy's disappearance and you are right to do so. But you are wrong to end our relationship. There are only two weeks left until the election. Please don't make any definite decision until then. I firmly believe that Izzy will be returned to us unhurt. I have people looking for her, trying to make contact with whoever might be holding her. The police have said they believe she's with people who will not wish to harm her.

Please trust me.

I love you.

Josh

He wasn't particularly happy with his fourth and final version of the letter but he decided to send it anyway. He would sneak out of the house later and slip it quietly through Kim's letterbox so that she would find it in the morning.

Izzy was thinking about her family. Tears ran down her cheeks and she made no attempt to stop them. They dripped onto her black leggings, glistened for a second and then sank into the stretchy material. Izzy wanted to be able to look out of the window but it was too high up. All she could see was the sky. She'd been told that no-one ever came up to the attic. She was fed up with eating biscuits and crisps and drinking fizzy drinks. It had all been a big mistake. Izzy put her head in her hands and cried silently.

CHAPTER
TWENTY-FIVE

'I keep thinking I should give up on the Internet Party, said Josh.

Maggie bit her lip and paced up and down in front of where he was sitting on her black leather sofa.

'Don't be pathetic. That's what they want.'

Josh felt weak in Maggie's strong presence.

'Whoever they are,' he said as he looked down and examined the pattern in the newly laid wooden floor. The Internet Party had given him a real sense of purpose for the first time in his life. He had been riding high on the crest of a wave, but now that the wave was crashing all around him he felt he was drowning in a sea of misery. He felt guilty for the self-pity that engulfed him when he should have felt compassion for Kim. But towards her he felt a mixture of anger, resentment and sadness, with all of his emotions so mixed up that none was recognisable.

'Why would anyone want to kidnap Izzy?' Josh shouted.

'To get at you, to wear you down and make you give up,' Maggie shouted back at him. 'That is why you should be more determined to succeed.'

She paused for a few seconds. 'For Izzy's sake.'

Josh envied Maggie for her clarity of purpose and the rigid dogma by which she led her life. Things were either wrong or right. People were either worth knowing or they were a waste of space. Maggie was cool and controlled where Kim was emotional and irrational. At that precise moment in time Josh wished he were Maggie. Her life wasn't cluttered with the obligations, responsibilities and uncertainties that came from living with a woman with teenage children. Izzy's disappearance had brought into sharp focus just how complicated Josh's life had become.

'What did the police say?' said Maggie in an attempt to shake Josh out of his thoughts and into the moment.

'The police? Oh yes, the police. They treated us as if we were suspects, not victims of a crime.'

'Seriously?' Maggie stopped pacing about and looked at Josh. 'That's awful!'

'Well it wasn't quite as straightforward as that,' said Josh. 'The police didn't actually accuse us of committing a crime, but they behaved as if we had.'

'They didn't suggest that you had anything to do with Izzy's disappearance did they? Do you remember that couple on TV? They were accused of kidnapping their own daughter to get money.'

'The police might think that the whole thing is a publicity stunt, to raise the profile of the Internet Party and attract sympathy,' said Josh.

'We'll need more than the sympathy vote to get elected.' Maggie spoke in a light-hearted tone of voice in the hope of cheering him up.

'I'm probably over-reacting. The police didn't actually say Kim and I were suspects. I just felt like we were. Maybe that's because I feel so guilty.'

'Guilty of what? Guilty of standing up for what you believe in and wanting to change society for the better? What is there to feel guilty about?'

Josh wondered how he could possibly convey to Maggie what it felt like to be responsible for the life of another human being. He had realised from the moment that he'd first met her that she felt responsible for nobody apart from herself. Despite the fact that she and Bruno had been involved in a relationship for several years Maggie seemed to be completely independent of him. She had friends with children, but by her own admission she had no concept of what it was like to be responsible for the life of a child. Josh had been exactly the same until he'd fallen in love with Kim and taken on the role of surrogate father to Dan and Izzy. There was no point in continuing this discussion, thought Josh, as Maggie would never understand.

'I'm sorry,' he said. 'Of course I'm committed to the success of the Internet Party. You're right. Whoever has kidnapped Izzy wants us to shut up shop. We'll do the opposite. The kidnapping is bound to generate publicity. Let's make the most of it.'

'That's fighting talk, Josh. Standing up to these people, whoever they are, is the only way of getting Izzy back.'

'I just keep wondering who 'they' might be. I can't believe anyone from the mainstream political parties would kidnap a child. So then I start thinking that some sort of crackpot must have taken her and I just can't bear to consider that possibility.'

'We're a threat to all of the main political parties, Josh. Not just because we might take votes from them, but because we could end up holding the balance of power between them. The smaller parties might be worried that people will vote for the Internet Party instead of them. But it's more likely that they'll be pleased if we take votes away from the larger parties, as that will make the smaller parties seem bigger and more influential.'

Josh loved listening to Maggie when she was in an analytical frame of mind. He started to feel better now that she was in full flow.

'What all of the existing political parties have to fear is disturbance of the status quo and the possibility of a complete change to the currently inadequate and undemocratic process and its institutions,' she said.

'There are a lot of other people who have a vested interest in the current political system continuing,' said Josh. 'There are the banks and insurance companies and the huge global companies that own a large part of the United Kingdom. How do you think they would react to the

Internet Party gaining a majority of the seats in Parliament or even holding the balance of power?'

Maggie rolled her eyes and smiled. 'Oh Josh. Whatever will you say next? Perhaps a foreign government has kidnapped Izzy. Maybe the CIA are involved. They might even be working closely with the British security services to stop the Internet Party from succeeding in its quest. I think you're starting to become a conspiracy theorist.'

'Well, some strange things have been happening. My diaries going missing without any sign of a break-in, for example,' said Josh.

He was partly teasing Maggie but there was also an element of truth in what he'd said. At least she'd cheered him up a little. He always enjoyed talking about politics and philosophy. He was reminded of the 'meaning of life' discussions he'd had in his self-satisfied student days, of late nights spent perched on uncomfortable beds or sitting on the floor in university halls of residence.

Suddenly Dan burst into the room making both Josh and Maggie jump and jolting them back into reality. He was wearing white cricket trousers with bright green stains on the areas around his knees and a white polo shirt, which was unbuttoned as far as it would go. Dan was carrying a large cricket bag, which he slung onto the floor in the middle of the room as he grabbed the remote control for the TV. He clicked the 'on' button and the huge black flat screen TV on the wall flickered into life as the newsreader announced the start of the six o'clock news.

'Izzy's going to be on TV,' Dan panted as he collapsed onto the sofa next to Josh.

'How do you know?' said Maggie.

'Mum called me on the mobile. She saw a trailer for the news a few minutes ago.'

'What did she say? Has Izzy been found?' said Josh.

Dan stared straight ahead at the screen and didn't

appear to have heard him speak.

'This is our top story,' said the newsreader. 'As the Internet Party increases in popularity the thirteen-year-old step-daughter of its leader, Josh Walker, is kidnapped.'

The TV screen was suddenly filled with a photograph of Izzy smiling. She had hated her latest school photo and had pleaded with Kim not to buy it when the order form was sent home. But Kim had liked the picture of her daughter in her navy blue jumper and white shirt, with her hair tied back in a ponytail, so she'd bought it without Izzy knowing. Josh thought how annoyed she would be if she knew Kim had given that particular photo to the police.

The newsreader explained that Izzy had now been missing for several days and that the threat had been made that she would only be returned if the Internet Party were disbanded. Josh was described as the party's 'leader' and his photograph flashed up onto the screen, which to his relief was one that had been taken from the Internet Party website.

'At least they've used decent photos of you and Izzy,' said Maggie. 'But it really annoys me when the media describe you as party leader. They just don't get it do they? We don't have a leader.'

Josh knew that Maggie wanted to be seen as the leader. The role came naturally to her. But they'd agreed when they set the party up that they wouldn't call themselves leaders. There was always too much emphasis put on leaders of political parties by the media.

'It annoys me too,' said Josh. He realised when he spoke that he sounded pathetic. The media constantly referred to him as the party leader and he secretly enjoyed the attention, although only on his own terms. He didn't like being stopped in the street or questioned in the supermarket. Josh knew Maggie was envious and in spite of all her strong words about the dangers of political leaders being given too much credence and power, almost to the point of deification, he knew that she would like more serious attention for herself. But not the type of attention she was getting from the media at present. This took the form of salacious photographs of Maggie in tight fitting shirts showing her cleavage or of her getting in and out of vehicles with her short skirt riding up and exposing her legs to the world.

Josh thought that most of these pictures were extremely flattering, but he kept his views on the subject to himself. Kim called it the 'sexification' of female politicians, although in reality most were portrayed as sexless. The truth of the matter was that it was difficult for an attractive and sexy woman to be taken seriously as a politician, even in the twenty-first century.

'It doesn't make sense,' said Dan, when the news feature on Izzy's disappearance had been replaced by one about a conflict abroad. He spoke quietly, as if he was holding a conversation with himself. 'There's something not quite right about Izzy going missing like that.'

'Like what?' said Josh.

'Oh, I'm not really sure. I just have this feeling.' Dan paused for what seemed an age.

'What sort of feeling?' said Maggie gently.

'Oh, I don't know. I'll work it out. I need to get home and have a shower.'

Without so much as a glance at either Josh or Maggie, Dan jumped up from the sofa, grabbed his cricket bag and dashed out of the room. They watched him as he hurried past the front window and disappeared. Josh looked at Maggie and noticed that she had thin worry lines across her forehead. He'd never noticed them before. Maggie was not a worrier by nature but something was obviously bothering her.

'What did Dan mean, Josh?'

'I've absolutely no idea,' he said, shrugging his shoulders.

'They're very close aren't they?'

'Who?'

'Dan and Izzy.'

'Are they?'

'Well, you should know. You live with them.'

'Did live with them,' said Josh.

He had never thought of Dan and Izzy as having a close relationship. They were so different from each other. Izzy was impulsive, extrovert and creative. She could also be irrational and when she got a 'bee in her bonnet' as Kim would describe it, she could continue an argument well beyond the limits of most people. In contrast, Dan was the calm member of the family. He took after neither his mother nor his father, who were both more like Izzy. Dan was in some ways old for his years and he took life much more seriously than most seventeen-year-olds.

'Dan and Izzy are very fond of each other. Dan must be going through hell,' said Josh.

Suddenly he jumped up from the sofa, rushed to the kitchen and banged his fist hard on the granite work surface. The intense pain he felt made him wail like a wounded animal. He clutched his hand and threw himself back onto the sofa weeping and moaning. Josh hadn't cried for years but now his tears were flooding into the crevices of the leather cushions in a torrent of self-pity. As he buried his face into the damp leather he felt a hand on his head, then two arms around his back and a woman's breasts pressing into him, engulfing him in a wave of emotion that he couldn't immediately identify.

'It's not your fault, Josh,' whispered Maggie. 'It's not your fault.'

Acceptance. That was what he felt. Maggie had accepted him for who he was. Not for the person he could or should be, but for who he was. Kim always wanted him to be someone he could never be.

CHAPTER
TWENTY-SIX

Josh got off the tube at Piccadilly Circus and examined his phone for directions. Then he took out the blue pastel coloured envelope with green handwriting scrawled across it and removed the single sheet of white paper from inside. 'Come Alone!' The words stood out on the page and the message was as clear as the green ink it was written in. Josh had been tempted to tell Kim about the letter. But he knew it would have upset her and she would probably have wanted to come with him. In any case her hopes would have been raised, perhaps unjustifiably, and he didn't want to take that risk. So Josh had done what the letter had ordered and he'd come alone.

He descended the wide stone steps that led down to the basement from the busy street. He pressed the buzzer at the front door and it opened to reveal a large doorman wearing a dinner suit. This attire seemed inappropriate for lunchtime on a weekday. The doorman nodded and looked Josh up and down before opening the door wide and ushering him into a dimly lit foyer with dark gold wallpaper and a deep red carpet. Josh had no idea what to do next as he'd never been to a place like this before. He stood still for a few seconds and allowed his eyes to adjust to the lack of light. He could hear the repetitive heartbeat sound of music and through the opaque glass of the double doors ahead of him he could just make out the silhouettes of shady figures moving about.

Suddenly a voice to his left said, 'Can I take your coat, sir?' Josh turned to see where the voice had come from. A tall, slim young woman stood behind the dark wooden counter of what appeared to be a cloakroom. She had the fine features and pale complexion of a porcelain doll and her face was fixed in a half smile as she reached out a long, thin arm that offered to take his coat. The woman's bleached blonde hair was strained back from her face and was tied up high on the back of her head in the longest ponytail Josh had ever seen. Her perfect figure was scantily clad in a tight-fitting leopard print leotard. He couldn't see her legs but he imagined them to be long and thin like her arms.

'I haven't seen you here before, have I, sir?'

The girl spoke in a soft Eastern European accent, which Josh thought might be Russian. On the other hand it could be Slovakian or Latvian. London was full of people of different nationalities and he wasn't very good at distinguishing one accent from another.

'I'll keep my coat with me if that's ok,' said Josh as he clutched it to him as if it gave him security.

'That's fine, sir.'

The girl's outstretched arm that should have taken his coat now pointed him in the direction of the double doors. Perhaps she's a clockwork doll, thought Josh as he walked forward. He pushed open the doors and was assaulted by a barrage of sound and light. He carefully entered the giant room that stood before him. As his eyes adjusted to the flashing lights he could see a large podium on which the bodies of three young women writhed and slid, climbed and hung in various positions on three tall poles. Josh wished that his coat had magical properties so that he could disappear inside. As he stood transfixed, a young woman with long legs and a huge bust thrust herself in front of him and offered to get him a drink. She was wearing the smallest waitress's outfit he'd ever seen. The woman led Josh to a table in front of the podium and left him sitting there.

He felt hot and uncomfortable even though the air conditioning was sending swathes of cool air down from the ceiling. He looked around and noticed several men in suits who were either staring at the dancers on the podium or being entertained by women who seemed to be determined to get as close as they could without actually touching the men's bodies.

Josh sat quietly sipping the non-alcoholic fruit punch that the waitress had brought him and waited for something to happen. He'd never been to a lap dancing club before and he stared partly in horror but also in admiration at the figures on the podium who were contorting themselves into the most weird positions.

Josh assumed that someone would approach him to tell him why he was there. He didn't have to wait long as after a few minutes a dark-haired woman of about twenty-five started to dance in front of him. Her skin was light brown in colour and her limbs were strong and muscular. There was something harsh about the woman's face despite her perfect make up and fixed smile. Her high heels made her legs look longer than they were. Josh eased himself back on his seat as the woman thrust her pelvis towards him. He fought the urge to escape by reminding himself why he'd come to such a place. He could feel the warmth of the woman's body and smell her perfume as she leaned forward so that her right breast gently touched his left cheek. Josh felt detached from his body, as if he were watching himself in a film.

'Come with me and I'll tell you about Izzy.'

The woman whispered the words so quietly and the music was so loud that Josh wondered whether he'd imagined them. Then she took his hand and led him away from the podium and along a dark corridor. A door opened and Josh found himself in a smaller version of the room he'd been in before. The woman gently pushed Josh onto a large leather sofa, climbed onto a small stage with a pole in the middle and began her routine.

He wanted to shout, 'Tell me about Izzy', but he stopped himself from uttering a word. The woman must have to pretend I'm a real client to avoid arousing suspicion, thought Josh. He cast his eyes around to see if there were surveillance cameras anywhere, but the room was dark. After a few minutes of sliding up and down the pole the woman slid off the podium and settled down on the sofa next to Josh. His feelings of vulnerability had subsided and he was now beginning to feel angry.

'Would you like another drink?'

'No. I want you to tell me where I can find Izzy.'

All kinds of images had been flashing through Josh's mind as he watched the woman dance. He thought he could see needle marks on her arms, but if he was right they were well disguised. Was Izzy involved in drugs? Was she being held against her will by people traffickers? Had she run away with someone she'd met on the Internet? Where did the lap dancing club fit into what was fast becoming a giant jigsaw puzzle that seemed impossible to piece together?

Josh couldn't imagine Izzy working in a place like this. She did look a lot older than her thirteen years when she went out all dressed up to meet her friends with her thick eye make-up, short skirts and high heels. No matter how much Kim went on about the fact that she hadn't been a feminist for most of her life so that Izzy could go out dressed like a prostitute it had made no difference to her daughter's appearance. Josh knew that some of Izzy's friends had managed to get into pubs and nightclubs, despite being under age, as several of them had false identification documents.

Josh flinched as he felt the woman's hand on his thigh. He removed it and stared straight at her.

'Tell me where Izzy is or I'm out of here and I'll call the police.'

Suddenly a bright light flashed and Josh caught sight of a shadowy figure in the corner of the room. It was a woman holding a camera and she was pointing it straight at him. As the dancer pulled him closer to her there was another flash. Josh pushed her away, grabbed his coat and looked around for the woman with the camera. He had to get it from her but she'd disappeared into the darkness. Josh hurried towards the dimly lit 'Exit' sign above the door.

What was going on? Where was Izzy? He cast his eyes back to the woman on the sofa. To his horror he saw that she looked dishevelled. Her hair was all over her face and one of the straps of her bikini top had been partly pulled down. Did she look like that when the photos were taken? A wave of panic swept over Josh and he found that he couldn't move. Suddenly he could hear the high pitched buzzing sound of an alarm over the loud thumping of the music. The door of the room flew open and the larger than life doorman appeared followed by two smaller men, all wearing the same style of dinner suit. Josh felt one of the doorman's enormous hands on his shoulder.

'Hang on there, sonny. What's going on?'

Josh stood still. As much as he wanted to escape from this alien environment, he was not going to try his luck with three men. Words failed him as he glanced behind him to see that the woman's hair and bikini strap had been put back in place. He breathed a sigh of relief, which he realised was misplaced when she spoke.

'He tried to leave without paying.'

Josh realised that the woman must have pressed a panic button to set off the alarm that he'd heard. What was she playing at? She hadn't asked him to pay. Was she the author of the letter written in green ink? If not, who had sent it? Was the woman working for someone else? If so, who were they? And most important of all, where did poor little Izzy fit into this puzzle? Josh thought quickly. The doorman was unlikely to be the smartest thing on two legs. He put on his best South London accent.

'Look mate. I've never been to one of these clubs before. I thought I had to pay outside.'

Josh smiled sheepishly and waited while the words

sank in. After what seemed forever, the doorman moved away and called to the woman.

'How much does he owe you?'

'Two hundred.'

Josh felt hot, sick and dizzy. His head was starting to spin and he thought his legs might give way at any moment.

'I've only got a hundred.'

'Got any cards?'

Josh opened his wallet to show the doorman that it was empty apart from five twenty pound notes that were poking out. He'd removed his bank card and a couple of store loyalty cards before he left home to avoid carrying anything with his name on that might identify him. He'd brought a hundred pounds in cash thinking that he might have to pay an extortionate amount for drinks or for information about Izzy.

'Give her the hundred,' said the doorman. 'I'll let you off this time but don't let it happen again.'

Josh nodded and took the money out of his wallet while trying to stop his hands from shaking. He walked towards the woman and saw that she had a smug grin on her face. As he handed her the notes he whispered.

'Please tell me if you know anything about Izzy.'

The woman shrugged her shoulders as she folded the notes and slipped them into the front of her bikini bottoms. Josh knew she was taunting him as she pulled them further out than she needed to. He didn't look down but continued to stare straight into her eyes.

'Why did that woman take photographs? Who is she?'

Josh's questions met with no response. The woman's eyes were cold and empty despite their beauty. As he stood close to her he could see evidence of drug abuse on her arms. She had covered up the scars with make up but had been unable to hide them completely. She looked older than Josh had first thought.

'Come on sonny. It's time to leave.' The doorman and his two friends escorted Josh out of the small room, back along the dark corridor and through the double doors of the huge red room with its thumping sounds and writhing women. As he passed the woman who resembled a porcelain doll he felt a surge of sadness and the sudden urge to take her away from this vile place. He feared for Izzy's safety in a way he'd never felt before, as if his eyes had been opened to the harsh realities of a world he'd never previously encountered.

Josh walked slowly up the stone steps and emerged into the sunlight. Suddenly he caught sight of a man clad in black leather from head to toe standing next to a motorbike on the other side of the busy road. As his eyes adjusted to the light he realised that the man was pointing a camera straight at him. Josh quickly turned away and put a hand over his face, but it was too late. The man put on his crash helmet, jumped onto his motorbike, sped off into a stream of traffic and disappeared.

As Josh walked to the tube station he tried to convince himself that it had been a coincidence that the man had been taking photos just at the time when he came out of the club. But he knew in his heart that he was being targeted by someone and he feared the worst.

Izzy pulled the sleeves of her hooded jacket down over her hands in the hope that the scars on her arms would disappear if they were out of sight. She was ashamed of herself for having caused so much trouble. It was all her fault, the arguments between Josh and her mother and him moving in with Maggie. If only Izzy hadn't been so difficult none of this would have happened. She tried to picture her bedroom with its pink walls covered in photos of her friends. She longed for her own bed with its fluffy blanket and teddy bear. Izzy banged her fists down onto her thighs over and over again. Then she pulled up the left sleeve of her hooded jacket and tore her nails into the flesh of her arm.

CHAPTER
TWENTY-SEVEN

Josh was regularly scouring the newspapers to see if the photos of him at the lap dancing club had been published. When he first arrived back in Wimbledon he'd contemplated telling Kim what had happened but there was never the right moment. Or perhaps he was just a coward. Josh had thought about asking Maggie for help but had been unable to relive the embarrassment he'd felt.

The first sign of trouble came when another envelope with its familiar green handwriting dropped through the letterbox. Josh didn't open it immediately but let it lie on a shelf in the spare room at Maggie's until he felt ready to confront what was inside.

The message was simple. *'If you pay one hundred thousand pounds Izzy wount be hurt and photos will be destructed.'* The word 'destructed', which should have read 'destroyed' and the misspelling of the word 'won't' made Josh feel uneasy. He knew that no matter what embarrassment he might suffer, he was going to have to speak to the police. Blackmail was not something he could deal with on his own.

What he couldn't decide was whether to tell Kim. She was already on the verge of a nervous breakdown. Josh hadn't wanted to raise her hopes that he was going to find Izzy when he had visited the lap dancing club. He'd hoped to return to Kim that fateful day with the good news that her daughter had been located and was safe. The last thing he'd expected was that he would become a victim of blackmail.

Later that day Josh walked out of Crown Road police station having described to Detective Sergeant Spalding the events leading up to the blackmail threat he'd received. He'd handed over the letters with their green handwriting, apologised for not contacting DS Spalding before and explained why he'd gone to the club. Josh had played down the details of what had actually happened to him there. But DS Spalding had been persistent in his questioning and had obviously enjoyed hearing about Josh's 'experience', as he described the visit. The detective sergeant had agreed to keep the information confidential for the time being but had urged Josh to tell Kim, as there was a strong likelihood that the photos would be published.

Unfortunately, DS Spalding's prediction was right. The first Josh knew that the photos were out in the public domain was when he received a call from Maggie on his mobile.

'What the hell's going on? Why on earth didn't you tell me about this? We could at least have been prepared and done some damage limitation. You do realise this could destroy the Internet Party.'

Josh listened as Maggie berated him in the same vein for what seemed forever until she promptly ended their conversation with the words,

'We need to meet. I'll be free in an hour. I'm going to prepare a press statement, which you'll have to agree. We'll need a PR strategy. I'll get on to Bob Wright. He's a heavyweight operator and his people are local. He's got loads of contacts in the media and they take him seriously. I'll put a call out now. Can you get back by 3 o'clock?'

Josh just kept saying 'Yes'. It was always the best strategy to adopt with Maggie. Once she was in campaign mode it was better to let her do what she wanted than to argue.

There were two photographs in the online edition of the Daily Post. The headline read **'Internet Party leader visits lap dancing club'**. As Josh sat looking at the screen he congratulated the Post on the simplicity of its headline. There were no emotive words like 'shock' or 'scandal', nothing blatant like **'Internet Party leader caught with**

pants down at lap dancing club.' But there didn't need to be, as Josh knew people would draw their own conclusions and they wouldn't be good. Even those who knew him would be unlikely to give him the benefit of the doubt, based on what the paper had written.

Josh had to admit that the photos of him were good, as whoever had taken them had achieved their objective of causing him as much embarrassment as possible. There was a full frontal shot of the dancer fondling his leg and appearing to whisper something in his ear, with her breasts in their tiny bikini top touching his chest. The other photo was of Josh leaving the club in a hurry with his hand in front of his face in an effort at disguise. He felt a tinge of relief that there was no picture of the dancer looking dishevelled with her breasts exposed but he assumed that was being kept in reserve by whoever had decided to blackmail him. Things couldn't get much worse, thought Josh. The pictures would be all over the Internet by now. He would have to tell Kim straight away. He called her mobile and left a message for her to get back to him urgently.

Josh and Maggie sat in Kim's kitchen waiting for her to arrive. She'd gone to pick up Dan from a cricket match and Josh had spoken to her briefly on the phone. All he'd said was that something had appeared in the Daily Post that he needed to speak to her about. Kim had pressed him for detail but Josh had managed to persuade her that it would be better if she saw what was in the paper before speaking to him.

Josh knew Kim would be unlikely to meet anyone at Dan's school who would already have seen the photos. She usually parked some distance away down a side road and Dan would meet her there. Kim didn't have a mobile with Internet access as she still used an old phone that she'd had for years. Her reasoning was that it was a waste of the world's resources to give up a perfectly good phone and she had no time to transfer all her contacts to a new one, although Josh suspected a degree of technophobia on her part.

As Josh and Maggie discussed how to deal with the bad publicity from the newspaper article he listened out for the noise of Kim's car pulling up outside the front of the house. When he heard the sound of a key turning in the front door lock he felt his body stiffen. He and Maggie stopped talking.

'We're in the kitchen,' called Josh.

They heard the thump of Dan dropping his enormous cricket bag onto the wooden floor of the hallway and then the sound of approaching footsteps. Josh glanced at Maggie, who looked as uncomfortable as he felt. Kim and Maggie greeted each other formally while Dan said 'Hi' to everyone and went straight to the sink to get a drink of water.

Josh pulled out a chair for Kim so she could sit facing his laptop. He clicked the mouse and the photo of him coming out of the club filled the screen. Kim looked at Josh with a quizzical expression.

'What are you doing coming out of a lap dancing club? I thought you disapproved of them.'

'There's worse to come,' said Josh. When he flashed up the photo of himself with the dancer Kim stared at him in horror. She was speechless.

'It's not as bad as it looks,' said Maggie, trying to be helpful.

Dan wandered over to see what all the fuss was about. He nearly choked on the mouthful of water he'd just taken.

'I can explain,' said Josh.

He was surprised that Kim hadn't been as angry as he thought she would be. The poor woman was in such a state of shock as he recounted the events that had led up to the photographs being published that all she could do was to nod. Fortunately Dan had been his usual helpful self. He'd completely understood why Josh had acted as his did. Josh had been trying to find Izzy and that was all that mattered. Maggie had come up with a plan as to how the bad publicity could be turned to their advantage. Her overriding concern, of course, was to salvage the reputation of the Internet Party. But she could also see an opportunity to publicise Izzy's disappearance in the hope that she might be found.

'We'll hold a press conference,' said Maggie to Josh. 'Then you can explain your side of the story. I'll also email the photos to my friend Helen Rogers. She's a solicitor who specialises in media law. I'll get a meeting arranged with her straight away. It will be useful to get her perspective on this wretched business.'

Izzy had no idea of the trouble her disappearance had caused. How could she? Her phone was out of battery and she had no way of charging it. She hadn't left the attic now for days. All of Izzy's food had been delivered to her. Not that she'd eaten much of it. She could feel her ribs when she pressed her hands against her body. She didn't want to eat. She wanted to die. The less she ate the sooner she would die. That was Izzy's thinking and the longer she felt imprisoned in the attic and the less she ate and the more she hated herself and the more she hurt herself, the more likely it became that she would not survive.

CHAPTER
TWENTY-EIGHT

Kim and Josh had travelled separately to the offices of Rogers, Tippets and Lovelace, Solicitors, which was near St James's park tube station on the District line. Josh sat in the waiting area and looked at Kim, who studiously avoided catching his eye as a young assistant poured them both cups of coffee. He had heard nothing back from her since he'd posted his handwritten letter through her letterbox a few days earlier. His eyes searched her face for some sort of sign but Kim stared blankly into the depths of her cup of coffee. She took small sips, clutching the cup with both hands, as if someone might try and snatch it from her grasp.

The assistant disappeared for a moment before reappearing and holding open a large, brown, wooden door.

'Mr Walker, Ms Clark, Ms Rogers will see you now if you'd like to come with me.' She gestured to them to follow her along a nondescript corridor lined with other wooden doors. At the end of the corridor the assistant knocked on a door with the initials 'HR' in gold letters on a square wooden plaque that was slotted into a wooden holder on the door. A voice inside said 'Come in' and the assistant ushered Kim and Josh into a large room that was surprisingly light and airy. It had cream coloured walls that were covered in large photographs of people in foreign countries. Kim and Josh found themselves staring at the walls, taking in the rich colours and interesting scenes.

'Holiday snaps,' said Helen as she held out her hand to welcome them. 'Travel photography is a hobby of mine, when I get the time.' Kim and Josh nodded, as one after the other they shook her hand. 'Hi, I'm Helen. I've known Maggie for a long time. She's told me about the problems you've been having with the media.'

Kim and Josh sat down on the chairs that had been laid out for them in front of the large wooden desk, behind which Helen sat in a comfortable armchair. She looks like a lawyer, thought Josh as she smiled and leaned slightly forward, placing her arms on the desk. He examined her face, with its fair skin, pink cheeks and a few freckles. Her eyes were an unusual mixture of green, blue, grey and brown. He felt reassured by Helen's kind manner and for the first time since he'd walked into her offices, he felt himself relax and breathe more easily.

'First of all I'd like to say how sorry I am about Izzy.' Helen spoke in a familiar tone, as if she were a family member, not the stranger they'd only just met. 'This must be a very worrying and stressful time for you both.'

Josh glanced sideways at Kim and saw a tear form in the corner of her right eye. She sat rigid, holding tightly onto the sides of her chair.

'And I'm sure the situation has not been helped by all the media coverage Izzy's disappearance has received, which is, of course why you're here.'

Josh watched as Helen, wearing a dark green dress with her brown wavy hair tied up in a ponytail, extracted several pieces of paper from the file on her desk.

'She's the best in the business,' Maggie had reassured him before he'd set off to Wimbledon Station to catch the tube to Helen's office.

Josh cast his mind back to the article that had appeared the day before in the London Messenger. It was of course described as an 'exclusive'. The headline read: **'Internet Party leader arrested on suspicion of child abduction.'** The very thought of what the article had said made Josh shiver. He'd read it so many times that he knew every word by heart.

'A police source has revealed that Kim Clark, 38 and her partner, Josh Walker, 39, leader of the Internet Party, are being treated as possible suspects in the

disappearance of Ms Clark's daughter, Izzy, 13.'

Helen dug out her copy of the offending article from her file of papers and waved it in front of her in a derisory manner.

'We, of course, know that what the Messenger has published is untrue. But most of the people who've read the article will believe it because they think that newspapers print the truth.'

'How could a journalist write such lies?' said Kim angrily, suddenly breaking her silence.

'They do it all the time,' said Helen. 'I'd be out of a job otherwise.'

'So what can we do?' asked Josh.

'First of all we need to write a letter to the Editor of the London Messenger accusing them of libel and asking that they print an apology and retraction.'

'What's that exactly?' said Josh.

'I will ask the Editor to agree a form of words to be printed in the paper on an agreed date stating that they got their facts wrong and apologising for doing so.'

'Will it go on the front page? It should do as that's where the article was that you said was...' Kim's voice trailed off into silence.

'Defamatory,' said Helen. 'I'm afraid you're going to be on a steep learning curve over the next few days. You'll be learning a whole new language.'

'Legal jargon,' said Josh.

'That's right. Libel is defamation that is written. Slander is defamation that is spoken. Defamation is something that is either written or spoken that is untrue and damages someone's reputation. That's it in a nutshell, although there are all kinds of variations, qualifications, reservations and all the other things that lawyers use to make the law as complicated as possible.'

Josh felt like adding, 'in order to enable them to charge extortionate fees to their clients', but he thought better of it as he didn't want to offend Helen, who was carefully laying out the contents of a file across the desk. She picked up a roll of papers that were tied together with pink ribbon and extracted a document, which she opened and placed in front of her. The sides kept rolling upwards so she held it tightly with both hands.

'I've obtained a preliminary advice from counsel, that's a barrister by another name. I'll read out what he says and you can interrupt me if you don't understand.'

Kim and Josh listened intently while Helen read out the words that described why they had a strong case against the newspaper that had defamed them.

'That sounds hopeful,' said Josh when she'd finished reading. 'Do you think the Messenger will agree to apologise and print the truth straight away?'

Helen looked up at Josh and frowned.

'Sadly, no, the Messenger never settles a case without court proceedings being issued.'

'But that's ridiculous,' said Josh.

'Even when the truth is staring them in the face?' added Kim.

'I've been dealing with that particular paper for fifteen years and have always had to take them to court, no matter how strong my client's case has been,' said Helen.

'But aren't court cases really expensive?' said Kim, looking worried.

'They are indeed. But I'm going to suggest that you instruct this firm to act for you on what is called a conditional fee basis.'

'What's that?' said Josh.

'It's all written down here,' said Helen as she waved a letter in front of him that consisted of several pages of closely typed wording.

'Is it no win, no fee?' Kim asked hopefully. She had no money to pay to lawyers.

'That's the basic principle,' said Helen. 'But there's

a bit more to it than that. The details are all set out in this letter, which I'll explain so that you understand. I've printed off a copy for each of you.'

Helen handed Kim a document headed 'Client Agreement' and then gave one to Josh. Just as they started reading Helen interrupted them.

'I need to mention at this stage that, on the basis of the information you've given me, I am quite happy to represent both of you. However, if at any point in the future I feel there's a conflict of interest between you, I will have to refer either one or both of you to other solicitors. Is that clear?'

'What do you mean by conflict of interest?' said Kim.

'Well, it's hard to describe in the abstract. But if I feel I can't do a proper job for one of you because it wouldn't be in the best interests of the other, then I'd have to stop acting for either both or one of you, with the other's agreement.' Helen looked at the blank expressions on their faces. 'Basically, if you decide you want different things.'

Kim and Josh glanced at each other for the first time since they'd walked into the offices of Rogers, Tippets and Lovelace. They both knew that they wanted many different things out of life. But there were some things on which they were firmly in agreement. Kim and Josh wanted Izzy back and they were determined to punish the London Messenger for printing lies about them.

'Now first I'll run through the details of the conditional fee agreements before getting you both to sign. Then I'll explain what happens next,' said Helen calmly.

The meeting with their solicitor had lasted for over two hours and Josh had a splitting headache by the time he and Kim found themselves on the pavement outside her offices, standing in the late afternoon sun.

'I could do with some fresh air,' said Josh. 'I think I'll take a walk through St James's Park.'

He hoped that Kim would agree to walk with him, but he didn't dare to ask her. Not after the way she had spoken to him a few days before when she'd told him their relationship was over. Josh was therefore pleasantly surprised when Kim said, 'It's not far to St James's Park,' and set off in the direction of Horse Guards Parade, gesturing to him to follow.

They walked along in silence for a while, breathing in the traffic fumes and mulling over the vast amount of information they'd been bombarded with that afternoon.

Josh waited until Kim broke the silence. 'I thought Helen was really nice.'

Josh usually objected when Kim described people as being 'really nice' and insisted that another adjective be found. But on this occasion he simply said, 'Yes, she was nice and she inspired confidence that she can sue the London Messenger and win.'

'I hope so,' said Kim quietly, almost as if she was speaking to herself. They walked in silence for the rest of their journey until they reached the café in St James's Park, where they stopped and sat down at a small table. Kim reserved seats while Josh went to get them both cups of strong tea and flapjacks. The air was warm and unusually humid for the time of year and mottled sunlight slipped through the fresh green leaves of the trees.

Not for the first time that day Josh observed that Kim had dressed smartly for the meeting with the solicitor. She was wearing a dark blue suit with black leather shoes that had fairly high heels. Kim must have borrowed them from a friend, thought Josh. She hardly ever wore a skirt and he couldn't recall the last time she'd worn heels. He felt a surge of sexual excitement as he found himself wondering whether Kim was wearing stockings or tights. The suit was slightly old fashioned, as was the fitted white blouse with its buttons straining over her chest.

Suddenly Josh felt like lurching across the small

round table and taking Kim into his arms. He longed to kiss her passionately and run his hands through her hair and over her body. He noticed that she'd applied the faintest trace of makeup to her eyes and lips and that she looked tired but beautiful as the last rays of the afternoon sun shone down on her.

Josh started to feel hot, so he loosened his collar and removed his jacket. He'd felt it was necessary to wear a suit and a striped shirt to see the solicitor, although he'd stopped short of wearing a tie. He'd even applied polish to his hardly worn smart black loafers.

'Josh,' said Kim suddenly, 'I'm pregnant.'

He stared at her and tried not to appear shocked, which was exactly how he felt.

'Well aren't you going to say something?'

Josh felt incapable of speaking, let alone saying anything that Kim might want to hear. Thoughts flashed through his brain like pictures across a TV screen. Eventually he managed to utter a few words in a weak voice that even he could hardly hear.

'That's amazing Kim. When is the baby due?'

'It's our baby, Josh.'

Kim began to cry. She buried her head in her hands and made huge sobbing noises. A few of the customers in the café looked away awkwardly as Josh stood up and moved towards her. He put his arms around Kim and hugged her tightly, but not too tightly in case he might damage the baby.

While Kim struggled to regain her composure Josh couldn't help wondering why she was crying at all. She'd often told him that she would like to have more children. Kim never went so far as to ask him directly whether he wanted his own kids, most likely because she knew that he would have said no. What she said instead was that she wanted a second chance at making a success of family life.

'It's ironic, isn't it?' said Kim as she extricated

herself from Josh's embrace. She took a packet of tissues out of her bag and blew her nose hard.

'What's ironic?'

'I've lost one child and gained another.' Kim started crying again. 'I miss Izzy so much.'

Josh took Kim gently into his arms and kissed the top of her head.

'So do I,' he whispered. 'But we'll find her and she'll come back safe. I know she will.'

Kim had gone straight to bed as soon as she and Josh had returned to Horatio Road. She'd fallen asleep leaning against him in the taxi that had brought them back to Wimbledon from St James's Park. Josh's mind had been in turmoil throughout the journey. He was finding it difficult to come to terms with being a father. He needed to speak to Kim about the state of their relationship after the words she'd spoken to him a few days ago. She had not responded to the letter he'd sent her. Was this a good or bad sign? Had she known she was pregnant when she told him their relationship was over? Would Kim want him to move back in with her? When was the baby due to be born?

Josh had found himself wondering when Kim had actually become pregnant. He knew from adverts he'd seen on TV that pregnancy tests were pretty accurate these days. It seemed disingenuous to be trying to recall the number of times he and Kim had made love over recent weeks. He even once stopped himself from wondering if the baby's father might be someone else, as he had no reason to think that was the case. Eventually Josh fell into a state of restless sleep, unable to find answers to the myriad of questions that presented themselves to him.

CHAPTER
TWENTY-NINE

'It's really irritating, not being able to go anywhere or do anything,' said Kim through gritted teeth. 'Can't you do something?'

Josh held his mobile phone slightly away from his left ear and tried to picture Kim, where she might be standing, what clothes she might be wearing. But the only image that came into his mind was of her face, with a cross expression, tired eyes, her mouth drooping at the corners with disappointment.

'Sorry.'

The word slipped out of Josh's lips automatically, limp and slippery like a fish escaping from the hand of a fisherman. If the word had been an object it would have lain on the ground in front of him, helpless and inadequate. That was how he felt now.

'Sorry! Is that all you can say? You must be able to do something. Tell these media people to go and camp somewhere else with their long lenses and cigarette butts.'

Kim was almost shouting now and Josh moved the phone even further from his head, accidentally pressing the loudspeaker button as he did so.

'I'll do what I can.' He tried to sound reassuring.

'Don't put me on loudspeaker,' Kim shrieked.

'Calm down,' said Josh, summoning up as much strength as he could in an effort to speak with authority.

'And don't tell me to calm down. It's all right for you. This is what you wanted, the attention, adulation, people hanging on your every word. All politicians want the eyes of the world's media upon them until such time as they're caught with their pants down, screwing someone else's wife or husband, ordering porn movies on expenses or paying fictitious mortgages with taxpayers' money. Isn't that right, Josh? Then they're nowhere to be seen, these so called guardians of the public interest, not in their constituencies, not in their 'second homes' that they've never even visited, let alone lived in. Then they just disappear into thin air, don't they, Josh? Into thin air, is that what you're going to do? You might be all high ideals and have huge ambitions for the good of humanity now. But give it a few years, Josh, maybe even only a year of being a member of that exclusive, mainly white, male-dominated 'gentleman's' club. You'll be having one too many drinks on the terrace overlooking the Thames subsidised by taxpayers' money. You will be corrupted by the place, if you get elected as an MP, just like the rest of them.'

Josh heard Kim stop for breath and seized the opportunity to speak.

'I understand what you're saying. You know my views on Parliament and if I'm elected as an MP I'll do everything in my power to make huge changes. And I mean HUGE. More women, more people from ethnic minorities, family friendly hours, no more subsidised drinking sessions, a fair and transparent system of claiming expenses. You know that's what the Internet Party stands for.'

Josh paused for a few seconds. He didn't want Kim to think he was giving her a lecture, but he felt he had to defend his position. He could hear her breathing at the other end of the phone as he spoke in a gentler tone.

'I realise it's a pain, having all these media people hanging around twenty-four seven. I know it's all because of me and I'm sorry. If I'd known what was going to happen I might never have started the whole business. But there are only two days now before the election. Things are bound to get worse before they get better as the media engage in a feeding frenzy. But once it's over, they'll all rush off like rats following the Pied Piper of Hamlyn to the next 'breaking news' story. You can be sure of that. And then you'll get your life back and you'll wonder if it was all a dream.'

'More like a nightmare,' said Kim, with an air of resignation. Josh heard her sigh. 'I'm so worried about Izzy.'

Kim sounded so pitiful that Josh wanted to run down the road and scoop her up into his arms. But he knew she wouldn't want him to. He might not exactly be classed as the enemy. That was the place Kim had reserved for whoever was holding Izzy. But he wasn't far away from it. He knew she regarded him as an alien being, as unknown a quantity as any of the prospective parliamentary candidates that graced the TV screens of the electorate night after night.

'Izzy will come back safe, I know she will,' said Josh, as much to convince himself as Kim. He spoke with as much conviction in his voice as he could summon up. He had no reason to believe the statement he'd just made and Kim had no reason to believe it either, but he nevertheless felt he needed to say something to her that was positive and encouraging.

The latest message from the kidnappers had read, **'Izzy safe. Stop Internet Party now!'** That had been two days ago and the police were still trying to trace the sender. They didn't know how long that might take or if they could trace them at all. Over the last week there had been some tense moments when the police had identified the senders of various messages that had said where Izzy was being held but they'd turned out to be hoaxes. One of the messages had been sent by a fifteen-year-old boy from Birmingham who, when the police turned up at his door had sheepishly admitted that he'd sent the message because he'd been bored and wanted to see what might happen. The tabloid newspapers had latched onto the story and expressed great enthusiasm for the Crown Prosecution Service decision to prosecute the young man for wasting police time.

Josh suddenly realised that neither he nor Kim had

spoken for over a minute. He listened to her irregular breathing and it occurred to him that she must be crying.

'I'll do what I can to keep the media away from you. But they do have their uses. The police said that Izzy is less likely to be harmed and more likely to be found while there's so much media interest in her disappearance. The kidnappers will be worried that they'll be discovered, as anyone who's seen Izzy's picture will be looking out for her. Neighbours will be keeping their eyes open for suspicious activity in nearby houses. People in shopping centres will be examining the faces of teenagers to see if they fit Izzy's description. We need to harness the good aspects of the media and if that means putting up with the inconvenience of being photographed every time we go out of the front door, then it's a small price to pay for Izzy's safe return.'

'Ok Josh,' said Kim weakly.

'Are you all right? Is Dan there?'

'No, but he'll be back soon.'

'You shouldn't be on your own.'

'It's ok. I don't mind being on my own. Sometimes it's worse having to talk to people.'

'I could always...'

'No,' said Kim firmly.

'Well, let me know if you hear anything.'

'And you. Bye.'

Kim rang off before Josh could say goodbye. There was a distance between them that was growing each day. He wondered what would happen to their relationship after the election. He could hardly visualise life beyond that point in time. What about the baby? A new life made from two lives that were being torn apart.

Izzy could hear noises from the room below. They were different from the sounds she'd heard over the last few days, since she'd been living in the attic. She knew this could mean only one thing. They were coming for her now. There was nothing she could do. She would have to go with them. She would have no choice, no choice at all. Izzy would have to face the consequences of the decision she'd made. She tried to scream but no sound came out of her mouth. No sound at all. The only sounds were of people moving around downstairs. They'd only just arrived but they must be getting ready for her to leave.

Izzy no longer cared what happened to her, where she was taken, what she did, what others might do to her. Everything had gone too far. There would be no going back. Izzy froze. Was that the sound of footsteps on the stairs? Creak followed by creak of someone else's feet, someone trying hard not to make a sound, treading carefully, attempting to hide their presence.

Izzy wrapped the sleeping bag around her shrinking frame and huddled in the farthest corner of the room. How she wished she could disappear into the plaster on the wall or slip down a crack in the bare floorboards. Another step, then another, the footsteps were coming nearer. Next she heard the sound of breathing and a voice without a body, a man's voice.

'Izzy,' he beckoned to her.

The girl stood up and slowly walked towards the man.

CHAPTER
THIRTY

After speaking to Kim about what she described as the 'media circus' outside her house, Josh had embarked on a long discussion with Maggie. She'd taken a hard and unemotional stance on the whole business that he'd found irritating and disappointing.

As he lay on the narrow bed in Maggie's spare room he felt like a sulky teenager who had stomped off after not getting his own way. Josh had noticed that, as the election got nearer, Maggie had become more and more full of her own self-importance. She directed operations downstairs in her 'Control Room' from six in the morning until past midnight, apart from when she had to attend an important press briefing or meeting with a journalist. At times Josh felt Maggie resembled some famous historical female figure like Helen of Troy or Cleopatra. She commanded her 'troops', the bevy of young volunteers who scurried back and forth between their laptops, clutching mobile phones tightly to their ears or frantically sending messages.

Maggie twittered, or was it tweeted? several times a day and she took great pleasure in telling Josh how many followers she had on Twitter and how that number increased by the minute. The young male volunteers swooned over Maggie whenever she asked them to help her and there was always at least one or two young women following her around. They would hang on her every word, ready to jump to attention and be given an important task, like a grateful dog receiving a much salivated over bone from its adored mistress.

'Call Jenny at the Sunday Echo to fix up an interview for tomorrow. Email this press release to Felix at the Morning News. Courier those photos to Verity at Gossip

Magazine, phone her in half an hour and find out which ones she wants to use so we can agree a caption.'

Josh described these helpers as Maggie's 'ladies in waiting', which she disliked, when he felt she was becoming too self-important.

'Someone's got to keep the media happy,' she would retort, sometimes in a more cutting tone of voice than he felt was strictly necessary.

Josh hadn't exactly found himself being eased out of the action by Maggie, but he certainly felt he was sidelined at times. It was still the case that the volunteers would refer to him for policy statements or comments to be given to journalists, especially in reply to criticism from politicians of other parties. But at times he felt as if Maggie had engineered herself into the position of chief executive while Josh took the role of chairman. Still, he knew she was right whenever she said, 'You can't have it both ways. You can't expect me to deal with the media around the clock and then be surprised if they come to me when they want a comment or a story.'

Not only did Josh know Maggie was right, he actually preferred to keep out of the limelight as much as possible. It suited his personality to be seen as accessible and yet at the same time to be enigmatic.

Josh stared up at the newly painted white ceiling with its perfectly symmetrical lights. Maggie loved symmetry. This was evident in each room of the house where lights were set into ceilings likes rows of soldiers standing to attention. Lamps were juxtaposed at either end of each room exactly opposite each other and the few ornaments and pictures were displayed in pairs. Maggie strived for order and balance in her surroundings. Josh smiled to himself as he tried to imagine how she might deal with the organised chaos of Kim's house. She would either bring about order or she'd be driven mad. Sometimes Josh wondered whether it was Maggie's controlling personality that had determined how she decorated her home, or perhaps she just had a keen interest in Feng Shui. It was a philosophy he knew little about and had no particular desire to find out more.

Josh was finding it impossible to get to sleep and that worried him, as he hadn't slept for more than a few hours on any night since Izzy disappeared. He knew the lack of sleep was taking its toll on his appearance. Even at the height of summer Josh's complexion tended to be somewhat pale. But he was surprised at how dreadful he looked when he caught sight of his face earlier that night in the unforgiving florescent light over the bathroom sink.

Josh's eyes had resembled the insides of volcanic craters, they were so dark and menacing. His skin had looked a pasty grey colour and he'd counted more wrinkles than ever before. As he lay awake with his eyes closed, Josh conjured up images in his mind of various political leaders such as presidents and prime ministers. It was invariably the case that they started their election campaigns fresh-faced and animated with bundles of energy. But how quickly their faces changed to become tired and worn after little sleep and weeks of campaigning. Then after only a few years as heads of state they would look as if they'd aged by several decades, their faces crumpled by worry and exhaustion, their hair grey and thinning, their minds empty of ideas. Josh found himself wondering if this would be his fate after the election.

Suddenly his mobile rang. He flung out his left arm to grab it from where it was perched on top of a cardboard box he was using as a makeshift bedside table. His arm missed its target and hit the box so that the phone flew off onto the floor and stopped ringing. Josh muttered to himself as he sat up, swung his legs over the side of the bed and fumbled around for the light switch. He screwed up his eyes as the lights beamed down on him, felt around on the floor and picked up the phone. He checked the time. It was twenty past one in the morning. Who would be calling him at this time of night? Josh immediately thought of his father and his heart sank. Perhaps he'd been taken ill. His father's neighbours had Josh's telephone numbers for emergencies but no-one had ever called him apart from on one occasion when his father had gone off on holiday leaving an upstairs window wide open.

Josh dialled 123 for his voicemail. There was one new message. He listened hard as the automatic voice ran through its usual spiel. Then there was the sound of someone breathing hard and smacking their lips together as if they were debating whether to leave a message. After a few seconds Josh heard the words: 'To listen to your message again, press one. To save your message, press two. To delete it press three.'

Josh did nothing. After a couple more seconds the voice said: 'Message saved. That was your last message. Thank you for using the service.'

Josh was about to examine the log to see who had called when the phone rang again. He stared at the small screen. The words 'unknown caller' flashed up before his eyes. He pressed the answer button, held the phone to his left ear and waited for someone to speak.

'Hello,' said a voice in a whispered tone that sounded familiar.

'Hello,' echoed Josh.

'Who's that?'

'Who do you want to speak to?'

There was a long pause.

'Josh?'

'Dan?'

'What the hell! Why didn't you speak?'

'Well, it could have been anyone. You came up as 'unknown caller', Dan.'

'That's because I'm using someone else's phone. Someone you don't know. They won't be in your contacts.'

'Why aren't you using your phone?'

'Look. That doesn't matter. We're wasting time.'

Josh paused for a few seconds. Why was Dan using someone else's phone? What did he mean about wasting time? Josh put on his best parental tone of voice. 'Well, what's going on? Are you drunk, or in trouble?'

Dan responded immediately with indignation. 'Thanks very much, Josh. I'm not drunk or in trouble. Actually, I'm with Izzy.'

'Izzy!' Josh just managed to stop himself from shouting out loud and waking up the whole house. He could feel his heart beating in his chest faster than it had ever done before and he could hardly catch his breath. 'Izzy' he muttered to himself as tears welled up in his eyes. 'Is she ok?'

'Sort of, but I need to get her out of here. Can you come now?' said Dan anxiously.

'Where are you?' said Josh.

'Ninety-three Sheepwash Place.'

'That's up in Wimbledon Village isn't it? What the hell's she doing there?'

'I can't answer any questions now. There isn't time. I need to get Izzy out of here fast. Can you come or shall I call Mum?'

Josh thought quickly. If he went rushing out of Maggie's house in the middle of the night and jumped into his car there was a risk that he'd be pursued by the media, like hounds chasing a fox. The park was locked so no one from the press or TV could be camping out there as they did during the day. But there might be any number of freelance reporters and photographers lurking in the cars and vans that seemed to be parked up and down Horatio Road both day and night.

Josh couldn't wake Kim and ask her to go and fetch Izzy and Dan as she'd be hysterical and would probably crash her car. He thought about waking Vicky and creeping out of her house into a cab but he didn't think it was fair to involve her and her family and it would just delay things.

'Josh. Are you coming or shall I phone Mum? We need to get out of here,' Dan insisted.

'I'll call a taxi to come and get you immediately. I can pay by credit card. There's a company I use. It's very reliable. I'll need a contact mobile number as the driver will text you as soon as he arrives outside the house. Number three, Sheepwash Place, is that what you said?'

'No. Ninety-three!'

'Ok. Ninety-three. Text me the number of the phone you're using.'

After Dan hung up Josh found that he couldn't move. He felt as if he was looking out from inside his own body like an alien who had just landed on Earth in a small spaceship. He knew that the emotions he was feeling were generally positive, a mixture of joy, relief and happiness. But at the other end of the spectrum he felt fear, anxiety and foreboding. Josh found himself thinking the worst. That Izzy had been harmed and was still in danger. Perhaps Dan was in danger too. How did he find her? Had she escaped from where she was being held? Had the kidnappers simply decided to let her go? Perhaps they'd realised that their plan had backfired.

The publicity generated by Izzy's disappearance had catapulted Josh and the Internet Party into the limelight, to the front of people's consciousness, to the number one spot on all the Internet news sites and onto the front pages of every newspaper. That had been the case for days now and if Izzy really did come back tonight, the whole of tomorrow would be taken up with the story.

Josh had told Dan to explain to the taxi driver that his sister had been taken ill while staying overnight with a friend and he'd come to take her home. He had also told Dan to disguise Izzy to avoid her being recognised. So, after a series of frantic phone calls – *Josh calling the taxi company to arrange a pick up from ninety-three Sheepwash*

Place; Dan calling Josh to say that Izzy was hysterical and had absolutely refused to get into a taxi in the middle of the night with 'some strange man', even if she was with her brother; Josh calling the taxi company again and cancelling the pick up – Josh found himself creeping quietly down the stairs, having thrown on a pair of dark grey jeans and a black sweater.

He quickly ran his fingers through his tousled mop of hair and grabbed a dark blue baseball cap from the understairs cupboard where the volunteers dumped their coats and bags. He pulled it down over his face and headed towards the front door. As Josh passed the living room doorway he stopped and took a detour to check the CCTV. He waited while the picture on the monitor moved from the fuzzy darkness of the back garden to the orange glow of the front of the house. The camera panned round and he could just make out the dim outline of his Saab parked in the road, slightly to the right of the house. There were a couple of vehicles parked opposite but they didn't look suspicious and Josh thought they probably belonged to people who lived in maisonettes around the corner in Holy Road. He could see that neither car had blacked out windows and no one was sitting or sleeping inside.

Josh took a deep breath as he quietly opened the front door. He walked down the newly laid chequered black and white Victorian-style path with a purposeful stride and glanced quickly up and down the road. Nothing moved apart from a young fox that appeared out of nowhere, stopped and stared at him and then disappeared through the park railings. Josh opened the driver's door, eased himself into the seat, closed the door as quietly as he could and turned his key in the ignition. He held his breath as the car engine spluttered into life and then gave a guttural roar as it sped off into the night. He checked his rear view mirror and let out a sigh of relief when he saw that no-one was following. Then he jammed his foot on the accelerator and set off in the direction of Wimbledon Village.

As soon as Josh turned into Sheepwash Place he stopped the car and reached for the small piece of paper on which he'd written the instructions Dan had given him. It was a wide, tree-lined road with huge houses of different shapes and sizes, mostly Victorian, with a few more modern ones in between. Some of the houses would have been built to replace those destroyed when London was bombed during the Second World War. Others had been squeezed in when people had sold off parts of their gardens. These were mostly odd-looking box-like buildings from the sixties and seventies.

As Josh drove slowly along Sheepwash Place looking out for the three storey red-brick building Dan had described, he thought how Wimbledon had changed over the years. A lot of green space had been filled in with extra houses or flats and there were more people and cars.

Josh stopped his car immediately outside an imposing Victorian detached house that was set back slightly from the road. It had a thick yew hedge at the front and a massive four by four vehicle parked at the side. Josh looked at the small piece of paper and tapped the number Dan had given him into his mobile phone. It rang a few times and then Dan's voice answered.

'Hello.'

'I'm outside.'

'Ok. Wait there. We'll come out.'

Josh could feel his whole body writhing inside of itself with anticipation and excitement. After what seemed hours, but could only have been a few minutes, the front door opened and two figures appeared, outlined by the light behind them. Josh immediately recognised Dan's tall and muscular frame. Close behind him a small frail figure stood wrapped in what looked like a blanket. 'Izzy,' Josh whispered to himself. The blanket came over her head and hid her face from view. He watched as one of Dan's long arms propelled the figure along the front pathway towards the car. As it came nearer Josh gently opened the driver's door and stepped into the road. A wave of cold night air surged into his lungs and made him feel more alert. He breathed in deeply and became aware of the aroma of freshly cut grass from Wimbledon Common at the far end of Sheepwash Place. Josh eased himself round to the other side of the car, opened the passenger door and tipped the seat forward. Then he saw Izzy's face. She looked tired and pale and tears were running down her cheeks. He wanted to throw his arms around her and squeeze her tightly but he felt she might break. He reached out and touched her gently on the shoulder.

'It's ok. You're safe now. I'm taking you home.'

'I'm sss…sorry.'

Dan helped his sister into the back seat of the car and wrapped the seatbelt around her slight frame while keeping her hidden beneath the blanket. Then he climbed into the front passenger seat, did up his seatbelt and, looking straight ahead, said, 'Let's go.'

Sitting in the brightly-lit kitchen at Kim's house, with Izzy safely tucked up in bed having consumed three glasses of chocolate milk, Josh wondered how he'd managed to drive back safely from the Village. He looked down at the two hands that were holding the mug of strong, sweet tea that Bruno had just made for him. They were shaking and the tea was sloshing around so that drops kept spilling onto the table. Josh removed his hands and placed them firmly onto his knees.

'I still can't get my head around the fact that Jessica's parents went off to Geneva leaving a fourteen-year-old girl alone in the house for a whole week,' said Bruno.

He sat down heavily at the head of the kitchen table.

His shirtsleeves were rolled up to reveal strong brown arms covered in thick black hair. The same type of hair that Josh could see sprouting up from Bruno's open necked shirt.

'She wasn't exactly alone,' said Dan, pouring himself a glass of water from the tap. 'Her older brother was supposed to be keeping an eye on her.'

'But he wasn't, was he?' said Bruno, leaning forward with his arms outstretched on the table in front of him in a proprietorial fashion, as if he were chairing a meeting. 'The brother only returned from his girlfriend's house tonight because his parents are due back home in a couple of hours.'

'He's called James,' said Dan, with a tone of irritation in his voice. 'He's nineteen and was in the year above me at school.'

'I don't care how old he is. James was given the job of looking after his sister, as a responsible adult and he singularly failed, in my book anyway.' Bruno leaned back and folded his arms across his chest.

'Well, at least he recognised Izzy and called me to say she was there,' said Dan, resting against the sink and taking sips from his glass of water.

Josh felt he should say something, but every time he tried to speak, a lump would form in his throat and he'd have to choke back the tears that were threatening to pour from his eyes at any moment, like a dam about to burst. He concentrated on his mug of tea and made a half-hearted attempt to pick it up before letting his hands fall back into his lap, limp and lifeless.

'So, let me get this right,' said Bruno. 'The girl, Jessica, didn't want to go with her parents to their holiday home in Geneva over half term. So the parents stocked up the fridge with ready meals, frozen pizza and the like and went off to enjoy themselves in Switzerland leaving their daughter to do god knows what with god knows who.'

Dan sighed. 'Lots of parents do it. They usually leave an older brother or sister in charge, or sometimes an au pair or cleaner.'

'Well, I wouldn't do that, if I had my own children, which I hope I will one day,' said Bruno. He deliberately took a large sip of his tea and made a loud, slurping noise as he put the mug back down on the table.

Various thoughts ran through Josh's mind. He tried to imagine the baby developing inside Kim's body. He'd seen pictures of foetuses inside the womb but couldn't quite identify with something like that being 'his' or rather 'his and Kim's baby'. He thought of Izzy and how she must have suffered during the time she'd spent hiding away at Jessica's house. To start with the feelings of empowerment and satisfaction she must have felt when she sent that first text, *'Stop the Internet Party or Izzy won't come back'*

Izzy must have believed that she'd regained control of her life after weeks of feeling she was a victim of the war that was raging around her. A war that had arisen between Kim and Josh due to the frustration and anger she felt as his long held political ambitions came to fruition.

'I thought that if I went away for a while, you and Mum would stop arguing. Nobody was listening to me... ever. No one cared about me, what I thought, how I was suffering.' Izzy's words echoed in Josh's mind.

'What I can't understand is how those girls didn't know the trouble they'd caused. Izzy's picture was all over the newspapers, on TV every day. It's illogical that Izzy stayed hidden for as long as she did,' said Bruno in a tone of exasperation, rubbing his forehead with his large right hand. He was catching up with the news of Izzy's return after being woken up by Kim when Izzy was put to bed. He'd thrown on some clothes and come downstairs at least an hour after the story had unfolded.

'The whole thing started as something of a practical joke,' said Josh, suddenly finding his voice again.

'A joke!' said Bruno loudly. Dan looked startled.

'Well, not a joke, but a prank. Izzy wanted to make

a point.'

'She certainly did that.'

'Izzy had called Jessica on her way home from school. She was very upset. She'd been given a detention for not handing in a piece of coursework on time,' said Dan, in defence of his sister. Bruno raised his eyebrows and took a slurp of his tea.

'Izzy was behind with her work because she wasn't sleeping properly or concentrating at school. She was worried about Mum and Josh breaking up,' said Dan. His eyes darted from left to right as he looked at the two grown men sitting at either end of the kitchen table. Neither of them spoke.

'Jessica told Izzy to go to her house because she didn't want to come home. As time went on the girls hatched a plan. They convinced themselves that if Izzy pretended to have been kidnapped, Josh would give up the Internet Party and move back in with Mum.'

Bruno stifled a laugh. 'That's unbelievable!' Josh and Dan exchanged glances. He obviously didn't know Izzy very well.

'Then the whole thing got out of hand,' said Josh. 'I suppose because there were no parents around and Jessica's brother was more interested in spending time with his girlfriend than keeping a check on his sister, the girls' imaginations took over and they started living a fantasy life.'

'But why didn't the police track down Jessica?' said Bruno. 'Surely they must have contacted Izzy's mobile company to find out who she'd been in contact with before she disappeared.'

'They did call Jessica but apparently she lied and said she'd talked to Izzy as she was leaving school and she believed her friend had gone straight home.'

'So the police didn't search her house,' said Bruno.

'Why should they?' said Josh. 'They had no reason

to believe Izzy was there.'

'What about the girls' phones? Didn't they use them to send those ridiculous messages?'

Josh was beginning to find Bruno's pious attitude and barrage of critical questions annoying. He was determined to defend Izzy's misjudgements, no matter how stupid she'd been. 'The girls knew that if they used their own phones to send texts from the supposed kidnappers, they'd be traced. So Jessica dug out an old pay as you go phone that hadn't been registered, which her brother had taken to a music festival several years ago.'

'Clever girl,' said Bruno. 'But surely the police or you and Kim contacted her friends. Why wasn't Jessica caught out?'

'She's a new friend,' said Dan. 'She only recently joined the school. She was expelled from boarding school, somewhere outside of London. Jessica was unhappy when she came to our school and Izzy took her under her wing. They formed a bond, probably because they were both unhappy. Mum and Josh don't really know Jessica.'

'That explains a lot,' said Bruno. 'Was Izzy pleased when her picture appeared all over the newspapers and on TV?'

'To start with she was,' said Dan. 'You know she's always going on about wanting to be a celebrity. Then as time went on Izzy began to realise the trouble she'd caused. But she couldn't see a way out.'

Dan's head dropped slightly as he relived the sadness he'd experienced when he first saw his sister's frail body huddled in a corner of the attic. She'd looked like a frightened animal awaiting capture and resigned to her fate, yet still with a desire to be free.

Josh could see that Dan was having trouble keeping his eyes open as his large head with its tousled mop of fair hair kept nodding forward like one of those dogs people put on the back shelves of their cars which nod their heads as the car moves. Josh came to his rescue.

'Go to bed, Dan. You need some rest.' The boy jerked himself upright as if to prove that he was anything but exhausted.

'I'm ok. Mum might need me.'

'Dan. It's four o'clock in the morning. Your mother has probably fallen asleep in bed with Izzy. You need to get some rest. Tomorrow, or rather today, will be a very busy day. Go to bed.'

Josh spoke in the most authoritative and fatherly tone he could manage, bearing in mind that he felt completely drained of all physical and emotional energy. Dan rose slowly to his feet and stretched out his arms. He pulled down his slightly too small polo shirt from where it had ridden up to reveal his toned stomach.

'I'll see if Mum needs anything. Night.'

Then Dan disappeared into the hallway. Josh and Bruno remained silent until he was out of earshot.

'Stupid girl,' said Bruno, draining his tea into his large mouth with a smack of his lips. Josh made another attempt to pick up his own mug and felt a surge of gratification when he managed to do so. He examined his hands and was pleased to see they had stopped shaking. He took a large gulp of tea. It was lukewarm but its sweetness felt comforting.

'Izzy's driven her mother half mad with worry. Such a selfish thing to do, going missing like that,' said Bruno, casting a glance at Josh. The two men had avoided eye contact with each other since Bruno had sat down at the table.

'I blame myself. Izzy's just a child,' said Josh, at last managing to speak without having to choke back tears. He'd done his fair share of crying that night.

As soon as the three of them had got safely into the house, without any sign of the world's media and with Izzy still wrapped from head to toe in the borrowed blanket, Dan had woken Kim. Then all hell had broken loose with Izzy and her mother crying hysterically, entwined in each others arms, while Dan and Josh stood by with tears flowing down their faces in a respectful silence. To Josh's surprise Bruno had managed to sleep through all the drama of Izzy's return. This included a visit from a doctor who'd come to check on her state of wellbeing and pronounced her to be generally in good health physically but in need of emotional support and counselling.

To his annoyance but to Josh and Dan's relief, Bruno had also slept through the arrival and departure of two police officers. Josh had called Detective Sergeant Spalding on his mobile phone minutes after arriving at Kim's house and he in turn had contacted the duty sergeant at Wimbledon Police Station. About ten minutes later two uniformed officers, one male and the other female, had arrived at the house. They'd taken brief statements from Josh, Kim, Dan and Izzy and had then been called away urgently to give back-up to other officers who were dealing with a fight on Wimbledon Broadway.

The female officer, a young woman with blonde hair tied back in a thick plait, had been very kind and sympathetic to Izzy, who kept saying how sorry she was for causing so much trouble. Josh knew that Detective Sergeant Spalding might not be quite so understanding. He'd advised Josh that he would be holding a press briefing in the afternoon and had requested that Josh and Kim should be present in order to give their side of the story. He said it was important that they should have an opportunity to clear up any misunderstandings and ensure that the media gave out correct information.

Josh was sure that Maggie would agree to Kim and himself taking part in the press briefing. She would no doubt wish to prepare statements for them. Suddenly Josh thought of Maggie sleeping peacefully in her bed in complete ignorance of the events unfolding along the road.

He wondered whether to wake her, but as soon as the thought came into his mind he sent it away again. Tomorrow, or rather today, would be demanding both mentally and physically. Maggie would need to have her wits about her, especially as Josh knew he'd be exhausted. He would tell Maggie about Izzy's return when she woke up.

'Well, I'm going back to bed,' Bruno announced as he pushed his empty mug away from him and heaved himself up from the chair. He gave Josh a long look with his slightly narrowed, dark and piercing eyes. 'You'd better get some sleep, if you can.'

Josh nodded. He waited until the large lumbering man had disappeared into the hallway and listened as he climbed the stairs. Then he heard the creaking groan of the door to the guest room being closed, the room that until only a few weeks ago had been Josh's territory. Most of Josh's belongings were still there but he hadn't seen much of them for a while. He continued to sit at the kitchen table and finished drinking his tea while he decided whether he could face going back to Maggie's house to sleep. It didn't take him long to decide that he couldn't, especially as the volunteers would be arriving soon, all full of eager youthfulness. But far more important was the fact that he wanted to be as close as he could legitimately be to Kim, Izzy and Dan.

Josh washed his and Bruno's mugs under the hot tap and left them upside down on the draining board. Then he tiptoed down the hallway, took a brief look into his study, slipped into the TV room, curled up on the sofa, buried his face into its green velvet covering and fell into a deep sleep.

CHAPTER
THIRTY-ONE

After a couple of hours Josh was woken up by the sound of his mobile phone ringing somewhere in his subconscious. The first time he ignored it but it kept ringing and ringing and by the time he'd summoned up enough energy to reach into his trouser pocket and switch it off, he was sufficiently curious to at least see who was calling him at six thirty in the morning. He looked at the illuminated screen with its slight tinge of green. 'Maggie'. Who else would it be?

'Hi Maggie.'

'Josh. Where are you?'

'Kim's sofa.'

'What?'

'I said, Kim's sofa. The green velvet one downstairs. It's a long story.'

'I don't have time for long stories, Josh. You're supposed to be here, now, for a briefing session with the team.'

He felt irritated by Maggie. How could she always be so resolute, so persistent? She was like one of those wind-up toys. Once she was set on a particular course she would continue in a straight line, no matter how many obstacles she encountered on her way.

'Josh.'

'Yes.'

'Did you hear me?'

'Maggie. It's been a long night. I got to sleep two hours ago. I'll be as quick as I can. Start the meeting without me. I'll explain when I get back.'

'Damn right you will. We've got an election to win today and it's not just about you, Josh.'

He bit his lip. 'I know.' He disliked Maggie for

being right and for making him feel guilty for letting the side down.'

'I know it's not all about me. Last night it was about…' He hesitated.

'About who, Josh?'

'Izzy. She came back.'

He could feel tears welling up in his eyes as he listened to the shocked silence at the other end of the phone. Then a quiet voice, quite unlike Maggie's said, 'Oh my…'

Josh switched off his phone. He'd explain everything to her later. But for a few minutes he would allow the tears to cascade down his cheeks, taking with them the stress and relief of the previous night.

The day of the election had been planned with the precision of a military operation. Maggie had made a few changes to Josh's busy schedule to accommodate an interview with Detective Sergeant Spalding, a press briefing and a meeting with a top PR guru, who'd offered to broker an exclusive deal with a newspaper.

Izzy's reappearance after an absence of seven days had, of course, generated a media feeding frenzy. Her school photo was on the front page of every newspaper and the twenty-four hour news channels were running the story every hour on the hour, with a 'breaking news' caption running across the screen in between. The tabloid newspapers, true to form, had dreamed up some weird and wonderful headlines such as:

'Ms Izzy mystery solved'

'Izzy text misstry uncovered'

One paper even had the caption **'WELCOME BACK IZ!'** in huge bold letters all over its front page with nothing else apart from Izzy's photo.

While the tabloids rejoiced in her safe return the broadsheets debated the impact of parents' busy lives on those of their kids. Subjects under discussion included how children react when their parents divorce and whether highly paid absent fathers should be allowed to make their much poorer estranged wives go through prolonged periods of suffering before agreeing to satisfactory financial settlements. Without specifically saying so they were of course referring to Richard.

Then there was debate about the stresses and strains faced by women who, after being supported financially when they were married and living with their husbands, suddenly found themselves working full time in demanding jobs while still bearing the bulk of responsibility for the welfare of their children. Josh was relieved to see that there was almost universal sympathy for Kim and that she was regarded as a victim of male selfishness and male ambition by most of the media.

There were allegations of 'Middle class neglect' in one prominent newspaper. These were not directed at Kim, Josh or Richard but at the parents of Jessica, who were portrayed as having facilitated the scenario whereby Izzy had been able to conceal herself at their house for a whole week. The paper cited other examples of what it described as 'overly liberal and utterly self-seeking middle class parents neglecting their responsibilities to their children'. These included parents supplying alcohol at parties for thirteen-year-olds or dishing out large amounts of money, regardless of the fact that this might be spent on drink, cigarettes or drugs. There was a story about a fifteen-year-old girl who had to be taken to hospital and put on a drip after drinking too much vodka. The paper also mentioned the case of an eleven-year old boy at a prominent independent school who'd been left alone at home for several days while his parents were away. The article went on to describe how a few years later the boy, who was still at the same expensive fee-paying school, had become a drug dealer.

There were discussions on the radio and TV about the pressures on family life of people in public office being hounded by the media. One commentator questioned how far the private lives of spouses or partners should come under scrutiny and whether it was morally acceptable for the wife of a former prime minister to be publicly castigated for buying and selling second hand items on eBay.

'The other parties are furious,' said Maggie gleefully as she and Josh sat comparing notes over a cup of coffee. 'They're accusing us of mounting a huge publicity stunt. Of course, it's backfiring on them because public sympathy for Izzy is astronomical.' Maggie raised her arms up in the air in a gesture of supremacy. 'The good thing is that everyone now knows about the Internet Party, what we stand for and why they should vote for us.'

The interview with Detective Sergeant Spalding at Wimbledon Police Station had gone much better than Josh expected. Once he and Kim managed to get through the throng of media people who had virtually blocked the entrance, they'd only been inside for just over ten minutes. The detective had spent most of that time telling them about the pressures of his own life. It turned out that he and his wife had separated because of the demands of their jobs. His wife had gone off with a car salesman who did not work antisocial hours and Detective Sergeant Spalding hardly ever saw his young daughter.

Before the interview Maggie had warned Josh that the issue of Izzy wasting police time might come up in relation to her disappearance, but thankfully it was never raised. On the contrary, DS Spalding advised Kim that Izzy might need counselling to help her come to terms with her ordeal. DC Emily Willis and another female police officer had interviewed the girl with both Kim and Richard present shortly after she woke up.

After their interview Josh and Kim accompanied DS Spalding to a press conference. The detective did most of the talking and Kim said nothing at all while Josh quietly took advantage of the PR opportunity that had been presented to him. It wasn't all plain sailing as he was subjected to some pretty tough questioning by a few of the journalists present. Although the media had been sympathetic to Izzy for effectively kidnapping herself, they made clear to Josh that he needed to realise the damage that had been caused to her family by his political ambitions. After all, that was why she'd run away.

Josh worked hard to convince his most ardent critics that he'd learned to value family life more than ever before. He tried to put a positive spin on the negative publicity by saying that he would ensure that family values came at the top of his political agenda. Josh openly admitted that he would like to have his own children and that he would do everything in his power to ensure that Izzy never felt under pressure again.

'We have to turn what has been the most horrific experience for you and Kim into something positive,' Maggie had urged Josh when he'd expressed distaste for her idea of transforming the police press conference into what he'd rudely described as an 'Internet Party roadshow.'

He'd immediately apologised to her as soon as the words had come out of his mouth and explained that he was tired and overwrought from the events of the previous night. Josh felt he had to hand it to Maggie. She had a way of getting people to do the things she wanted. By twelve o'clock mid-day Maggie and the PR guru had brokered a deal with a national newspaper for exclusive contact with Josh and Kim in relation to Izzy's disappearance in return for a large six figure sum each, enough in fact to set them both up nicely over the next few years. Josh had agreed to donate some of his money to pay for a proper headquarters for the Internet Party after the election.

To Maggie's horror Kim had rejected the first offer made by a newspaper. This was because she'd been required to wear a skirt or dress together with 'kitten heels' in any photographs, in accordance with the paper's editorial policy. Kim had no idea what 'kitten heels' were but she'd no intention of being pictured wearing anything other than her standard 'uniform' of black trousers, flat black shoes and a plain sweater or shirt.

Kim's wardrobe contained only a few current items and she often bought clothes in duplicate or triplicate so she could wear the same outfit day in and day out. She always chose classic and unobtrusive clothing and eschewed anything fashionable. In contrast Maggie's wardrobe consisted of a myriad of different styles and colours and she chucked out anything remotely out of fashion at regular intervals. She had huffed and puffed about how stubborn and ungrateful Kim was until the PR guru managed to negotiate an even better deal with another newspaper with no particular dress requirement. There was talk of a potential book deal, depending on the outcome of the election. With the prospect of a large amount of money in sight that was not dependant on Richard's beneficence and which would relieve some of the pressures on her, Kim began to recover from the trauma of Izzy's disappearance.

Every time Josh crossed paths with Kim throughout the morning he thought about her pregnancy. On several occasions he found himself staring at her stomach, which she always kept covered in baggy shirts or sweaters. He hadn't had an opportunity to have a proper conversation with Kim since the day they'd both returned to her house in a taxi after their visit to the solicitor. The day when she'd told Josh she was pregnant and that he was the father of her child. It seemed to him that there had always been someone else present. He wondered whether Kim had mentioned her pregnancy to anyone apart from him. It was early days yet, he kept telling himself. Anything could happen in the first few weeks. Josh knew all the possible pitfalls of pregnancy as he'd carried out research on the Internet and terrified himself in the process with all the horror stories he'd read about things that could go wrong.

The whole of the afternoon had been taken up with

press briefings, live chat and blogging on the Internet and directing Maggie's team in the control centre. Six hours of Josh's existence had passed in what seemed like six minutes.

'Why don't you go and lie down for an hour or so? It's going to be a long night,' Maggie had suggested during a lull in activity at around six o'clock. 'You can come and join us later.'

Josh looked at himself in the mirror of the downstairs cloakroom. No wonder Maggie had been uncharacteristically sympathetic. The dark rings around his eyes made him look as if he hadn't slept for days. His hair was bedraggled and he needed a shave. Maggie's house was unusually quiet now that she and her entourage had decamped to a suite of rooms in a large hotel, next door to where the count for the constituency of Wimbledon would be held, in the early hours of the following morning.

Maggie had reminded Josh that she would be leaving the hotel to attend the count in Wandsworth, where she was standing as the prospective parliamentary candidate. As usual Maggie had everything worked out down to the minutest detail. She had even given Josh a watch, which she'd sent one of her helpers out to buy and had herself wrapped around Josh's right wrist before she left the house.

'Now don't forget to put it back on after you've showered.' Maggie had spoken to Josh in the tone of voice of a mother addressing her son.

'But I've got the time on my mobile,' Josh had protested. Maggie had raised her eyebrows.

'If you remember to bring it.'

Josh ambled into Maggie's kitchen and surveyed its spotless surfaces. There were no dirty coffee cups or plates covered in the remnants of the doughnuts that had been consumed in great quantities that afternoon. The cups and plates had been dutifully placed in the dishwasher that was now quietly humming away in the far corner of the kitchen. Josh removed a yellow and green striped mug from a cupboard, lifted the lid of a matching jar, took out a teabag and dropped it into the mug. Then he filled the kettle with water, switched it on, perched himself on a stool and surveyed the garden.

Over the last few weeks it had been transformed from a dirty patch of builder's rubble surrounded by a mass of overgrown shrubbery into an oasis of order and beauty. There was a patch of newly laid turf in an attractive oval shape in the middle of the garden that was bright green from having been religiously watered by one of Maggie's most diligent helpers each day. Around the outside of the oval lawn bedding plants of all colours, shapes and sizes had been planted to make a symmetrical pattern. The shrubs had been cut back and tamed to create a pleasant green frame inside a perfectly executed light brown fence.

Josh heard the kettle switch itself off. He poured boiling water over the teabag and watched as the brown colour of the tea seeped into the clear water. He thought he heard the sound of a key in the front door and listened as the door opened and closed again.

'Anyone here?'

'In the kitchen.'

'Oh. Hi Josh,' said Bruno, appearing at the doorway.

'Tea? I've just made myself one.'

'Thanks.'

Bruno walked slowly across to the glass topped table, pulled out a chair and sat down heavily. Josh thought he looked like a man who was carrying a heavy burden of responsibility on his shoulders. Why should that be? Josh wondered. To the outside world Bruno appeared to have a charmed existence. He was a partner in a successful surveying business. As far as Josh was aware he had no money worries or family responsibilities. Maggie wasn't a burden to him either financially or emotionally, being independent and self-sufficient with her own successful career. In addition to that she was attractive, vivacious and had a body most men would die for. Momentarily the thought of Maggie's toned and curvy physique distracted Josh so that he almost spilled Bruno's tea as he placed it down on the table.

'I thought you'd be at the hotel with the others,' said Bruno.

'I'm running late. I'm supposed to be getting ready. What are your plans?'

Bruno hesitated for a while before speaking and stared down into his mug of tea, deep in thought.

'There's something I need to tell you.'

Josh pulled out a chair and sat down at the table opposite Bruno.

'Fire away,' he said as casually as possible. What could Bruno want to talk about? Something to do with Izzy, perhaps. Suddenly it occurred to Josh that Bruno and Maggie might be having problems with their relationship. They'd hardly spent any time together since Bruno had moved into Kim's house several weeks ago. But there didn't seem to be any antagonism towards each other when Josh had seen them together.

'It's about the baby.'

Josh felt as if he'd been punched in the stomach. He stared down into his tea. Kim must have told Bruno she was pregnant. What about the baby? What business was it of Bruno's to even speak about the baby? Josh looked up at the man's wide handsome face with its perfectly coiffed dark brown hair resting on top.

'Kim asked me to tell you.' Bruno paused.

What? A voice screamed in Josh's head. What? But no word came out of his mouth.

'This is difficult.' Bruno rubbed his face with his right hand. Then he leaned back slightly, put both hands firmly on the table and looked straight at Josh. 'Kim asked me to tell you that she's not going to have your baby.'

'Not going to have your baby.' The words resonated in Josh's mind. He felt shocked and could hardly speak.

'She hasn't had a... an...' He wrestled with the words 'miscarriage', 'abortion', but they wouldn't come out of his mouth.

'No,' said Bruno quickly. 'God, no, nothing like that.'

'Well, what then?'

There was a long pause before Bruno spoke.

'Josh. I'm so sorry. The baby is mine.'

'Yours?'

'Yes. Kim and I, we...I can't explain everything but we've fallen in love. We're going to get married.'

'Married?' Josh shouted.

'Yes, when Kim's divorce comes through. Since the business with Izzy going missing Richard is a changed man. He's at last agreed a reasonable financial settlement with Kim. The house in Horatio Road will be sold and we'll be moving to Surrey.'

'Surrey!' Josh banged his fists down on the glass table sending drops of tea flying into the air. 'You're moving to Surrey...with Kim. What about Dan and Izzy? What do they think about this grand plan of yours? You and Kim have only known each other for a few weeks.'

Bruno sighed. 'I know that. But we're not children, Josh. We know what we want. Kim is going to give up work and stay at home to look after Izzy and the baby. Perhaps we'll have another child. I'm not going to put any pressure on her. I'll be delighted with just one.'

'What about Maggie?'

A pained expression came across Bruno's face.

'Maggie and I want different things. That became obvious once she started all this Internet Party business. For a short time I hoped it would be a flash in the pan, another of her mad escapades. There have been a few over the years, believe you me.' Bruno shifted awkwardly in his seat as if he was trying to extricate himself from a large patch of chewing gum that had become attached to his trousers. 'But gradually I realised that I wanted someone to belong to, someone who would belong to me. And then I met Kim, that evening when Maggie and I first met you both at Kim's house. We hit it off immediately and, gradually, we fell in love.' Bruno sucked in a huge breath of air, looked straight at Josh, shrugged his shoulders and held out his arms with his palms upturned. 'Kim and I want the same thing, Josh. A boring, stable home life. Maggie will never want that. She'll never belong to anyone. People will belong to her for as long as it suits her to own them.'

'That's harsh,' said Josh.

'I know you're fond of Maggie but she's a free spirit. There are so many good things about her but being in a relationship with her isn't something I'd recommend.'

Josh had gone from feeling numb with the pain of being told he was not going to be a father after all, just when he was beginning to get used to the idea, to feeling anger and resentment towards Bruno.

'You didn't answer my question. Do Dan and Izzy know or not?' said Josh through gritted teeth.

Bruno let out a long slow breath. 'I can understand your shock and anger, Josh.'

'Don't patronise me.'

'No, of course Dan and Izzy don't know yet and we'd be grateful if you didn't tell them. Izzy is still in a fragile state and Dan is about to sit his A levels. But they'll be ok about it. Dan will be going to university in September, or taking a gap year, depending on his grades. We won't be moving far away from Wimbledon. There are trains every few minutes.'

'What about Izzy's school?'

'She doesn't want to go back. Not after everything that's happened. Kim's going to teach Izzy at home for a while. Then she'll start a new school when we find a house.'

'What about her friends?'

'She'll make new ones.'

'It's not that easy, especially for a girl of her age.'

'We're going to enrol Izzy in a riding school over the summer, near to where we want to live. Maybe we'll buy her a pony.'

'A pony!'

Josh stood up and paced around the kitchen. He wondered if he was going mad, or perhaps he'd fallen asleep and was in the middle of a terrible nightmare. He looked at Bruno. If there was any glimmer of pleasure on that man's face Josh would punch him fair and square between the eyes, even if Bruno were to hit him back. No amount of physical pain could equate with the mental anguish Josh was feeling. But Bruno was crying. The large, handsome and hairy man, always calm and in control, was rubbing his eyes as tears flowed silently down his masculine cheeks.

'This is hard for me too,' he sobbed. 'I loved Maggie. I still love her and I know that you still love Kim. But you and Maggie have chosen a particular path, a certain lifestyle that Kim and I have no desire to buy into.'

Josh sat back down at the table. Both men were crying now, wiping their eyes on their shirtsleeves and sniffing loudly.

'What will I do? Where will I go?' said Josh weakly.

'In all probability you'll be elected as an MP, judging by the latest exit polls. Or, if you don't get elected, you'll carry on in your job and stand again in the future. You'll continue to play an important role in the lives of Dan and Izzy. You can buy a flat in Wimbledon with the money you get from selling your story to the newspaper. The kids will come and stay with you. They love you, Josh. You've been a good father figure and the fact that you no longer live with their mother won't change that.'

Josh turned over Bruno's words in his mind. Yes,

he had been a good father figure. He'd always been there when Dan or Izzy had needed a lift or someone to talk to. He'd tried to instil in them some of the moral values he'd been brought up with by his own parents. He'd challenged their consumer-led beliefs and encouraged them to consider the lives of those who were less fortunate. Josh may not have been able to give Dan and Izzy expensive gifts or large amounts of money like Richard, but together with Kim he'd helped to give them a moral framework by which to lead their lives and he would continue to do so.

'I expect you'll hate me for a while,' said Bruno, wiping his eyes with several pieces of kitchen paper.

'Not hate. Envy perhaps,' said Josh.

'Envy?' said Bruno, looking surprised.

'I wanted the baby. Well, I wasn't sure when Kim first told me. But I got used to the idea. Then I wanted it.'

'You can share it with us,' said Bruno gently. He smiled tentatively at Josh, who didn't notice.

'Is it a boy or a girl?'

'A girl.'

'Izzy will be pleased.'

Bruno nodded.

'Just one more question and then I'd better go and get ready,' said Josh. 'How can you be sure the baby is yours?'

'Kim had a DNA test, a few days ago, after she visited the hospital. They gave her the exact date of conception and she worked out that the baby was most likely mine so she had the test.'

'Oh.' Josh let the information sink in.

'Kim's very upset. She feels she misled you. That's why she asked me to speak to you.'

'Tell her I forgive her.'

'I will,' said Bruno. He rose to his feet. 'I'm just going upstairs to get some clothes and then I'm off to Wandsworth to give Maggie moral support at the count. I'll see you at the hotel later. Best of luck,' said Bruno as he shot a glance at Josh and disappeared into the hallway.

'Thanks,' said Josh after him. He looked down at the watch Maggie had given him. He had a couple of hours to get showered and dressed before making his way to the hotel. He would watch the election programmes when they started at nine o'clock. Josh felt surprisingly calm. Perhaps the news he'd received from Bruno had been welcome in an odd sort of way. He knew in his heart of hearts that his relationship with Kim was over. A baby might have brought them together for a while. But for how long? Josh was about to embark on a new and exciting journey, to take a path that he was destined to take at some point in his life, into the political arena where he might make a difference in a positive way to people's lives. Suddenly Maggie's house phone rang.

'Josh?'

'Dad.'

'Your mobile's not working. I've been phoning you for ages. I had to call Kim to get this number.'

'Sorry. It's probably out of battery.'

'Well, charge it up, son. I might need to speak to you.'

'Ok. I'll do it now.'

'I just wanted to wish you luck. I'm very proud of you. Your mother would be even prouder than I am.'

'Thanks, Dad.'

'I'll be watching the result of the count on TV.'

'I'll wave.'

'Don't be stupid.'

'I'm joking.'

'Good. Now charge up that wretched phone, son. I'll call you again later.'

After Josh had replaced the handset it suddenly occurred to him that Bruno hadn't mentioned whether he'd told Maggie that he intended to marry Kim and move to

Surrey, or that Kim was going to have his baby. He called upstairs to see if Bruno was still in the house, but there was no reply. He must have slipped out quietly while Josh had been talking to his father on the phone. He tried to block out all thoughts of Maggie, Kim and Bruno as he showered and dressed, locked up the empty house and climbed into his Saab.

Josh drove off in the direction of the hotel that was being used as an overnight base for the Internet Party supporters who'd worked so hard over the last few weeks to get him and Maggie elected as MPs. The car journey seemed timeless and Josh felt detached from his own body, as if he were watching himself in a film. He was too shocked by what Bruno had told him to feel either happy or sad, or indeed, anything at all. His head was telling him that this was his big moment, his chance to show the world that he was a man and not a mouse. But his heart was devoid of emotion.

Josh parked his car down a side road and slipped into the hotel lobby and up to the room on the second floor that had been reserved for him. He eased open the heavy door and entered a room that could have been anywhere in the world. It was decorated in neutral colours and had no distinguishing features. Even the artwork on the walls looked anonymous and detached from its surroundings, rather like Josh felt himself. He hung his jacket on the back of a chair and lay down on the bed as a wave of exhaustion came over him. He grabbed the remote and switched on the TV, but his eyes were so tired they could hardly focus on the images on the screen. Josh looked wearily at the watch that Maggie had given him. He could rest for a couple of hours before going downstairs to meet the others. Josh fell into a deep sleep.

CHAPTER
THIRTY-TWO

Josh was woken by the screams and shouts of the joyful crowd in the suite on the floor below. He shot a glance at the large TV that sat heavily on the standard hotel issue chest of drawers. His eyes were drawn to the screen where lights were flashing and words were sliding across from one side to the other. Josh watched as a large group of political commentators, tightly clutching their microphones, were jostled by the crowd. He'd turned down the volume on the TV and all he could hear was the dull buzz of the air conditioning and the noise below, an indescribable babble of voices that seemed to get louder with each of his heartbeats.

Josh watched motionless as the election results skidded across the screen. They were coming thick and fast now. His eyes widened as the names of familiar towns and cities appeared before him - Exeter, Newcastle, Leicester, Plymouth, Nottingham and Southampton – each of them carrying memories, hopes and dreams. Josh held his breath – Bristol North West – his heart thudded as beads of sweat formed at his temples and he waited for a number. It was a landslide victory – twenty thousand, three hundred and sixty votes.

The air rushed from Josh's lungs as he sat up, his eyes transfixed by the constant procession of names, numbers and a myriad of colours. They were red, blue, yellow, purple and green. But most of all they were turquoise, rich and dark like the depths of the ocean or light and translucent like the crest of a wave.

A raft of emotions swept over Josh so that at one moment he felt elated and yet seconds later he found himself in the depths of despondency. He turned his eyes to the mirror on the wall next to the TV screen and watched himself as he sat motionless.

'Do you want to be part of this or not? What are you going to do? Make a decision,' he said out loud. There was no answer.

Josh stood up suddenly and moved quickly towards the heavy fireproof door to his room. As he opened it the shouts and screams from the floor below became deafening. He had to get away. He could feel his heart pounding in his chest. His head was throbbing and he could hardly breath.

'What have you done?'

He heard a voice and quickly looked around, but the voice was in his head.

'Is this some sort of game you've been playing?'

'Did you in your wildest dreams think this would happen?' said the voice.

Josh looked quickly from side to side. The corridor was empty. Everyone else was downstairs. This was his last chance to escape. He hurried towards the fire exit breathing fast, anxious to leave behind the pain he could feel in his chest. Suddenly, as he wrenched open the fire door, Josh felt himself spinning. There was a ringing sound in his ears and his vision was blurred. Adrenalin rushed through his veins and yet he seemed to be moving in slow motion. Fight or flight? Flight or fight? Was there a choice or had his body taken over his mind?

'Josh! Josh!'

A voice was calling him. It was a female voice. Josh's life over the last few weeks flashed before his eyes. Now the voice was running towards him he felt a rush of fresh air filling his lungs and the sensation that he was falling, spinning in space. Suddenly the voice had a face and it was staring at him.

'Josh. You're not leaving are you?'

'Kim. What are you doing here?'

'I came to find you. Are you ok?'

Josh opened and closed his eyes a few times until his

surroundings came back into focus. He was aware of his irregular breathing pattern as he took sudden sharp gasps of air into his lungs.

'Take deep breaths,' said Kim as she gently rested her hand on his shoulder. 'Four breaths in,' she counted. 'Six breaths out. As slowly as you can.'

'I thought I was going to pass out,' said Josh, trying to stand up. Kim held his arm to steady him.

'Be careful. Don't rush to get up. How do you feel?'

He sat back down again. 'I had a pain in my chest but it's gone now. I thought I was having a heart attack.' He wiped his forehead with the back of his left hand.

'More likely a panic attack,' said Kim reassuringly. 'If you were having a heart attack you'd be feeling worse, not better.'

Josh eased himself onto his feet. 'I'm ok now.' He slowly headed back in the direction of his hotel room. Kim followed him.

'Where were you going?'

'I don't really know. I just had this sudden urge to leave, to get away and an overwhelming feeling of panic, as if my very survival depended on escaping. Fight or flight. That sort of feeling.'

Josh opened the door to his room and went inside. Kim followed. He looked at her with a quizzical expression, as if he was trying to remember something. 'Why did you come?'

Kim glanced down at her watch. 'I came to tell you that you're needed next door at the Town Hall, where the votes are being counted. The election results are due to be announced in around half an hour. Everyone's been wondering where you are.' She paused and looked up at Josh with her wide green eyes and an earnest expression on her face.

'I also came to apologise.'

'Apologise, for what?'

Kim hesitated and smoothed down her hair, which immediately sprang back up again into tight brown curls.

'Bruno told me he'd spoken to you. He wasn't supposed to tell you until after the election.' Kim paused. 'I felt you had enough to deal with.' She looked straight at Josh. 'But he said that when he saw you, when he came to collect his clothes, he felt it was unfair that you thought you were going to be a father when you weren't.'

Josh noticed that Kim had one hand resting on her abdomen as she spoke and a tinge of disappointment rose up from somewhere deep inside his body. He took a deep breath.

'Bruno was right. I didn't exactly thank him at the time. I was shocked, sad, disappointed and angry. But he did the right thing.'

Kim wrung her hands together and sighed loudly. 'I should have told you myself.'

It occurred to Josh that he could use sarcastic words, accuse her of misleading him and tell her how deceptive and selfish she'd been. But he had no desire to do any such thing. He felt numb and a little light-headed but he didn't feel any animosity towards Kim.

'It doesn't matter. I almost feel...' Josh paused.

'What?' she said, looking anxious.

'Relieved.' He glanced at Kim. She looked tired but she also seemed happier and more relaxed than she had for weeks. Hardly surprising really, thought Josh. Izzy was safely back at home and Kim would soon be starting a new life with Bruno, not to mention giving up work and having a baby. It was what she had desired for a long time.

'I couldn't give you what you wanted, what you deserve,' said Josh with a tinge of sadness in his voice.

'And I wouldn't have made a very good MP's wife.'

'If I get elected.'

Kim smiled. 'That reminds me. I need to get you to the Town Hall or they'll announce the election results without you.' She grabbed Josh's arm and pulled him in the direction of the lift. He came willingly and she was relieved to see that he was smiling.

'That wouldn't be the best start to my political career, would it?'

'Not in front of millions of people watching on TV. No, it wouldn't.'

Josh took Kim's hand as they waited for the lift. 'I still love you,' he said gently. 'I think I always will love you.' He turned to face her and let her hand fall away. 'But I recognise that our relationship is over.'

The lift arrived and they stepped inside. Fortunately it was empty.

'I love you too Josh and I want you to stay involved with Dan and Izzy. Whatever difficulties we've had, they've never stopped caring for you.' Kim paused. 'You've been a good father to them.'

'I love Dan and Izzy and they've taught me a lot about myself over the last few weeks.'

'What do you mean?'

'They've made me realise that I want my own children one day. I never thought I would. I always felt there was something lacking in me, that I could never be a good father. But when Izzy went missing I thought my heart would break.' Josh wiped a tear from one eye before it had the chance to drop down and leave a mark on his shirt.

'You'll meet someone and have a family. I know you will. You're about to embark on a new and exciting journey. Women will be falling at your feet.' Kim squeezed his arm, reassuringly.

'I hope you're right,' said Josh as they walked out of the lift and through the revolving door of the hotel lobby in the direction of the Town Hall.

Josh climbed onto the podium with the other prospective parliamentary candidates. They were all proudly wearing their brightly coloured rosettes – red, blue, yellow, purple, green…Josh touched the shiny satin of his own turquoise rosette that was clipped to the left lapel of his light grey suit jacket. Underneath he wore a white open-necked shirt. As he looked at the other male candidates standing to his left and right he wondered if he should have worn a tie. They were all wearing ties. Somehow they seemed inhibited and constrained by convention. The Internet Party was about breaking free of conventions.

As the returning officer read out various instructions from the sheet of paper in front of her, Josh cast his eyes over the sea of faces that surrounded the podium. He spotted Dan, who stood out from the crowd, his fair hair glinting in the bright lights of the TV crews. He must be well over six feet tall, Josh thought as he beamed a smile across the room.

Dan gave a wave and a 'thumbs up' sign with both hands, which made Josh smile even more. He looked around for Bruno and Maggie. He knew the count at Wandsworth Town Hall was running late because there had been so many people trying to vote late into the evening that some of the ballot boxes had been delayed.

Josh looked to see if there was anyone else he knew among the writhing mass of bodies, some headed this way, others that way. All trying to reach the places they wanted to be before they were required to stand still for the announcement of the results. There were a few familiar faces, friends and neighbours, fellow supporters of the Internet Party.

Suddenly Josh was surprised to see Christine, standing on her own at the back of the hall. She hadn't told him she'd be coming to the count. She was wearing a smart cream coloured suit and a turquoise blouse. Josh caught Christine's eye and watched as her lips curled into a smile. He felt excited by her presence and pleased that she'd come to see him. For a moment he was transported to another place, somewhere in his past. He was a young man again starting out on a new life.

Christine raised her right hand as if to wave and then quickly put it back down by her side. Josh couldn't take his eyes off her soft brown hair, which she'd obviously had styled for the occasion. It rested gently on her shoulders and glowed in the stark lighting of the hall. Josh wanted to mouth the word 'thanks' but he knew he was under the gaze of TV cameras and journalists. He didn't want to make Christine feel uncomfortable. He kept glancing at her out of the corner of his eye. Her presence made him feel safe and supported, as if she was his ally.

The crowd in the hall became virtually silent as the returning officer announced that she was ready to read the results. Josh could hear his heart beating in his chest. He reminded himself to breath. Four breaths in and six breaths out. The returning officer peered at the assembled company over her reading glasses and rustled the papers in her hand, as if she were a head teacher trying to get the attention of a few recalcitrant pupils before embarking on a school assembly. Someone at the back of the hall stifled a cough, a few people whispered and when there was complete silence the returning officer opened her mouth to speak.

'Robert Cooper, British National Party, two hundred and fifteen votes, lost deposit.'

There was a rumble of satisfaction in the hall as the BNP candidate grinned defiantly at the audience and shifted his feet awkwardly from side to side.

'Quiet please,' said the returning officer. When the babble of voices had calmed down she continued.

'Jonathan Brown, UK Independence Party, nine hundred and sixty-two votes, lost deposit.'

Josh heard the murmur of a few male voices that seemed to belong to a group of well-dressed middle-aged men standing near the front of the crowd. He saw them turn towards each other as if they were sharing some deep secret.

'Jane Howard, Green Party, five thousand one hundred and seventy-three votes.'

A small rotund woman aged about thirty wearing a green and white patterned dress made of silk or some other shiny material stepped forward to the sound of whoops and laughter from her supporters. She gave a broad smile as she tossed her golden curls back in an attractive manner as if she couldn't care less how many votes she'd polled.

'Thank you,' said the returning officer as she waited for the crowd to calm itself down.

'Andrew Cross, Liberal Democrat Party, three thousand, seven hundred and fifty-one votes, lost deposit.'

Josh heard sharp intakes of breath from some of the crowd and saw glances being exchanged across the hall. Well, that was much lower than expected, he thought as he took a deep breath himself. He started to add up the votes that had been declared so far and then gave up.

'Susan Wilding, Labour Party, five thousand, one hundred and two votes.'

The returning officer had given up trying to maintain a dignified silence in the hall and had instead raised her voice over the chattering crowd.

'Dominic Berry, Conservative Party,' she almost shouted. Then she waited for a few seconds. Josh held his breath. There had been so much debate in the media as to whether the opinion polls that had been held in the run up to the election could possibly be correct. Political commentators had failed to agree on what effect the Internet Party might have on the other parties. Josh looked at the returning officer and saw that she was mouthing some words, but he heard nothing. All he could hear was the heavy pounding of his heart and a ringing sound in his ears. Then he heard his name.

'Joshua Walker, Internet Party.'

The returning officer turned to him and smiled as the

hall fell silent.

'Fifty thousand, four hundred and twenty-five votes. I am therefore proud to announce that Joshua Walker has been duly elected as Member of Parliament for the constituency of Wimbledon.'

Josh could hardly believe his ears. He stood rigid as the returning officer and the other candidates came forward to shake his hand. The crowd caught its collective breath and then there was mayhem as everyone tried to move somewhere else.

Suddenly there was commotion by the main entrance and Josh spotted Maggie and Bruno followed by an entourage of supporters hurrying into the hall, chattering loudly and giving 'thumbs up' signs in all directions. Maggie had been elected as the MP for Wandsworth.

Josh felt a surge of excitement and the urge to jump up in the air and wave at her with both arms, but he knew it would be inappropriate. So he gave her the biggest smile he felt he could get away with before she disappeared into a sea of faces.

A mass of Internet Party supporters chanted with joy, 'Josh Walker, Josh Walker, Josh Walker...' over and over again. Election pundits from various newspapers and TV companies jostled for position as they tried to plough their way through the crowd to get to Josh for what they hoped might be an exclusive comment on his landslide victory.

Suddenly a wave of relief swept over his body and the anxieties and uncertainties of the past lay around him like discarded clothes. As Josh tried to make his way across the hall, he found himself being patted on the back and his hands being grasped and shaken in every direction.

'There must have been around an eighty per cent turnout of voters in this constituency,' Josh heard one commentator say as he was carried past by a sea of bodies. Eventually he managed to reach the small huddle that consisted of Maggie, Bruno, Kim and Dan, who immediately embraced him into their midst.

'Congratulations,' said Maggie triumphantly as she put up her hand for a high five.

'Congratulations to you too and thanks for everything you've done to get us both elected,' said Josh. Their palms and their eyes met making him feel vindicated and happy, not to mention a host of other emotions he couldn't begin to describe. Maggie and Josh stood for a few seconds, their faces flushed with pride at their own and each other's success and holding hands above their heads, to the cheers of their supporters.

Bruno grabbed Josh's other hand and shook it furiously. 'Well done.'

Suddenly Josh felt a tap on the shoulder from behind. He turned around and Dan gave him a massive bear hug that nearly knocked him off his feet. As they held each other Dan whispered in Josh's ear. 'I've got your diaries, the ones that went missing from your desk drawer. They're safely hidden.'

Josh froze for a second.

'I found Izzy snooping around so I grabbed the diaries before she could look at them.'

Josh pulled away from Dan.

'I hope you don't mind. I didn't read them.'

Dan winked conspiratorially and Josh felt a wave of relief engulf him. He grabbed the boy's right arm.

'I don't know how to thank you.'

'Can I be your private secretary or whatever it's called, in my gap year?'

'You bet,' said Josh, tapping Dan on the arm warmly as politicians often do. Then he caught sight of Kim. She was standing next to Bruno, whose largeness made her look small and vulnerable. Her brown curls framed her round face and he felt pleased to see that the colour that had been so absent from her cheeks over recent weeks had returned. Kim's green eyes shone out like beacons and for a moment

Josh felt a deep sense of longing for the happy times they'd spent together.

Suddenly he felt his mobile phone vibrate in his jacket pocket. He'd remembered to charge it up before he left for the count and had put it on 'silent'. It must be Dad, Josh thought as he pulled the phone out of his pocket. No, it was a text. His father had mastered the art of making and receiving calls but had decided that texting was not appropriate for a man of eighty-six years old.

Josh looked at the message. 'It's a text from Izzy,' he shouted so that Kim and the others might hear him. 'It says, **Saw you on TV. Josh for PM!'**

'Wow, Prime Minister. That's cool,' said Dan.

'It's a bit premature. We don't know how many seats we've won yet,' laughed Maggie.

Kim reached out her hand and gently touched Josh on his arm. 'You'd be a great Prime Minister,' she said and smiled warmly. Josh noticed that Bruno's hand rested proprietorially on Kim's shoulder. Then he felt himself being pushed and pummelled by the crowd as arms reached out to him and microphones were shoved in front of his face. He held his phone tightly and quickly texted Izzy a reply.

'Mr Walker. Suzy Bradshaw, Sunshine News. Could I have a few words, please?' A smartly dressed female held a large microphone in front of Josh and he recognised her familiar face from one of the twenty-four hour news stations. She seemed smaller than she was on TV and wore heavy make-up with a bright orange suit and enormous black high-heeled shoes. Josh found himself face to face with a large camera surrounded by bright lights and noticed that a tall man with a beard was waving something that looked like a furry animal on the end of a long pole over his head. He assumed this must be some sort of sound device.

'Mr Walker. How do you feel about your amazing victory this evening?'

Josh heard himself saying the things that he and Maggie had discussed, argued over, agreed, prepared and rehearsed, as if he was detached from his own body. He felt as if he'd been on a long journey and had finally reached his destination. He knew there would be other journeys to come, new and exciting challenges to face and, at times, mountains to climb. But he was ready for them. Josh felt a greater sense of purpose than he had ever before felt in his life.

THE END

ACKNOWLEDGEMENTS

There are two dear friends I wish to thank, who together are the sine qua non of The Internet Party. If it hadn't been for them, this novel would never have been finished, let alone published. They are Judy Turner, former Publicity Director of Transworld Publishers and Martin Fletcher, Editor and former Publisher at Headline Publishing.

I am grateful to my family and the friends who've encouraged me. Particular thanks go to Caroline Toft for giving me a special pen to get me started on my writing career. Thank you also to freelance journalist, Deborah Dooley for her wonderfully nurturing 'Retreats for You' writers' retreats in Devon.

I would also like to express my gratitude to Richard Chalkley, Media Manager and James Willis, Creative Director at Spiffing Covers. Richard's endless patience and James' excellent design skills, together with their sound advice, have helped to make my journey as a self-published author as painless as it could be.

THE INTERNET PARTY - AUTHOR'S NOTE

I started writing The Internet Party in the summer of 2004 during a family holiday in Mallorca. The UK local elections had taken place on 10 June with interesting results. The Labour Party had been in government since 1998 but was becoming increasingly unpopular. Its decision to invade Iraq in 2003 did not have widespread public support. The Conservative opposition had supported the invasion but not Liberal Democrat MPs. None of the parties would have achieved an overall majority if the local election results had been replicated at a general election.

In the London Borough of Merton, where I've lived for over thirty years, there is a political party called the Merton Park Ward Independent Residents. The party started as a pressure group in 1990, campaigning to stop a ring road being built in a residential area. It subsequently became a political party and three councillors have been elected every year since it was formed. In the 2004 local election the Merton Park Independents held the balance of power between the Conservative and Labour Party councillors. In other words, there was a hung council. This was becoming more frequent in local elections around the UK with Liberal Democrats often holding the balance of power.

I found the concept of a hung council very interesting as, in effect, a small group of people had a lot of power and influence. I considered how this concept might be translated into a national setting. I knew that there had been a couple of hung parliaments in UK national elections but that the coalition governments had been short-lived and somewhat ineffectual. What if a minority party held the balance of power at a national level? How would that change the face of British politics? It would happen sooner or later, I was sure. People's voting habits were changing. As the electorate became more disillusioned with politicians of all parties, fewer people voted. It became a valid choice to not vote, something I can never understand, as if politicians would care. On the contrary, I believe that the only way of holding them to account is to vote, even if there's a limited choice of parties and candidates and the opportunity only exists once every few years.

So, going back to my holiday in Mallorca, I predicted the likelihood of a hung parliament and I intended to finish my novel in time for the next general election. I imagined that the party holding the balance of power would be a new party, independent of vested interests and truly democratic. How could that happen? Well, somehow the idea came into my mind that it could come about by someone deciding to set up a political party based on the Internet. The party would come from nowhere, catch the public imagination, increase in popularity and challenge the existing political parties in a way never seen before in British politics. It would be called The Internet Party.

Unfortunately, for various domestic reasons, the writing of my novel ended up at the bottom of my 'to do' list. I therefore missed the opportunity of publishing it before the 2010 General Election when no single party was able to form a majority government. The Liberal Democrats held the balance of power between the Conservative Party and Labour and decided to join with the Conservatives to form the first coalition government in the UK since 1940.

Over the last ten years the social and political landscape both inside and outside the UK has changed dramatically. While the Internet at times showcases the worst aspects of human behaviour I believe it will ultimately be the saviour of humanity. It allows people to access knowledge and information like never before. This gives them more power and control over their lives. The Internet is a platform for freedom of expression that allows the individual to publicise his or her research, ideas, opinions, music, writing or artwork. Organisations such as Hacked Off and 38 Degrees are bringing about real social change through people signing online petitions or emailing their MPs.

When I started writing The Internet Party in 2004 I wasn't aware of any Internet based political parties. If I carried out a google search there were entries relating to actual parties that had been organised over the Internet but nothing else. However, over the years a few have appeared. The first one I noticed is in the Ukraine, which according to Wikipedia was set up in 2007 and registered as a political party in 2010. The second is the Internet Party (Spain) that Wikipedia says was founded in 2009. In 2014 the Internet Party (New Zealand) hit the headlines. There is a facebook based Internet Party that claims to be the first worldwide Internet based party.

I firmly believe that Internet democracy is the way of the future. All over the world organisations are forming with the aim of allowing people to directly influence their own lives and political decisions by exerting influence online. In the UK the prime example of this is an organisation called 38 Degrees. It describes itself as 'a community of citizens working together to bring about real change in the UK by taking action on the issues that we all care about.' It 'is inspired by the impact of advocacy groups like MoveOn in the United States, GetUp in Australia and Avaaz around the world.'

38 Degrees has over 2 million supporters in the UK and has been instrumental in affecting UK government policy. In contrast to this example of truly democratic people power, membership of political parties is generally in decline and there is little opportunity for members to directly influence their policies. When I vote as a member of 38 Degrees on an important local or national issue to create an online petition or send thousands of emails to a

politician, I feel I matter, that my vote counts. But I don't get the same feeling of empowerment when I vote in a local or general election.

I strongly believe that people should be able to elect their political representatives on line and take part in determining government policies by regularly voting on key issues that affect their daily lives. Despite what politicians might think, I am confident that people would make the right decisions.